JAIME HERNANDEZ
THE DEATH OF
SPEEDY

JAIME HERNANDEZ
THE DEATH OF
SPEEDY

FANTAGRAPHICS BOOKS

FANTAGRAPHICS BOOKS
7563 Lake City Way N.E.
Seattle, WA 98115

Editor: Gary Groth
Art Director: Mark Thompson
Front cover colored by Monster X; separations by
Mark Thompson; films supplied by Port Publications
Back cover colored by Monster X

First Fantagraphics Books edition: November, 1989.
1 3 5 7 9 10 8 6 4 2

ISBN (soft): 1-56097-003-0. ISBN (hard): 1-56097-004-9.
Printed in Singapore through Palace Press.

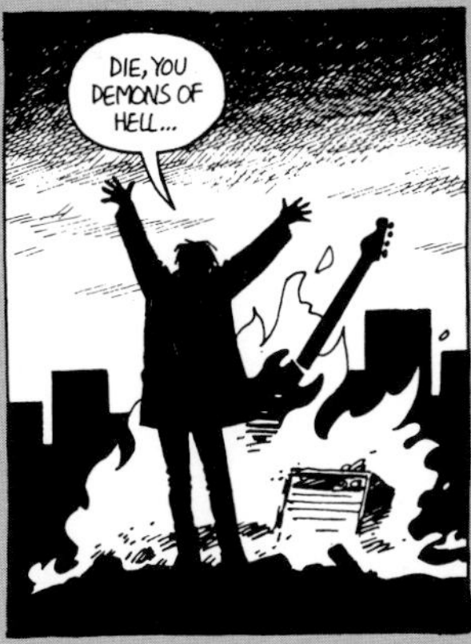
DIE, YOU DEMONS OF HELL...

CONTENTS

FANTAGRAPHICS BOOKS

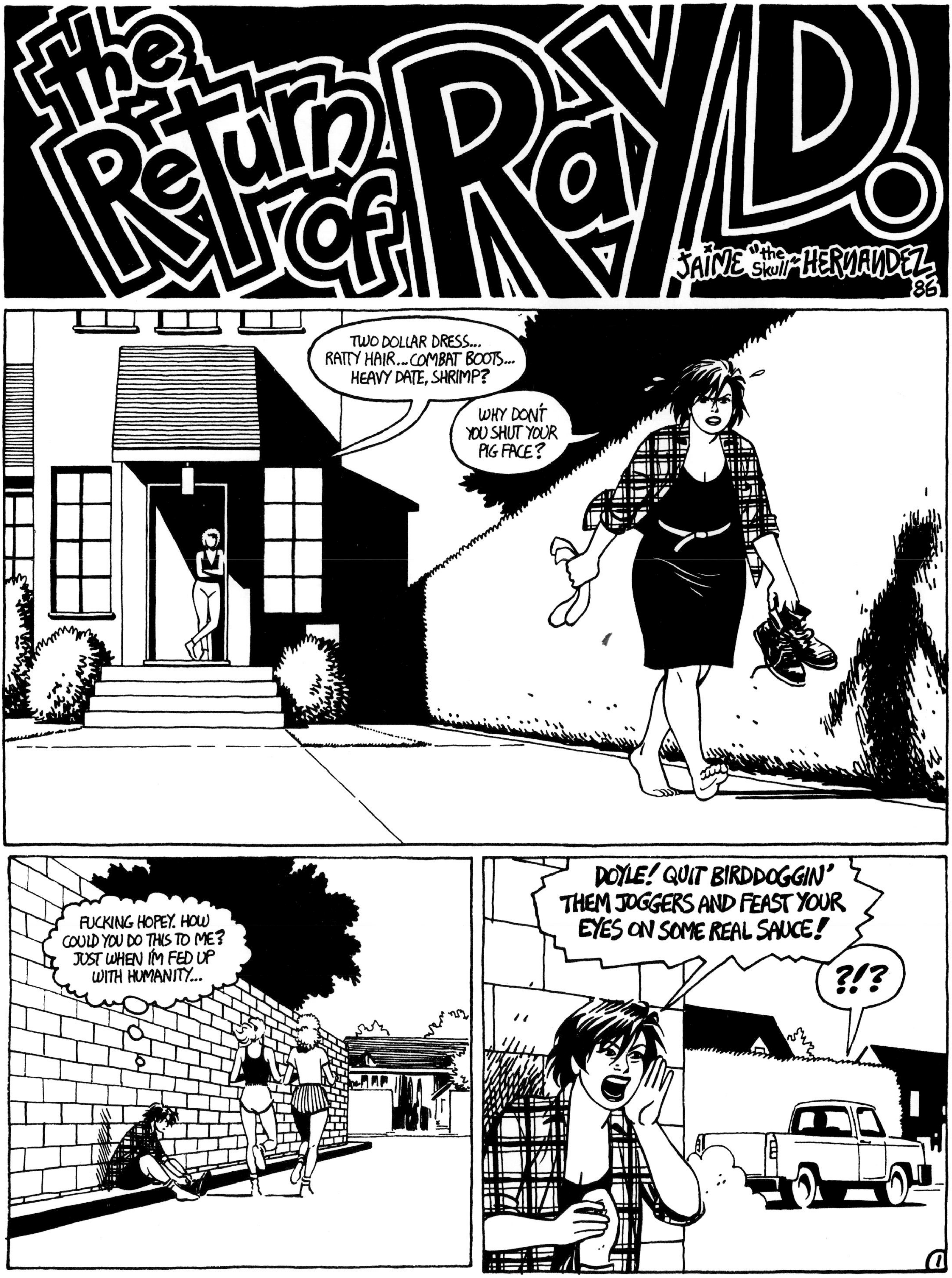
the Return of Ray D.
JAIME "the Skull" HERNANDEZ 86
TWO DOLLAR DRESS... RATTY HAIR... COMBAT BOOTS... HEAVY DATE, SHRIMP?
WHY DON'T YOU SHUT YOUR PIG FACE?
FUCKING HOPEY. HOW COULD YOU DO THIS TO ME? JUST WHEN I'M FED UP WITH HUMANITY...
DOYLE! QUIT BIRDDOGGIN' THEM JOGGERS AND FEAST YOUR EYES ON SOME REAL SAUCE!
?!?

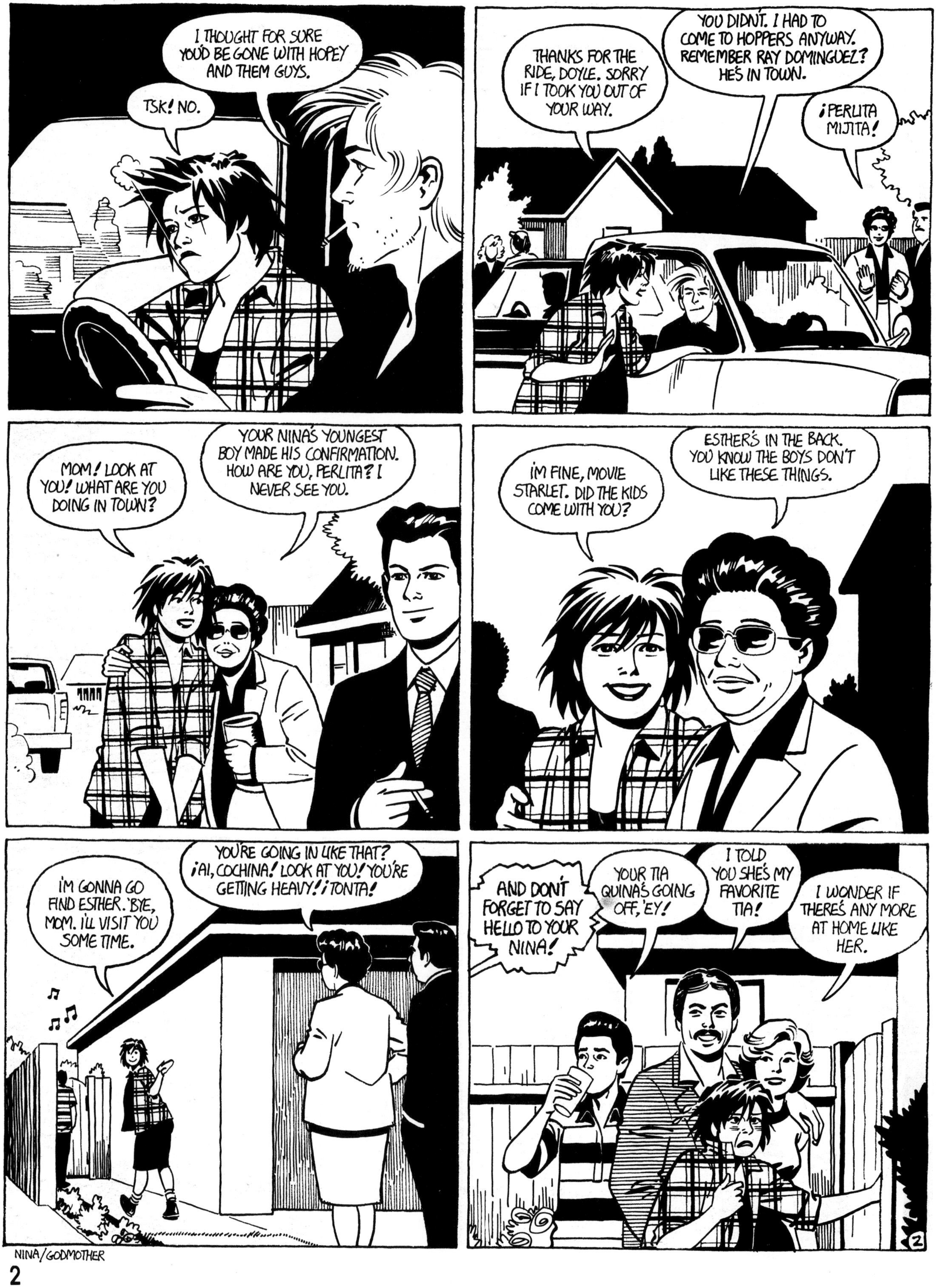
I THOUGHT FOR SURE YOU'D BE GONE WITH HOPEY AND THEM GUYS.
TSK! NO.
THANKS FOR THE RIDE, DOYLE. SORRY IF I TOOK YOU OUT OF YOUR WAY.
YOU DIDN'T. I HAD TO COME TO HOPPERS ANYWAY. REMEMBER RAY DOMINGUEZ? HE'S IN TOWN.
¡PERLITA MIJITA!
MOM! LOOK AT YOU! WHAT ARE YOU DOING IN TOWN?
YOUR NINA'S YOUNGEST BOY MADE HIS CONFIRMATION. HOW ARE YOU, PERLITA? I NEVER SEE YOU.
I'M FINE, MOVIE STARLET. DID THE KIDS COME WITH YOU?
ESTHER'S IN THE BACK. YOU KNOW THE BOYS DON'T LIKE THESE THINGS.
I'M GONNA GO FIND ESTHER. 'BYE, MOM. I'LL VISIT YOU SOME TIME.
YOU'RE GOING IN LIKE THAT? ¡AI, COCHINA! LOOK AT YOU! YOU'RE GETTING HEAVY! ¡TONTA!
AND DON'T FORGET TO SAY HELLO TO YOUR NINA!
YOUR TIA QUINA'S GOING OFF, 'EY!
I TOLD YOU SHE'S MY FAVORITE TIA!
I WONDER IF THERE'S ANY MORE AT HOME LIKE HER.
2

NINA/GODMOTHER

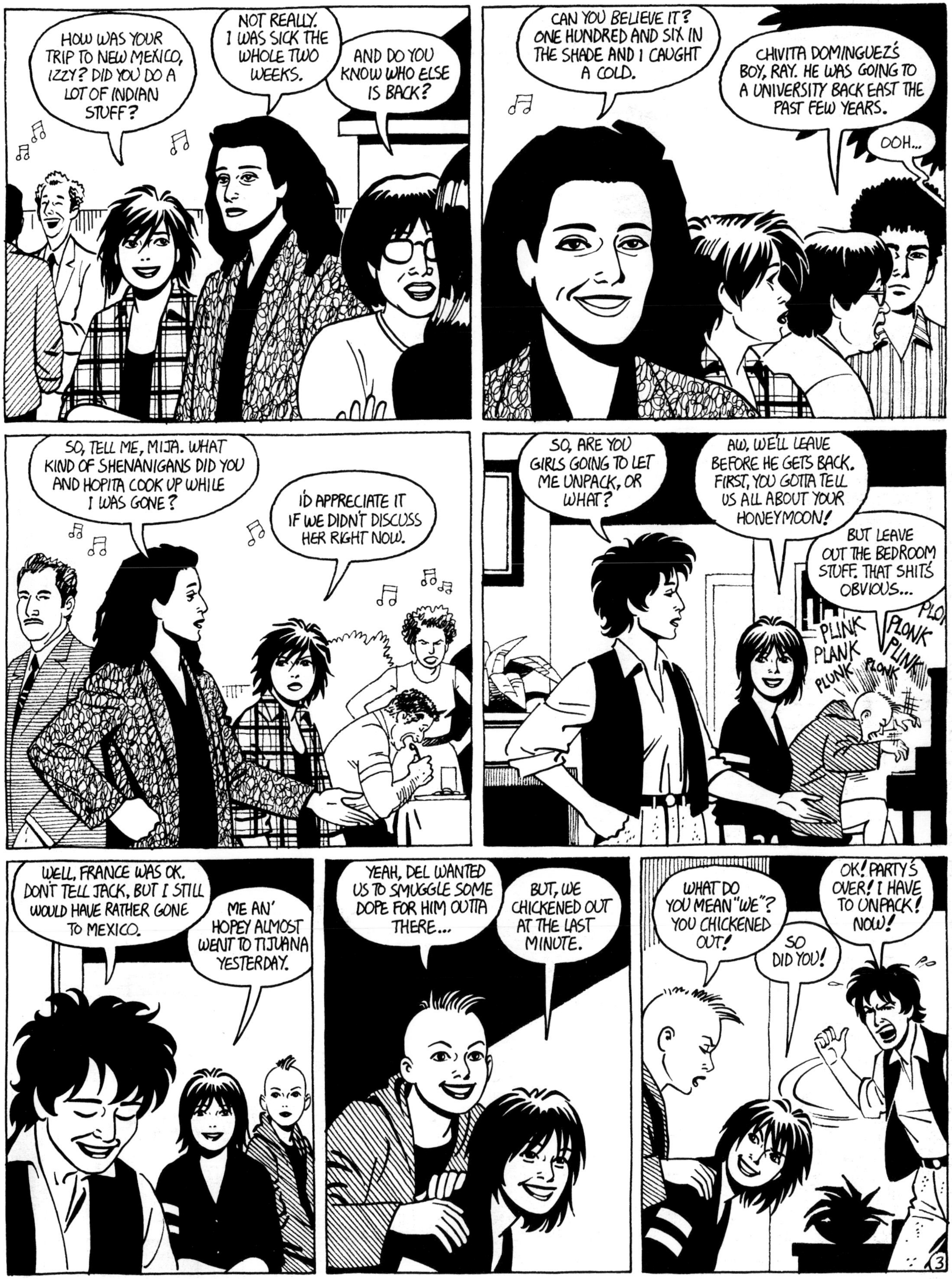

HOW WAS YOUR TRIP TO NEW MEXICO, IZZY? DID YOU DO A LOT OF INDIAN STUFF?
NOT REALLY. I WAS SICK THE WHOLE TWO WEEKS.
AND DO YOU KNOW WHO ELSE IS BACK?
CAN YOU BELIEVE IT? ONE HUNDRED AND SIX IN THE SHADE AND I CAUGHT A COLD.
CHIVITA DOMINGUEZ'S BOY, RAY. HE WAS GOING TO A UNIVERSITY BACK EAST THE PAST FEW YEARS.
OOH...
SO, TELL ME, MIJA. WHAT KIND OF SHENANIGANS DID YOU AND HOPITA COOK UP WHILE I WAS GONE?
I'D APPRECIATE IT IF WE DIDN'T DISCUSS HER RIGHT NOW.
SO, ARE YOU GIRLS GOING TO LET ME UNPACK, OR WHAT?
AW, WE'LL LEAVE BEFORE HE GETS BACK. FIRST, YOU GOTTA TELL US ALL ABOUT YOUR HONEYMOON!
BUT LEAVE OUT THE BEDROOM STUFF. THAT SHIT'S OBVIOUS...
PLINK PLANK PLUNK PLONK PLONK PLINK
WELL, FRANCE WAS OK. DON'T TELL JACK, BUT I STILL WOULD HAVE RATHER GONE TO MEXICO.
ME AN' HOPEY ALMOST WENT TO TIJUANA YESTERDAY.
YEAH, DEL WANTED US TO SMUGGLE SOME DOPE FOR HIM OUTTA THERE...
BUT, WE CHICKENED OUT AT THE LAST MINUTE.
WHAT DO YOU MEAN "WE"? YOU CHICKENED OUT!
SO DID YOU!
OK! PARTY'S OVER! I HAVE TO UNPACK! NOW!
3

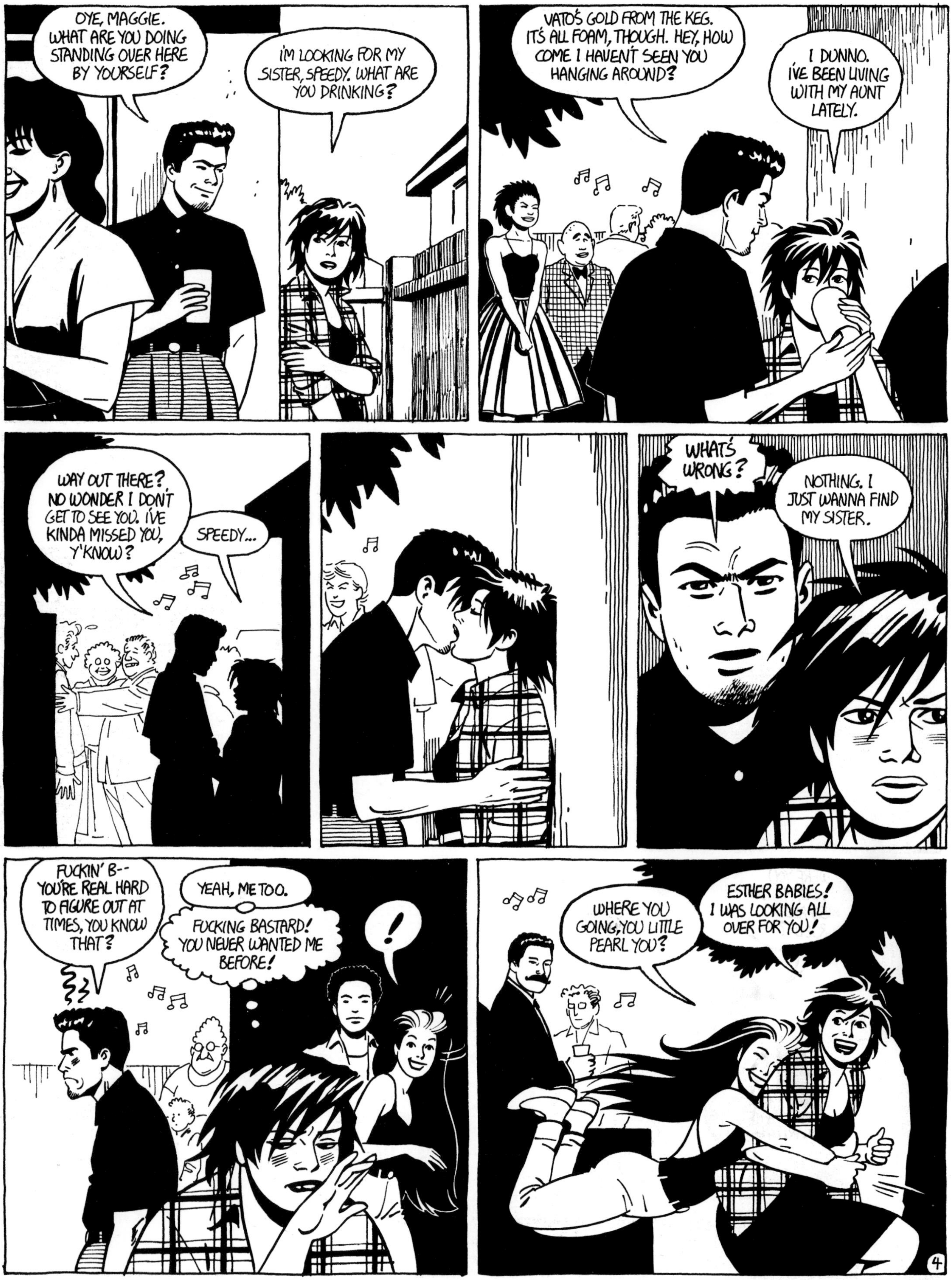
OYE, MAGGIE. WHAT ARE YOU DOING STANDING OVER HERE BY YOURSELF?
I'M LOOKING FOR MY SISTER, SPEEDY. WHAT ARE YOU DRINKING?
VATO'S GOLD FROM THE KEG. IT'S ALL FOAM, THOUGH. HEY, HOW COME I HAVEN'T SEEN YOU HANGING AROUND?
I DUNNO. I'VE BEEN LIVING WITH MY AUNT LATELY.
WAY OUT THERE? NO WONDER I DON'T GET TO SEE YOU. I'VE KINDA MISSED YOU, Y'KNOW?
SPEEDY...
WHAT'S WRONG?
NOTHING. I JUST WANNA FIND MY SISTER.
FUCKIN' B-- YOU'RE REAL HARD TO FIGURE OUT AT TIMES, YOU KNOW THAT?
YEAH, ME TOO.
FUCKING BASTARD! YOU NEVER WANTED ME BEFORE!
!
WHERE YOU GOING, YOU LITTLE PEARL YOU?
ESTHER BABIES! I WAS LOOKING ALL OVER FOR YOU!
4

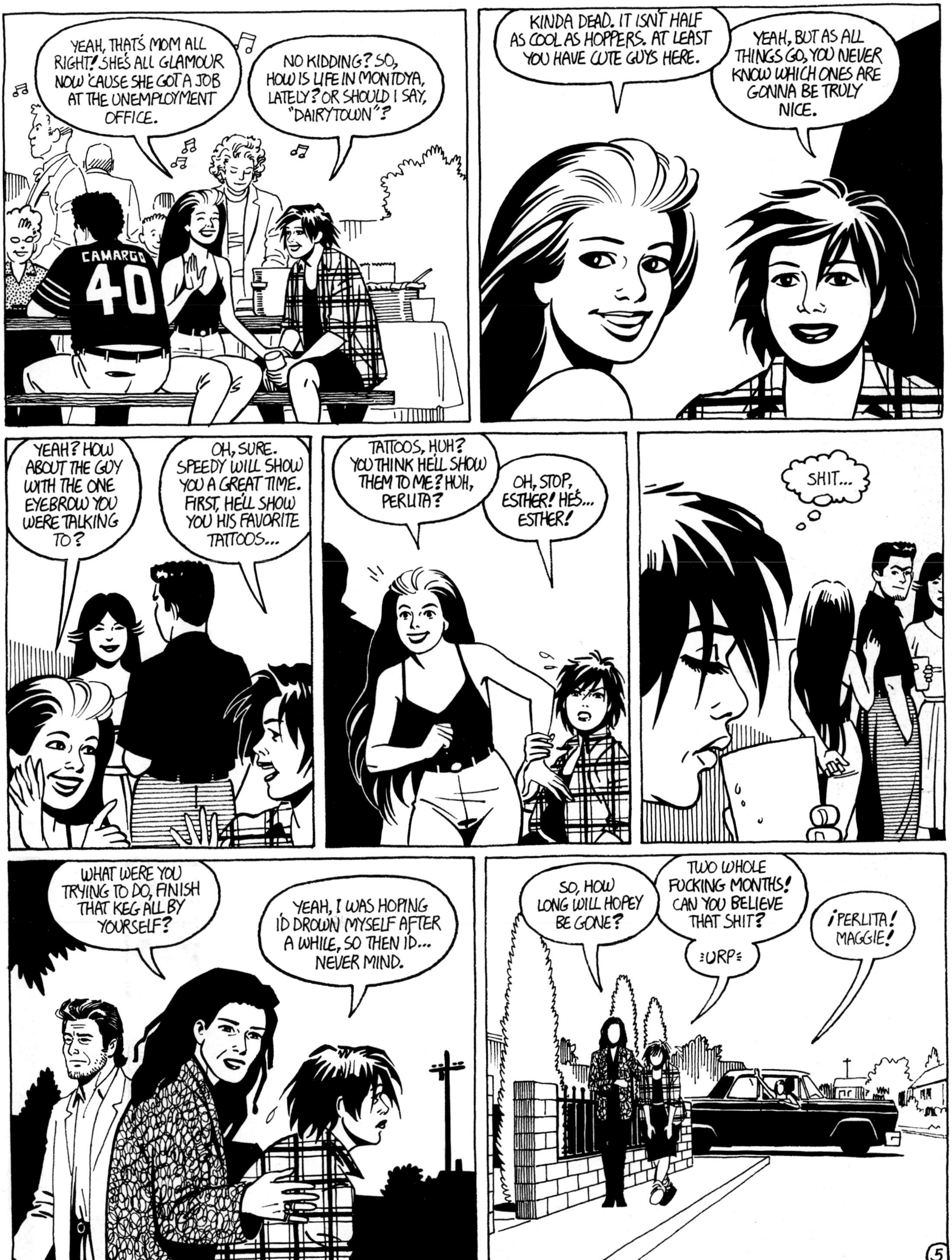
YEAH, THAT'S MOM ALL RIGHT! SHE'S ALL GLAMOUR NOW 'CAUSE SHE GOT A JOB AT THE UNEMPLOYMENT OFFICE.
NO KIDDING? SO, HOW IS LIFE IN MONTOYA, LATELY? OR SHOULD I SAY, "DAIRYTOWN"?
CAMARGO
40
KINDA DEAD. IT ISN'T HALF AS COOL AS HOPPERS. AT LEAST YOU HAVE CUTE GUYS HERE.
YEAH, BUT AS ALL THINGS GO, YOU NEVER KNOW WHICH ONES ARE GONNA BE TRULY NICE.
YEAH? HOW ABOUT THE GUY WITH THE ONE EYEBROW YOU WERE TALKING TO?
OH, SURE. SPEEDY WILL SHOW YOU A GREAT TIME. FIRST, HE'LL SHOW YOU HIS FAVORITE TATTOOS...
TATTOOS, HUH? YOU THINK HE'LL SHOW THEM TO ME? HUH, PERLITA?
OH, STOP, ESTHER! HE'S... ESTHER!
SHIT...
WHAT WERE YOU TRYING TO DO, FINISH THAT KEG ALL BY YOURSELF?
YEAH, I WAS HOPING I'D DROWN MYSELF AFTER A WHILE, SO THEN I'D... NEVER MIND.
SO, HOW LONG WILL HOPEY BE GONE?
TWO WHOLE FUCKING MONTHS! CAN YOU BELIEVE THAT SHIT?
URP
¡PERLITA! MAGGIE!
5

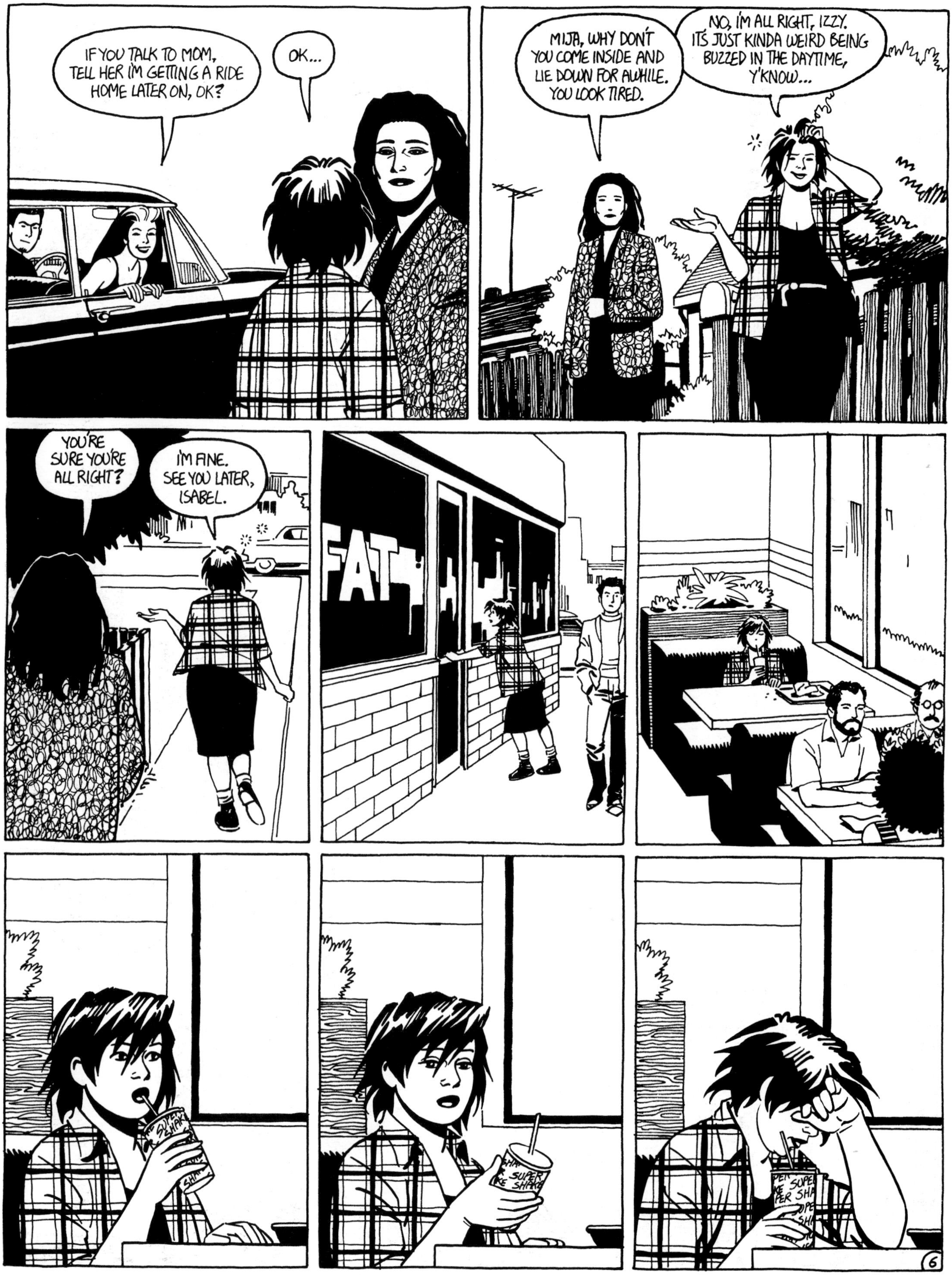

IF YOU TALK TO MOM, TELL HER I'M GETTING A RIDE HOME LATER ON, OK?
OK...
MIJA, WHY DON'T YOU COME INSIDE AND LIE DOWN FOR AWHILE. YOU LOOK TIRED.
NO, I'M ALL RIGHT, IZZY. IT'S JUST KINDA WEIRD BEING BUZZED IN THE DAYTIME, Y'KNOW...
YOU'RE SURE YOU'RE ALL RIGHT?
I'M FINE. SEE YOU LATER, ISABEL.
EAT
SUPER SHAKE
SUPER SHAKE
SUPER SHAKE
6

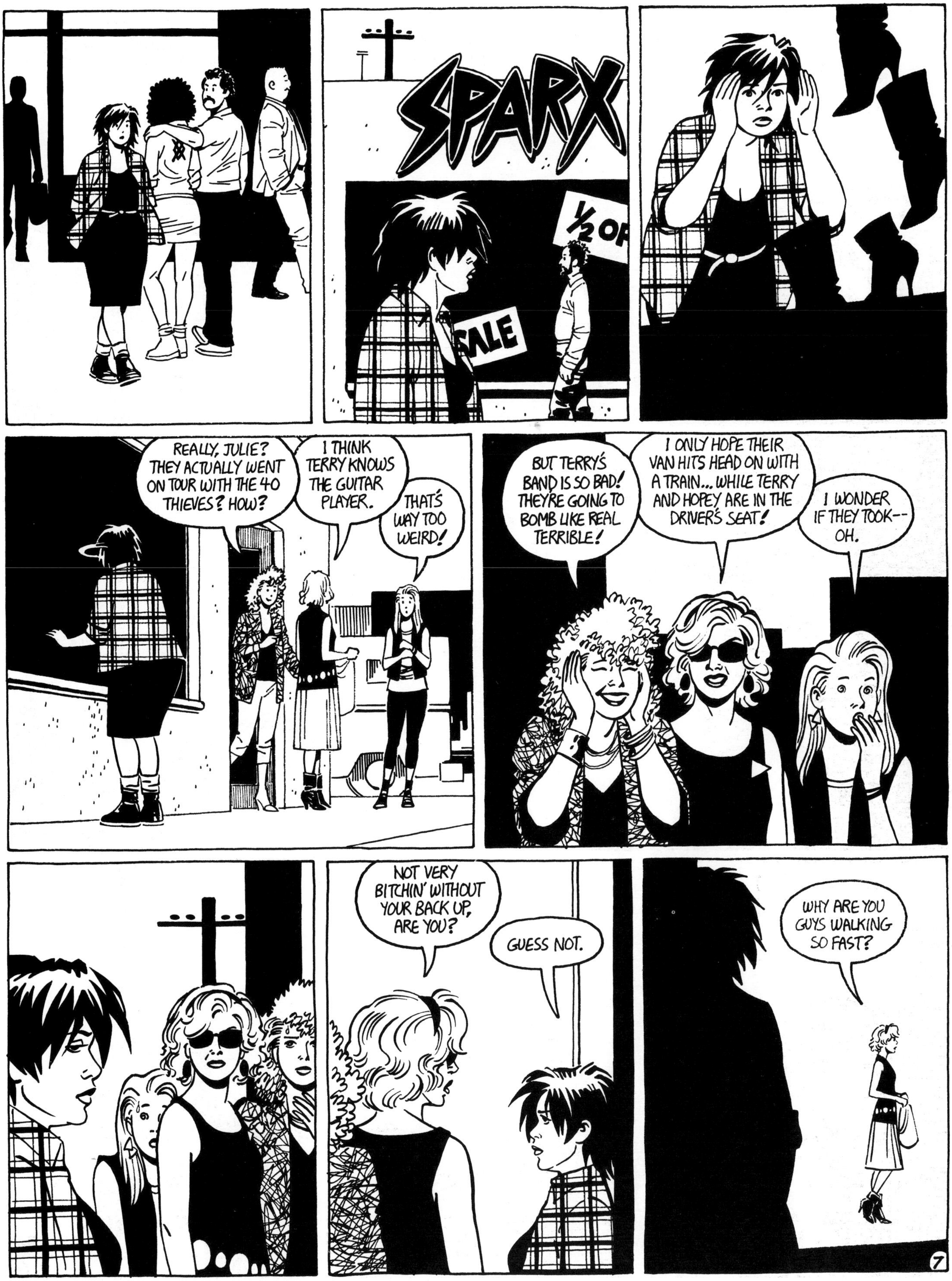
SPARX
1/2 OF
SALE
REALLY, JULIE? THEY ACTUALLY WENT ON TOUR WITH THE 40 THIEVES? HOW?
I THINK TERRY KNOWS THE GUITAR PLAYER.
THAT'S WAY TOO WEIRD!
BUT TERRY'S BAND IS SO BAD! THEY'RE GOING TO BOMB LIKE REAL TERRIBLE!
I ONLY HOPE THEIR VAN HITS HEAD ON WITH A TRAIN... WHILE TERRY AND HOPEY ARE IN THE DRIVER'S SEAT!
I WONDER IF THEY TOOK-- OH.
NOT VERY BITCHIN' WITHOUT YOUR BACK UP, ARE YOU?
GUESS NOT.
WHY ARE YOU GUYS WALKING SO FAST?
7

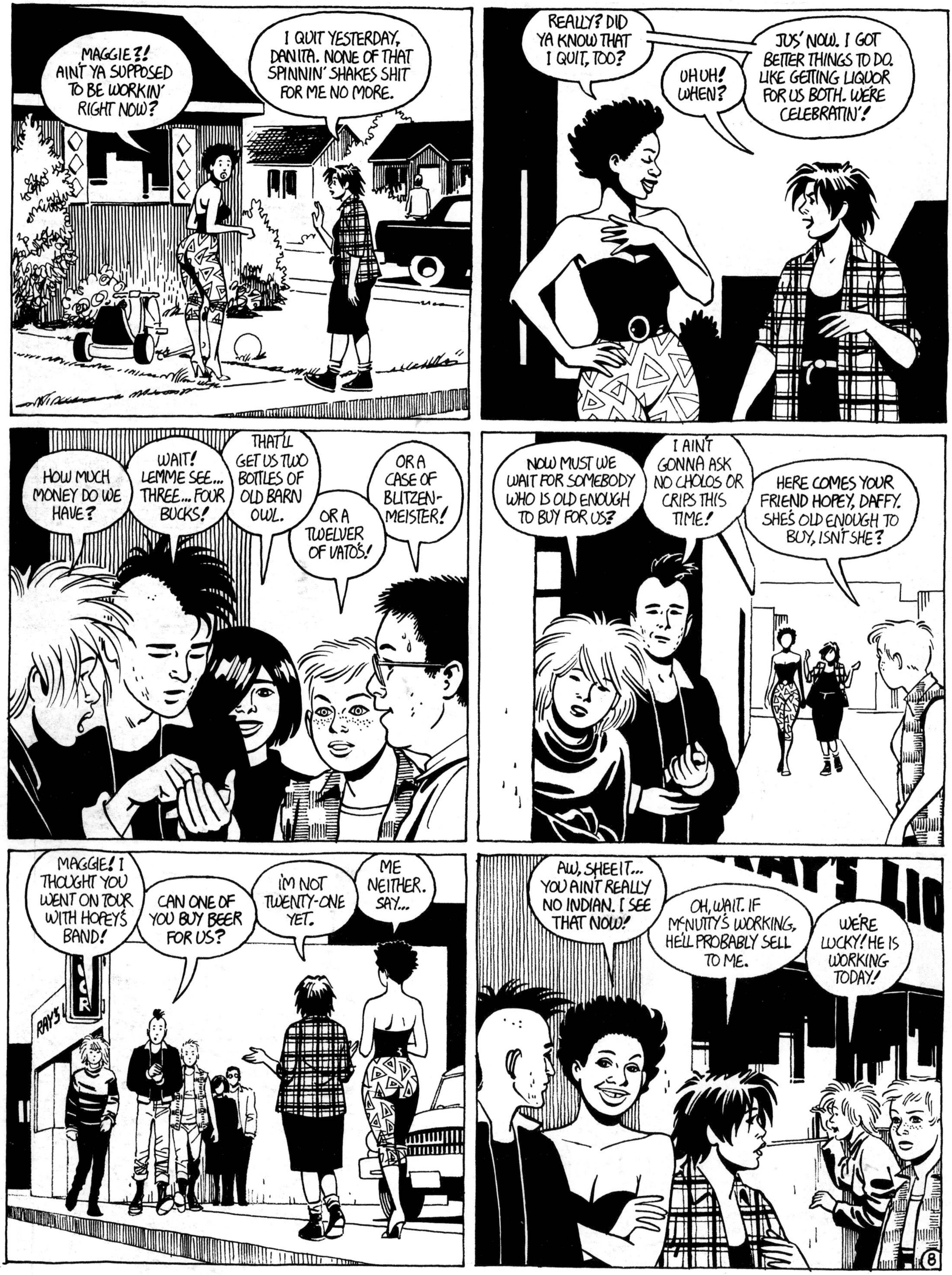
MAGGIE?! AIN'T YA SUPPOSED TO BE WORKIN' RIGHT NOW?
I QUIT YESTERDAY, DANITA. NONE OF THAT SPINNIN' SHAKES SHIT FOR ME NO MORE.
REALLY? DID YA KNOW THAT I QUIT, TOO?
UH UH! WHEN?
JUS' NOW. I GOT BETTER THINGS TO DO. LIKE GETTING LIQUOR FOR US BOTH. WE'RE CELEBRATIN'!
HOW MUCH MONEY DO WE HAVE?
WAIT! LEMME SEE... THREE... FOUR BUCKS!
THAT'LL GET US TWO BOTTLES OF OLD BARN OWL.
OR A TWELVER OF VATO'S!
OR A CASE OF BLITZEN-MEISTER!
NOW MUST WE WAIT FOR SOMEBODY WHO IS OLD ENOUGH TO BUY FOR US?
I AIN'T GONNA ASK NO CHOLOS OR CRIPS THIS TIME!
HERE COMES YOUR FRIEND HOPEY, DAFFY. SHE'S OLD ENOUGH TO BUY, ISN'T SHE?
MAGGIE! I THOUGHT YOU WENT ON TOUR WITH HOPEY'S BAND!
CAN ONE OF YOU BUY BEER FOR US?
I'M NOT TWENTY-ONE YET.
ME NEITHER. SAY...
RAY'S
AW, SHEEIT... YOU AIN'T REALLY NO INDIAN. I SEE THAT NOW!
OH, WAIT. IF McNUTTY'S WORKING, HE'LL PROBABLY SELL TO ME.
WE'RE LUCKY! HE IS WORKING TODAY!
8

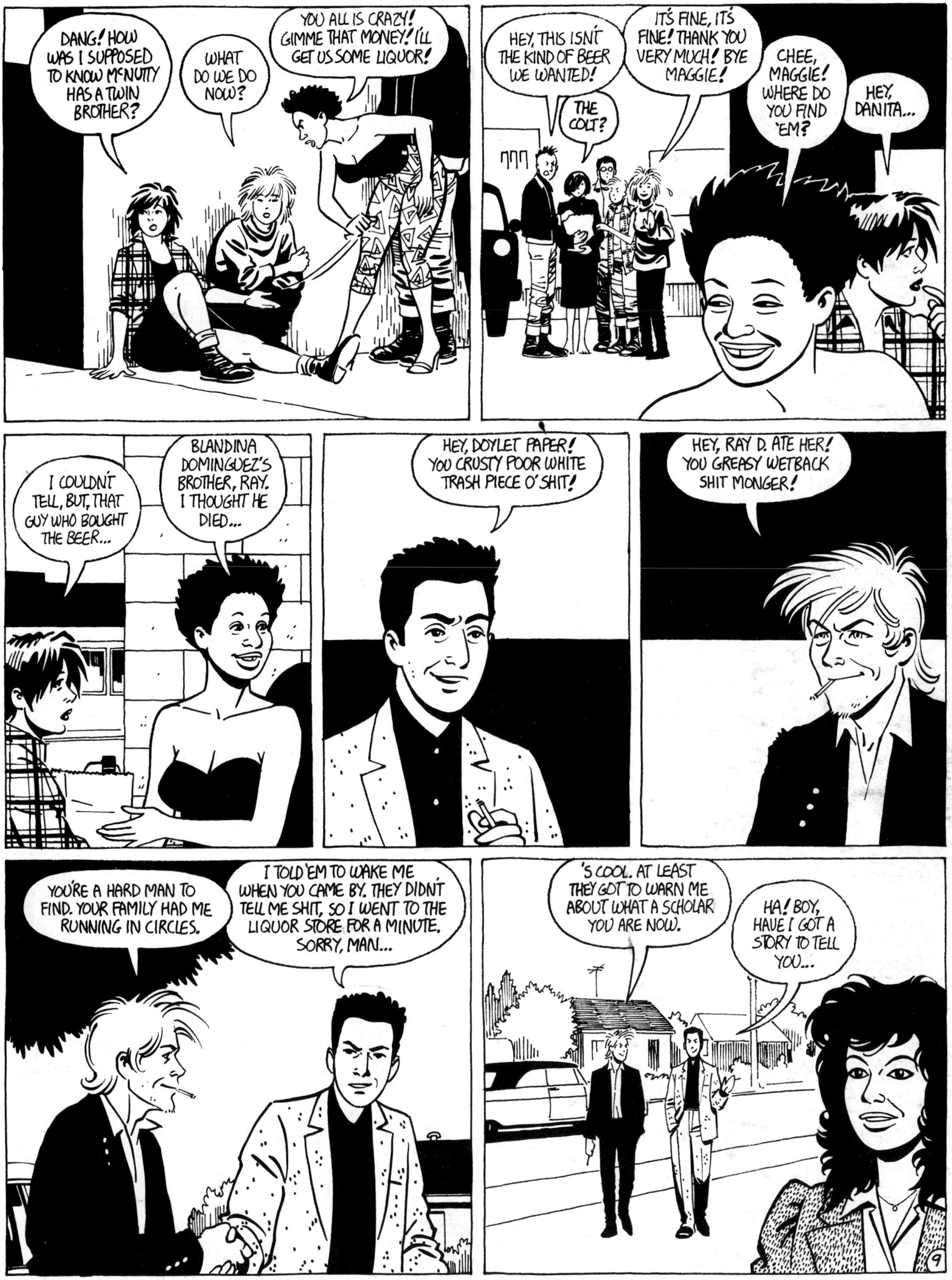
DANG! HOW WAS I SUPPOSED TO KNOW McNUTTY HAS A TWIN BROTHER?
WHAT DO WE DO NOW?
YOU ALL IS CRAZY! GIMME THAT MONEY! I'LL GET US SOME LIQUOR!
HEY, THIS ISN'T THE KIND OF BEER WE WANTED!
THE COLT?
IT'S FINE, IT'S FINE! THANK YOU VERY MUCH! BYE MAGGIE!
CHEE, MAGGIE! WHERE DO YOU FIND 'EM?
HEY, DANITA...
I COULDN'T TELL, BUT, THAT GUY WHO BOUGHT THE BEER...
BLANDINA DOMINGUEZ'S BROTHER, RAY. I THOUGHT HE DIED...
HEY, DOYLET PAPER! YOU CRUSTY POOR WHITE TRASH PIECE O' SHIT!
HEY, RAY D. ATE HER! YOU GREASY WETBACK SHIT MONGER!
YOU'RE A HARD MAN TO FIND. YOUR FAMILY HAD ME RUNNING IN CIRCLES.
I TOLD 'EM TO WAKE ME WHEN YOU CAME BY. THEY DIDN'T TELL ME SHIT, SO I WENT TO THE LIQUOR STORE FOR A MINUTE. SORRY, MAN...
'S COOL. AT LEAST THEY GOT TO WARN ME ABOUT WHAT A SCHOLAR YOU ARE NOW.
HA! BOY, HAVE I GOT A STORY TO TELL YOU...
9

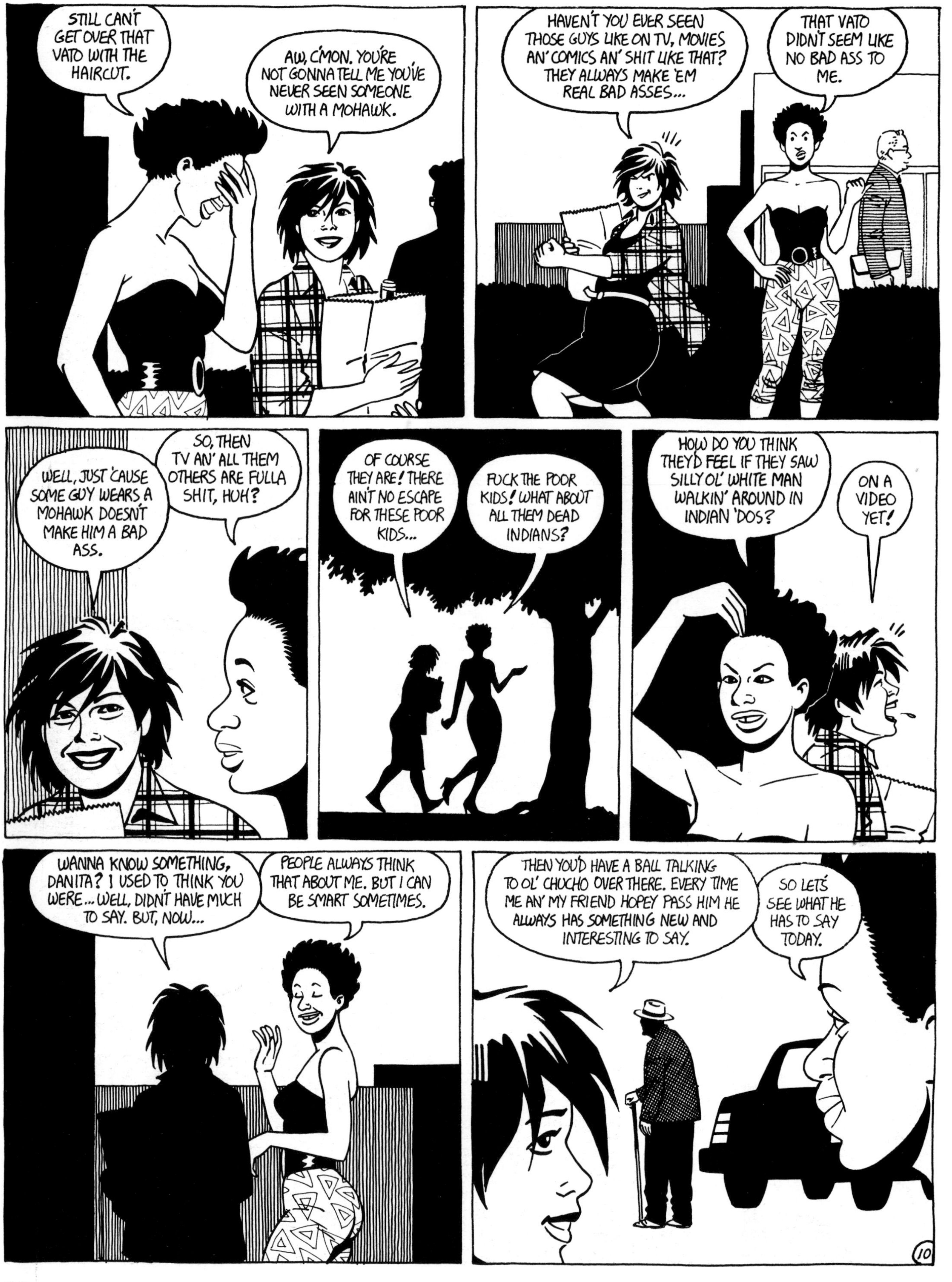
STILL CAN'T GET OVER THAT VATO WITH THE HAIRCUT.
AW, C'MON. YOU'RE NOT GONNA TELL ME YOU'VE NEVER SEEN SOMEONE WITH A MOHAWK.
HAVEN'T YOU EVER SEEN THOSE GUYS LIKE ON TV, MOVIES AN' COMICS AN' SHIT LIKE THAT? THEY ALWAYS MAKE 'EM REAL BAD ASSES...
THAT VATO DIDN'T SEEM LIKE NO BAD ASS TO ME.
WELL, JUST 'CAUSE SOME GUY WEARS A MOHAWK DOESN'T MAKE HIM A BAD ASS.
SO, THEN TV AN' ALL THEM OTHERS ARE FULLA SHIT, HUH?
OF COURSE THEY ARE! THERE AIN'T NO ESCAPE FOR THESE POOR KIDS...
FUCK THE POOR KIDS! WHAT ABOUT ALL THEM DEAD INDIANS?
HOW DO YOU THINK THEY'D FEEL IF THEY SAW SILLY OL' WHITE MAN WALKIN' AROUND IN INDIAN 'DOS?
ON A VIDEO YET!
WANNA KNOW SOMETHING, DANITA? I USED TO THINK YOU WERE... WELL, DIDN'T HAVE MUCH TO SAY. BUT, NOW...
PEOPLE ALWAYS THINK THAT ABOUT ME. BUT I CAN BE SMART SOMETIMES.
THEN YOU'D HAVE A BALL TALKING TO OL' CHUCHO OVER THERE. EVERY TIME ME AN' MY FRIEND HOPEY PASS HIM HE ALWAYS HAS SOMETHING NEW AND INTERESTING TO SAY.
SO LET'S SEE WHAT HE HAS TO SAY TODAY.
10

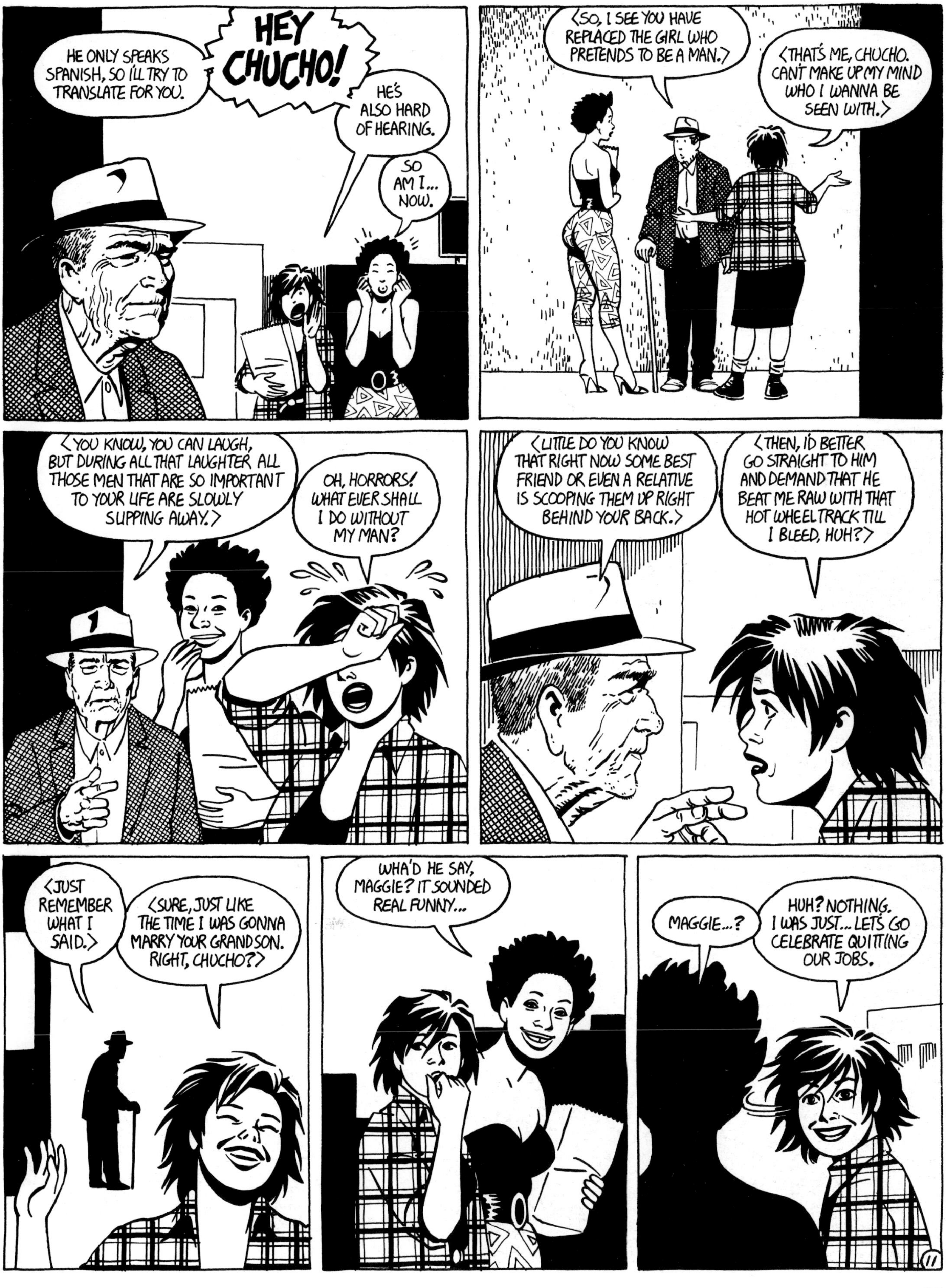

HE ONLY SPEAKS SPANISH, SO I'LL TRY TO TRANSLATE FOR YOU.
HEY CHUCHO!
HE'S ALSO HARD OF HEARING.
SO AM I... NOW.
<SO, I SEE YOU HAVE REPLACED THE GIRL WHO PRETENDS TO BE A MAN.>
<THAT'S ME, CHUCHO. CAN'T MAKE UP MY MIND WHO I WANNA BE SEEN WITH.>
<YOU KNOW, YOU CAN LAUGH, BUT DURING ALL THAT LAUGHTER ALL THOSE MEN THAT ARE SO IMPORTANT TO YOUR LIFE ARE SLOWLY SLIPPING AWAY.>
OH, HORRORS! WHAT EVER SHALL I DO WITHOUT MY MAN?
<LITTLE DO YOU KNOW THAT RIGHT NOW SOME BEST FRIEND OR EVEN A RELATIVE IS SCOOPING THEM UP RIGHT BEHIND YOUR BACK.>
<THEN, I'D BETTER GO STRAIGHT TO HIM AND DEMAND THAT HE BEAT ME RAW WITH THAT HOT WHEEL TRACK TILL I BLEED, HUH?>
<JUST REMEMBER WHAT I SAID.>
<SURE, JUST LIKE THE TIME I WAS GONNA MARRY YOUR GRANDSON. RIGHT, CHUCHO?>
WHA'D HE SAY, MAGGIE? IT SOUNDED REAL FUNNY...
MAGGIE...?
HUH? NOTHING. I WAS JUST... LET'S GO CELEBRATE QUITTING OUR JOBS.
11

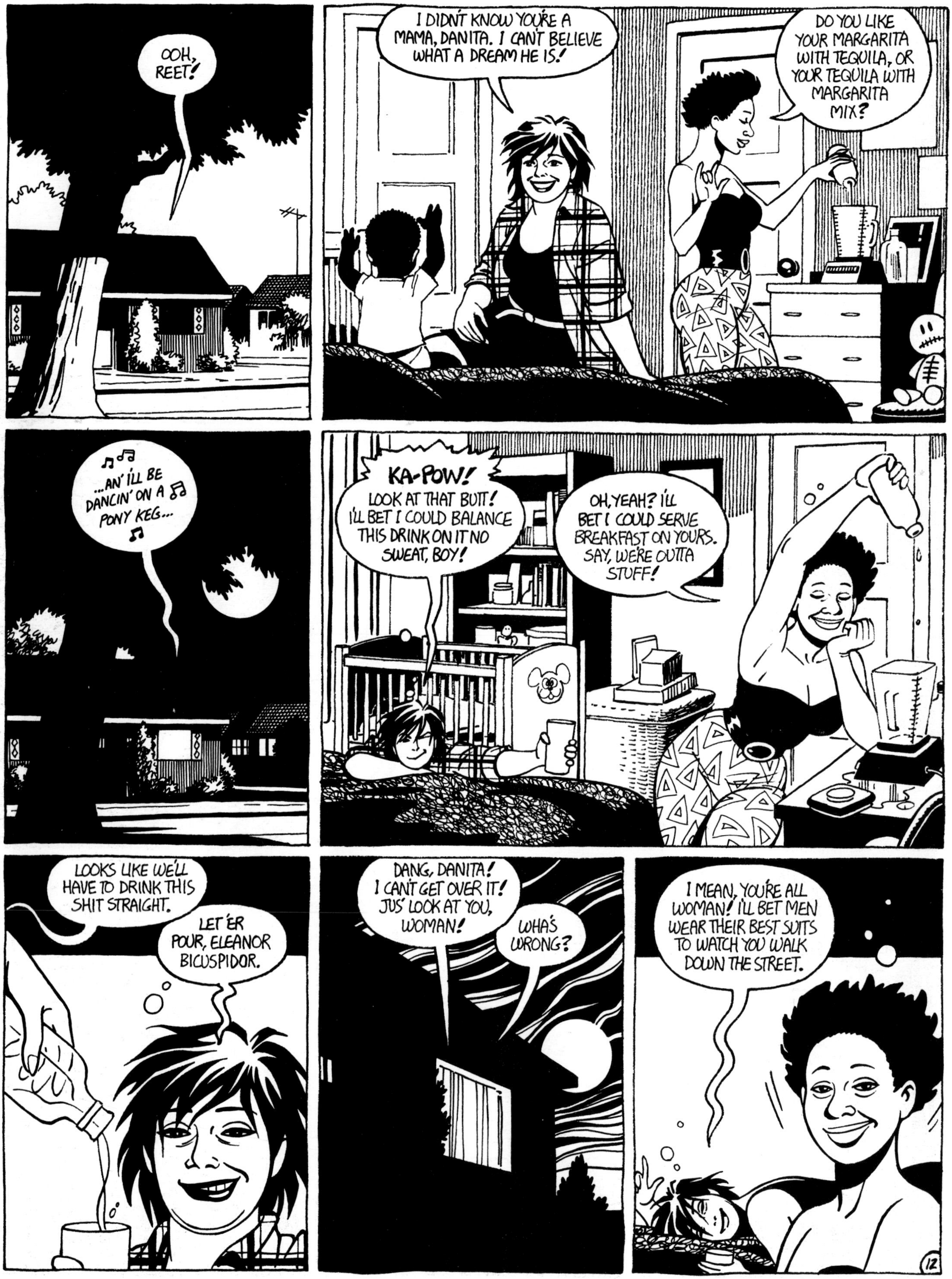

OOH, REET!
I DIDN'T KNOW YOU'RE A MAMA, DANITA. I CAN'T BELIEVE WHAT A DREAM HE IS!
DO YOU LIKE YOUR MARGARITA WITH TEQUILA, OR YOUR TEQUILA WITH MARGARITA MIX?
...AN' I'LL BE DANCIN' ON A PONY KEG...
KA-POW!
LOOK AT THAT BUTT! I'LL BET I COULD BALANCE THIS DRINK ON IT NO SWEAT, BOY!
OH, YEAH? I'LL BET I COULD SERVE BREAKFAST ON YOURS. SAY, WE'RE OUTTA STUFF!
LOOKS LIKE WE'LL HAVE TO DRINK THIS SHIT STRAIGHT.
LET 'ER POUR, ELEANOR BICUSPIDOR.
DANG, DANITA! I CAN'T GET OVER IT! JUS' LOOK AT YOU, WOMAN!
WHA'S WRONG?
I MEAN, YOU'RE ALL WOMAN! I'LL BET MEN WEAR THEIR BEST SUITS TO WATCH YOU WALK DOWN THE STREET.
12

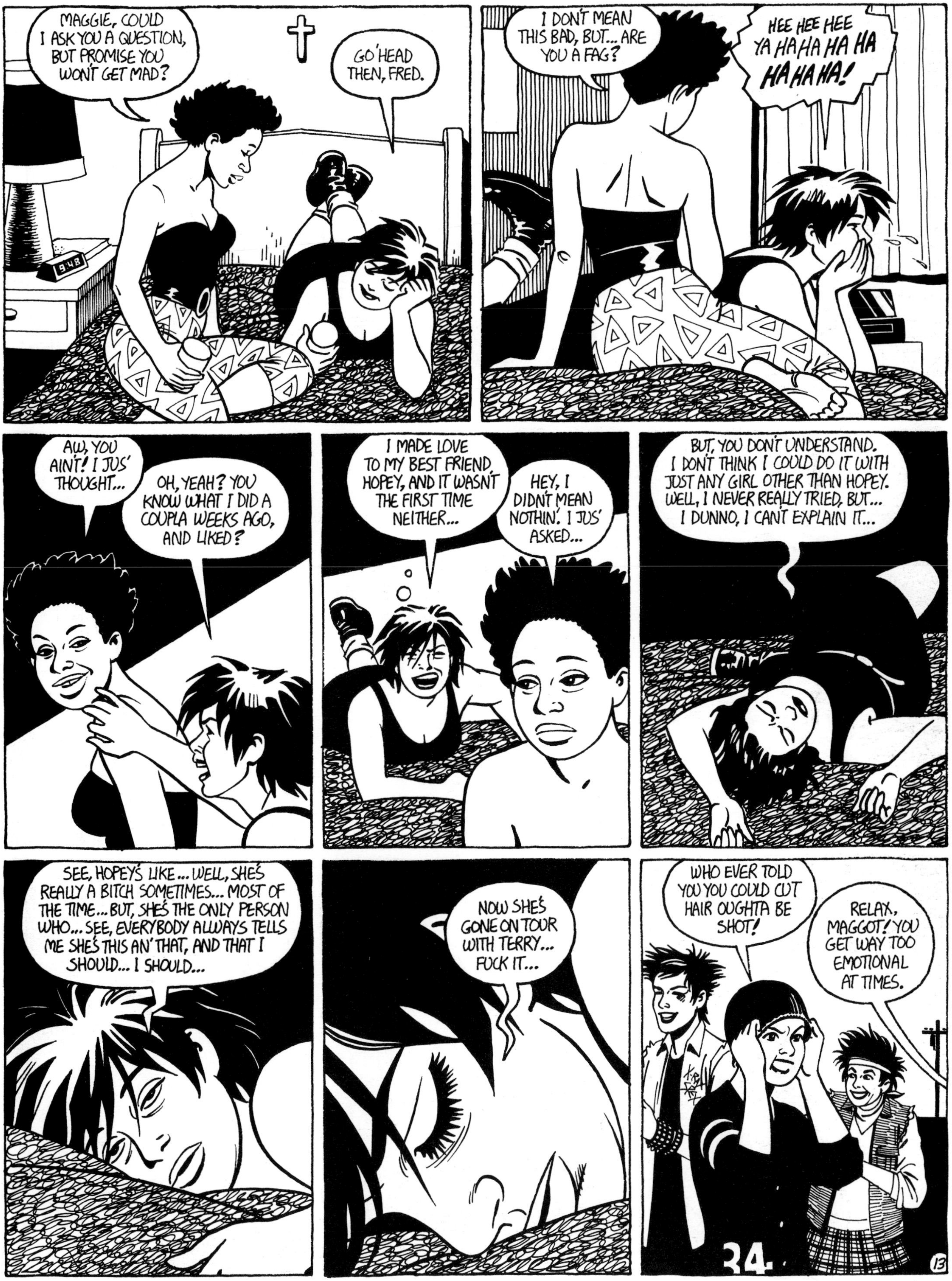
MAGGIE, COULD I ASK YOU A QUESTION, BUT PROMISE YOU WON'T GET MAD?
GO'HEAD THEN, FRED.
I DON'T MEAN THIS BAD, BUT... ARE YOU A FAG?
HEE HEE HEE YA HA HA HA HA HA HA HA HA!
AW, YOU AIN'T! I JUS' THOUGHT...
OH, YEAH? YOU KNOW WHAT I DID A COUPLA WEEKS AGO, AND LIKED?
I MADE LOVE TO MY BEST FRIEND, HOPEY, AND IT WASN'T THE FIRST TIME NEITHER...
HEY, I DIDN'T MEAN NOTHIN'. I JUS' ASKED...
BUT, YOU DON'T UNDERSTAND. I DON'T THINK I COULD DO IT WITH JUST ANY GIRL OTHER THAN HOPEY. WELL, I NEVER REALLY TRIED, BUT... I DUNNO, I CAN'T EXPLAIN IT...
SEE, HOPEY'S LIKE... WELL, SHE'S REALLY A BITCH SOMETIMES... MOST OF THE TIME... BUT, SHE'S THE ONLY PERSON WHO... SEE, EVERYBODY ALWAYS TELLS ME SHE'S THIS AN' THAT, AND THAT I SHOULD... I SHOULD...
NOW SHE'S GONE ON TOUR WITH TERRY... FUCK IT...
WHO EVER TOLD YOU YOU COULD CUT HAIR OUGHTA BE SHOT!
RELAX, MAGGOT! YOU GET WAY TOO EMOTIONAL AT TIMES.
34
13

I SUPPOSE TERRY SAID THAT, TOO?
AS A MATTER OF FACT, SHE DID, MAGGOT.
WHAT DID YOU WRITE? LEMME DO SOME!
AH, LET'S GO. THAT CEMENT IS DRY ALREADY.
WET CEMENT
GOD, THIS DAY IS SO BORING! WE SHOULD GO MEET SOME GUYS OR SOMETHING.
GUYS?
YEAH! DON'T TELL ME MEETING GUYS AIN'T THE "PUNK" THING TO DO.
THUTHUTHU THUTHUTHUTHU... AWRIGHT, AWRIGHT!
OK, SO LET'S GO MEET SOME "GUYS".
OH, SHUT... HEY, LOOKIT, HOKEY!
SEE THAT GUY? THAT'S RAY DOMINGUEZ. HE'S MY BOYFRIEND.
THAT GUY?
WELL, SHOOT! THEN DON'T YA THINK IT'S TIME FOR A FEW INTRODUCTIONS?
WAIT! NO, HOPEY! DON'T SAY ANYTHING TO HIM...
HE'S NOT MY REAL BOYFRIEND. WE JUST KINDA... AH, SHIT! I'M DEAD!
C'MON, I AIN'T PLAYIN', MAGGIE! YOU GOTTA GO LIKE, RIGHT NOW!
14

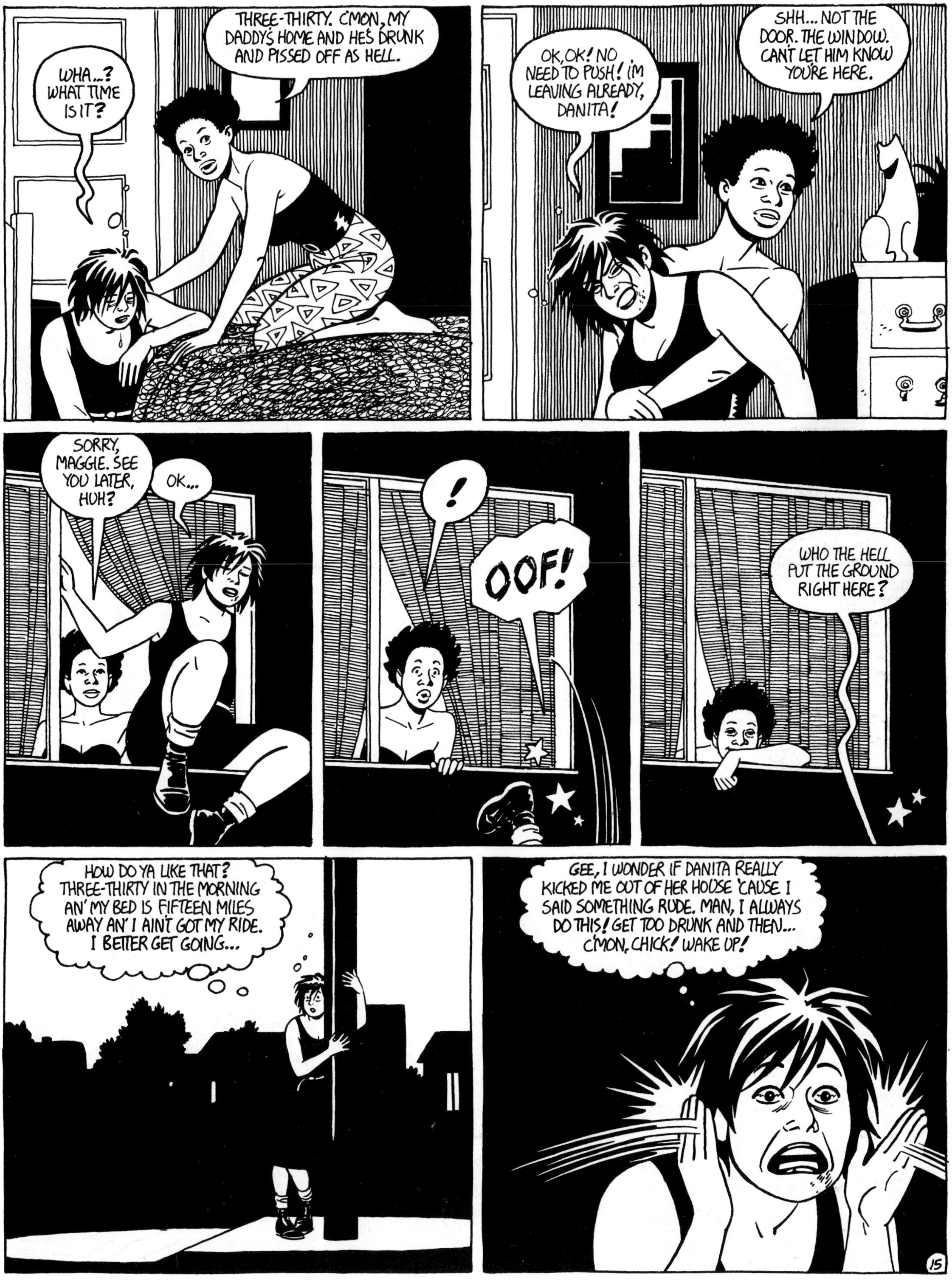
WHA...? WHAT TIME IS IT?
THREE-THIRTY. C'MON, MY DADDY'S HOME AND HE'S DRUNK AND PISSED OFF AS HELL.
OK, OK! NO NEED TO PUSH! I'M LEAVING ALREADY, DANITA!
SHH... NOT THE DOOR. THE WINDOW. CAN'T LET HIM KNOW YOU'RE HERE.
SORRY, MAGGIE. SEE YOU LATER, HUH?
OK...
!
OOF!
WHO THE HELL PUT THE GROUND RIGHT HERE?
HOW DO YA LIKE THAT? THREE-THIRTY IN THE MORNING AN' MY BED IS FIFTEEN MILES AWAY AN' I AIN'T GOT MY RIDE. I BETTER GET GOING...
GEE, I WONDER IF DANITA REALLY KICKED ME OUT OF HER HOUSE 'CAUSE I SAID SOMETHING RUDE. MAN, I ALWAYS DO THIS! GET TOO DRUNK AND THEN... C'MON, CHICK! WAKE UP!
15

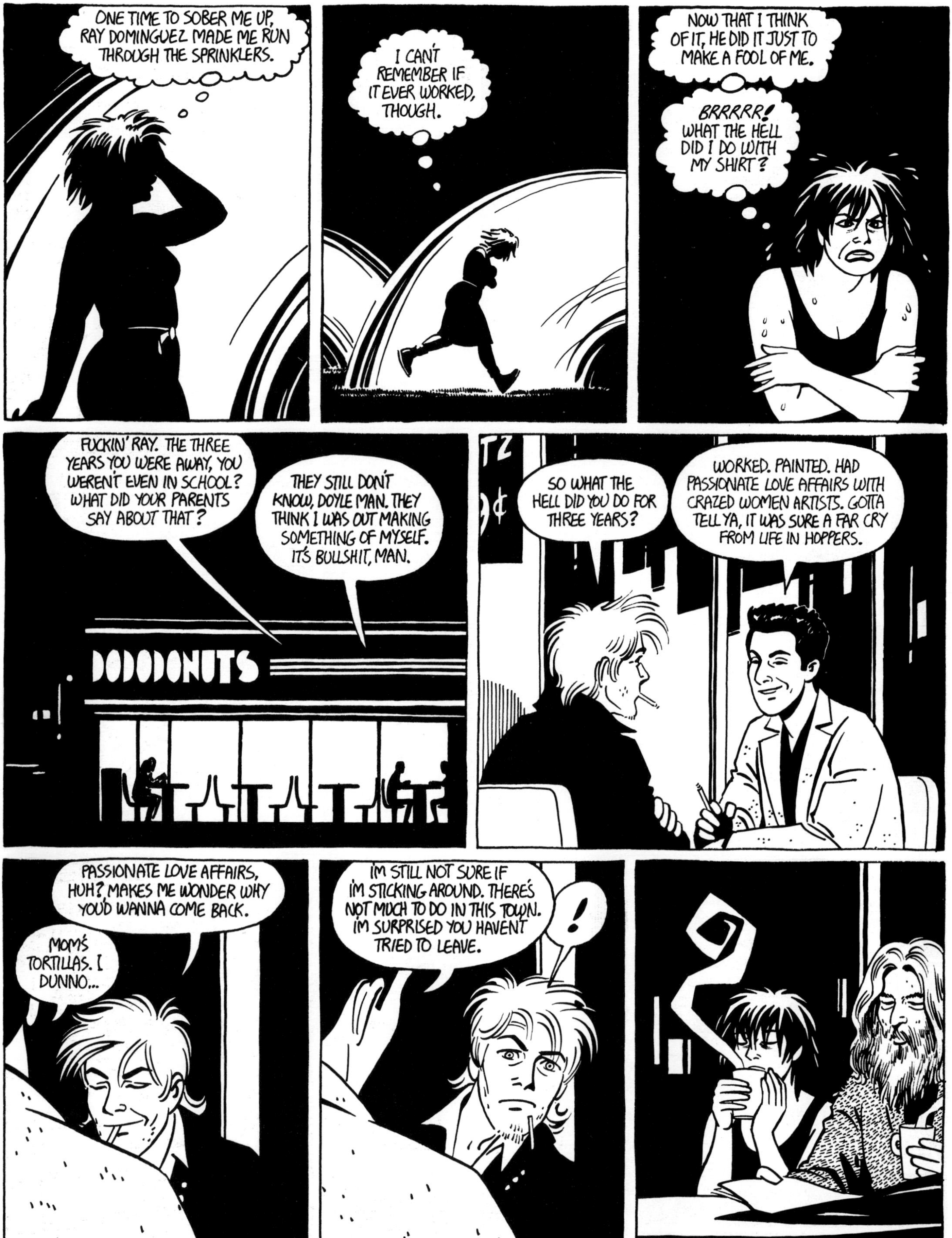
ONE TIME TO SOBER ME UP, RAY DOMINGUEZ MADE ME RUN THROUGH THE SPRINKLERS.
I CAN'T REMEMBER IF IT EVER WORKED, THOUGH.
NOW THAT I THINK OF IT, HE DID IT JUST TO MAKE A FOOL OF ME.
BRRRRR! WHAT THE HELL DID I DO WITH MY SHIRT?
FUCKIN' RAY. THE THREE YEARS YOU WERE AWAY, YOU WEREN'T EVEN IN SCHOOL? WHAT DID YOUR PARENTS SAY ABOUT THAT?
THEY STILL DON'T KNOW, DOYLE MAN. THEY THINK I WAS OUT MAKING SOMETHING OF MYSELF. IT'S BULLSHIT, MAN.
DODODONUTS
SO WHAT THE HELL DID YOU DO FOR THREE YEARS?
WORKED. PAINTED. HAD PASSIONATE LOVE AFFAIRS WITH CRAZED WOMEN ARTISTS. GOTTA TELL YA, IT WAS SURE A FAR CRY FROM LIFE IN HOPPERS.
PASSIONATE LOVE AFFAIRS, HUH? MAKES ME WONDER WHY YOU'D WANNA COME BACK.
MOM'S TORTILLAS. I DUNNO...
I'M STILL NOT SURE IF I'M STICKING AROUND. THERE'S NOT MUCH TO DO IN THIS TOWN. I'M SURPRISED YOU HAVEN'T TRIED TO LEAVE.
!
16

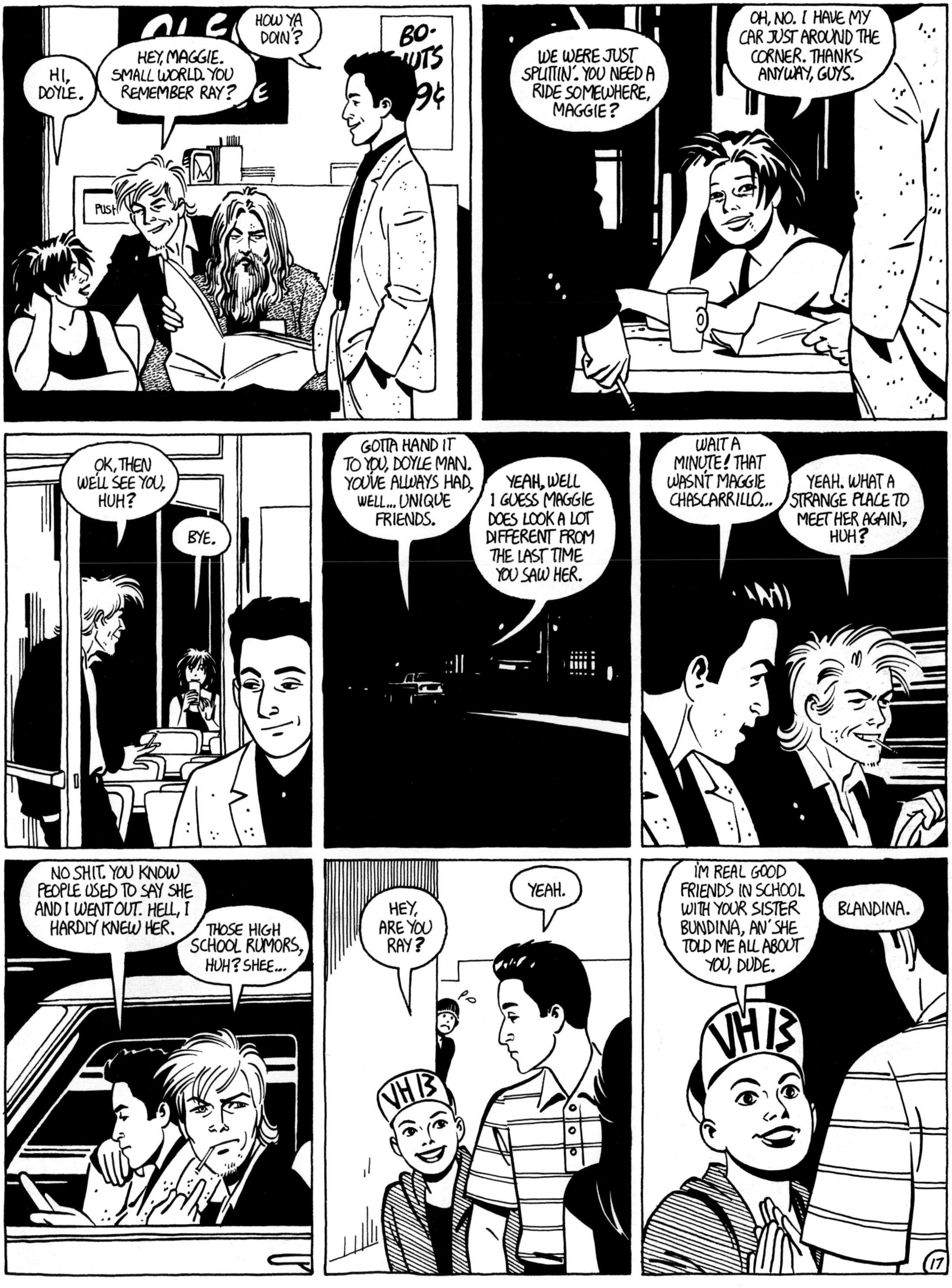
HI, DOYLE.
HEY, MAGGIE. SMALL WORLD. YOU REMEMBER RAY?
HOW YA DOIN'?
WE WERE JUST SPLITTIN'. YOU NEED A RIDE SOMEWHERE, MAGGIE?
OH, NO. I HAVE MY CAR JUST AROUND THE CORNER. THANKS ANYWAY, GUYS.
OK, THEN WE'LL SEE YOU, HUH?
BYE.
GOTTA HAND IT TO YOU, DOYLE MAN. YOU'VE ALWAYS HAD, WELL... UNIQUE FRIENDS.
YEAH, WELL I GUESS MAGGIE DOES LOOK A LOT DIFFERENT FROM THE LAST TIME YOU SAW HER.
WAIT A MINUTE! THAT WASN'T MAGGIE CHASCARRILLO...
YEAH. WHAT A STRANGE PLACE TO MEET HER AGAIN, HUH?
NO SHIT. YOU KNOW PEOPLE USED TO SAY SHE AND I WENT OUT. HELL, I HARDLY KNEW HER.
THOSE HIGH SCHOOL RUMORS, HUH? SHEE...
HEY, ARE YOU RAY?
YEAH.
I'M REAL GOOD FRIENDS IN SCHOOL WITH YOUR SISTER BUNDINA, AN' SHE TOLD ME ALL ABOUT YOU, DUDE.
BLANDINA.
VH13
VH13
17

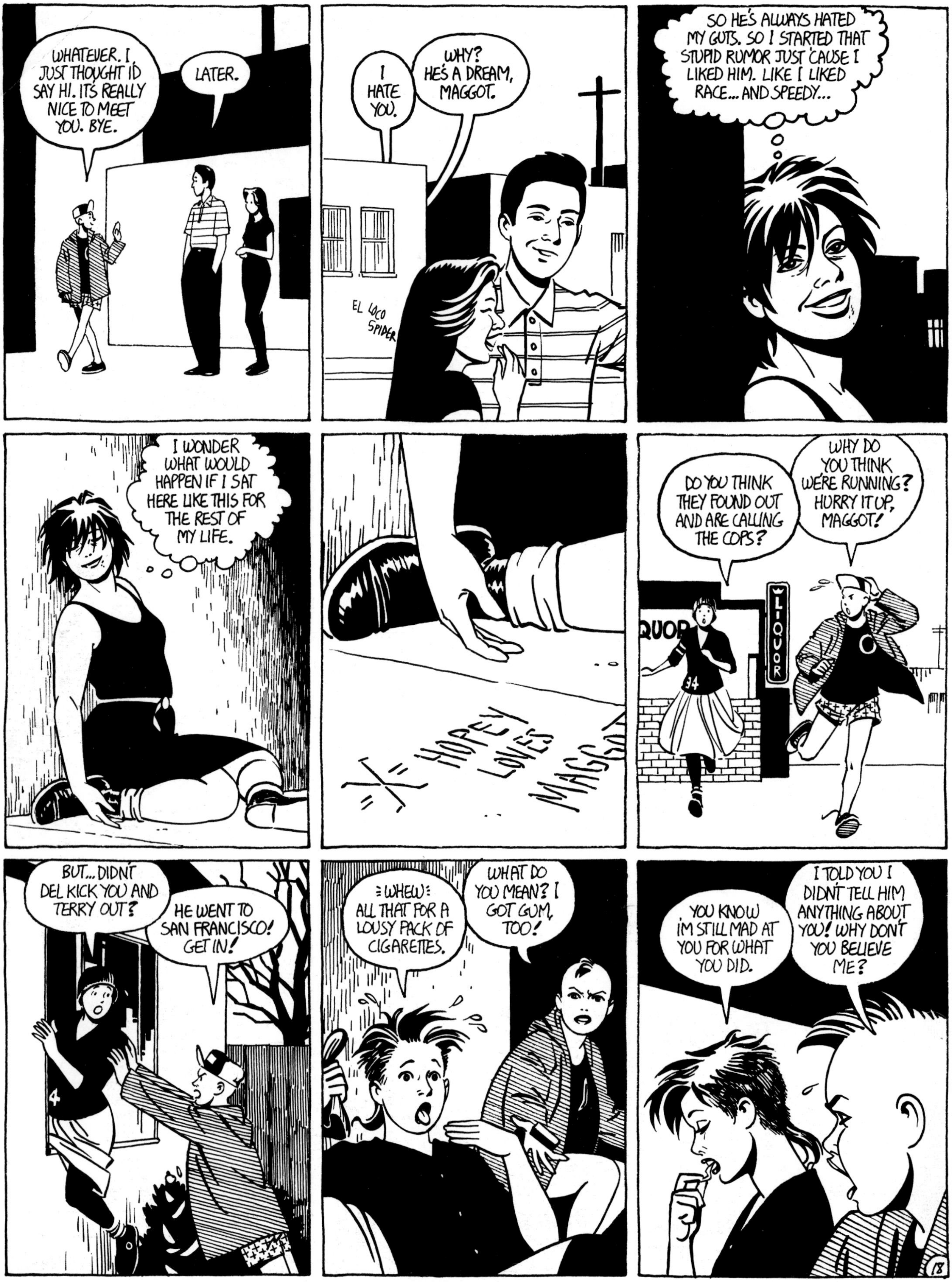
WHATEVER. I JUST THOUGHT I'D SAY HI. IT'S REALLY NICE TO MEET YOU. BYE.
LATER.
I HATE YOU.
WHY? HE'S A DREAM, MAGGOT.
EL LOCO SPIDER
SO HE'S ALWAYS HATED MY GUTS. SO I STARTED THAT STUPID RUMOR JUST 'CAUSE I LIKED HIM. LIKE I LIKED RACE... AND SPEEDY...
I WONDER WHAT WOULD HAPPEN IF I SAT HERE LIKE THIS FOR THE REST OF MY LIFE.
HOPEY LOVES MAGGOT
DO YOU THINK THEY FOUND OUT AND ARE CALLING THE COPS?
WHY DO YOU THINK WE'RE RUNNING? HURRY IT UP, MAGGOT!
LIQUOR
BUT... DIDN'T DEL KICK YOU AND TERRY OUT?
HE WENT TO SAN FRANCISCO! GET IN!
WHEW
ALL THAT FOR A LOUSY PACK OF CIGARETTES.
WHAT DO YOU MEAN? I GOT GUM, TOO!
YOU KNOW I'M STILL MAD AT YOU FOR WHAT YOU DID.
I TOLD YOU I DIDN'T TELL HIM ANYTHING ABOUT YOU! WHY DON'T YOU BELIEVE ME?
18

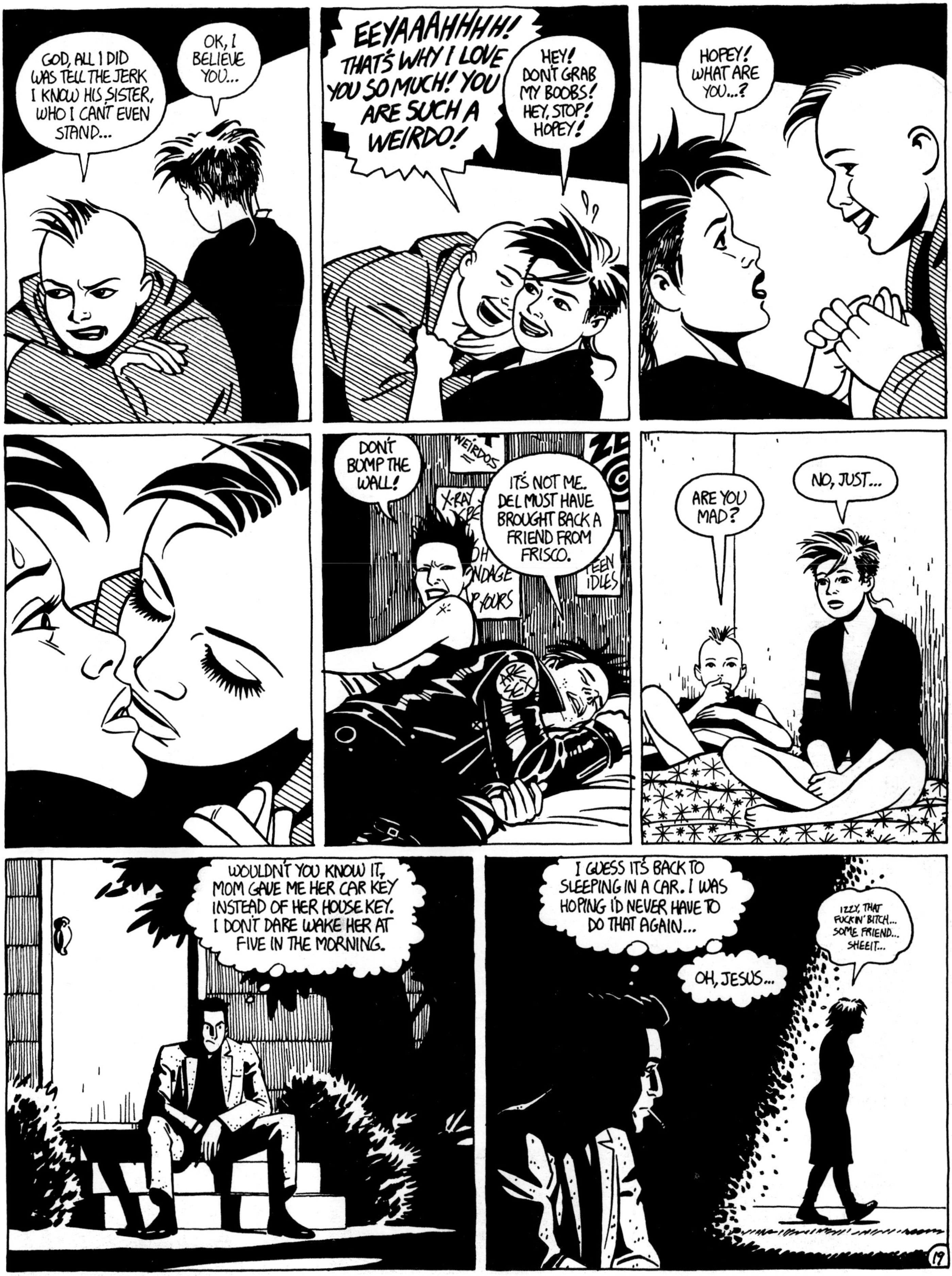
GOD, ALL I DID WAS TELL THE JERK I KNOW HIS SISTER, WHO I CAN'T EVEN STAND...
OK, I BELIEVE YOU...
EEYAAAHHHH! THAT'S WHY I LOVE YOU SO MUCH! YOU ARE SUCH A WEIRDO!
HEY! DON'T GRAB MY BOOBS! HEY, STOP! HOPEY!
HOPEY! WHAT ARE YOU...?
DON'T BUMP THE WALL!
IT'S NOT ME. DEL MUST HAVE BROUGHT BACK A FRIEND FROM FRISCO.
WEIRDOS
X-RAY
TEEN IDLES
ARE YOU MAD?
NO, JUST...
WOULDN'T YOU KNOW IT, MOM GAVE ME HER CAR KEY INSTEAD OF HER HOUSE KEY. I DON'T DARE WAKE HER AT FIVE IN THE MORNING.
I GUESS IT'S BACK TO SLEEPING IN A CAR. I WAS HOPING I'D NEVER HAVE TO DO THAT AGAIN...
OH, JESUS...
IZZY, THAT FUCKIN' BITCH... SOME FRIEND... SHEEIT...
19

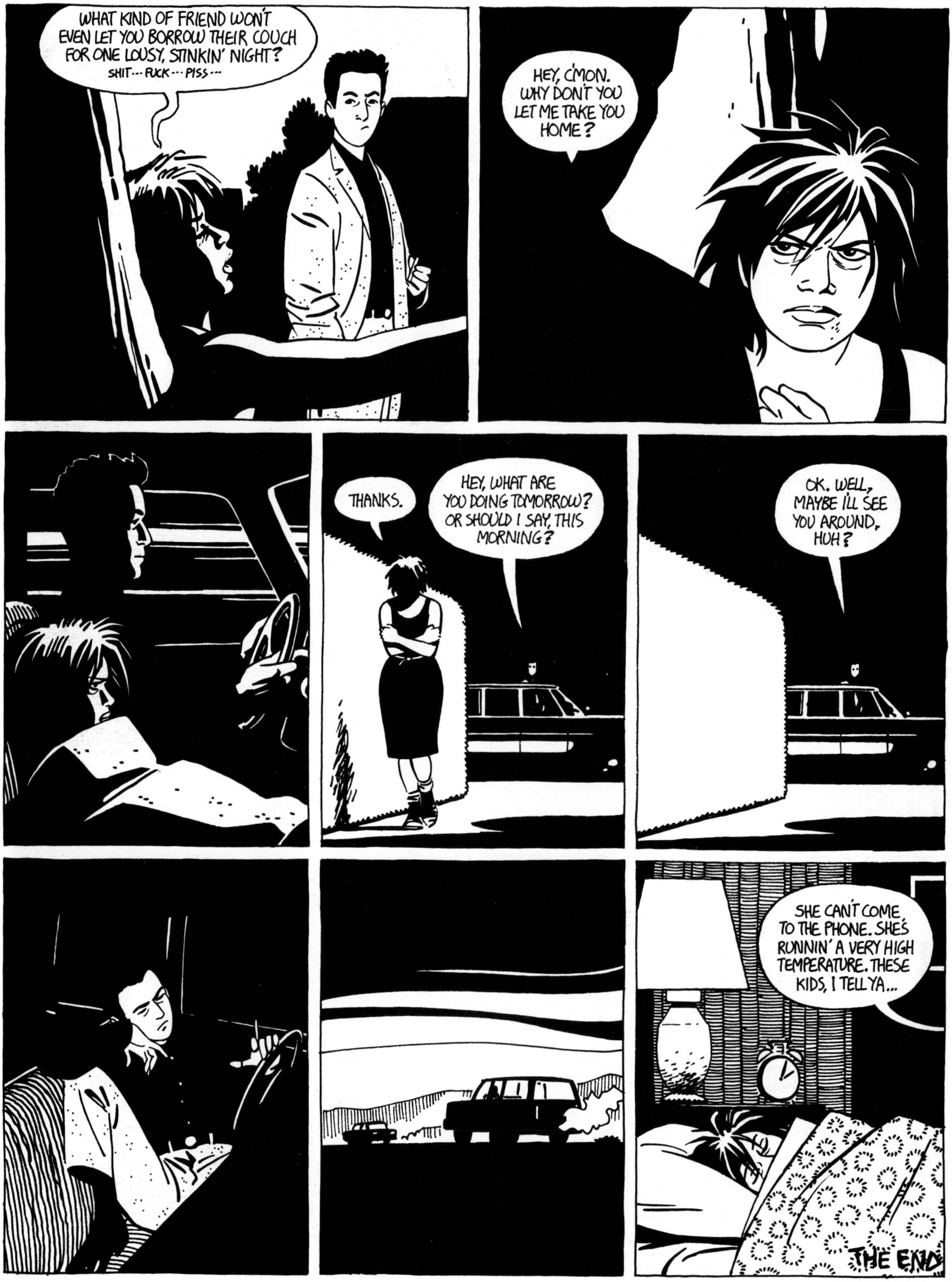
WHAT KIND OF FRIEND WON'T EVEN LET YOU BORROW THEIR COUCH FOR ONE LOUSY, STINKIN' NIGHT?
SHIT--- FUCK--- PISS---
HEY, C'MON. WHY DON'T YOU LET ME TAKE YOU HOME?
THANKS.
HEY, WHAT ARE YOU DOING TOMORROW? OR SHOULD I SAY, THIS MORNING?
OK. WELL, MAYBE I'LL SEE YOU AROUND, HUH?
SHE CAN'T COME TO THE PHONE. SHE'S RUNNIN' A VERY HIGH TEMPERATURE. THESE KIDS, I TELL YA...
THE END

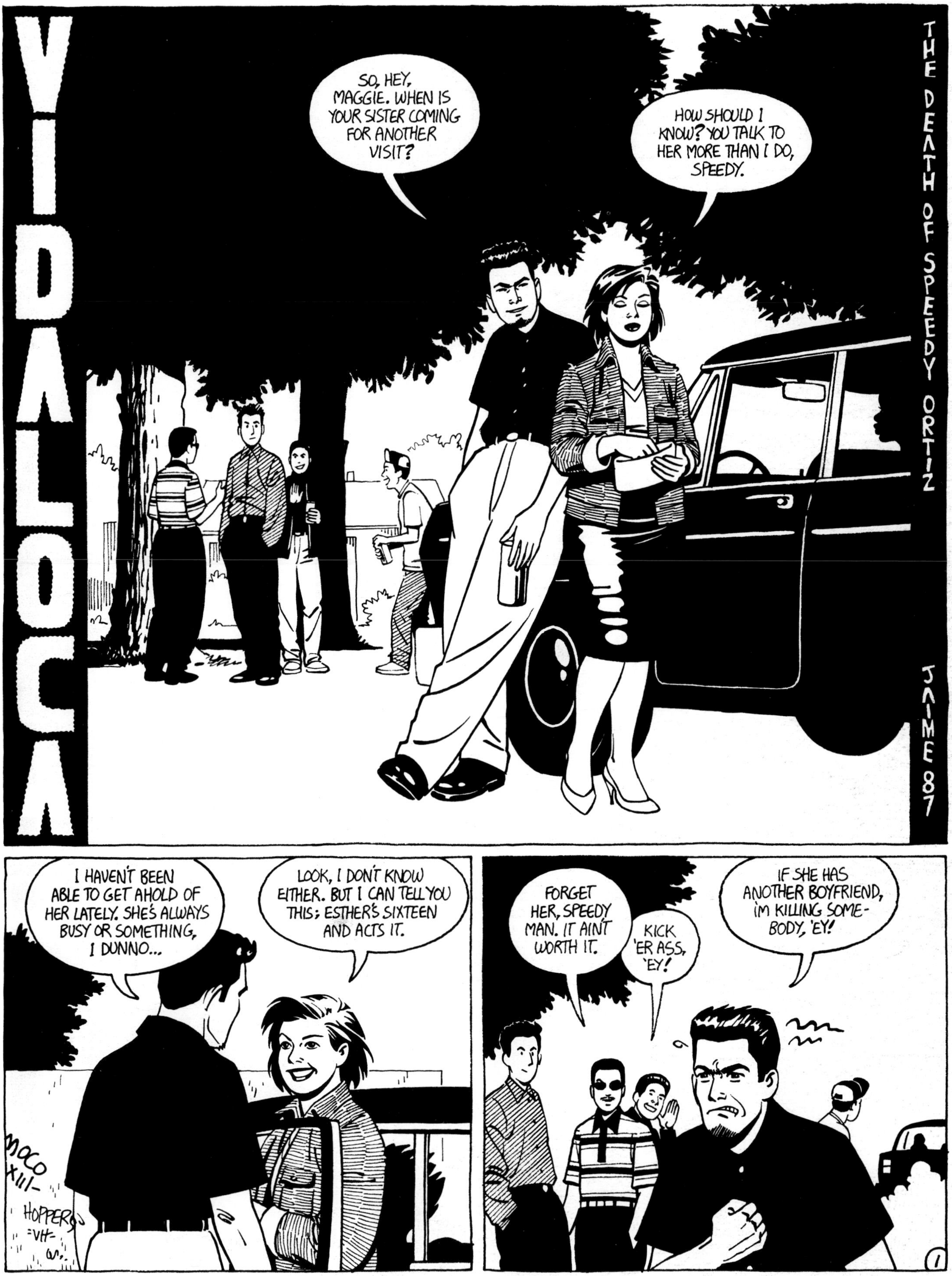
VIDALOCA
THE DEATH OF SPEEDY ORTIZ
SO, HEY, MAGGIE. WHEN IS YOUR SISTER COMING FOR ANOTHER VISIT?
HOW SHOULD I KNOW? YOU TALK TO HER MORE THAN I DO, SPEEDY.
JAIME 87
I HAVEN'T BEEN ABLE TO GET AHOLD OF HER LATELY. SHE'S ALWAYS BUSY OR SOMETHING, I DUNNO...
LOOK, I DON'T KNOW EITHER. BUT I CAN TELL YOU THIS; ESTHER'S SIXTEEN AND ACTS IT.
FORGET HER, SPEEDY MAN. IT AIN'T WORTH IT.
KICK 'ER ASS, 'EY!
IF SHE HAS ANOTHER BOYFRIEND, I'M KILLING SOME-BODY, 'EY!
1

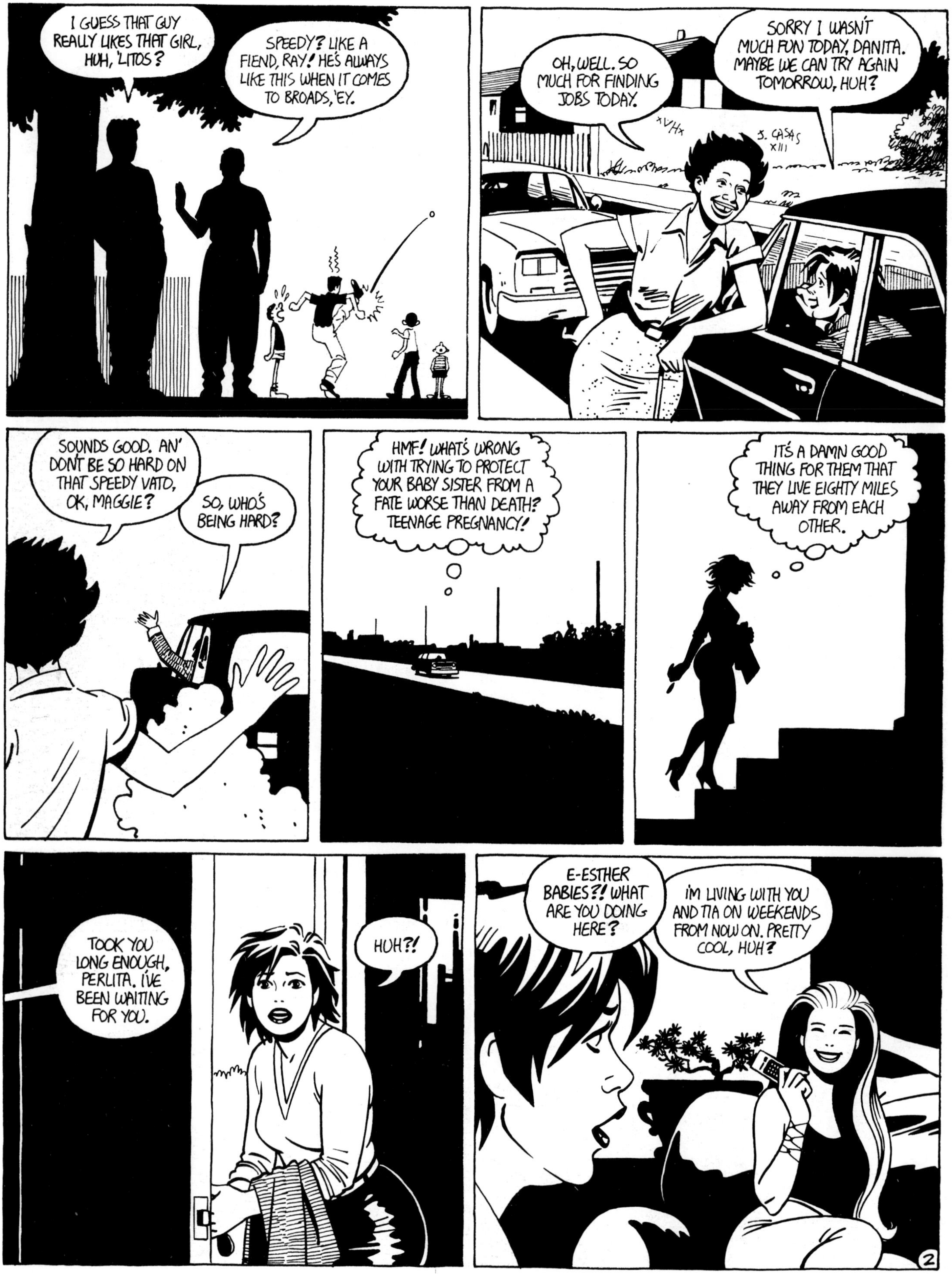

I GUESS THAT GUY REALLY LIKES THAT GIRL, HUH, 'LITOS?
SPEEDY? LIKE A FIEND, RAY! HE'S ALWAYS LIKE THIS WHEN IT COMES TO BROADS, 'EY.
OH, WELL. SO MUCH FOR FINDING JOBS TODAY.
SORRY I WASN'T MUCH FUN TODAY, DANITA. MAYBE WE CAN TRY AGAIN TOMORROW, HUH?
xVHx
J. CASAS XIII
SOUNDS GOOD. AN' DON'T BE SO HARD ON THAT SPEEDY VATO, OK, MAGGIE?
SO, WHO'S BEING HARD?
HMF! WHAT'S WRONG WITH TRYING TO PROTECT YOUR BABY SISTER FROM A FATE WORSE THAN DEATH? TEENAGE PREGNANCY!
IT'S A DAMN GOOD THING FOR THEM THAT THEY LIVE EIGHTY MILES AWAY FROM EACH OTHER.
TOOK YOU LONG ENOUGH, PERLITA. I'VE BEEN WAITING FOR YOU.
HUH?!
E-ESTHER BABIES?! WHAT ARE YOU DOING HERE?
I'M LIVING WITH YOU AND TIA ON WEEKENDS FROM NOW ON. PRETTY COOL, HUH?
2

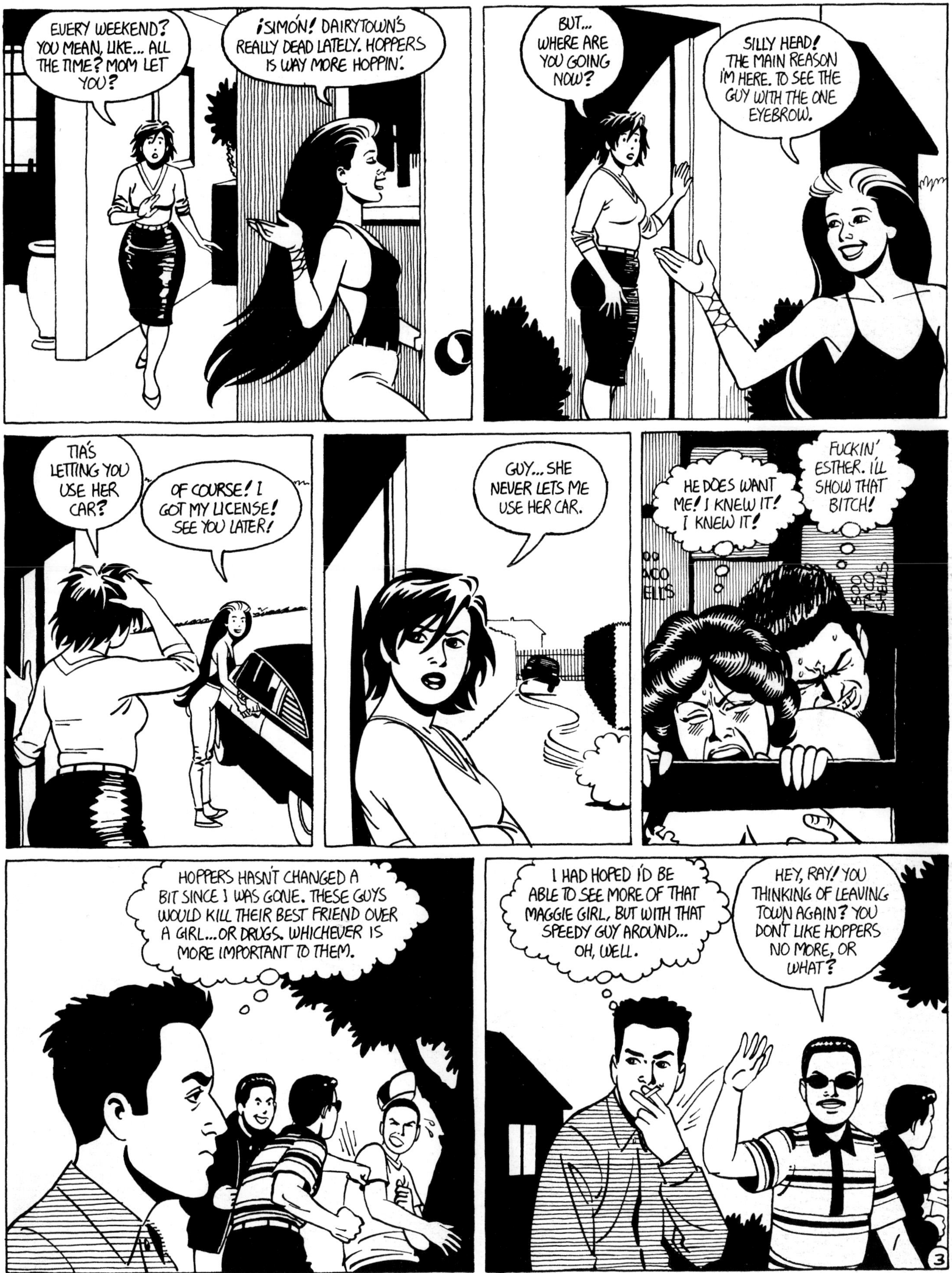
EVERY WEEKEND? YOU MEAN, LIKE... ALL THE TIME? MOM LET YOU?
¡SIMÓN! DAIRYTOWN'S REALLY DEAD LATELY. HOPPERS IS WAY MORE HOPPIN'.
BUT... WHERE ARE YOU GOING NOW?
SILLY HEAD! THE MAIN REASON I'M HERE. TO SEE THE GUY WITH THE ONE EYEBROW.
TIA'S LETTING YOU USE HER CAR?
OF COURSE! I GOT MY LICENSE! SEE YOU LATER!
GUY... SHE NEVER LETS ME USE HER CAR.
HE DOES WANT ME! I KNEW IT! I KNEW IT!
FUCKIN' ESTHER. I'LL SHOW THAT BITCH!
HOPPERS HASN'T CHANGED A BIT SINCE I WAS GONE. THESE GUYS WOULD KILL THEIR BEST FRIEND OVER A GIRL... OR DRUGS. WHICHEVER IS MORE IMPORTANT TO THEM.
I HAD HOPED I'D BE ABLE TO SEE MORE OF THAT MAGGIE GIRL, BUT WITH THAT SPEEDY GUY AROUND... OH, WELL.
HEY, RAY! YOU THINKING OF LEAVING TOWN AGAIN? YOU DON'T LIKE HOPPERS NO MORE, OR WHAT?
3

SIMÓN/OF COURSE!

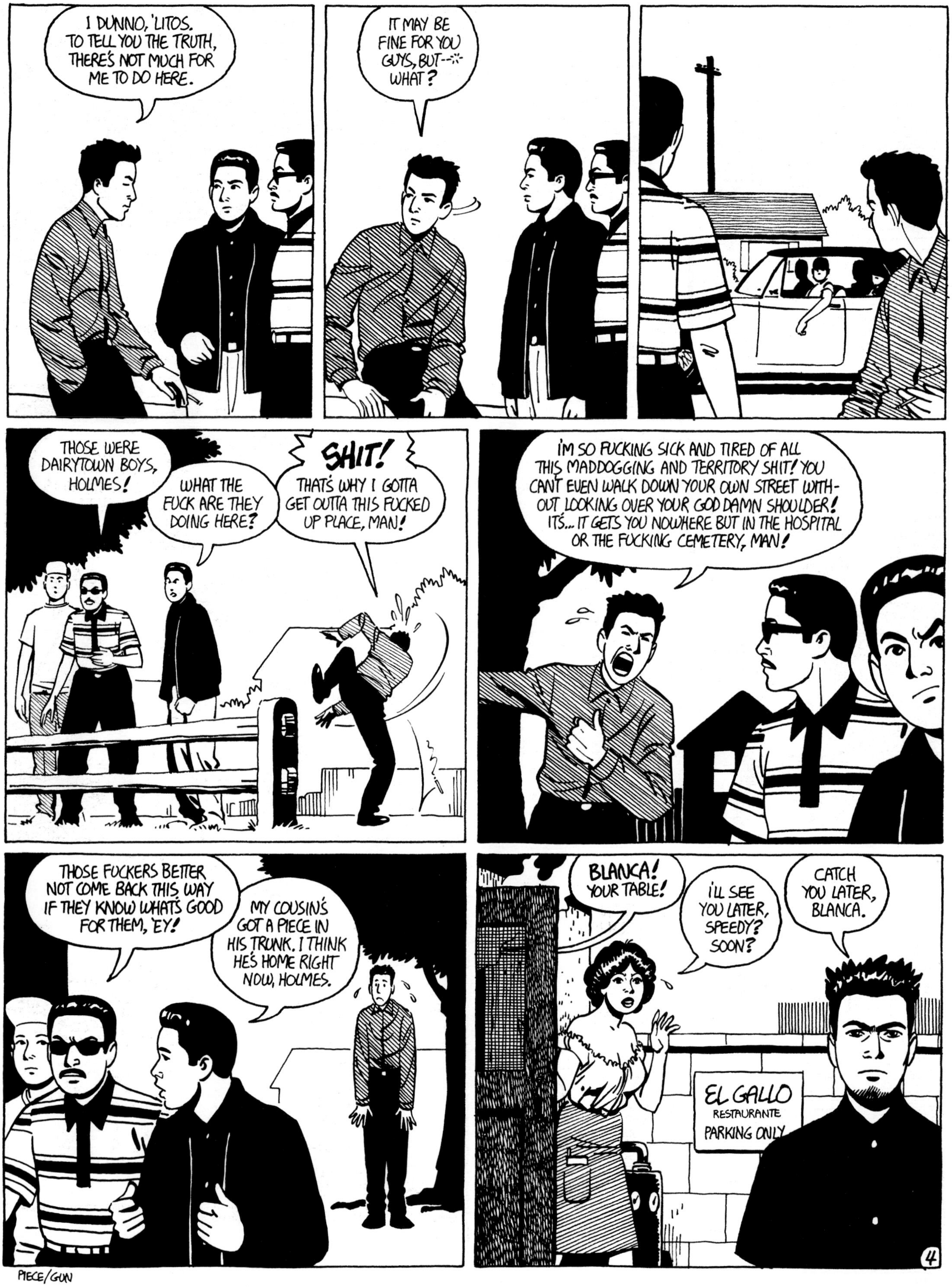

I DUNNO, 'LITOS. TO TELL YOU THE TRUTH, THERE'S NOT MUCH FOR ME TO DO HERE.
IT MAY BE FINE FOR YOU GUYS, BUT-- WHAT?
THOSE WERE DAIRYTOWN BOYS, HOLMES!
WHAT THE FUCK ARE THEY DOING HERE?
SHIT!
THAT'S WHY I GOTTA GET OUTTA THIS FUCKED UP PLACE, MAN!
I'M SO FUCKING SICK AND TIRED OF ALL THIS MADDOGGING AND TERRITORY SHIT! YOU CAN'T EVEN WALK DOWN YOUR OWN STREET WITHOUT LOOKING OVER YOUR GOD DAMN SHOULDER! IT'S... IT GETS YOU NOWHERE BUT IN THE HOSPITAL OR THE FUCKING CEMETERY, MAN!
THOSE FUCKERS BETTER NOT COME BACK THIS WAY IF THEY KNOW WHAT'S GOOD FOR THEM, EY!
MY COUSIN'S GOT A PIECE IN HIS TRUNK. I THINK HE'S HOME RIGHT NOW, HOLMES.
BLANCA! YOUR TABLE!
I'LL SEE YOU LATER, SPEEDY? SOON?
CATCH YOU LATER, BLANCA.
EL GALLO
RESTAURANTE
PARKING ONLY
4

PIECE/GUN

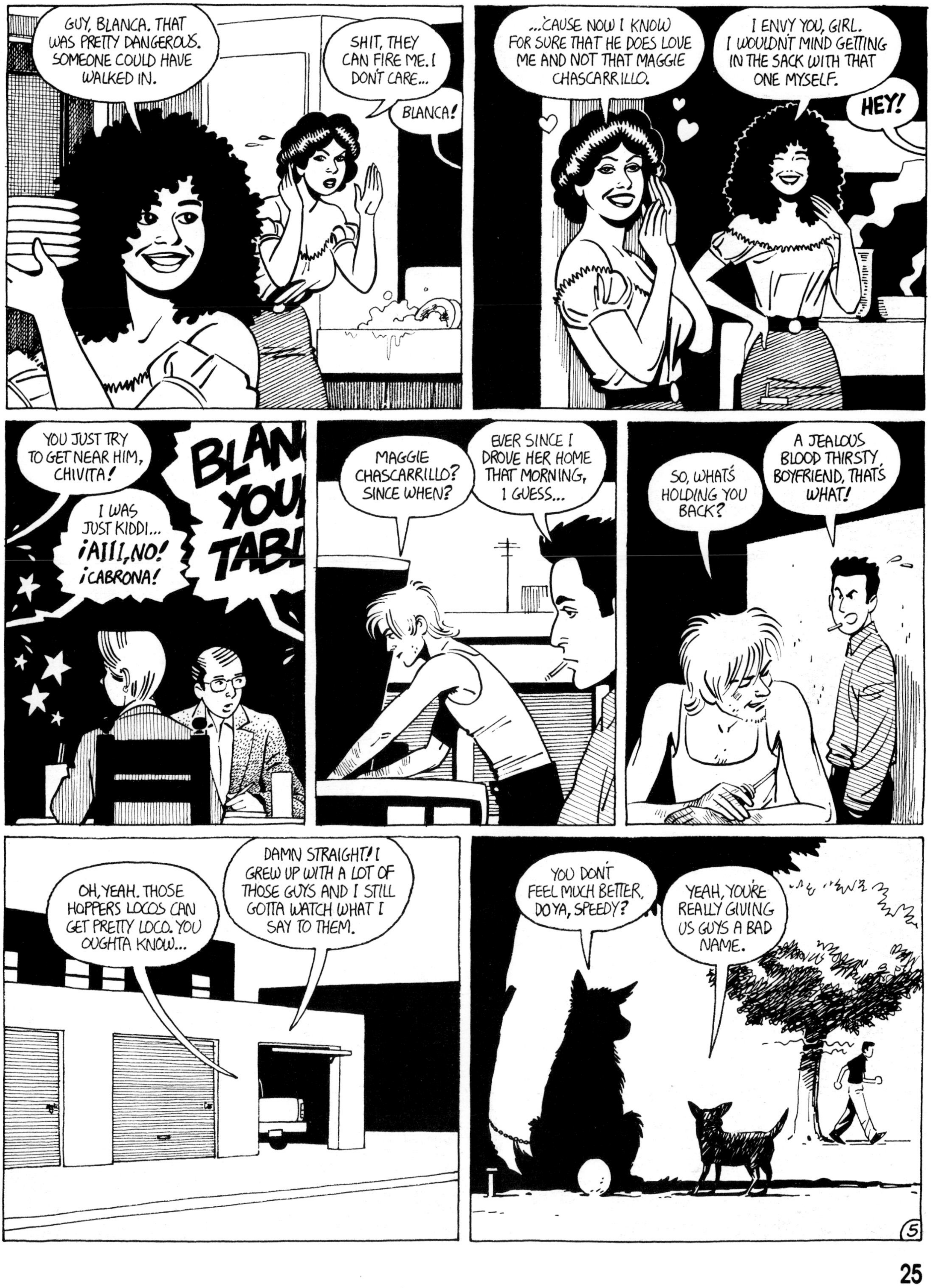
GUY, BLANCA. THAT WAS PRETTY DANGEROUS. SOMEONE COULD HAVE WALKED IN.
SHIT, THEY CAN FIRE ME. I DON'T CARE...
BLANCA!
...'CAUSE NOW I KNOW FOR SURE THAT HE DOES LOVE ME AND NOT THAT MAGGIE CHASCARRILLO.
I ENVY YOU, GIRL. I WOULDN'T MIND GETTING IN THE SACK WITH THAT ONE MYSELF.
HEY!
YOU JUST TRY TO GET NEAR HIM, CHIVITA!
I WAS JUST KIDDI... ¡AIII, NO! ¡CABRONA!
BLAN YOU TABL
MAGGIE CHASCARRILLO? SINCE WHEN?
EVER SINCE I DROVE HER HOME THAT MORNING, I GUESS...
SO, WHAT'S HOLDING YOU BACK?
A JEALOUS BLOOD THIRSTY BOYFRIEND, THAT'S WHAT!
OH, YEAH. THOSE HOPPERS LOCOS CAN GET PRETTY LOCO. YOU OUGHTA KNOW...
DAMN STRAIGHT! I GREW UP WITH A LOT OF THOSE GUYS AND I STILL GOTTA WATCH WHAT I SAY TO THEM.
YOU DON'T FEEL MUCH BETTER, DO YA, SPEEDY?
YEAH, YOU'RE REALLY GIVING US GUYS A BAD NAME.
5

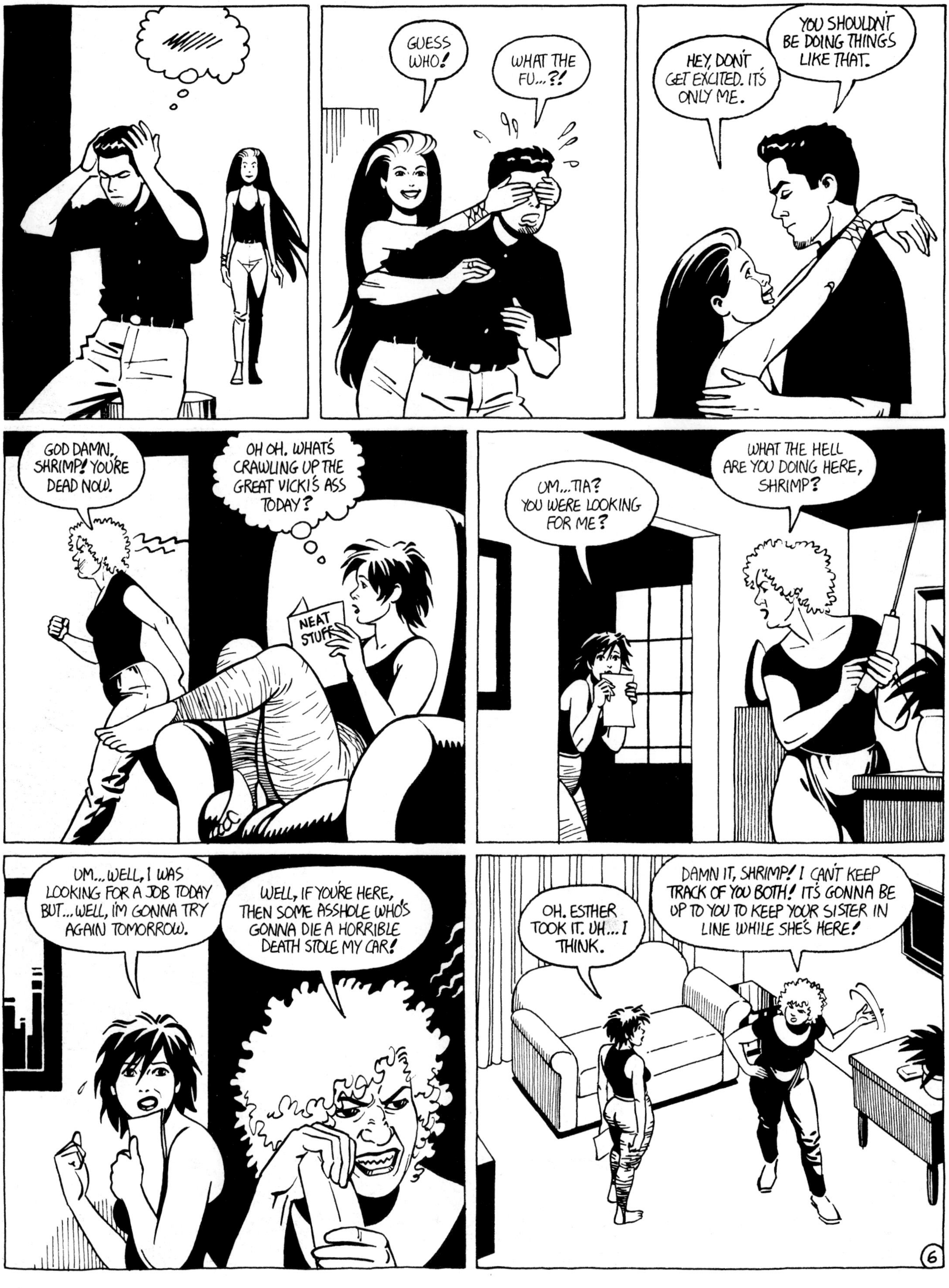
GUESS WHO!
WHAT THE FU...?!
HEY, DON'T GET EXCITED. IT'S ONLY ME.
YOU SHOULDN'T BE DOING THINGS LIKE THAT.
GOD DAMN, SHRIMP! YOU'RE DEAD NOW.
OH OH. WHAT'S CRAWLING UP THE GREAT VICKI'S ASS TODAY?
NEAT STUFF
UM...TIA? YOU WERE LOOKING FOR ME?
WHAT THE HELL ARE YOU DOING HERE, SHRIMP?
UM... WELL, I WAS LOOKING FOR A JOB TODAY BUT... WELL, I'M GONNA TRY AGAIN TOMORROW.
WELL, IF YOU'RE HERE, THEN SOME ASSHOLE WHO'S GONNA DIE A HORRIBLE DEATH STOLE MY CAR!
OH. ESTHER TOOK IT. UH... I THINK.
DAMN IT, SHRIMP! I CAN'T KEEP TRACK OF YOU BOTH! IT'S GONNA BE UP TO YOU TO KEEP YOUR SISTER IN LINE WHILE SHE'S HERE!
6

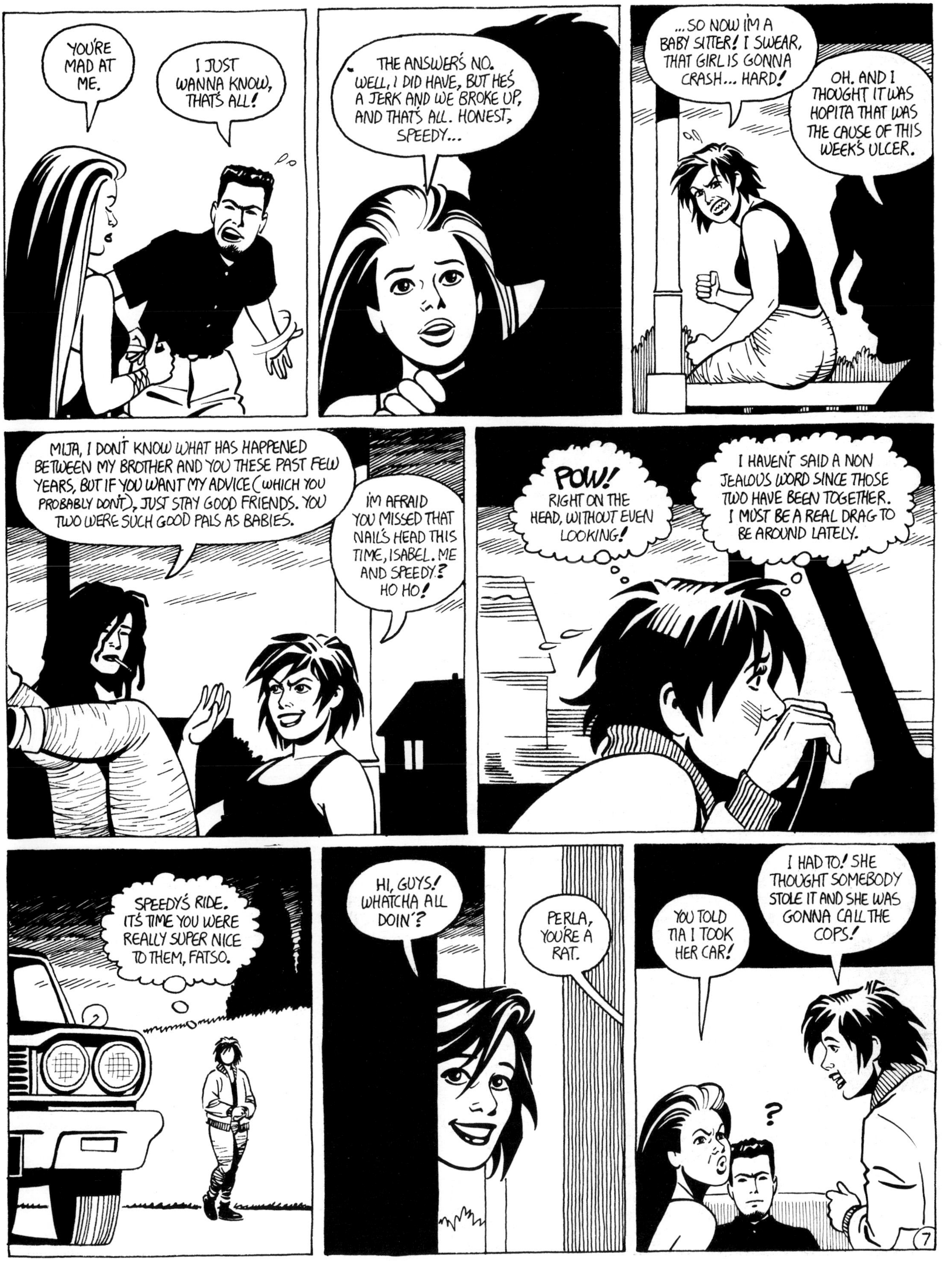
YOU'RE MAD AT ME.
I JUST WANNA KNOW, THAT'S ALL!
THE ANSWER'S NO. WELL, I DID HAVE, BUT HE'S A JERK AND WE BROKE UP, AND THAT'S ALL. HONEST, SPEEDY...
...SO NOW I'M A BABY SITTER! I SWEAR, THAT GIRL IS GONNA CRASH... HARD!
OH. AND I THOUGHT IT WAS HOPITA THAT WAS THE CAUSE OF THIS WEEK'S ULCER.
MIJA, I DON'T KNOW WHAT HAS HAPPENED BETWEEN MY BROTHER AND YOU THESE PAST FEW YEARS, BUT IF YOU WANT MY ADVICE (WHICH YOU PROBABLY DON'T), JUST STAY GOOD FRIENDS. YOU TWO WERE SUCH GOOD PALS AS BABIES.
I'M AFRAID YOU MISSED THAT NAIL'S HEAD THIS TIME, ISABEL. ME AND SPEEDY? HO HO!
POW! RIGHT ON THE HEAD, WITHOUT EVEN LOOKING!
I HAVEN'T SAID A NON JEALOUS WORD SINCE THOSE TWO HAVE BEEN TOGETHER. I MUST BE A REAL DRAG TO BE AROUND LATELY.
SPEEDY'S RIDE. IT'S TIME YOU WERE REALLY SUPER NICE TO THEM, FATSO.
HI, GUYS! WHATCHA ALL DOIN'?
PERLA, YOU'RE A RAT.
YOU TOLD TIA I TOOK HER CAR!
I HAD TO! SHE THOUGHT SOMEBODY STOLE IT AND SHE WAS GONNA CALL THE COPS!
?
7

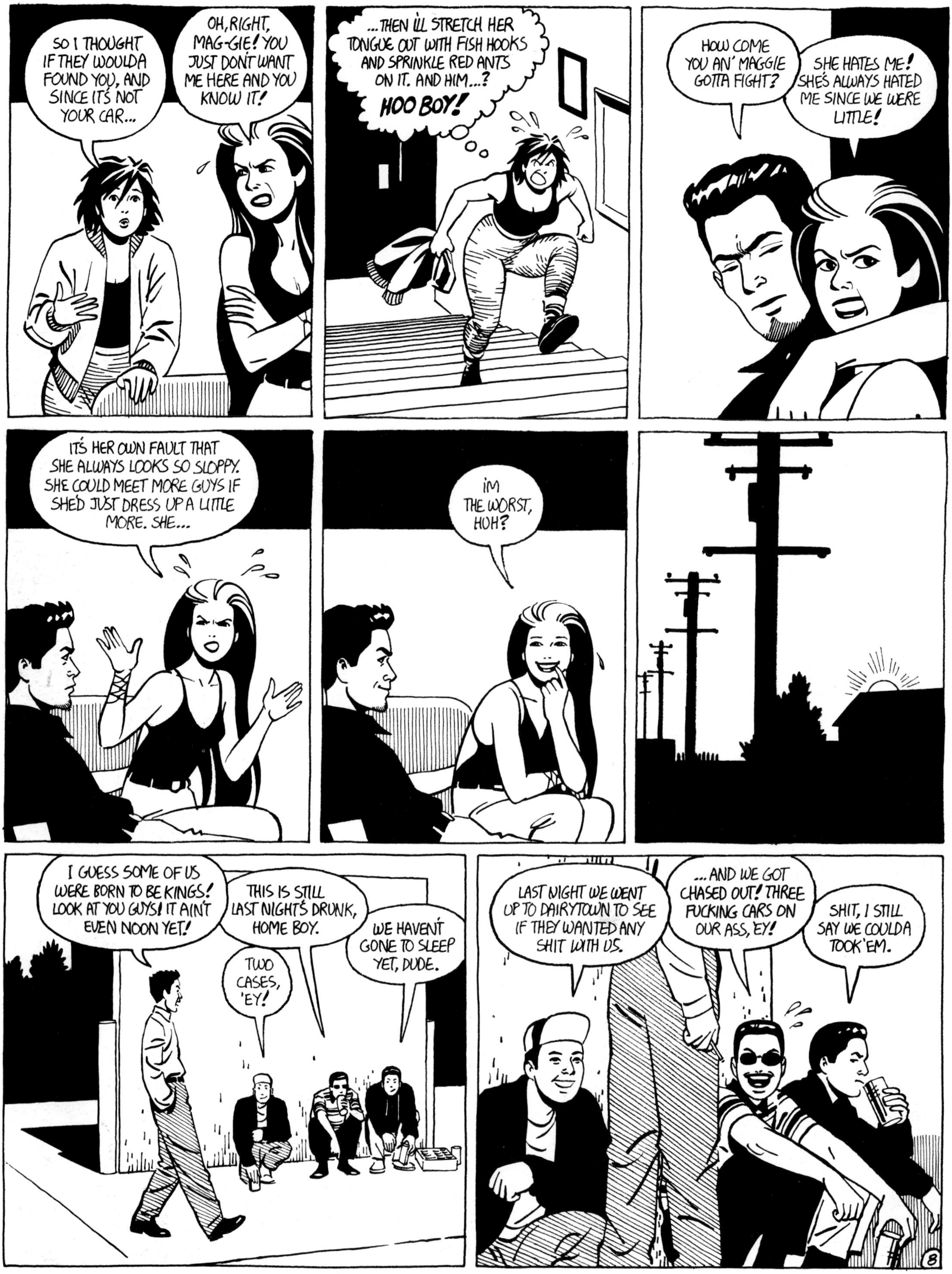
SO I THOUGHT IF THEY WOULDA FOUND YOU, AND SINCE IT'S NOT YOUR CAR...
OH, RIGHT, MAG-GIE! YOU JUST DON'T WANT ME HERE AND YOU KNOW IT!
...THEN I'LL STRETCH HER TONGUE OUT WITH FISH HOOKS AND SPRINKLE RED ANTS ON IT. AND HIM...? HOO BOY!
HOW COME YOU AN' MAGGIE GOTTA FIGHT?
SHE HATES ME! SHE'S ALWAYS HATED ME SINCE WE WERE LITTLE!
IT'S HER OWN FAULT THAT SHE ALWAYS LOOKS SO SLOPPY. SHE COULD MEET MORE GUYS IF SHE'D JUST DRESS UP A LITTLE MORE. SHE...
I'M THE WORST, HUH?
I GUESS SOME OF US WERE BORN TO BE KINGS! LOOK AT YOU GUYS! IT AIN'T EVEN NOON YET!
THIS IS STILL LAST NIGHT'S DRUNK, HOME BOY.
TWO CASES, 'EY!
WE HAVEN'T GONE TO SLEEP YET, DUDE.
LAST NIGHT WE WENT UP TO DAIRYTOWN TO SEE IF THEY WANTED ANY SHIT WITH US.
...AND WE GOT CHASED OUT! THREE FUCKING CARS ON OUR ASS, 'EY!
SHIT, I STILL SAY WE COULDA TOOK 'EM.
8

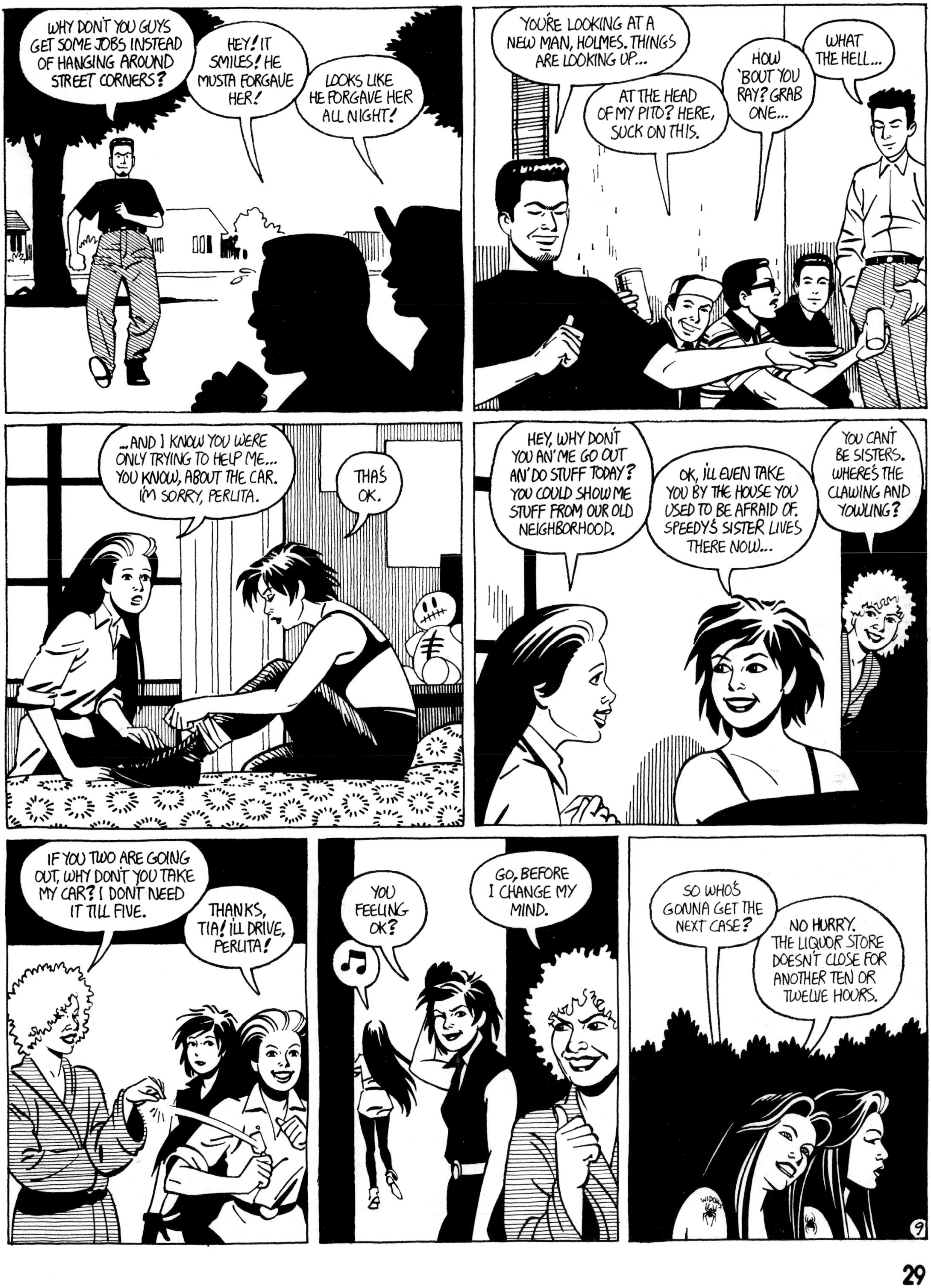
WHY DON'T YOU GUYS GET SOME JOBS INSTEAD OF HANGING AROUND STREET CORNERS?
HEY! IT SMILES! HE MUSTA FORGAVE HER!
LOOKS LIKE HE FORGAVE HER ALL NIGHT!
YOU'RE LOOKING AT A NEW MAN, HOLMES. THINGS ARE LOOKING UP...
AT THE HEAD OF MY PITO? HERE, SUCK ON THIS.
HOW 'BOUT YOU RAY? GRAB ONE...
WHAT THE HELL...
...AND I KNOW YOU WERE ONLY TRYING TO HELP ME... YOU KNOW, ABOUT THE CAR. I'M SORRY, PERLITA.
THA'S OK.
HEY, WHY DON'T YOU AN' ME GO OUT AN' DO STUFF TODAY? YOU COULD SHOW ME STUFF FROM OUR OLD NEIGHBORHOOD.
OK, I'LL EVEN TAKE YOU BY THE HOUSE YOU USED TO BE AFRAID OF. SPEEDY'S SISTER LIVES THERE NOW...
YOU CAN'T BE SISTERS. WHERE'S THE CLAWING AND YOWLING?
IF YOU TWO ARE GOING OUT, WHY DON'T YOU TAKE MY CAR? I DON'T NEED IT TILL FIVE.
THANKS, TIA! I'LL DRIVE, PERLITA!
YOU FEELING OK?
GO, BEFORE I CHANGE MY MIND.
SO WHO'S GONNA GET THE NEXT CASE?
NO HURRY. THE LIQUOR STORE DOESN'T CLOSE FOR ANOTHER TEN OR TWELVE HOURS.
WIDOWS
9

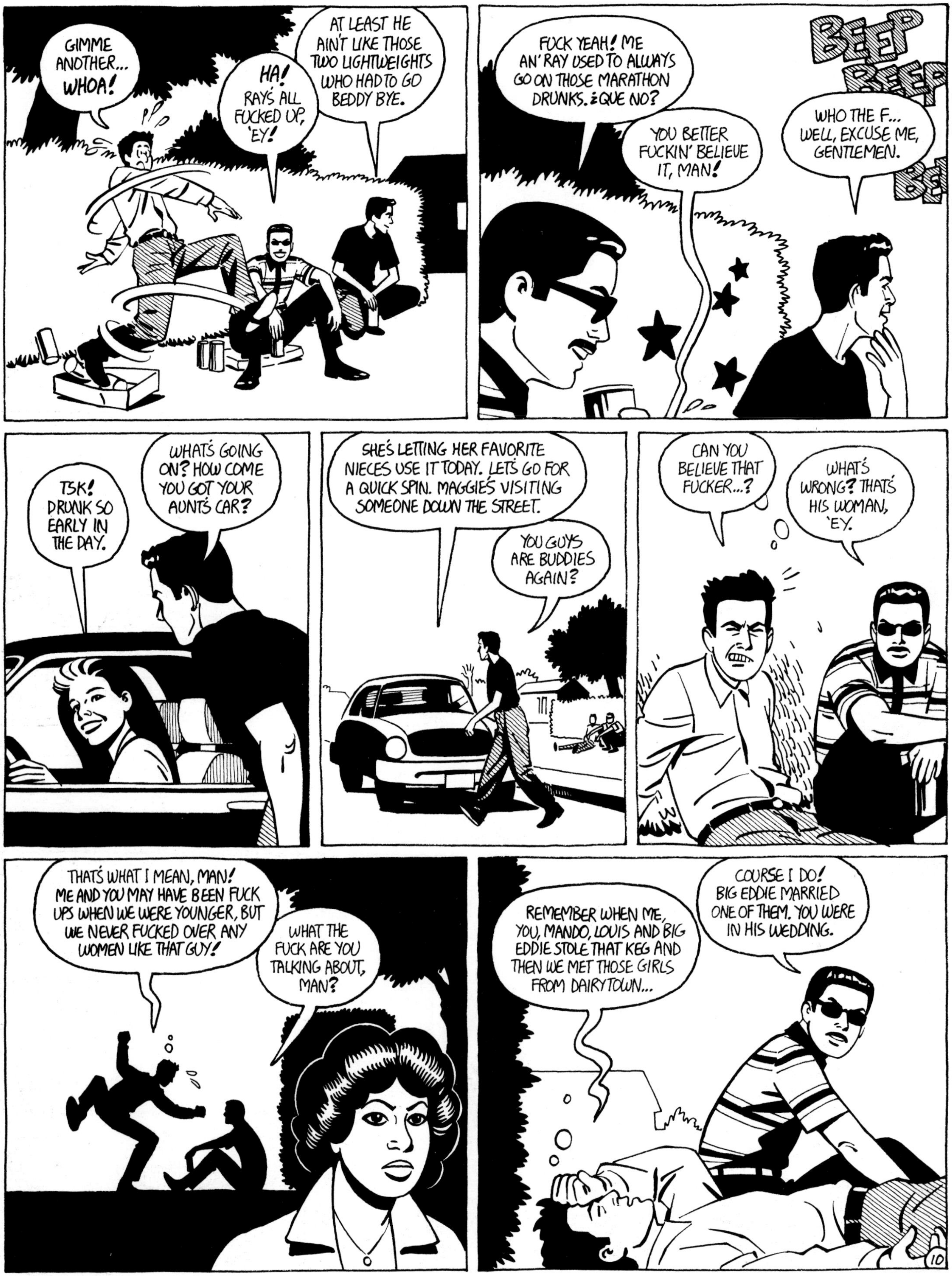
GIMME ANOTHER... WHOA!
HA! RAY'S ALL FUCKED UP, 'EY!
AT LEAST HE AIN'T LIKE THOSE TWO LIGHTWEIGHTS WHO HAD TO GO BEDDY BYE.
FUCK YEAH! ME AN' RAY USED TO ALWAYS GO ON THOSE MARATHON DRUNKS. ¿QUE NO?
YOU BETTER FUCKIN' BELIEVE IT, MAN!
BEEP
BEEP
BE
WHO THE F... WELL, EXCUSE ME, GENTLEMEN.
TSK! DRUNK SO EARLY IN THE DAY.
WHAT'S GOING ON? HOW COME YOU GOT YOUR AUNT'S CAR?
SHE'S LETTING HER FAVORITE NIECES USE IT TODAY. LET'S GO FOR A QUICK SPIN. MAGGIE'S VISITING SOMEONE DOWN THE STREET.
YOU GUYS ARE BUDDIES AGAIN?
CAN YOU BELIEVE THAT FUCKER...?
WHAT'S WRONG? THAT'S HIS WOMAN, 'EY.
THAT'S WHAT I MEAN, MAN! ME AND YOU MAY HAVE BEEN FUCK UPS WHEN WE WERE YOUNGER, BUT WE NEVER FUCKED OVER ANY WOMEN LIKE THAT GUY!
WHAT THE FUCK ARE YOU TALKING ABOUT, MAN?
REMEMBER WHEN ME, YOU, MANDO, LOUIS AND BIG EDDIE STOLE THAT KEG AND THEN WE MET THOSE GIRLS FROM DAIRYTOWN...
COURSE I DO! BIG EDDIE MARRIED ONE OF THEM. YOU WERE IN HIS WEDDING.
10

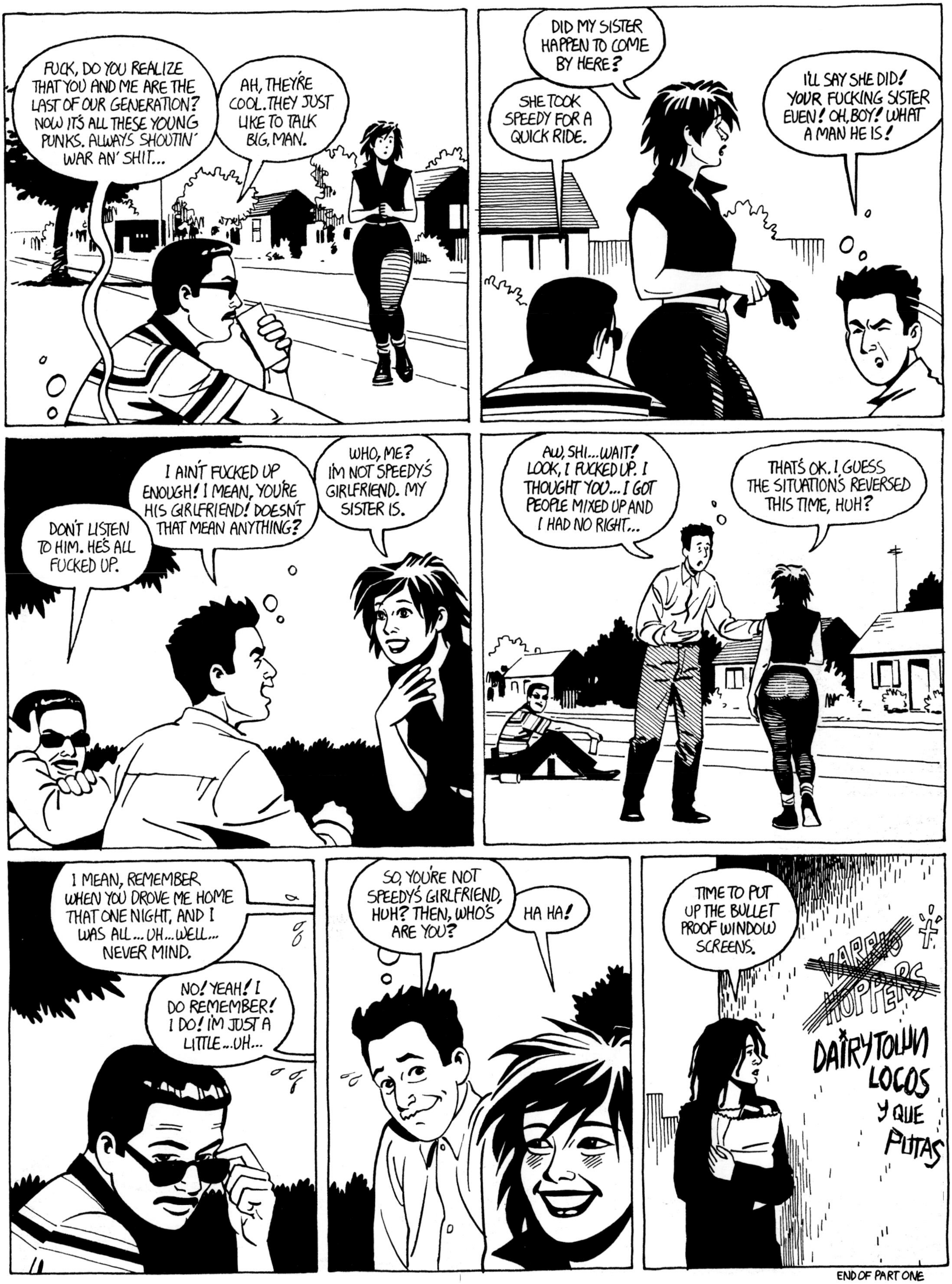
FUCK, DO YOU REALIZE THAT YOU AND ME ARE THE LAST OF OUR GENERATION? NOW IT'S ALL THESE YOUNG PUNKS. ALWAYS SHOUTIN' WAR AN' SHIT...
AH, THEY'RE COOL. THEY JUST LIKE TO TALK BIG, MAN.
DID MY SISTER HAPPEN TO COME BY HERE?
SHE TOOK SPEEDY FOR A QUICK RIDE.
I'LL SAY SHE DID! YOUR FUCKING SISTER EVEN! OH, BOY! WHAT A MAN HE IS!
DON'T LISTEN TO HIM. HE'S ALL FUCKED UP.
I AIN'T FUCKED UP ENOUGH! I MEAN, YOU'RE HIS GIRLFRIEND! DOESN'T THAT MEAN ANYTHING?
WHO, ME? I'M NOT SPEEDY'S GIRLFRIEND. MY SISTER IS.
AW, SHI... WAIT! LOOK, I FUCKED UP. I THOUGHT YOU... I GOT PEOPLE MIXED UP AND I HAD NO RIGHT...
THAT'S OK. I GUESS THE SITUATION'S REVERSED THIS TIME, HUH?
I MEAN, REMEMBER WHEN YOU DROVE ME HOME THAT ONE NIGHT, AND I WAS ALL... UH... WELL... NEVER MIND.
NO! YEAH! I DO REMEMBER! I DO! I'M JUST A LITTLE... UH...
SO, YOU'RE NOT SPEEDY'S GIRLFRIEND, HUH? THEN, WHO'S ARE YOU?
HA HA!
TIME TO PUT UP THE BULLET PROOF WINDOW SCREENS.
VARRIO HOPPERS
DAIRYTOWN LOCOS Y QUE PUTAS

END OF PART ONE

VIDALOCA2

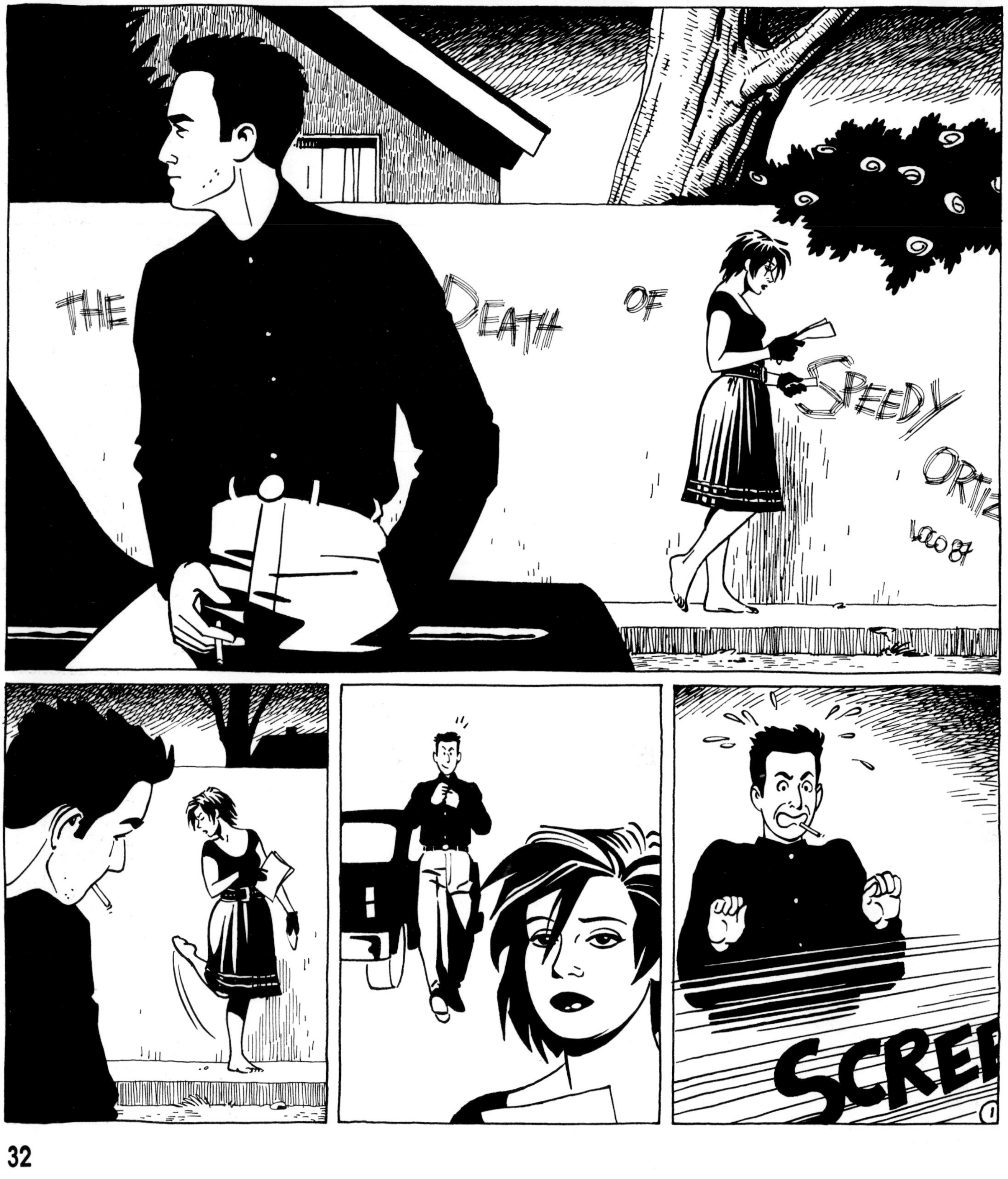

THE DEATH OF SPEEDY ORTIZ
LOCO 87
SCREE

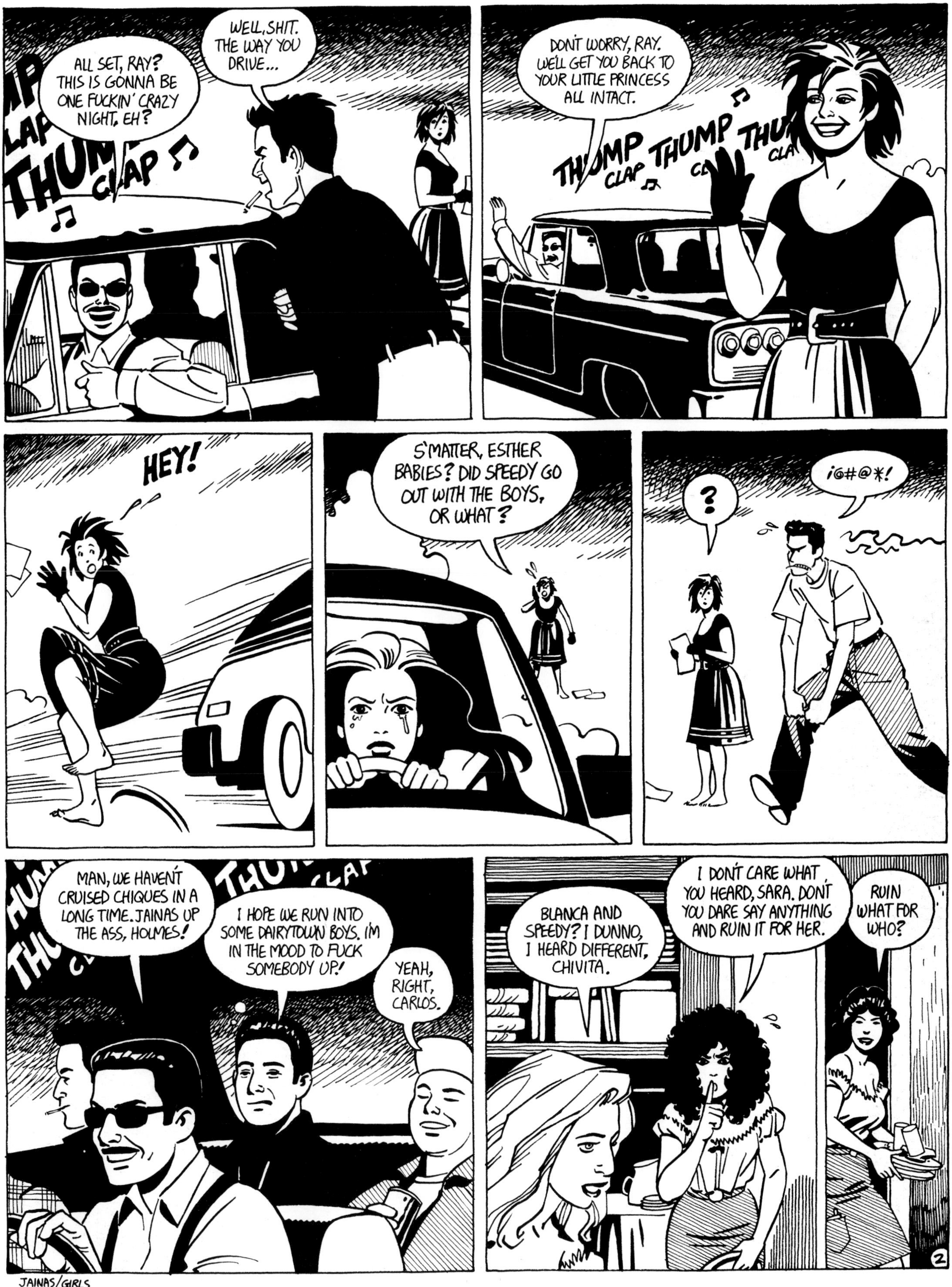
ALL SET, RAY? THIS IS GONNA BE ONE FUCKIN' CRAZY NIGHT, EH?
WELL, SHIT. THE WAY YOU DRIVE...
THUMP CLAP
DON'T WORRY, RAY. WE'LL GET YOU BACK TO YOUR LITTLE PRINCESS ALL INTACT.
THUMP CLAP THUMP
HEY!
S'MATTER, ESTHER BABIES? DID SPEEDY GO OUT WITH THE BOYS, OR WHAT?
?
¡@#@*!
MAN, WE HAVEN'T CRUISED CHIQUES IN A LONG TIME. JAINAS UP THE ASS, HOLMES!
I HOPE WE RUN INTO SOME DAIRYTOWN BOYS. I'M IN THE MOOD TO FUCK SOMEBODY UP!
YEAH, RIGHT, CARLOS.
BLANCA AND SPEEDY? I DUNNO, I HEARD DIFFERENT, CHIVITA.
I DON'T CARE WHAT YOU HEARD, SARA. DON'T YOU DARE SAY ANYTHING AND RUIN IT FOR HER.
RUIN WHAT FOR WHO?
2

JAINAS/GIRLS

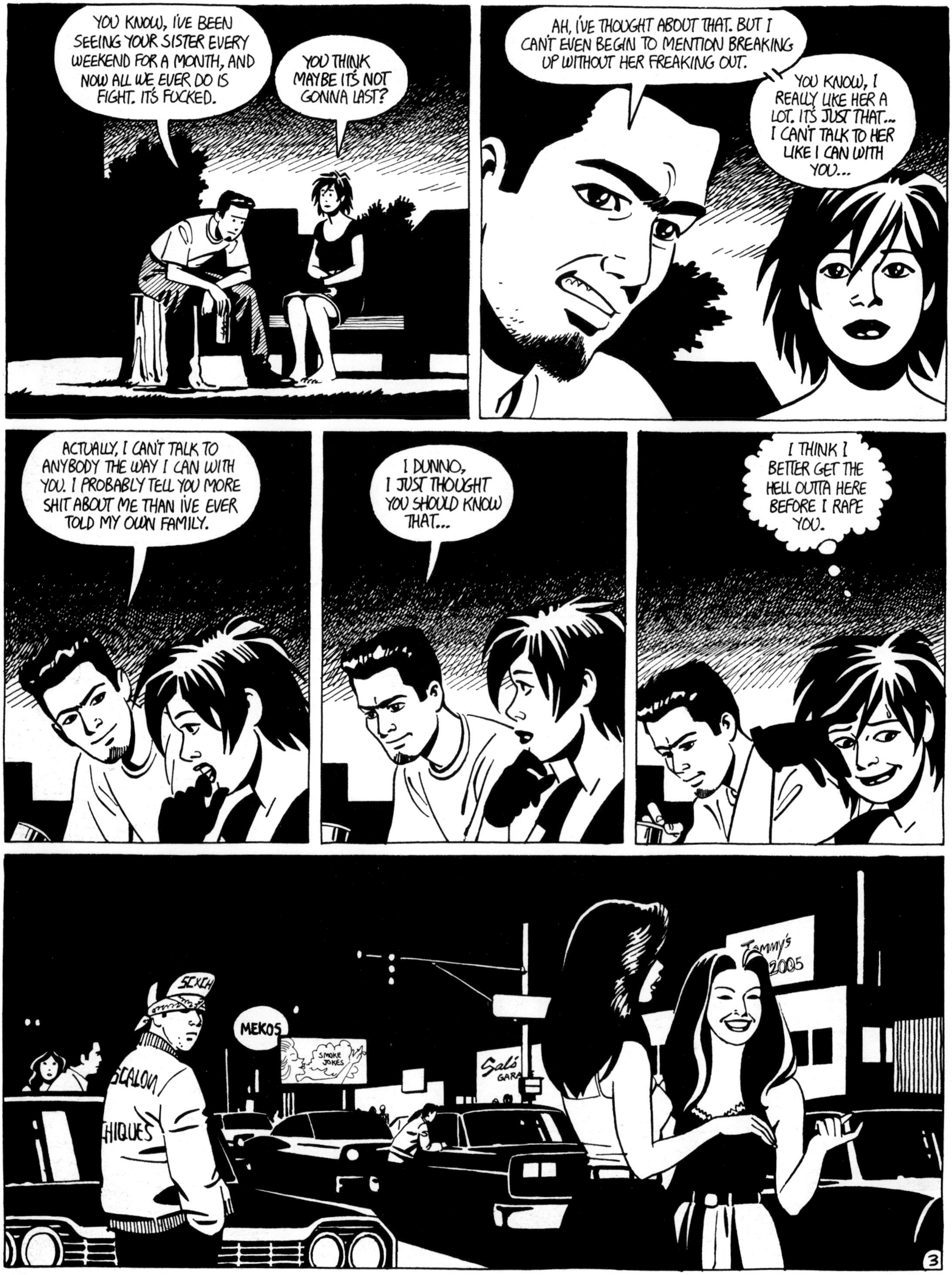
YOU KNOW, I'VE BEEN SEEING YOUR SISTER EVERY WEEKEND FOR A MONTH, AND NOW ALL WE EVER DO IS FIGHT. IT'S FUCKED.
YOU THINK MAYBE IT'S NOT GONNA LAST?
AH, I'VE THOUGHT ABOUT THAT. BUT I CAN'T EVEN BEGIN TO MENTION BREAKING UP WITHOUT HER FREAKING OUT.
YOU KNOW, I REALLY LIKE HER A LOT. IT'S JUST THAT... I CAN'T TALK TO HER LIKE I CAN WITH YOU...
ACTUALLY, I CAN'T TALK TO ANYBODY THE WAY I CAN WITH YOU. I PROBABLY TELL YOU MORE SHIT ABOUT ME THAN I'VE EVER TOLD MY OWN FAMILY.
I DUNNO, I JUST THOUGHT YOU SHOULD KNOW THAT...
I THINK I BETTER GET THE HELL OUTTA HERE BEFORE I RAPE YOU.
MEKOS
SMOKE JOKES
Sal's
3

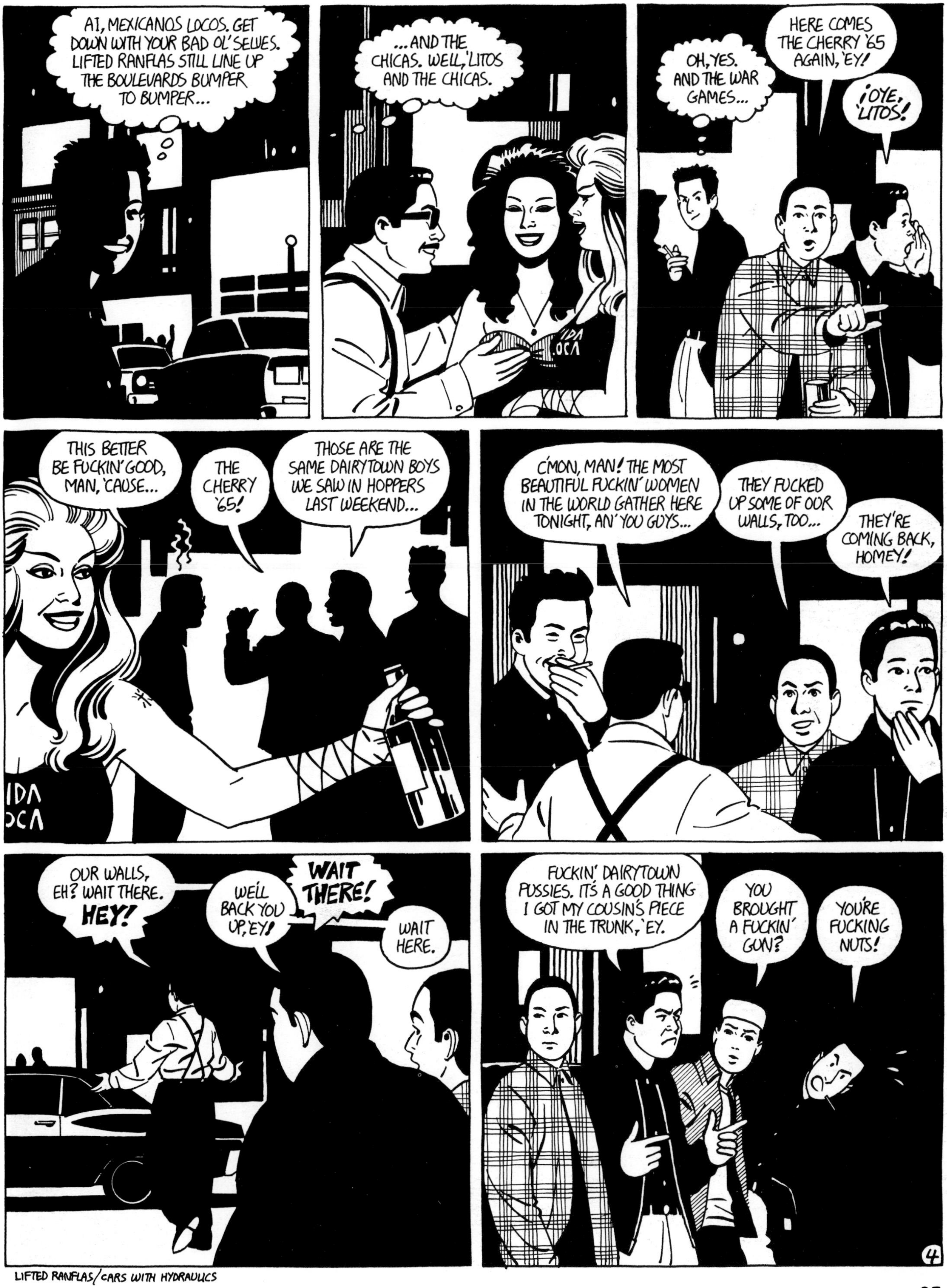
AI, MEXICANOS LOCOS. GET DOWN WITH YOUR BAD OL' SELVES. LIFTED RANFLAS STILL LINE UP THE BOULEVARDS BUMPER TO BUMPER...
...AND THE CHICAS. WELL, 'LITOS AND THE CHICAS.
OH, YES. AND THE WAR GAMES...
HERE COMES THE CHERRY '65 AGAIN, 'EY!
¡OYE, 'LITOS!
IDA
OCA
THIS BETTER BE FUCKIN' GOOD, MAN, 'CAUSE...
THE CHERRY '65!
THOSE ARE THE SAME DAIRYTOWN BOYS WE SAW IN HOPPERS LAST WEEKEND...
IDA
OCA
C'MON, MAN! THE MOST BEAUTIFUL FUCKIN' WOMEN IN THE WORLD GATHER HERE TONIGHT, AN' YOU GUYS...
THEY FUCKED UP SOME OF OUR WALLS, TOO...
THEY'RE COMING BACK, HOMEY!
OUR WALLS, EH? WAIT THERE. HEY!
WE'LL BACK YOU UP, 'EY!
WAIT THERE!
WAIT HERE.
FUCKIN' DAIRYTOWN PUSSIES. IT'S A GOOD THING I GOT MY COUSIN'S PIECE IN THE TRUNK, 'EY.
YOU BROUGHT A FUCKIN' GUN?
YOU'RE FUCKING NUTS!
4

LIFTED RANFLAS/CARS WITH HYDRAULICS

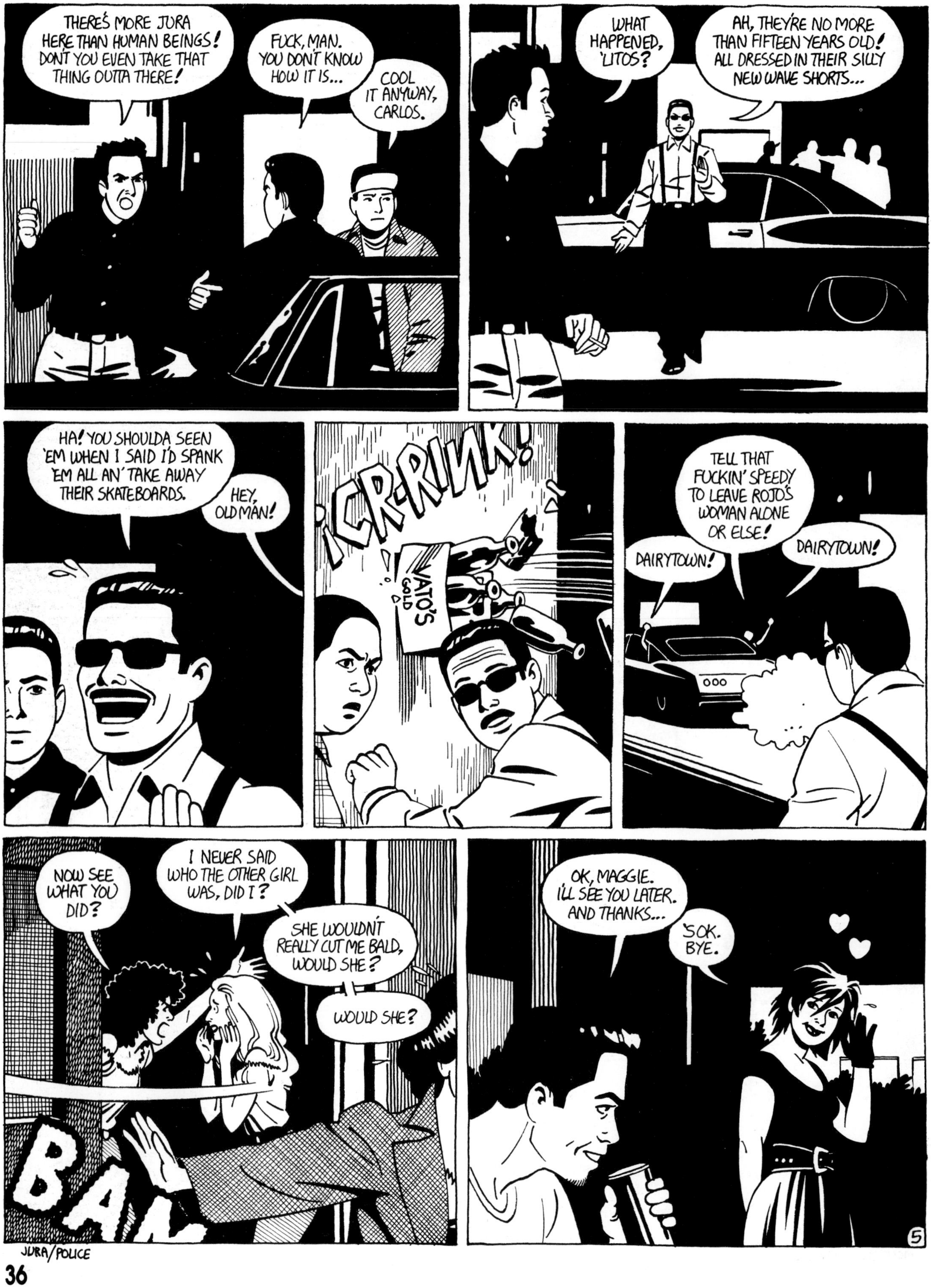

THERE'S MORE JURA HERE THAN HUMAN BEINGS! DON'T YOU EVEN TAKE THAT THING OUTTA THERE!
FUCK, MAN. YOU DON'T KNOW HOW IT IS...
COOL IT ANYWAY, CARLOS.
WHAT HAPPENED, 'LITOS?
AH, THEY'RE NO MORE THAN FIFTEEN YEARS OLD! ALL DRESSED IN THEIR SILLY NEW WAVE SHORTS...
HA! YOU SHOULDA SEEN 'EM WHEN I SAID I'D SPANK 'EM ALL AN' TAKE AWAY THEIR SKATEBOARDS.
HEY, OLD MAN!
¡CR-RINK!
VATO'S GOLD
TELL THAT FUCKIN' SPEEDY TO LEAVE ROJO'S WOMAN ALONE OR ELSE!
DAIRYTOWN!
DAIRYTOWN!
NOW SEE WHAT YOU DID?
I NEVER SAID WHO THE OTHER GIRL WAS, DID I?
SHE WOULDN'T REALLY CUT ME BALD, WOULD SHE?
WOULD SHE?
BAM
OK, MAGGIE. I'LL SEE YOU LATER. AND THANKS...
'S OK. BYE.
5
JURA/POLICE

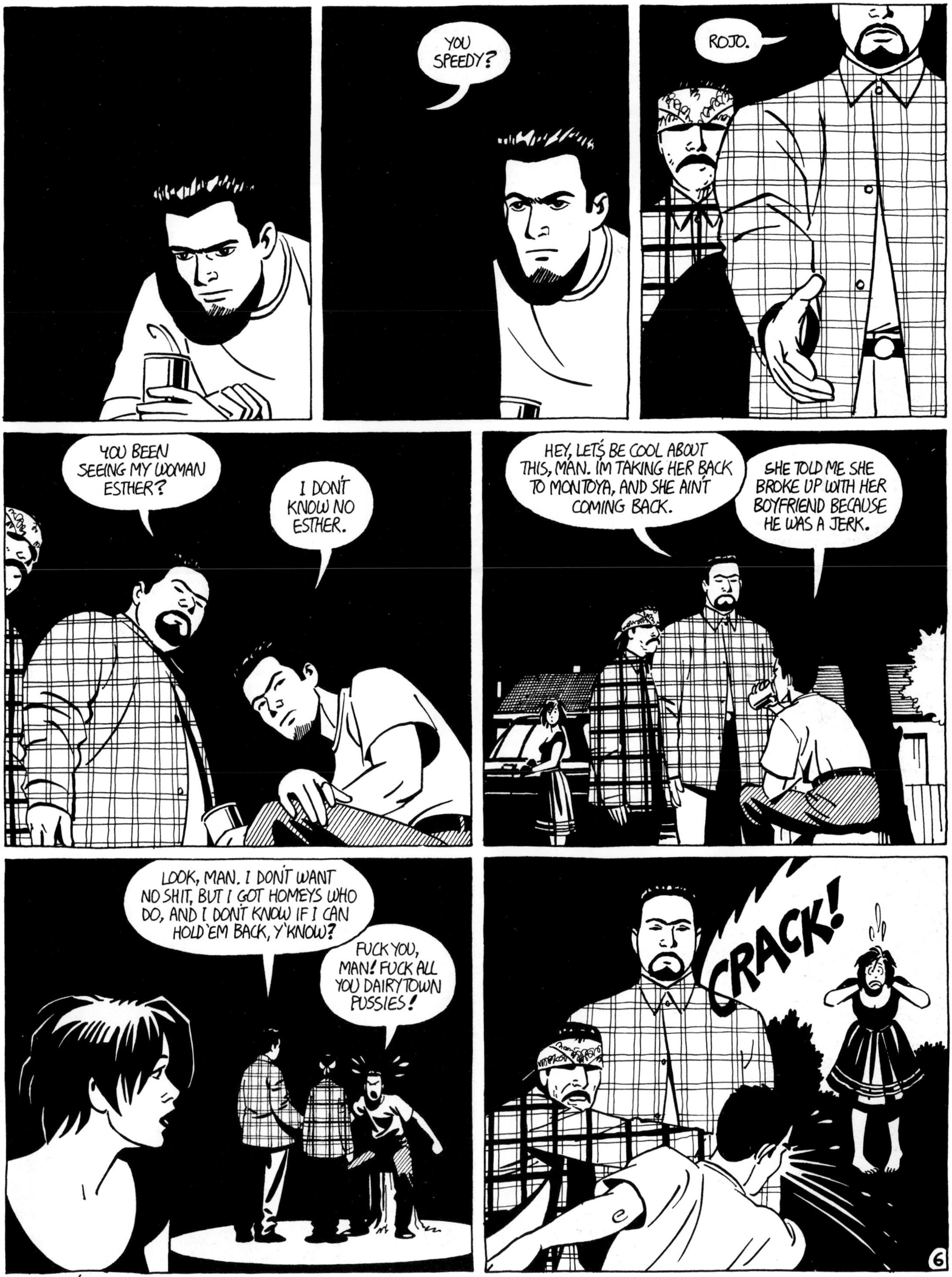

YOU SPEEDY?
ROJO.
YOU BEEN SEEING MY WOMAN ESTHER?
I DON'T KNOW NO ESTHER.
HEY, LET'S BE COOL ABOUT THIS, MAN. I'M TAKING HER BACK TO MONTOYA, AND SHE AIN'T COMING BACK.
SHE TOLD ME SHE BROKE UP WITH HER BOYFRIEND BECAUSE HE WAS A JERK.
LOOK, MAN. I DON'T WANT NO SHIT, BUT I GOT HOMEYS WHO DO, AND I DON'T KNOW IF I CAN HOLD 'EM BACK, Y'KNOW?
FUCK YOU, MAN! FUCK ALL YOU DAIRYTOWN PUSSIES!
CRACK!
6
MONTOYA/DAIRYTOWN

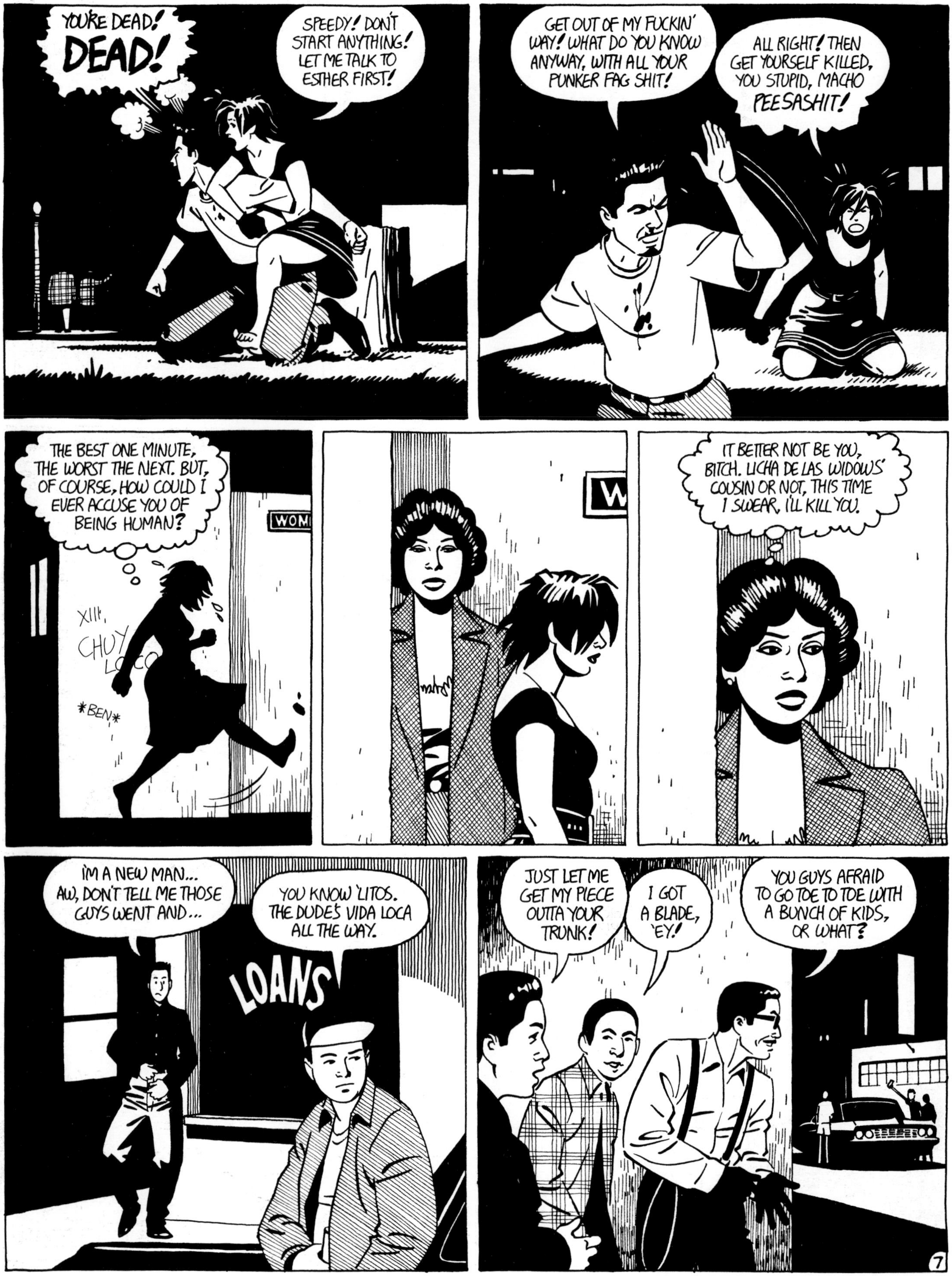
YOU'RE DEAD! DEAD!
SPEEDY! DON'T START ANYTHING! LET ME TALK TO ESTHER FIRST!
GET OUT OF MY FUCKIN' WAY! WHAT DO YOU KNOW ANYWAY, WITH ALL YOUR PUNKER FAG SHIT!
ALL RIGHT! THEN GET YOURSELF KILLED, YOU STUPID, MACHO PEESASHIT!
THE BEST ONE MINUTE, THE WORST THE NEXT. BUT, OF COURSE, HOW COULD I EVER ACCUSE YOU OF BEING HUMAN?
WOM
XIII
CHUY LOCO
BEN
W
IT BETTER NOT BE YOU, BITCH. LICHA DE LAS WIDOWS' COUSIN OR NOT, THIS TIME I SWEAR, I'LL KILL YOU.
I'M A NEW MAN... AW, DON'T TELL ME THOSE GUYS WENT AND...
YOU KNOW 'LITOS. THE DUDE'S VIDA LOCA ALL THE WAY.
LOANS
JUST LET ME GET MY PIECE OUTTA YOUR TRUNK!
I GOT A BLADE, 'EY!
YOU GUYS AFRAID TO GO TOE TO TOE WITH A BUNCH OF KIDS, OR WHAT?
7

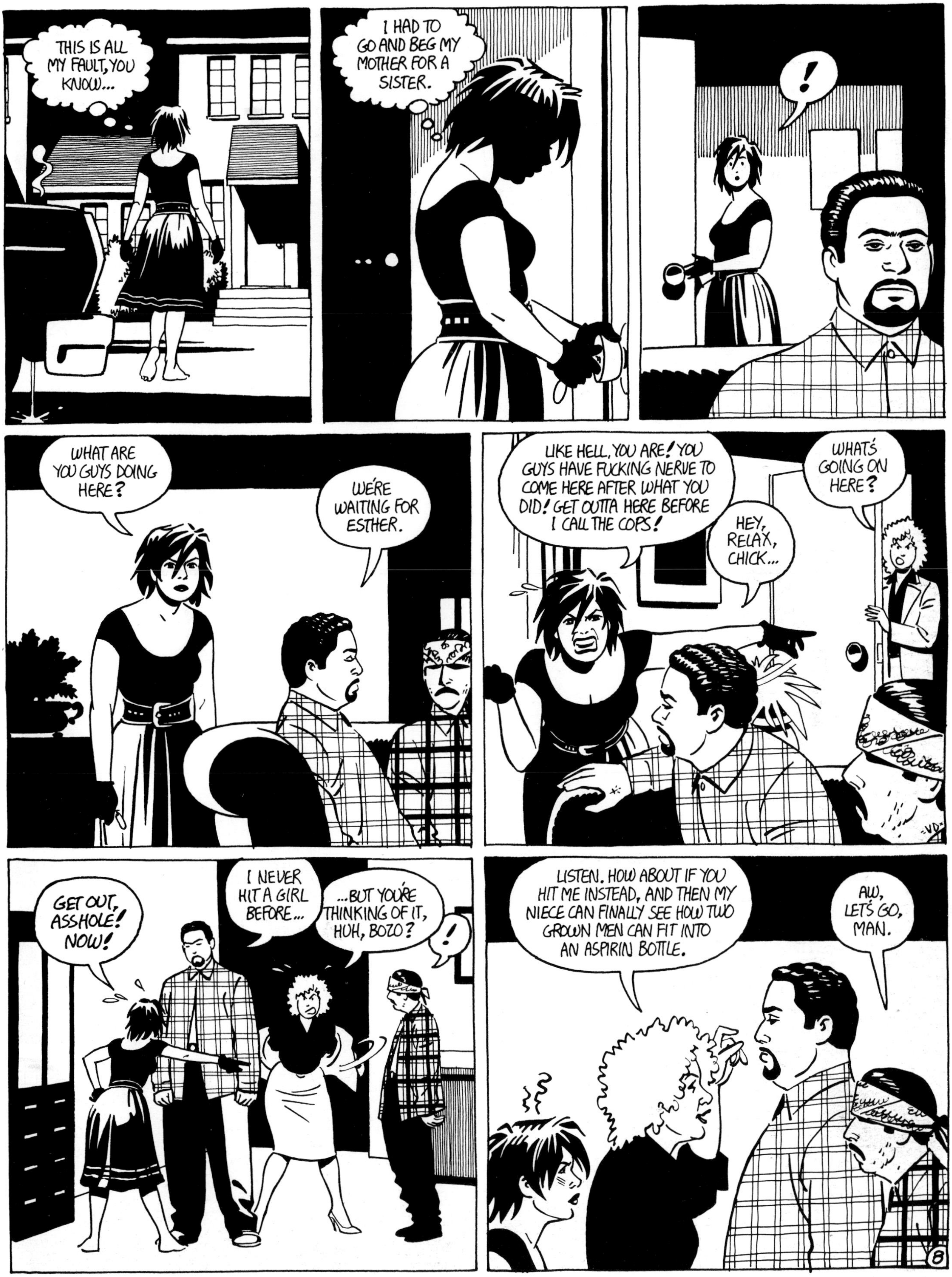

THIS IS ALL MY FAULT, YOU KNOW...
I HAD TO GO AND BEG MY MOTHER FOR A SISTER.
!
WHAT ARE YOU GUYS DOING HERE?
WE'RE WAITING FOR ESTHER.
LIKE HELL, YOU ARE! YOU GUYS HAVE FUCKING NERVE TO COME HERE AFTER WHAT YOU DID! GET OUTTA HERE BEFORE I CALL THE COPS!
HEY, RELAX, CHICK...
WHAT'S GOING ON HERE?
GET OUT, ASSHOLE! NOW!
I NEVER HIT A GIRL BEFORE...
...BUT YOU'RE THINKING OF IT, HUH, BOZO?
!
LISTEN. HOW ABOUT IF YOU HIT ME INSTEAD, AND THEN MY NIECE CAN FINALLY SEE HOW TWO GROWN MEN CAN FIT INTO AN ASPIRIN BOTTLE.
AW, LET'S GO, MAN.
8

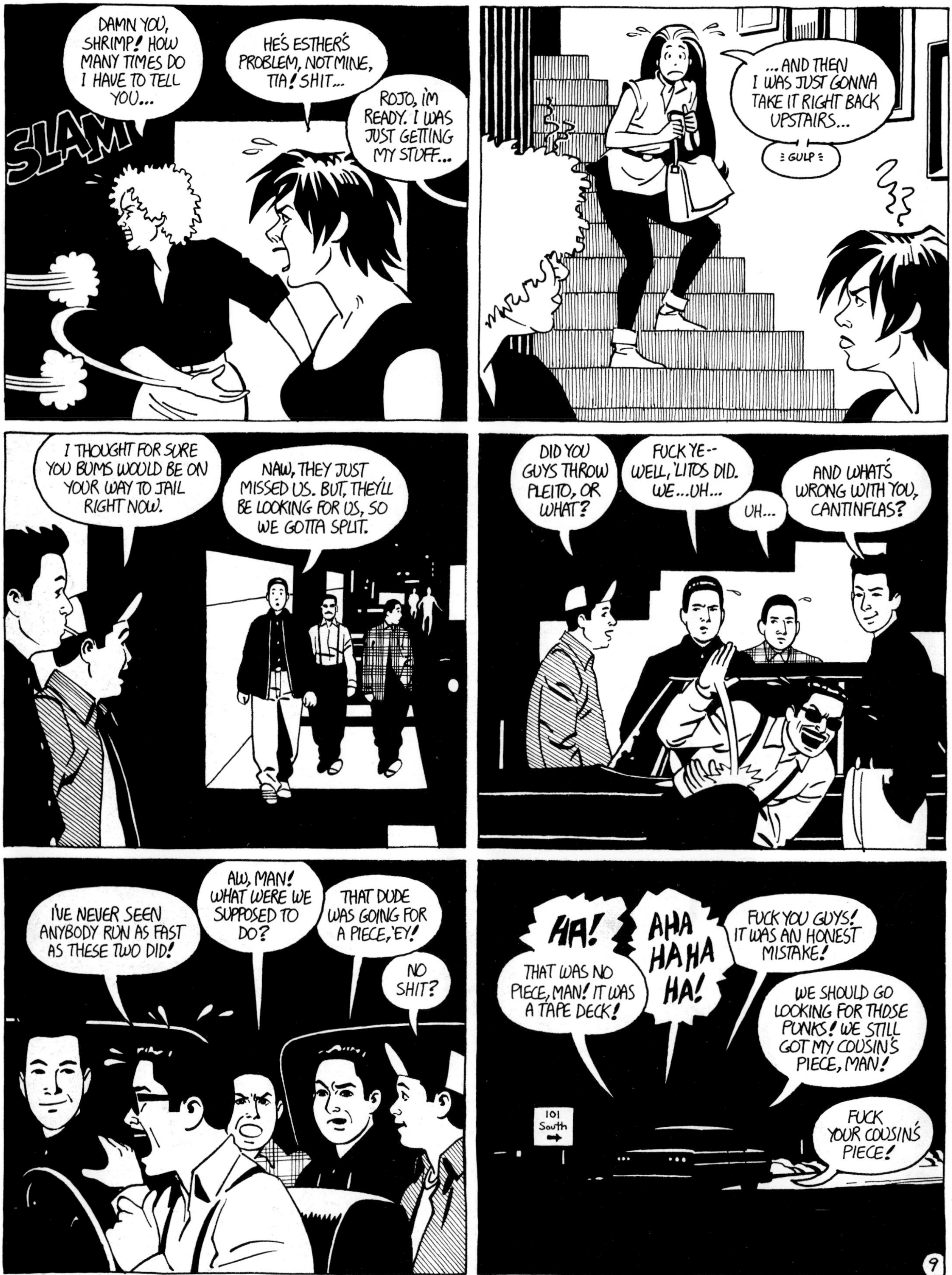
DAMN YOU, SHRIMP! HOW MANY TIMES DO I HAVE TO TELL YOU...
SLAM
HE'S ESTHER'S PROBLEM, NOT MINE, TIA! SHIT...
ROJO, I'M READY. I WAS JUST GETTING MY STUFF...
...AND THEN I WAS JUST GONNA TAKE IT RIGHT BACK UPSTAIRS...
GULP
I THOUGHT FOR SURE YOU BUMS WOULD BE ON YOUR WAY TO JAIL RIGHT NOW.
NAW, THEY JUST MISSED US. BUT, THEY'LL BE LOOKING FOR US, SO WE GOTTA SPLIT.
DID YOU GUYS THROW PLEITO, OR WHAT?
FUCK YE-- WELL, 'LITOS DID. WE...UH...
UH...
AND WHAT'S WRONG WITH YOU, CANTINFLAS?
I'VE NEVER SEEN ANYBODY RUN AS FAST AS THESE TWO DID!
AW, MAN! WHAT WERE WE SUPPOSED TO DO?
THAT DUDE WAS GOING FOR A PIECE, 'EY!
NO SHIT?
HA!
THAT WAS NO PIECE, MAN! IT WAS A TAPE DECK!
AHA HAHA HA!
FUCK YOU GUYS! IT WAS AN HONEST MISTAKE!
WE SHOULD GO LOOKING FOR THOSE PUNKS! WE STILL GOT MY COUSIN'S PIECE, MAN!
101 South
FUCK YOUR COUSIN'S PIECE!
9

THROW PLEITO/FIGHT

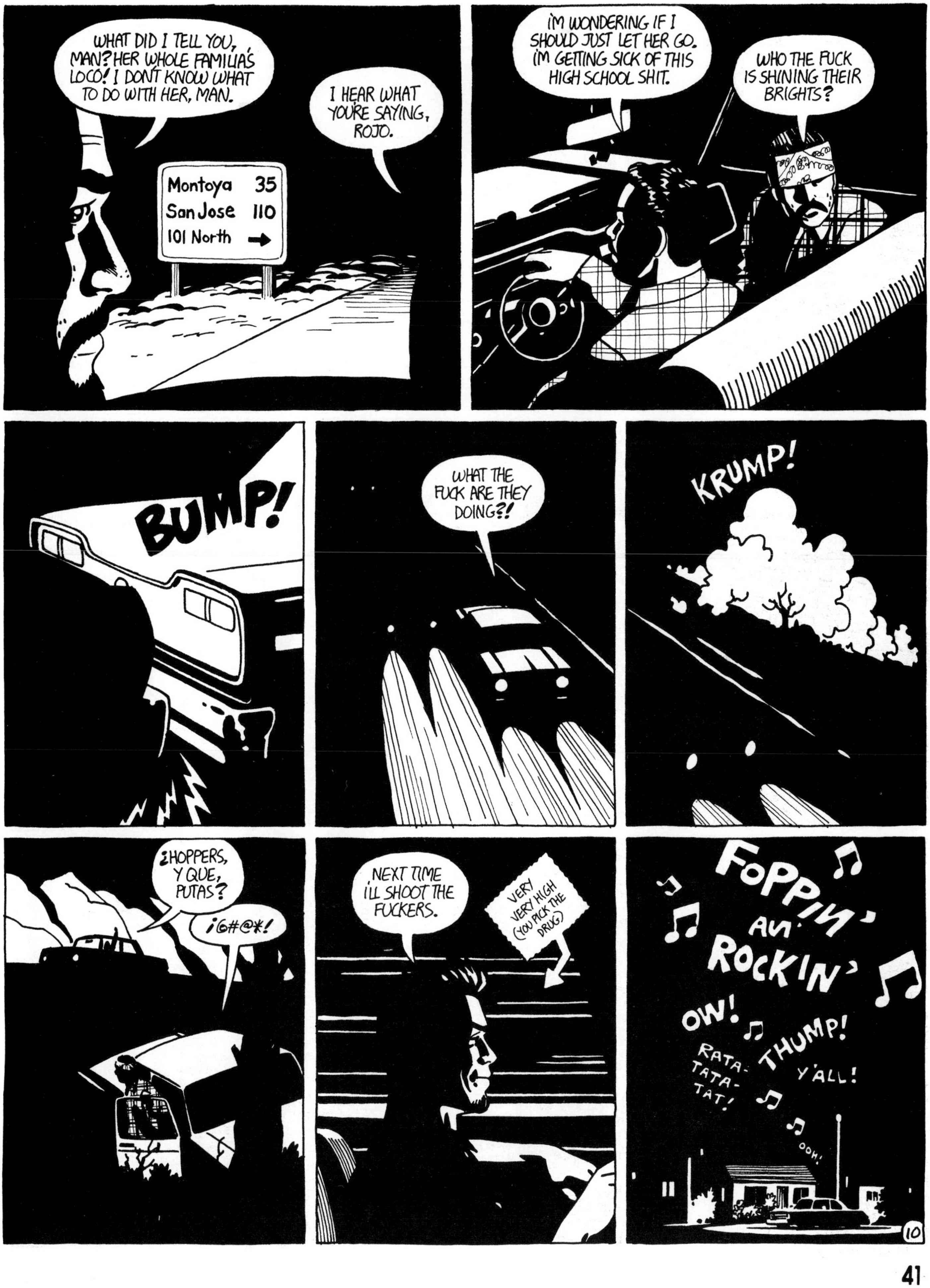

WHAT DID I TELL YOU, MAN? HER WHOLE FAMILIA'S LOCO! I DON'T KNOW WHAT TO DO WITH HER, MAN.
Montoya 35
San Jose 110
101 North
I HEAR WHAT YOU'RE SAYING, ROJO.
I'M WONDERING IF I SHOULD JUST LET HER GO. I'M GETTING SICK OF THIS HIGH SCHOOL SHIT.
WHO THE FUCK IS SHINING THEIR BRIGHTS?
BUMP!
WHAT THE FUCK ARE THEY DOING?!
KRUMP!
¿HOPPERS, Y QUE, PUTAS?
¡G#@*!
NEXT TIME I'LL SHOOT THE FUCKERS.
VERY VERY HIGH (YOU PICK THE DRUG)
FOPPIN' AN' ROCKIN'
OW!
THUMP!
RATA-TATA-TAT!
Y'ALL!
OOH!
10

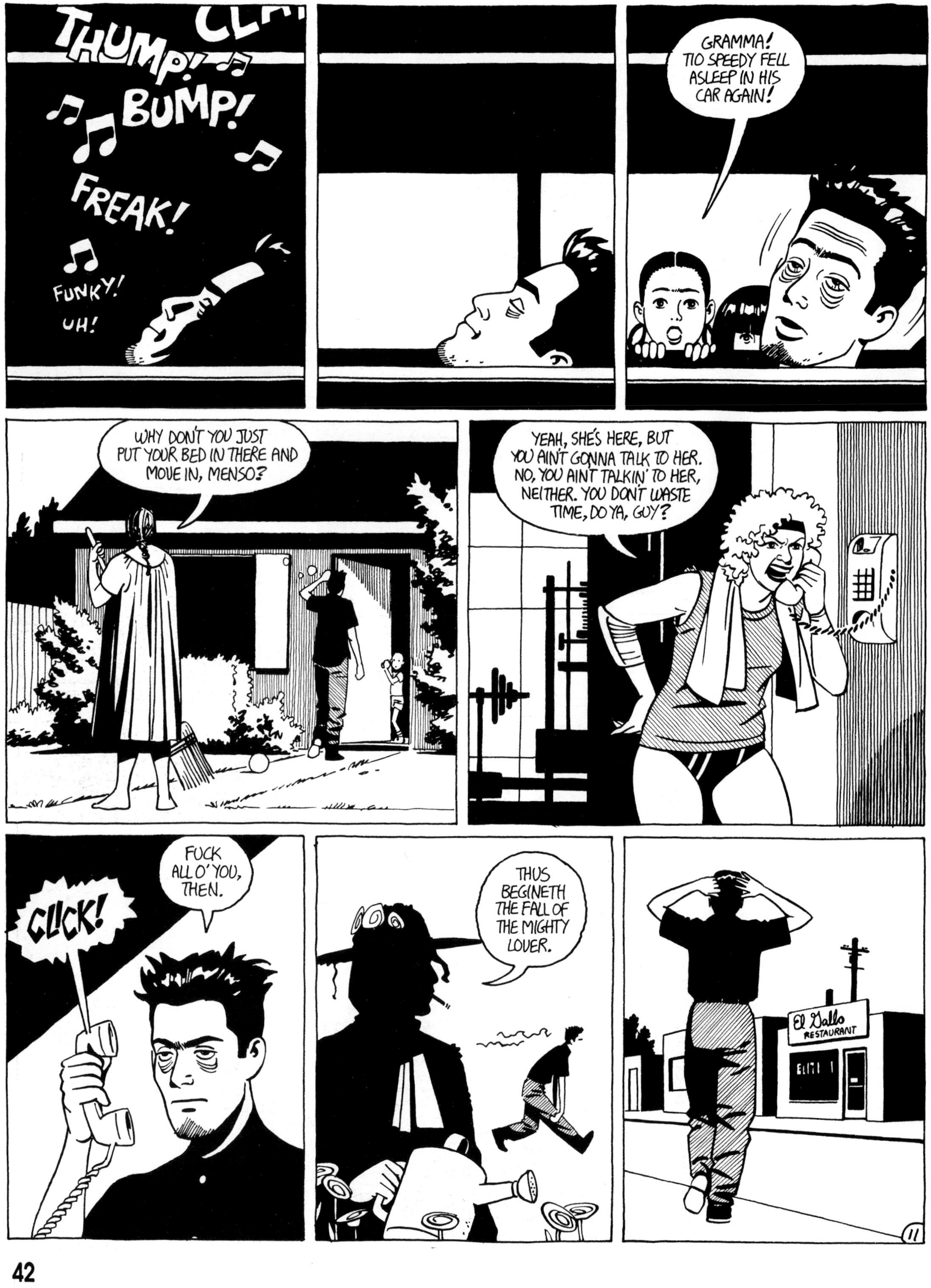
THUMP! CLA
BUMP!
FREAK!
FUNKY!
UH!
GRAMMA! TIO SPEEDY FELL ASLEEP IN HIS CAR AGAIN!
WHY DON'T YOU JUST PUT YOUR BED IN THERE AND MOVE IN, MENSO?
YEAH, SHE'S HERE, BUT YOU AIN'T GONNA TALK TO HER. NO, YOU AIN'T TALKIN' TO HER, NEITHER. YOU DON'T WASTE TIME, DO YA, GUY?
CLICK!
FUCK ALL O' YOU, THEN.
THUS BEGINETH THE FALL OF THE MIGHTY LOVER.
El Gallo RESTAURANT
11

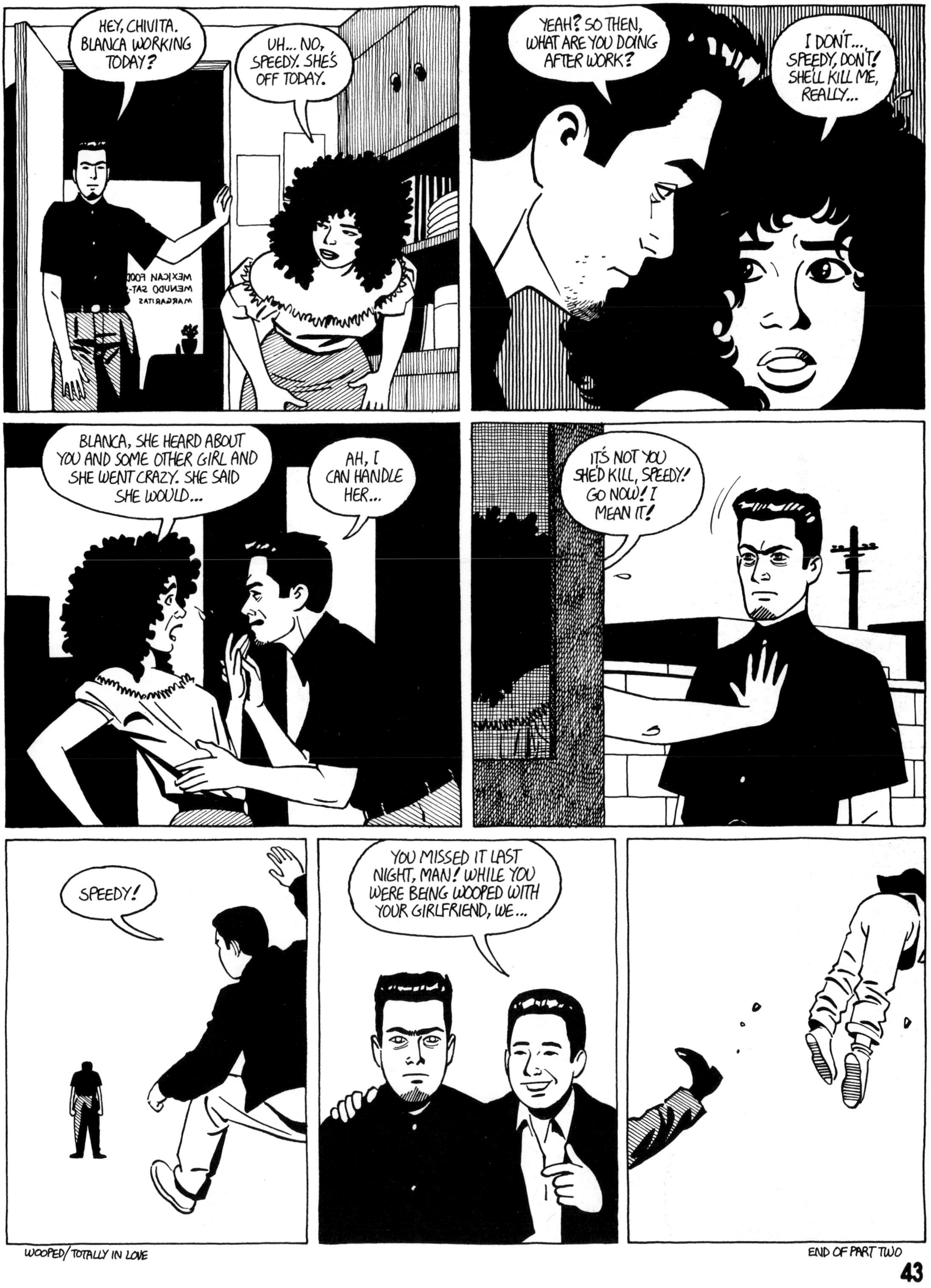

HEY, CHIVITA. BLANCA WORKING TODAY?
UH... NO, SPEEDY. SHE'S OFF TODAY.
YEAH? SO THEN, WHAT ARE YOU DOING AFTER WORK?
I DON'T... SPEEDY, DON'T! SHE'LL KILL ME, REALLY...
BLANCA, SHE HEARD ABOUT YOU AND SOME OTHER GIRL AND SHE WENT CRAZY. SHE SAID SHE WOULD...
AH, I CAN HANDLE HER...
IT'S NOT YOU SHE'D KILL, SPEEDY! GO NOW! I MEAN IT!
SPEEDY!
YOU MISSED IT LAST NIGHT, MAN! WHILE YOU WERE BEING WOOPED WITH YOUR GIRLFRIEND, WE...

WOOPED/ TOTALLY IN LOVE

END OF PART TWO

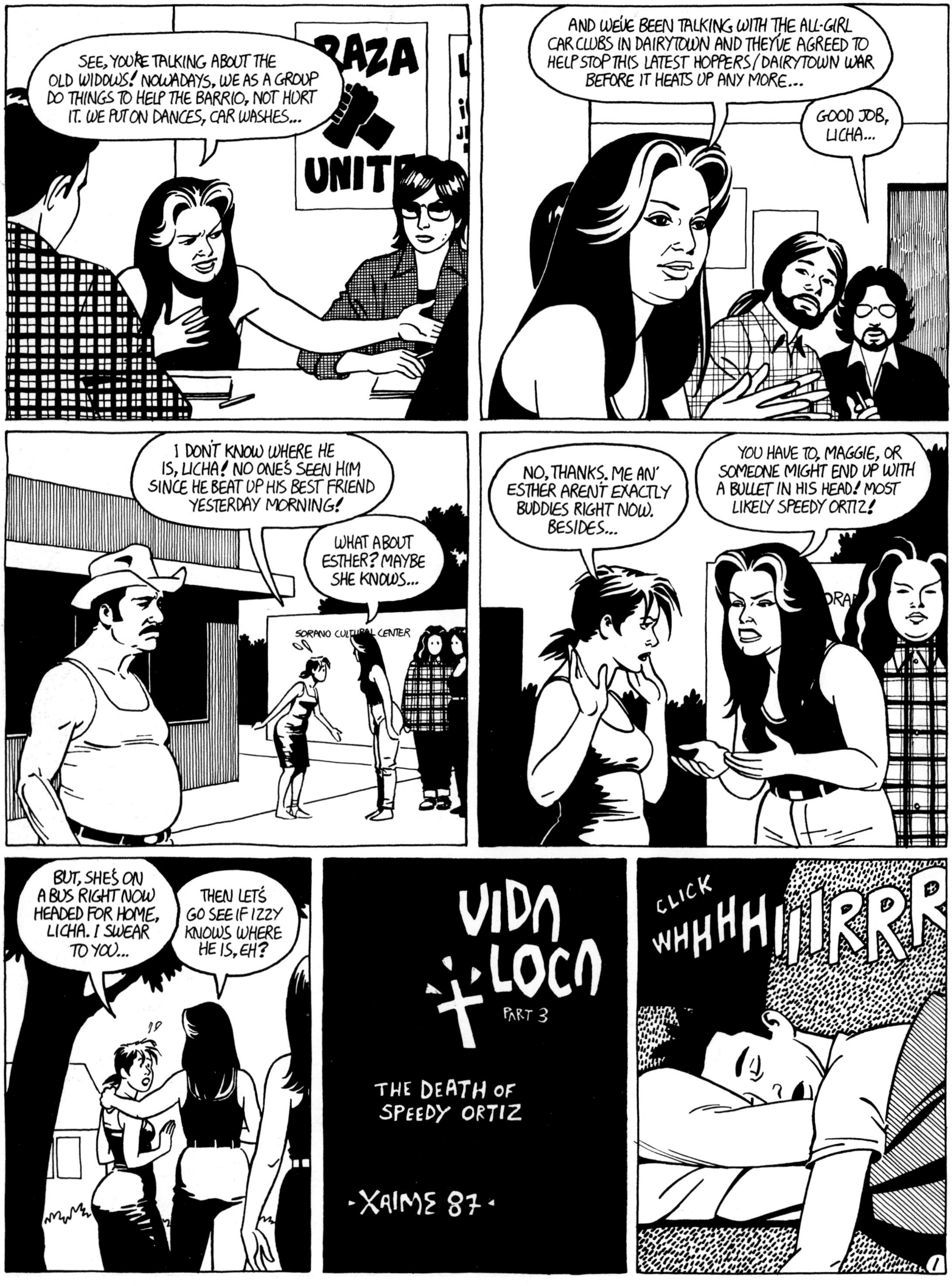
SEE, YOU'RE TALKING ABOUT THE OLD WIDOWS! NOWADAYS, WE AS A GROUP DO THINGS TO HELP THE BARRIO, NOT HURT IT. WE PUT ON DANCES, CAR WASHES...
RAZA
UNIT
AND WE'VE BEEN TALKING WITH THE ALL-GIRL CAR CLUBS IN DAIRYTOWN AND THEY'VE AGREED TO HELP STOP THIS LATEST HOPPERS/DAIRYTOWN WAR BEFORE IT HEATS UP ANY MORE...
GOOD JOB, LICHA...
I DON'T KNOW WHERE HE IS, LICHA! NO ONE'S SEEN HIM SINCE HE BEAT UP HIS BEST FRIEND YESTERDAY MORNING!
WHAT ABOUT ESTHER? MAYBE SHE KNOWS...
SORANO CULTURAL CENTER
NO, THANKS. ME AN' ESTHER AREN'T EXACTLY BUDDIES RIGHT NOW. BESIDES...
YOU HAVE TO, MAGGIE, OR SOMEONE MIGHT END UP WITH A BULLET IN HIS HEAD! MOST LIKELY SPEEDY ORTIZ!
BUT, SHE'S ON A BUS RIGHT NOW HEADED FOR HOME, LICHA. I SWEAR TO YOU...
THEN LET'S GO SEE IF IZZY KNOWS WHERE HE IS, EH?
VIDA LOCA
PART 3
THE DEATH OF SPEEDY ORTIZ
·XAIME 87·
CLICK
WHHHHIIRRR
1

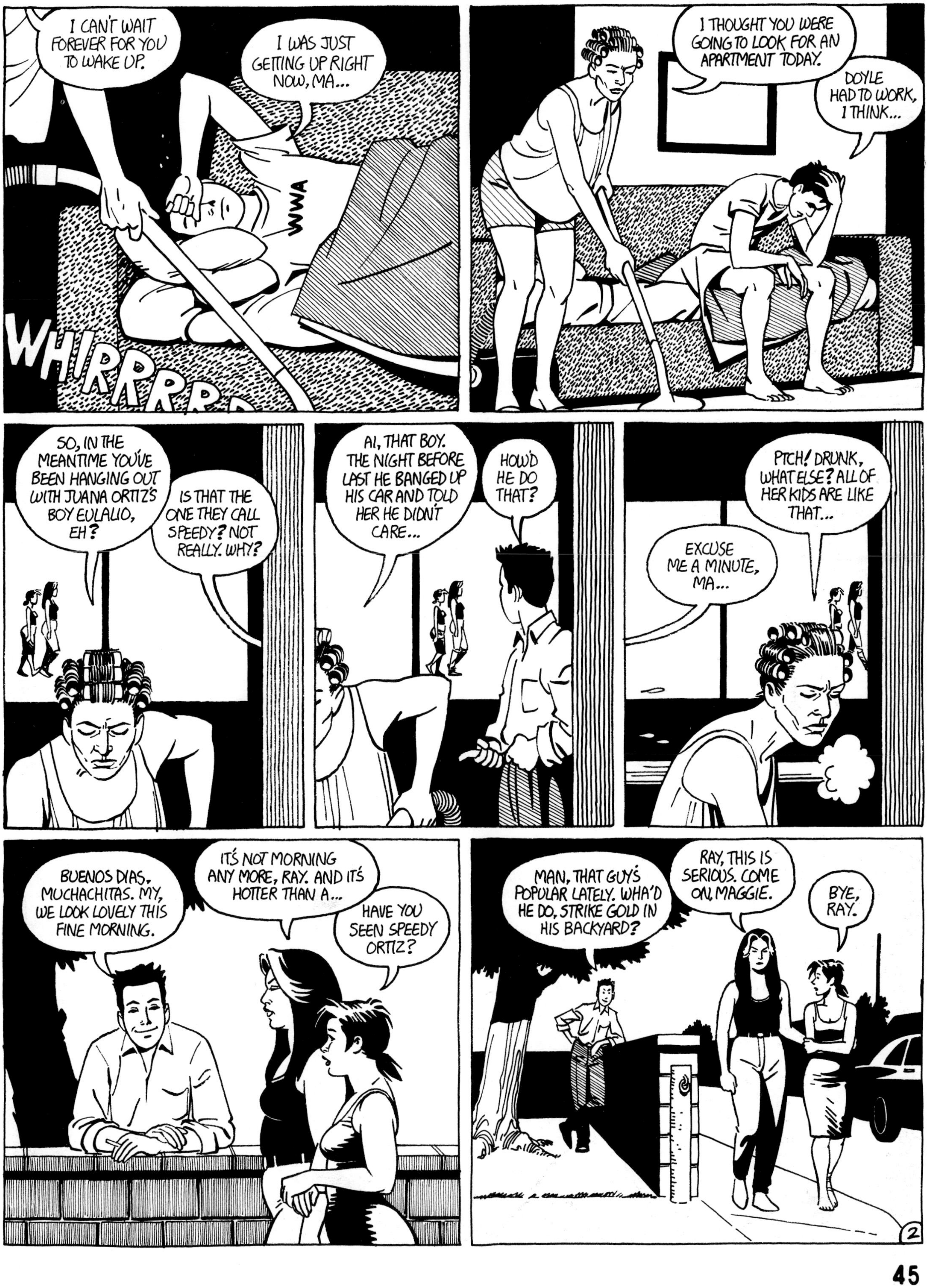
I CAN'T WAIT FOREVER FOR YOU TO WAKE UP.
I WAS JUST GETTING UP RIGHT NOW, MA...
WWA
WHIRRRRR
I THOUGHT YOU WERE GOING TO LOOK FOR AN APARTMENT TODAY.
DOYLE HAD TO WORK, I THINK...
SO, IN THE MEANTIME YOU'VE BEEN HANGING OUT WITH JUANA ORTIZ'S BOY EULALIO, EH?
IS THAT THE ONE THEY CALL SPEEDY? NOT REALLY. WHY?
AI, THAT BOY. THE NIGHT BEFORE LAST HE BANGED UP HIS CAR AND TOLD HER HE DIDN'T CARE...
HOW'D HE DO THAT?
PTCH! DRUNK, WHAT ELSE? ALL OF HER KIDS ARE LIKE THAT...
EXCUSE ME A MINUTE, MA...
BUENOS DIAS, MUCHACHITAS. MY, WE LOOK LOVELY THIS FINE MORNING.
IT'S NOT MORNING ANY MORE, RAY. AND IT'S HOTTER THAN A...
HAVE YOU SEEN SPEEDY ORTIZ?
MAN, THAT GUY'S POPULAR LATELY. WHA'D HE DO, STRIKE GOLD IN HIS BACKYARD?
RAY, THIS IS SERIOUS. COME ON, MAGGIE.
BYE, RAY.
2

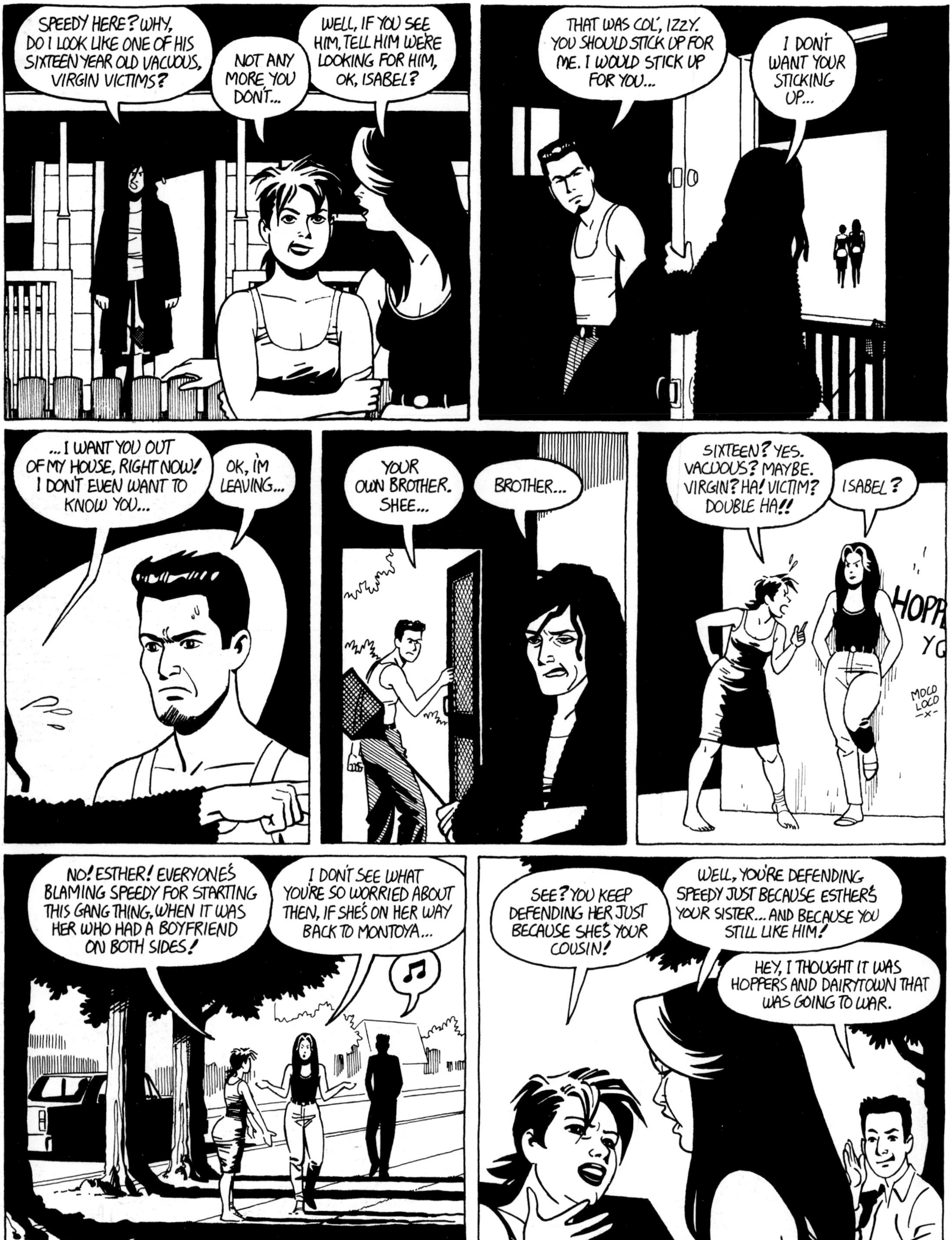
SPEEDY HERE? WHY, DO I LOOK LIKE ONE OF HIS SIXTEEN YEAR OLD VACUOUS, VIRGIN VICTIMS?
NOT ANY MORE YOU DON'T...
WELL, IF YOU SEE HIM, TELL HIM WE'RE LOOKING FOR HIM, OK, ISABEL?
THAT WAS COL', IZZY. YOU SHOULD STICK UP FOR ME. I WOULD STICK UP FOR YOU...
I DON'T WANT YOUR STICKING UP...
...I WANT YOU OUT OF MY HOUSE, RIGHT NOW! I DON'T EVEN WANT TO KNOW YOU...
OK, I'M LEAVING...
YOUR OWN BROTHER. SHEE...
BROTHER...
SIXTEEN? YES. VACUOUS? MAYBE. VIRGIN? HA! VICTIM? DOUBLE HA!!
ISABEL?
HOPP
YO
MOCO LOCO -X-
NO! ESTHER! EVERYONE'S BLAMING SPEEDY FOR STARTING THIS GANG THING, WHEN IT WAS HER WHO HAD A BOYFRIEND ON BOTH SIDES!
I DON'T SEE WHAT YOU'RE SO WORRIED ABOUT THEN, IF SHE'S ON HER WAY BACK TO MONTOYA...
♫
SEE? YOU KEEP DEFENDING HER JUST BECAUSE SHE'S YOUR COUSIN!
WELL, YOU'RE DEFENDING SPEEDY JUST BECAUSE ESTHER'S YOUR SISTER... AND BECAUSE YOU STILL LIKE HIM!
HEY, I THOUGHT IT WAS HOPPERS AND DAIRYTOWN THAT WAS GOING TO WAR.
3

MONTOYA/DAIRYTOWN

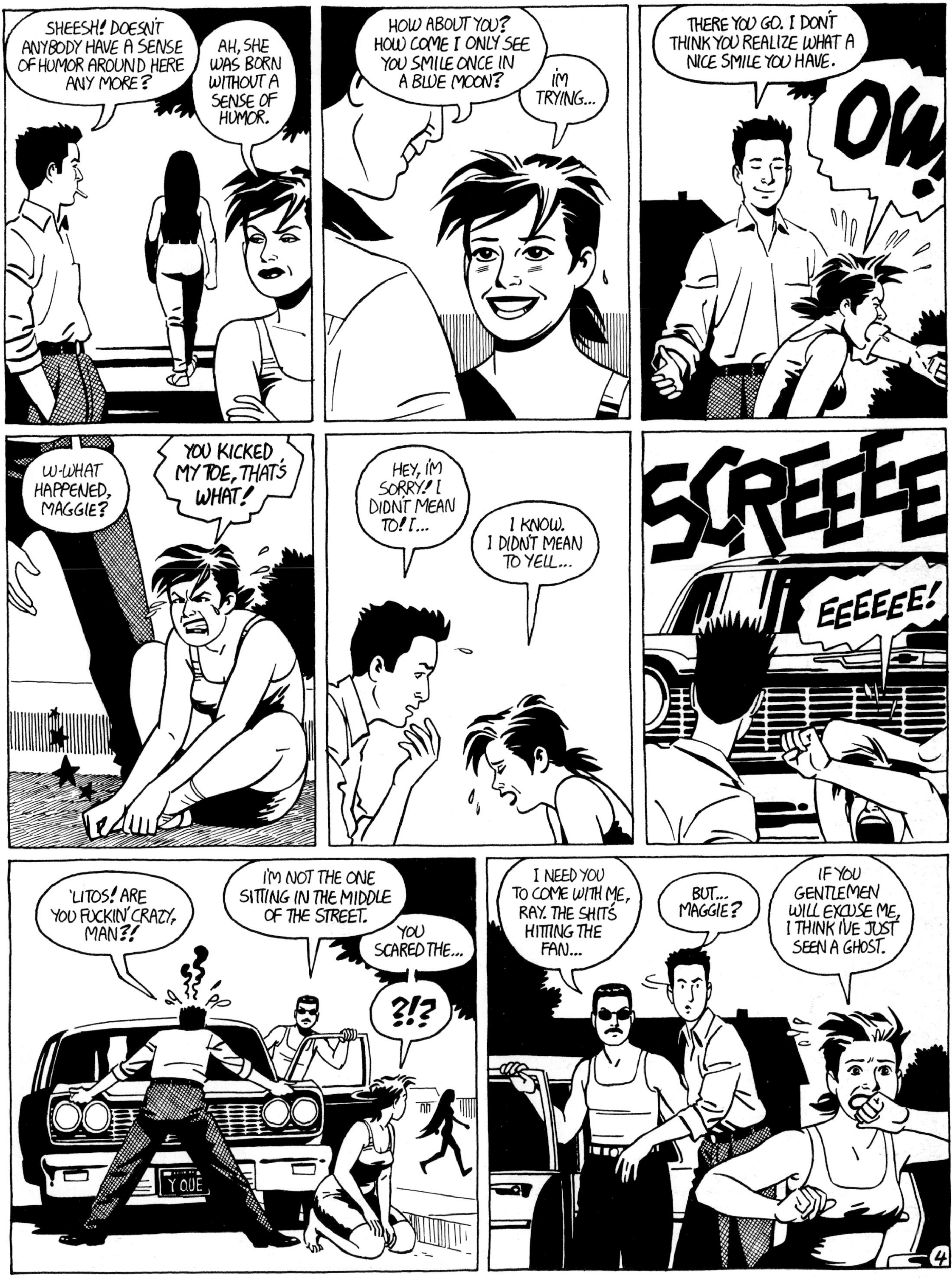
SHEESH! DOESN'T ANYBODY HAVE A SENSE OF HUMOR AROUND HERE ANY MORE?
AH, SHE WAS BORN WITHOUT A SENSE OF HUMOR.
HOW ABOUT YOU? HOW COME I ONLY SEE YOU SMILE ONCE IN A BLUE MOON?
I'M TRYING...
THERE YOU GO. I DON'T THINK YOU REALIZE WHAT A NICE SMILE YOU HAVE.
OW!
W-WHAT HAPPENED, MAGGIE?
YOU KICKED MY TOE, THAT'S WHAT!
HEY, I'M SORRY! I DIDN'T MEAN TO! I...
I KNOW. I DIDN'T MEAN TO YELL...
SCREEEE
EEEEEE!
'LITOS! ARE YOU FUCKIN' CRAZY, MAN?!
I'M NOT THE ONE SITTING IN THE MIDDLE OF THE STREET.
YOU SCARED THE...
?!?
Y QUE
I NEED YOU TO COME WITH ME, RAY. THE SHIT'S HITTING THE FAN...
BUT... MAGGIE?
IF YOU GENTLEMEN WILL EXCUSE ME, I THINK I'VE JUST SEEN A GHOST.
4

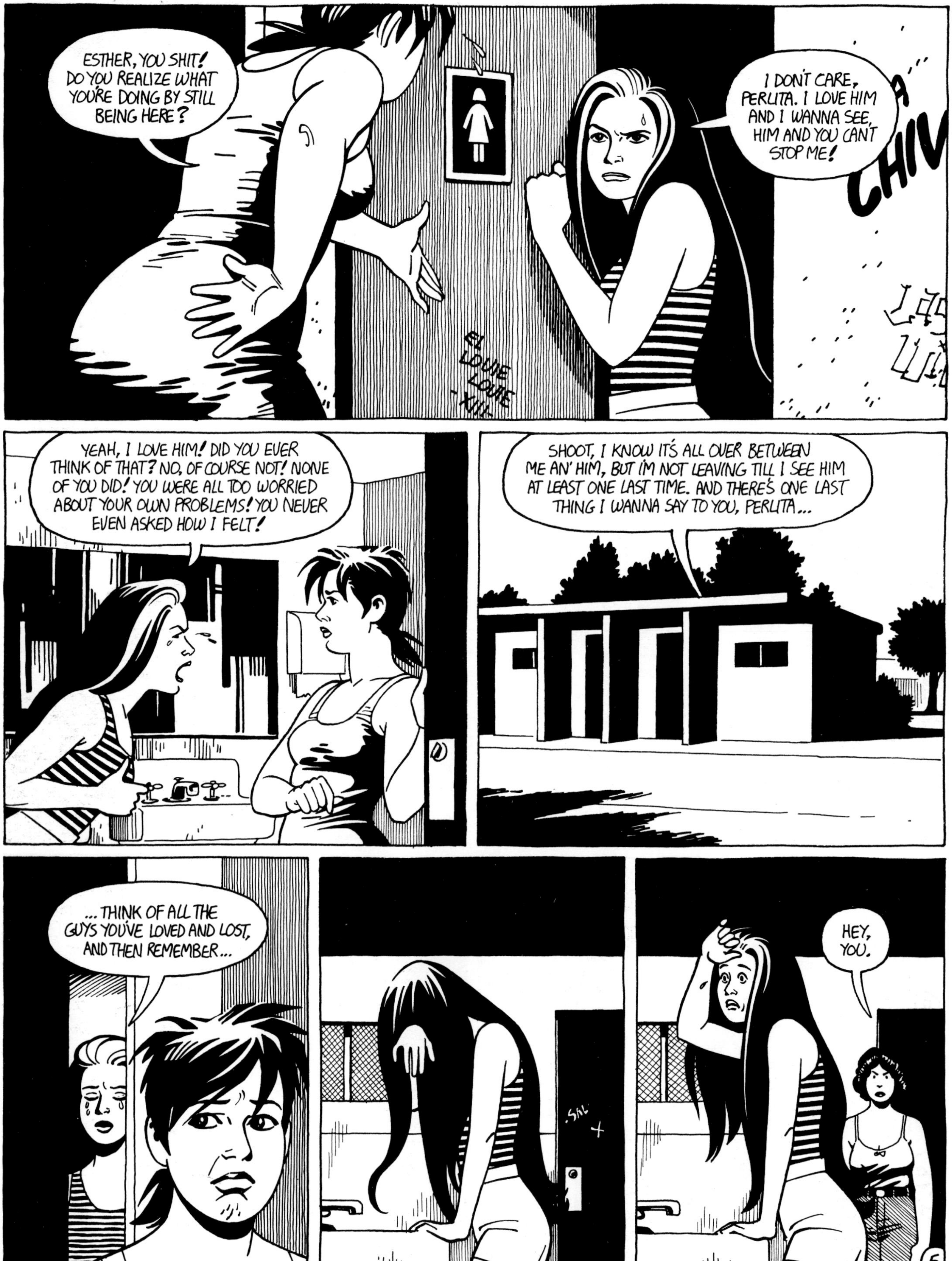
ESTHER, YOU SHIT! DO YOU REALIZE WHAT YOU'RE DOING BY STILL BEING HERE?
I DON'T CARE, PERLITA. I LOVE HIM AND I WANNA SEE, HIM AND YOU CAN'T STOP ME!
YEAH, I LOVE HIM! DID YOU EVER THINK OF THAT? NO, OF COURSE NOT! NONE OF YOU DID! YOU WERE ALL TOO WORRIED ABOUT YOUR OWN PROBLEMS! YOU NEVER EVEN ASKED HOW I FELT!
SHOOT, I KNOW IT'S ALL OVER BETWEEN ME AN' HIM, BUT I'M NOT LEAVING TILL I SEE HIM AT LEAST ONE LAST TIME. AND THERE'S ONE LAST THING I WANNA SAY TO YOU, PERLITA...
...THINK OF ALL THE GUYS YOU'VE LOVED AND LOST, AND THEN REMEMBER...
HEY, YOU.

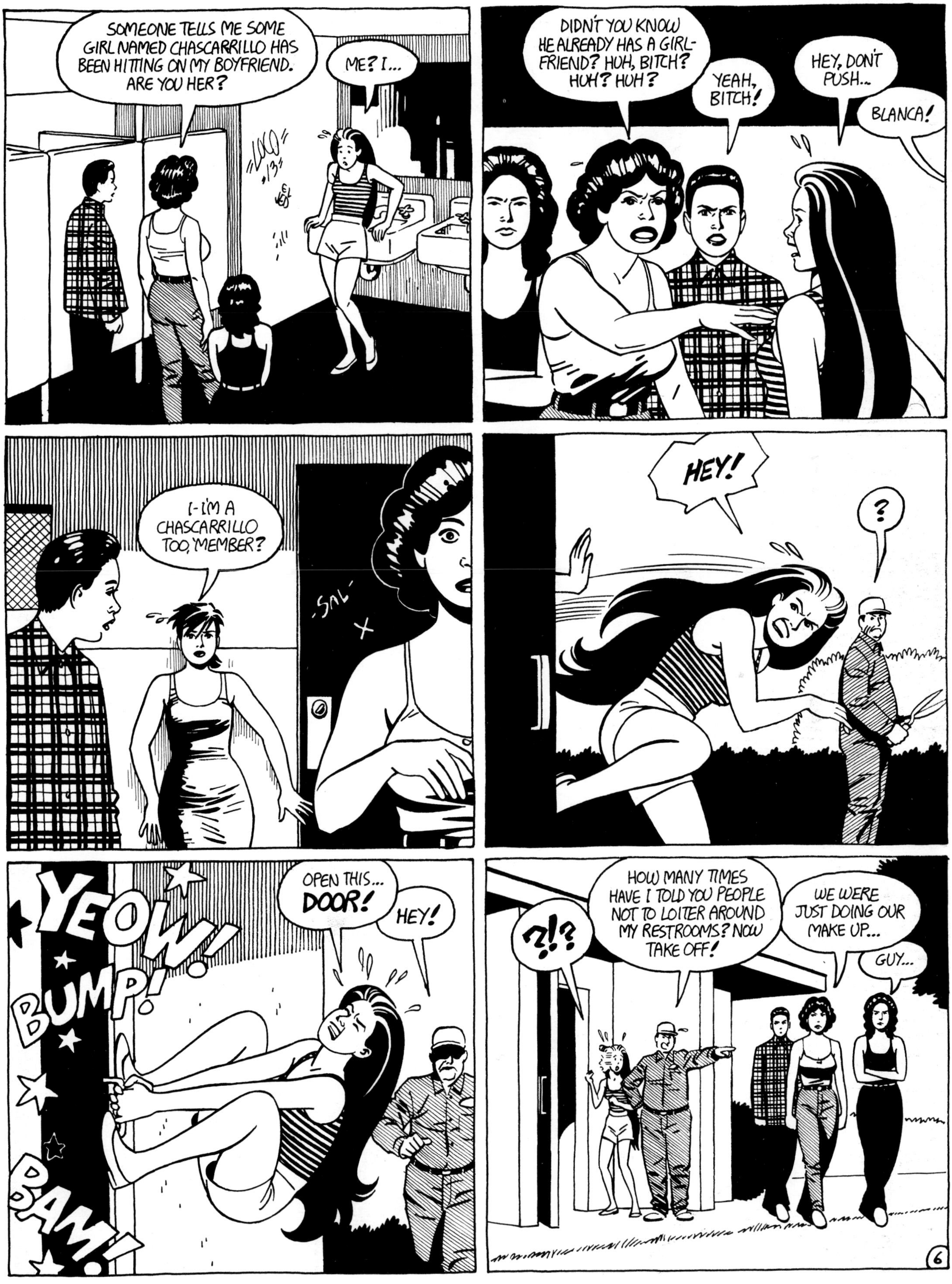
SOMEONE TELLS ME SOME GIRL NAMED CHASCARRILLO HAS BEEN HITTING ON MY BOYFRIEND. ARE YOU HER?
ME? I...
LOCO 13
DIDN'T YOU KNOW HE ALREADY HAS A GIRL-FRIEND? HUH, BITCH? HUH? HUH?
YEAH, BITCH!
HEY, DON'T PUSH...
BLANCA!
I-I'M A CHASCARRILLO TOO, 'MEMBER?
SAL
HEY!
?
YEOW!
BUMP!
BAM!
OPEN THIS... DOOR!
HEY!
?!?
HOW MANY TIMES HAVE I TOLD YOU PEOPLE NOT TO LOITER AROUND MY RESTROOMS? NOW TAKE OFF!
WE WERE JUST DOING OUR MAKE UP...
GUY...
6

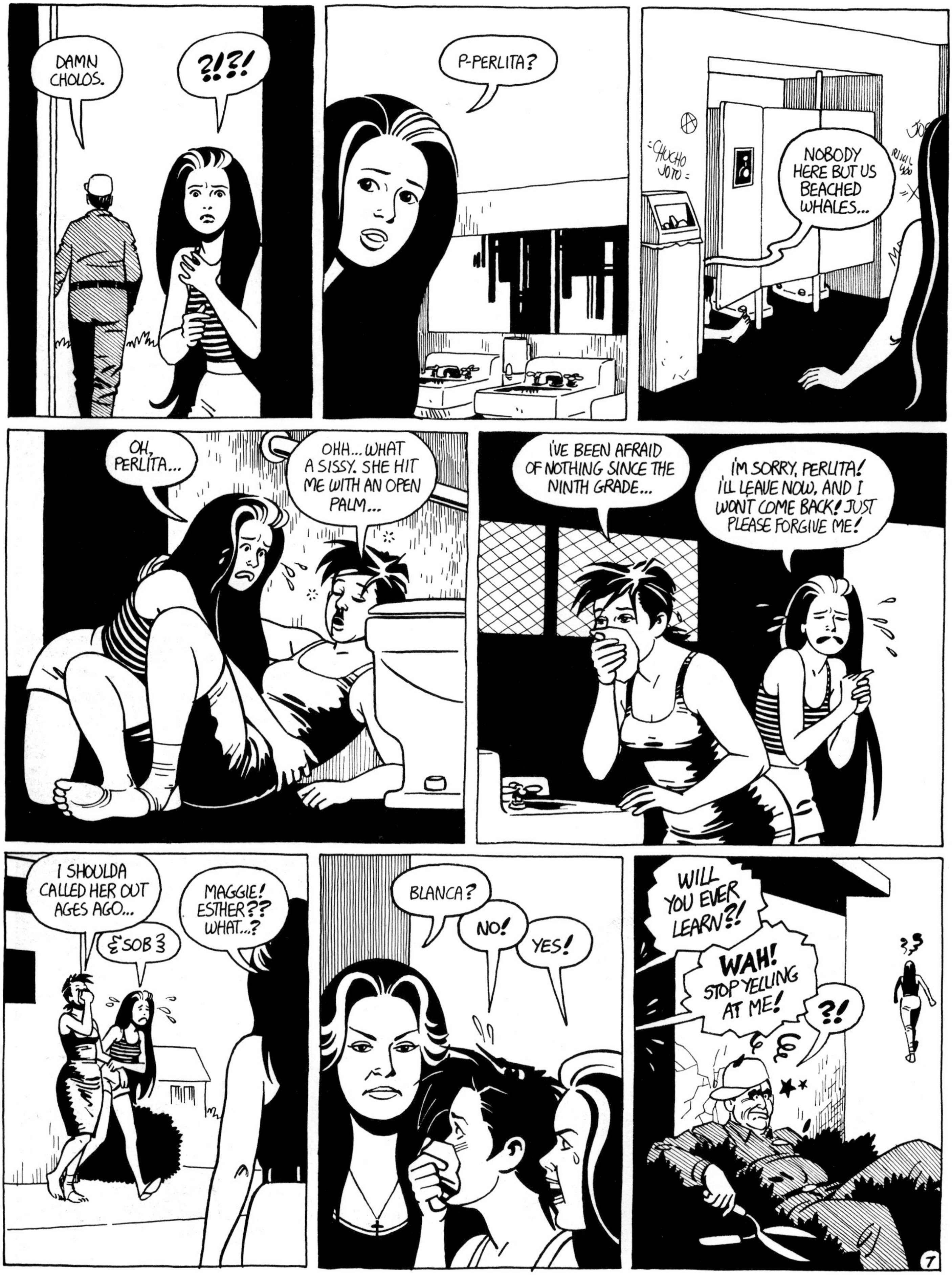
DAMN CHOLOS.
?!?!
P-PERLITA?
NOBODY HERE BUT US BEACHED WHALES...
OH, PERLITA...
OHH... WHAT A SISSY. SHE HIT ME WITH AN OPEN PALM...
I'VE BEEN AFRAID OF NOTHING SINCE THE NINTH GRADE...
I'M SORRY, PERLITA! I'LL LEAVE NOW, AND I WON'T COME BACK! JUST PLEASE FORGIVE ME!
I SHOULDA CALLED HER OUT AGES AGO...
{ SOB }
MAGGIE! ESTHER?? WHAT...?
BLANCA?
NO!
YES!
WILL YOU EVER LEARN?!
WAH! STOP YELLING AT ME!
?!
7

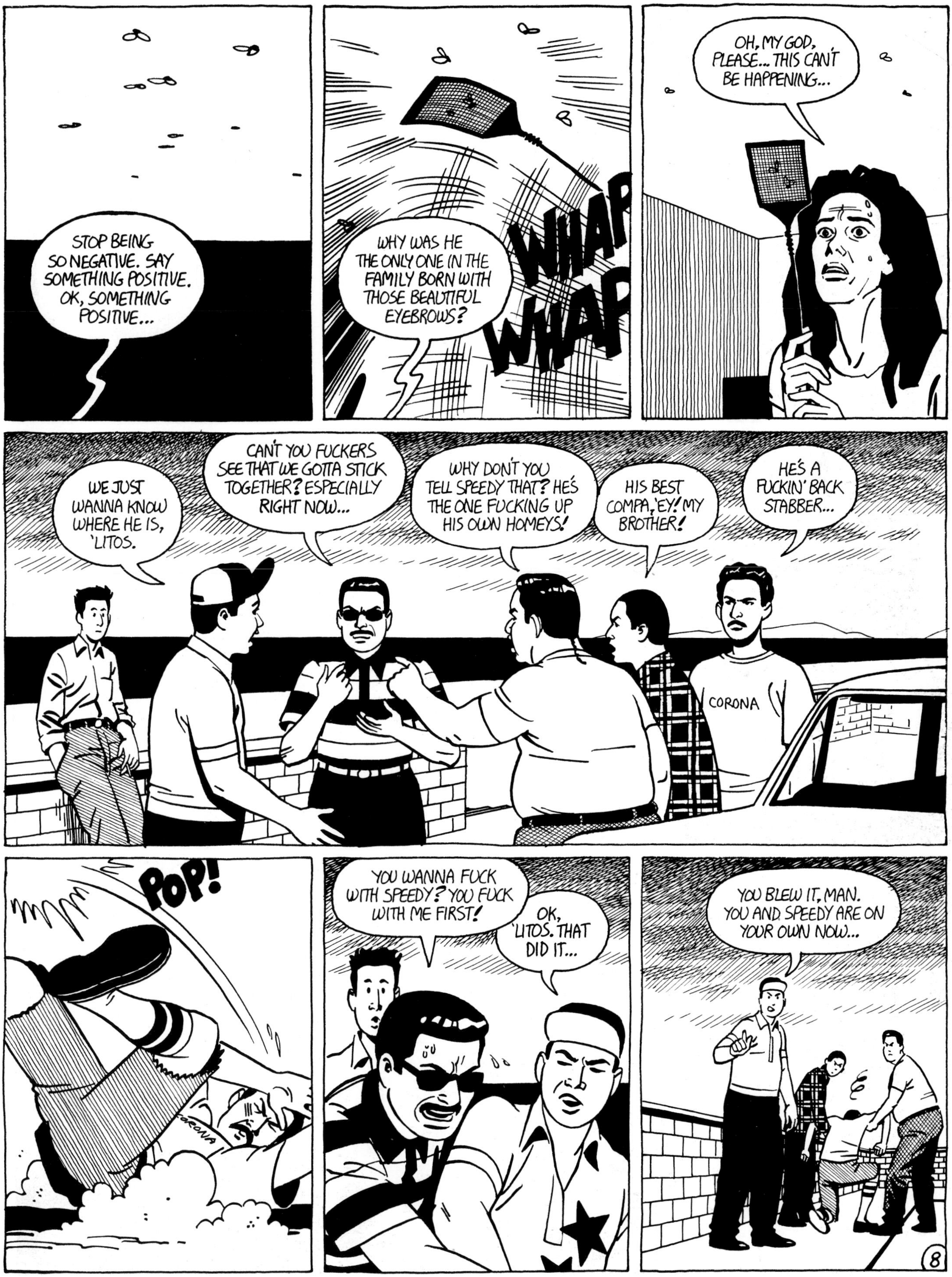
STOP BEING SO NEGATIVE. SAY SOMETHING POSITIVE. OK, SOMETHING POSITIVE...
WHY WAS HE THE ONLY ONE IN THE FAMILY BORN WITH THOSE BEAUTIFUL EYEBROWS?
WHAP
WHAP
OH, MY GOD, PLEASE... THIS CAN'T BE HAPPENING...
WE JUST WANNA KNOW WHERE HE IS, 'LITOS.
CAN'T YOU FUCKERS SEE THAT WE GOTTA STICK TOGETHER? ESPECIALLY RIGHT NOW...
WHY DON'T YOU TELL SPEEDY THAT? HE'S THE ONE FUCKING UP HIS OWN HOMEYS!
HIS BEST COMPA, 'EY! MY BROTHER!
HE'S A FUCKIN' BACK STABBER...
CORONA
POP!
CORONA
YOU WANNA FUCK WITH SPEEDY? YOU FUCK WITH ME FIRST!
OK, 'LITOS. THAT DID IT...
YOU BLEW IT, MAN. YOU AND SPEEDY ARE ON YOUR OWN NOW...
8

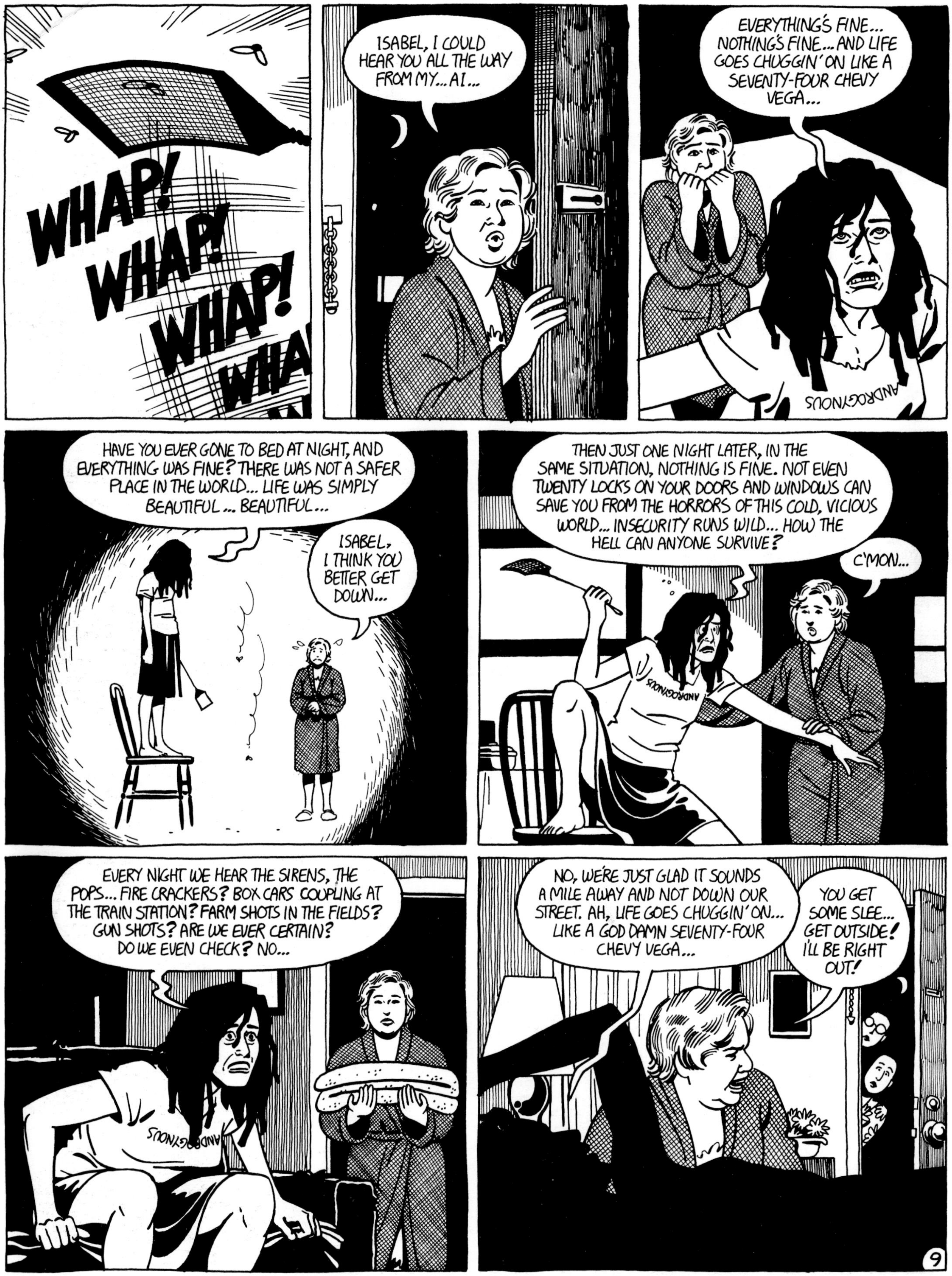
WHAP! WHAP! WHAP! WHA
ISABEL, I COULD HEAR YOU ALL THE WAY FROM MY...AI...
EVERYTHING'S FINE... NOTHING'S FINE...AND LIFE GOES CHUGGIN' ON LIKE A SEVENTY-FOUR CHEVY VEGA...
ANDROGYNOUS
HAVE YOU EVER GONE TO BED AT NIGHT, AND EVERYTHING WAS FINE? THERE WAS NOT A SAFER PLACE IN THE WORLD... LIFE WAS SIMPLY BEAUTIFUL... BEAUTIFUL...
ISABEL, I THINK YOU BETTER GET DOWN...
THEN JUST ONE NIGHT LATER, IN THE SAME SITUATION, NOTHING IS FINE. NOT EVEN TWENTY LOCKS ON YOUR DOORS AND WINDOWS CAN SAVE YOU FROM THE HORRORS OF THIS COLD, VICIOUS WORLD... INSECURITY RUNS WILD... HOW THE HELL CAN ANYONE SURVIVE?
C'MON...
ANDROGYNOUS
EVERY NIGHT WE HEAR THE SIRENS, THE POPS... FIRE CRACKERS? BOX CARS COUPLING AT THE TRAIN STATION? FARM SHOTS IN THE FIELDS? GUN SHOTS? ARE WE EVER CERTAIN? DO WE EVEN CHECK? NO...
ANDROGYNOUS
NO, WE'RE JUST GLAD IT SOUNDS A MILE AWAY AND NOT DOWN OUR STREET. AH, LIFE GOES CHUGGIN' ON... LIKE A GOD DAMN SEVENTY-FOUR CHEVY VEGA...
YOU GET SOME SLEE... GET OUTSIDE! I'LL BE RIGHT OUT!
9

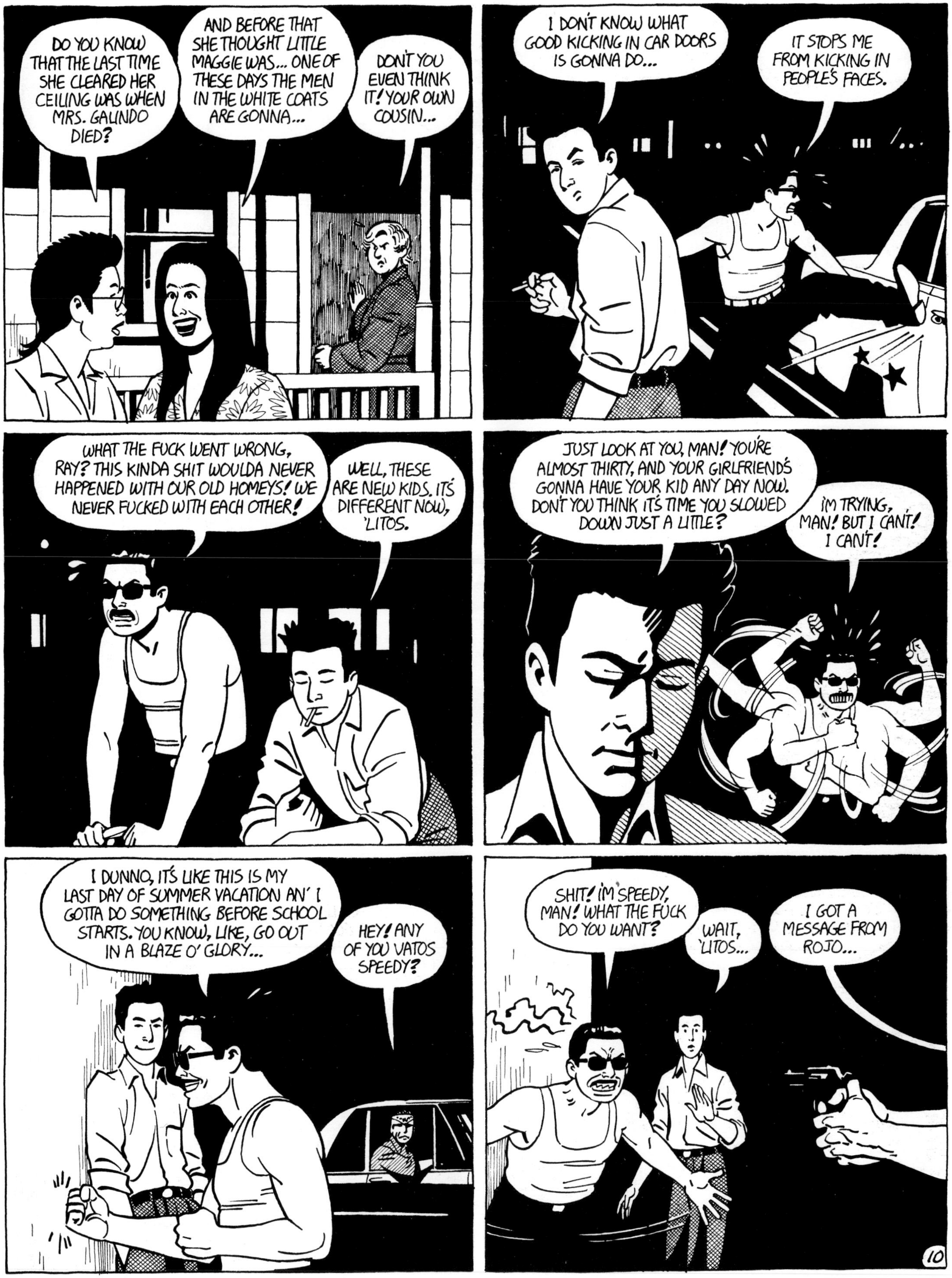
DO YOU KNOW THAT THE LAST TIME SHE CLEARED HER CEILING WAS WHEN MRS. GALINDO DIED?
AND BEFORE THAT SHE THOUGHT LITTLE MAGGIE WAS... ONE OF THESE DAYS THE MEN IN THE WHITE COATS ARE GONNA...
DON'T YOU EVEN THINK IT! YOUR OWN COUSIN...
I DON'T KNOW WHAT GOOD KICKING IN CAR DOORS IS GONNA DO...
IT STOPS ME FROM KICKING IN PEOPLE'S FACES.
WHAT THE FUCK WENT WRONG, RAY? THIS KINDA SHIT WOULDA NEVER HAPPENED WITH OUR OLD HOMEYS! WE NEVER FUCKED WITH EACH OTHER!
WELL, THESE ARE NEW KIDS. IT'S DIFFERENT NOW, 'LITOS.
JUST LOOK AT YOU, MAN! YOU'RE ALMOST THIRTY, AND YOUR GIRLFRIEND'S GONNA HAVE YOUR KID ANY DAY NOW. DON'T YOU THINK IT'S TIME YOU SLOWED DOWN JUST A LITTLE?
I'M TRYING, MAN! BUT I CAN'T! I CAN'T!
I DUNNO, IT'S LIKE THIS IS MY LAST DAY OF SUMMER VACATION AN' I GOTTA DO SOMETHING BEFORE SCHOOL STARTS. YOU KNOW, LIKE, GO OUT IN A BLAZE O' GLORY...
HEY! ANY OF YOU VATOS SPEEDY?
SHIT! I'M SPEEDY, MAN! WHAT THE FUCK DO YOU WANT?
WAIT, 'LITOS...
I GOT A MESSAGE FROM ROJO...
10

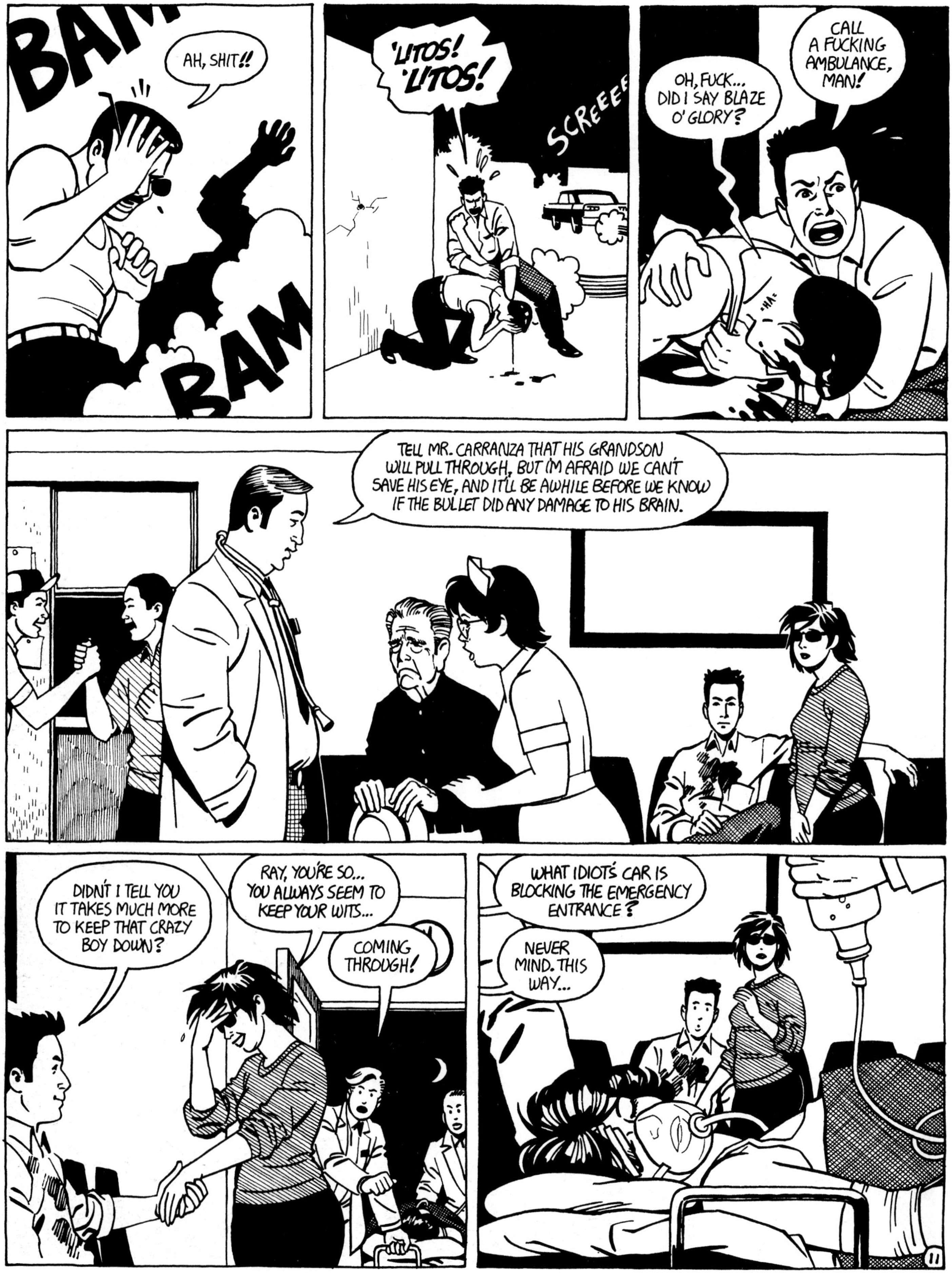
BAM
AH, SHIT!!
BAM
'LITOS! 'LITOS!
SCREEEE
OH, FUCK... DID I SAY BLAZE O' GLORY?
CALL A FUCKING AMBULANCE, MAN!
HA
TELL MR. CARRANZA THAT HIS GRANDSON WILL PULL THROUGH, BUT I'M AFRAID WE CAN'T SAVE HIS EYE, AND IT'LL BE AWHILE BEFORE WE KNOW IF THE BULLET DID ANY DAMAGE TO HIS BRAIN.
DIDN'T I TELL YOU IT TAKES MUCH MORE TO KEEP THAT CRAZY BOY DOWN?
RAY, YOU'RE SO... YOU ALWAYS SEEM TO KEEP YOUR WITS...
COMING THROUGH!
WHAT IDIOT'S CAR IS BLOCKING THE EMERGENCY ENTRANCE?
NEVER MIND. THIS WAY...
11

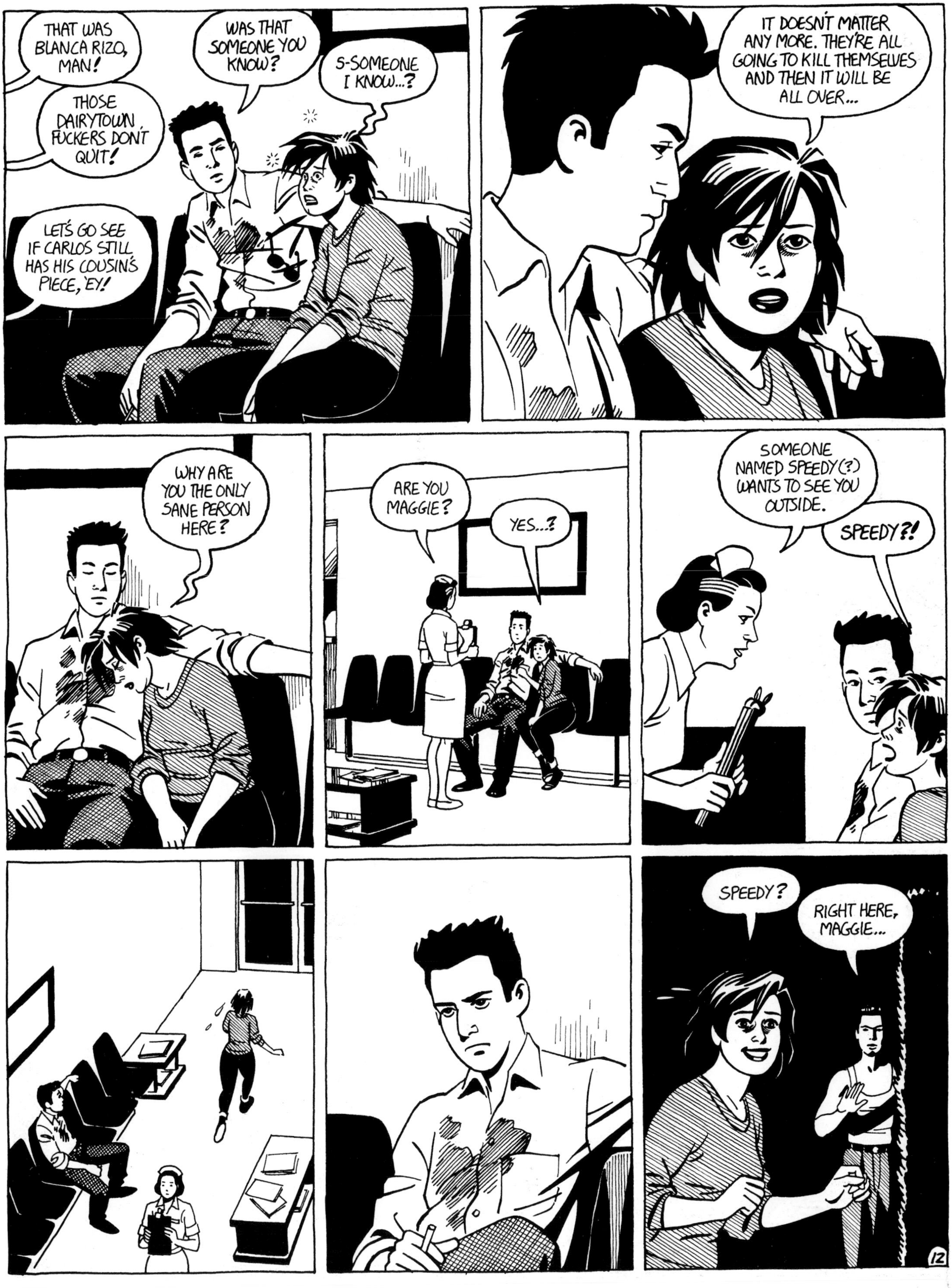
THAT WAS BLANCA RIZO, MAN!
THOSE DAIRYTOWN FUCKERS DON'T QUIT!
WAS THAT SOMEONE YOU KNOW?
S-SOMEONE I KNOW...?
LET'S GO SEE IF CARLOS STILL HAS HIS COUSIN'S PIECE, 'EY!
IT DOESN'T MATTER ANY MORE. THEY'RE ALL GOING TO KILL THEMSELVES AND THEN IT WILL BE ALL OVER...
WHY ARE YOU THE ONLY SANE PERSON HERE?
ARE YOU MAGGIE?
YES...?
SOMEONE NAMED SPEEDY (?) WANTS TO SEE YOU OUTSIDE.
SPEEDY?!
SPEEDY?
RIGHT HERE, MAGGIE...
12

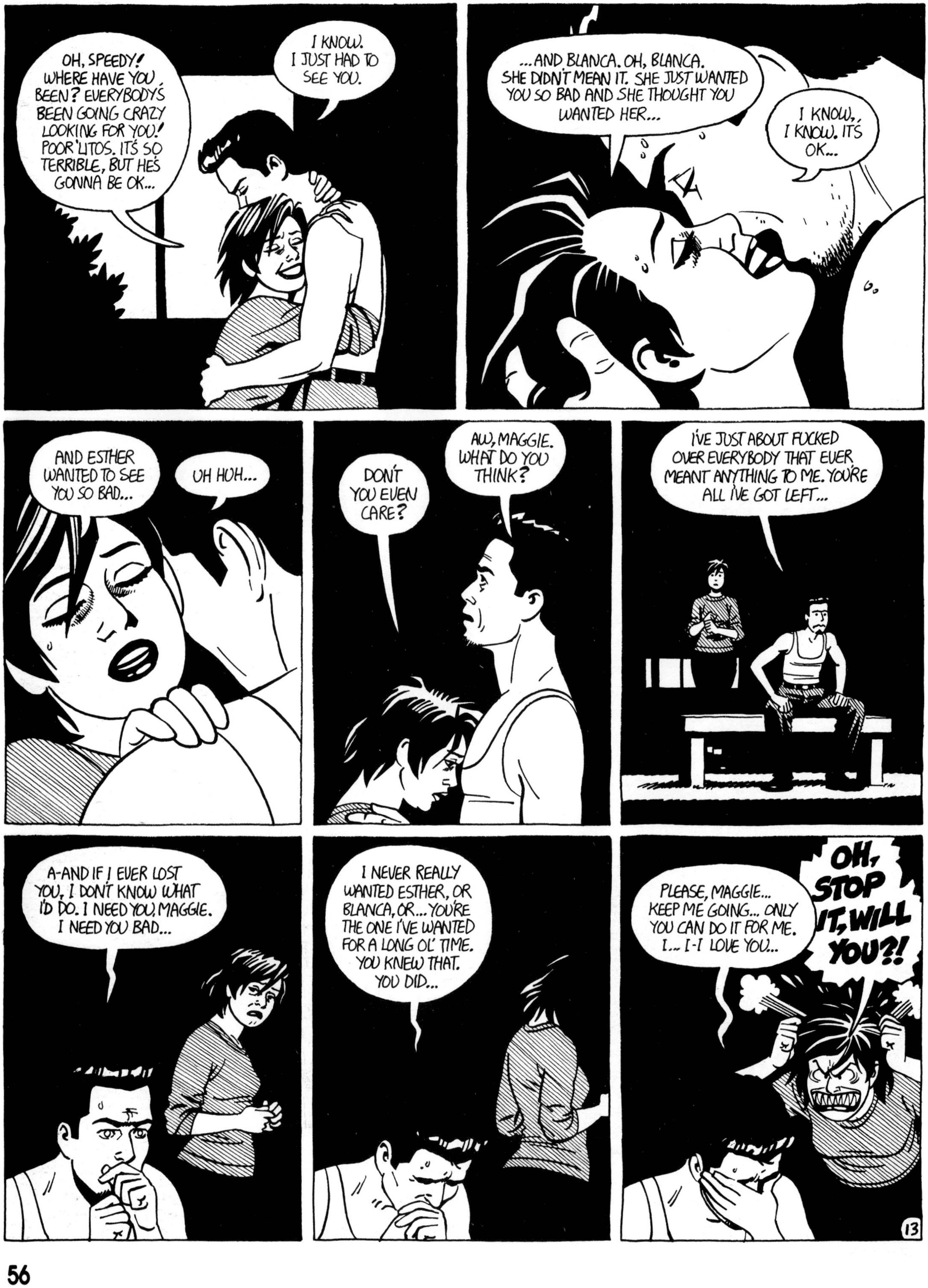
OH, SPEEDY! WHERE HAVE YOU BEEN? EVERYBODY'S BEEN GOING CRAZY LOOKING FOR YOU! POOR 'LITOS. IT'S SO TERRIBLE, BUT HE'S GONNA BE OK...
I KNOW. I JUST HAD TO SEE YOU.
...AND BLANCA. OH, BLANCA. SHE DIDN'T MEAN IT. SHE JUST WANTED YOU SO BAD AND SHE THOUGHT YOU WANTED HER...
I KNOW, I KNOW. IT'S OK...
AND ESTHER WANTED TO SEE YOU SO BAD...
UH HUH...
DON'T YOU EVEN CARE?
AW, MAGGIE. WHAT DO YOU THINK?
I'VE JUST ABOUT FUCKED OVER EVERYBODY THAT EVER MEANT ANYTHING TO ME. YOU'RE ALL I'VE GOT LEFT...
A-AND IF I EVER LOST YOU, I DON'T KNOW WHAT I'D DO. I NEED YOU, MAGGIE. I NEED YOU BAD...
I NEVER REALLY WANTED ESTHER, OR BLANCA, OR... YOU'RE THE ONE I'VE WANTED FOR A LONG OL' TIME. YOU KNEW THAT. YOU DID...
PLEASE, MAGGIE... KEEP ME GOING... ONLY YOU CAN DO IT FOR ME. I... I-I LOVE YOU...
OH, STOP IT, WILL YOU?!
13

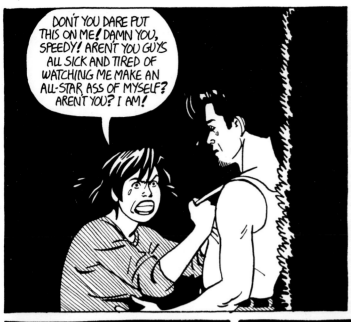

DON'T YOU DARE PUT THIS ON ME! DAMN YOU, SPEEDY! AREN'T YOU GUYS ALL SICK AND TIRED OF WATCHING ME MAKE AN ALL-STAR ASS OF MYSELF? AREN'T YOU? I AM!

I DON'T WANT TO WANT YOU ANY MORE, SPEEDY. I DON'T WANT TO WANT RAND RACE ANY MORE. I CAN'T... I CAN'T DO IT ANY MORE. IT HURTS TOO MUCH...

EMERGENCY

ISN'T THAT THAT ORTIZ KID'S CAR?

YEAH, WHAT'S HE UP TO SO LATE, OR SHOULD I SAY SO EARLY?

SAY, BUDDY! YOU CAN'T PARK HERE! C'MON, LET'S GO! MOVE IT, BAH-TOE...

AW, JEEZ... JERRY, GET ON THE RADIO...

WHAT'S UP?

BAH-TOE/VATO

(14)

57

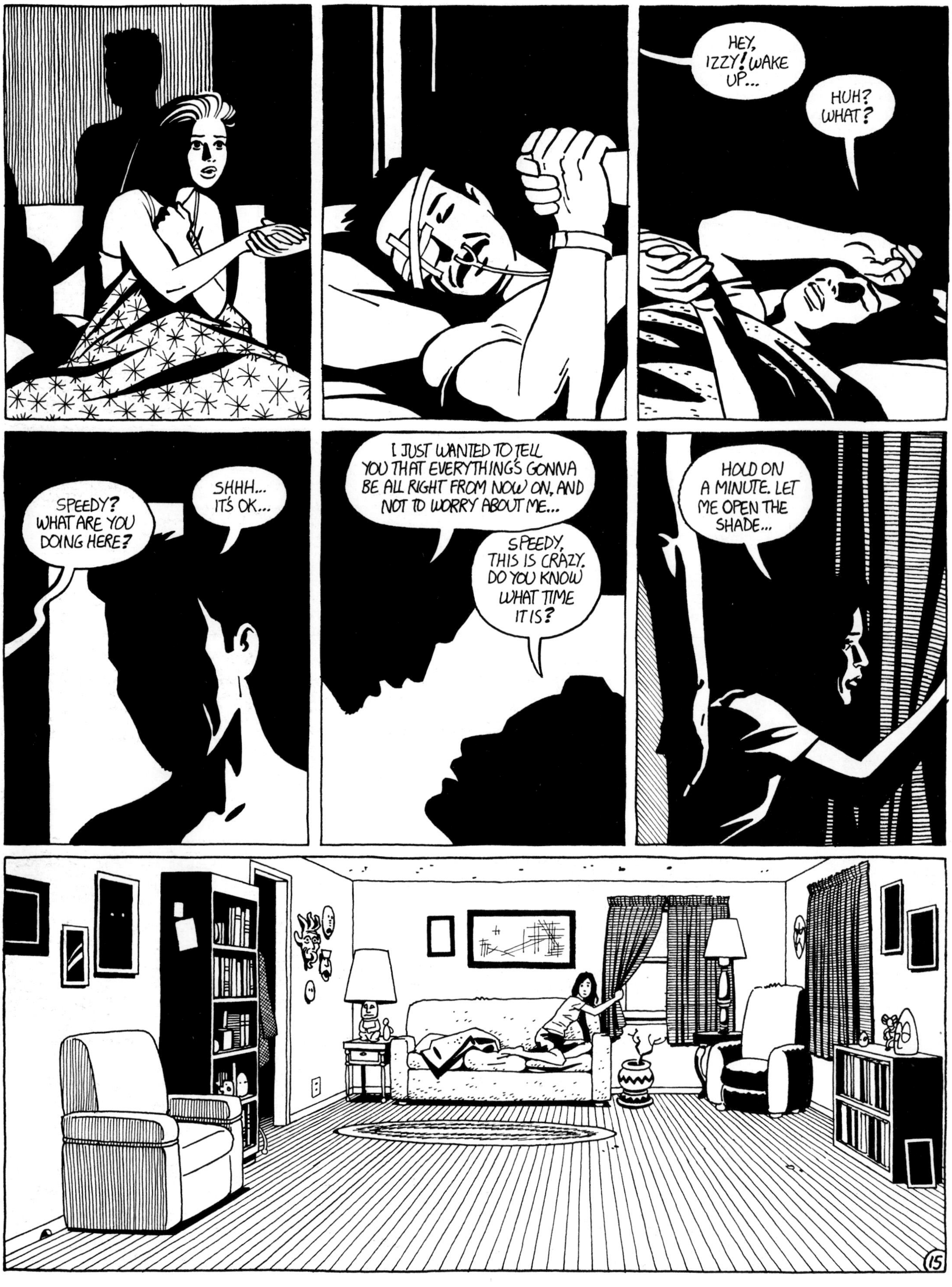
HEY, IZZY! WAKE UP...
HUH? WHAT?
SPEEDY? WHAT ARE YOU DOING HERE?
SHHH... IT'S OK...
I JUST WANTED TO TELL YOU THAT EVERYTHING'S GONNA BE ALL RIGHT FROM NOW ON, AND NOT TO WORRY ABOUT ME...
SPEEDY, THIS IS CRAZY. DO YOU KNOW WHAT TIME IT IS?
HOLD ON A MINUTE. LET ME OPEN THE SHADE...
15

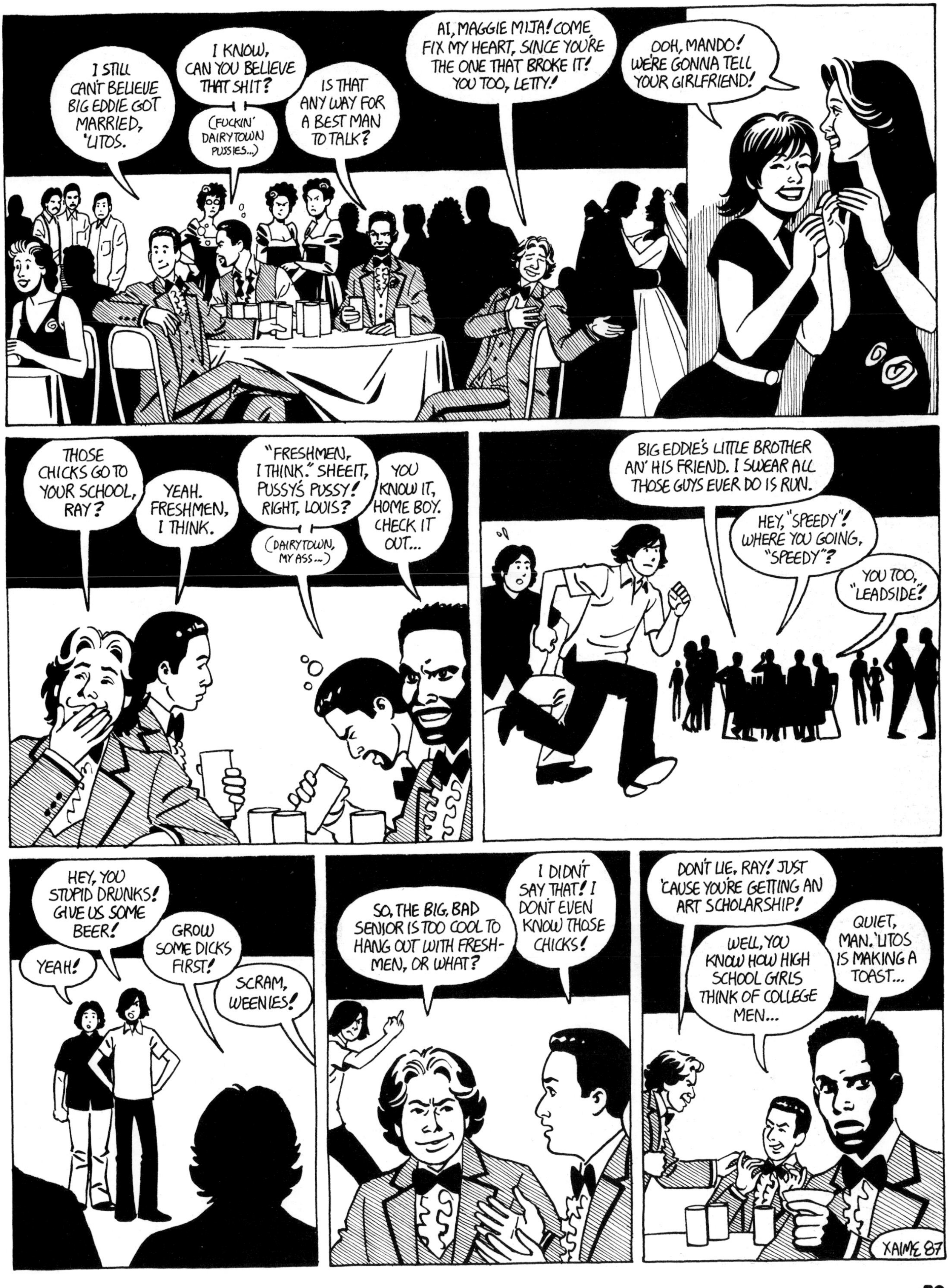

I STILL CAN'T BELIEVE BIG EDDIE GOT MARRIED, 'LITOS.
I KNOW, CAN YOU BELIEVE THAT SHIT?
(FUCKIN' DAIRYTOWN PUSSIES...)
IS THAT ANY WAY FOR A BEST MAN TO TALK?
AI, MAGGIE MIJA! COME FIX MY HEART, SINCE YOU'RE THE ONE THAT BROKE IT! YOU TOO, LETTY!
OOH, MANDO! WE'RE GONNA TELL YOUR GIRLFRIEND!
THOSE CHICKS GO TO YOUR SCHOOL, RAY?
YEAH. FRESHMEN, I THINK.
"FRESHMEN, I THINK." SHEEIT, PUSSY'S PUSSY! RIGHT, LOUIS?
(DAIRYTOWN, MY ASS...)
YOU KNOW IT, HOME BOY. CHECK IT OUT...
BIG EDDIE'S LITTLE BROTHER AN' HIS FRIEND. I SWEAR ALL THOSE GUYS EVER DO IS RUN.
HEY, "SPEEDY"! WHERE YOU GOING, "SPEEDY"?
YOU TOO, "LEADSIDE"!
HEY, YOU STUPID DRUNKS! GIVE US SOME BEER!
YEAH!
GROW SOME DICKS FIRST!
SCRAM, WEENIES!
SO, THE BIG, BAD SENIOR IS TOO COOL TO HANG OUT WITH FRESH-MEN, OR WHAT?
I DIDN'T SAY THAT! I DON'T EVEN KNOW THOSE CHICKS!
DON'T LIE, RAY! JUST 'CAUSE YOU'RE GETTING AN ART SCHOLARSHIP!
WELL, YOU KNOW HOW HIGH SCHOOL GIRLS THINK OF COLLEGE MEN...
QUIET, MAN. 'LITOS IS MAKING A TOAST...
XAIME 87

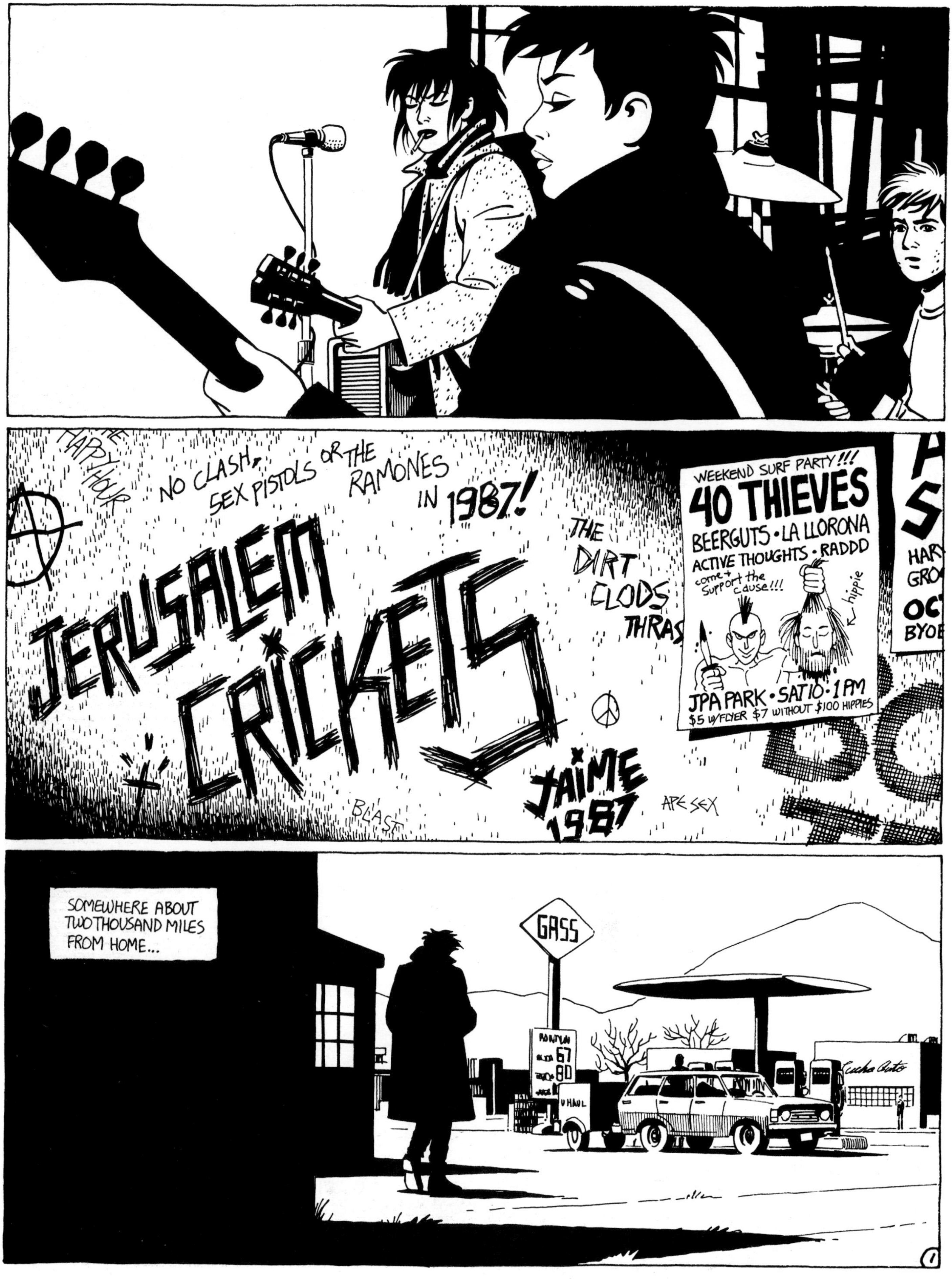
HAPPY HOUR
NO CLASH, SEX PISTOLS OR THE RAMONES IN 1987!
JERUSALEM CRICKETS
THE DIRT CLODS
WEEKEND SURF PARTY!!!
40 THIEVES
BEERGUTS • LA LLORONA
ACTIVE THOUGHTS • RADDD
come + support the cause!!!
hippie
JPA PARK • SAT 10 • 1 PM
$5 W/FLYER $7 WITHOUT $100 HIPPIES
BYOB
JAIME 1987
BLAST
APE SEX
SOMEWHERE ABOUT TWO THOUSAND MILES FROM HOME...
GASS
U HAUL
1

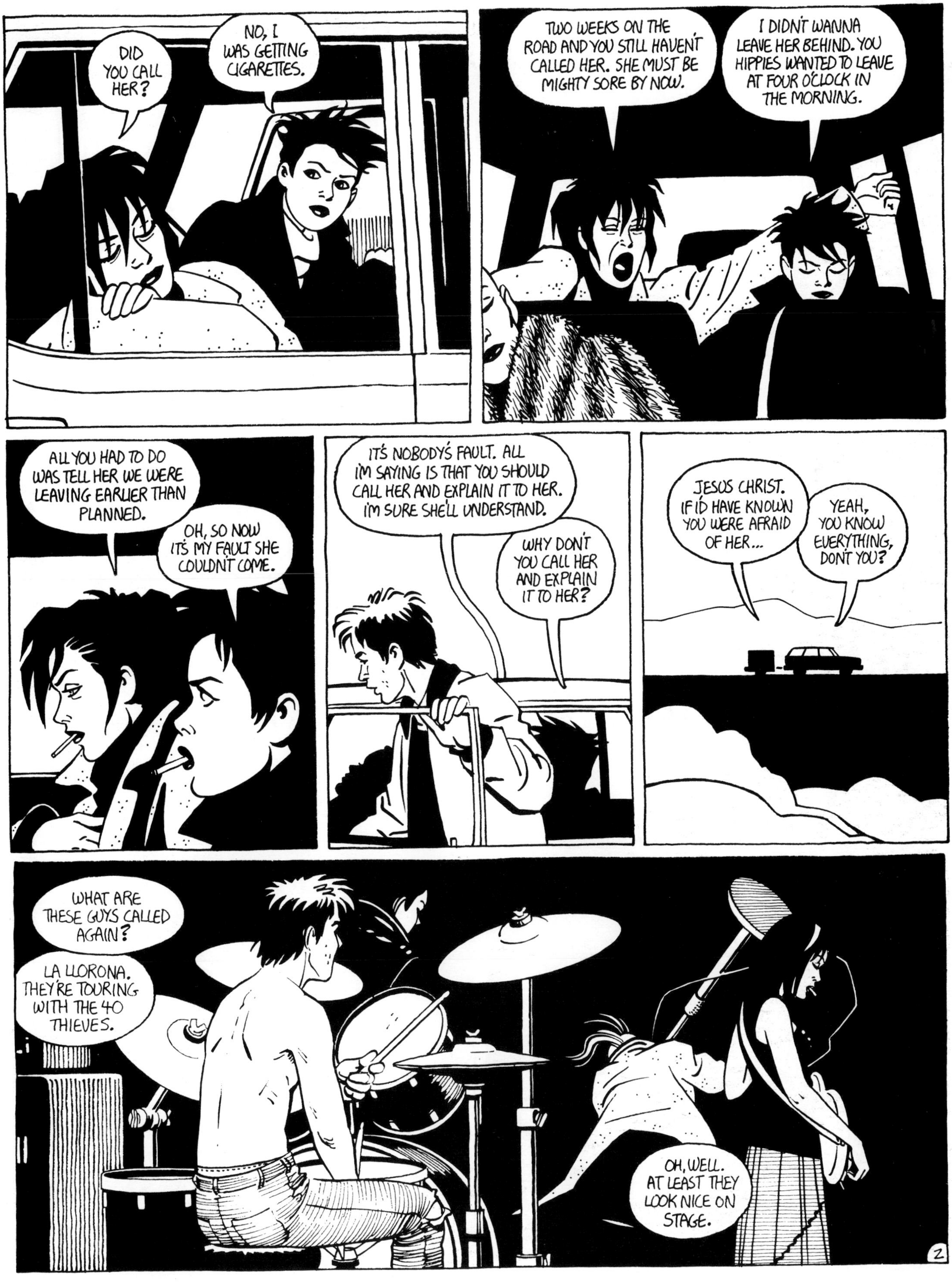
DID YOU CALL HER?
NO, I WAS GETTING CIGARETTES.
TWO WEEKS ON THE ROAD AND YOU STILL HAVEN'T CALLED HER. SHE MUST BE MIGHTY SORE BY NOW.
I DIDN'T WANNA LEAVE HER BEHIND. YOU HIPPIES WANTED TO LEAVE AT FOUR O'CLOCK IN THE MORNING.
ALL YOU HAD TO DO WAS TELL HER WE WERE LEAVING EARLIER THAN PLANNED.
OH, SO NOW IT'S MY FAULT SHE COULDN'T COME.
IT'S NOBODY'S FAULT. ALL I'M SAYING IS THAT YOU SHOULD CALL HER AND EXPLAIN IT TO HER. I'M SURE SHE'LL UNDERSTAND.
WHY DON'T YOU CALL HER AND EXPLAIN IT TO HER?
JESUS CHRIST. IF I'D HAVE KNOWN YOU WERE AFRAID OF HER...
YEAH, YOU KNOW EVERYTHING, DON'T YOU?
WHAT ARE THESE GUYS CALLED AGAIN?
LA LLORONA. THEY'RE TOURING WITH THE 40 THIEVES.
OH, WELL. AT LEAST THEY LOOK NICE ON STAGE.
2

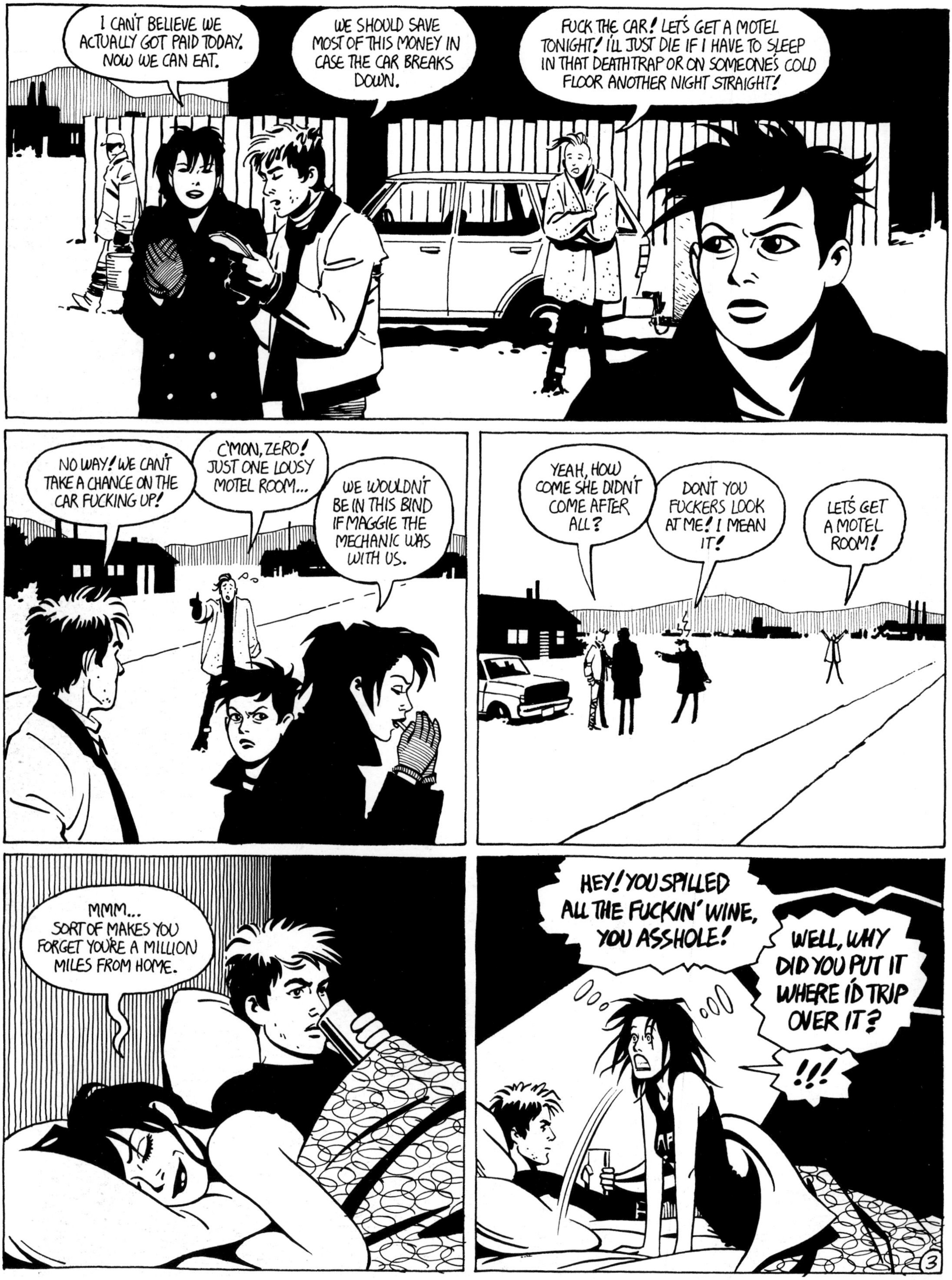

I CAN'T BELIEVE WE ACTUALLY GOT PAID TODAY. NOW WE CAN EAT.
WE SHOULD SAVE MOST OF THIS MONEY IN CASE THE CAR BREAKS DOWN.
FUCK THE CAR! LET'S GET A MOTEL TONIGHT! I'LL JUST DIE IF I HAVE TO SLEEP IN THAT DEATHTRAP OR ON SOMEONE'S COLD FLOOR ANOTHER NIGHT STRAIGHT!
NO WAY! WE CAN'T TAKE A CHANCE ON THE CAR FUCKING UP!
C'MON, ZERO! JUST ONE LOUSY MOTEL ROOM...
WE WOULDN'T BE IN THIS BIND IF MAGGIE THE MECHANIC WAS WITH US.
YEAH, HOW COME SHE DIDN'T COME AFTER ALL?
DON'T YOU FUCKERS LOOK AT ME! I MEAN IT!
LET'S GET A MOTEL ROOM!
MMM... SORT OF MAKES YOU FORGET YOU'RE A MILLION MILES FROM HOME.
HEY! YOU SPILLED ALL THE FUCKIN' WINE, YOU ASSHOLE!
WELL, WHY DID YOU PUT IT WHERE I'D TRIP OVER IT?
!!!
3

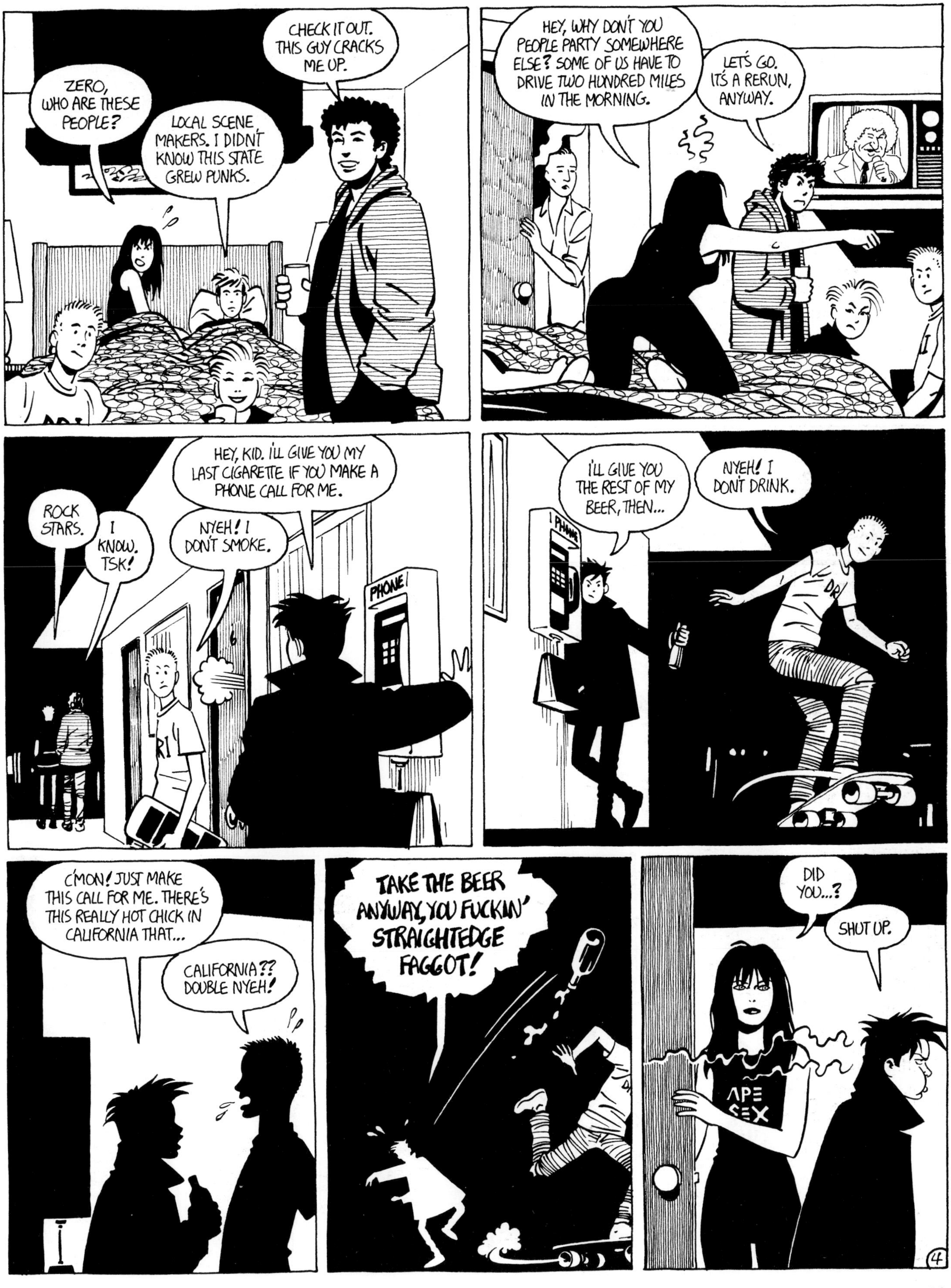
ZERO, WHO ARE THESE PEOPLE?
LOCAL SCENE MAKERS. I DIDN'T KNOW THIS STATE GREW PUNKS.
CHECK IT OUT. THIS GUY CRACKS ME UP.
HEY, WHY DON'T YOU PEOPLE PARTY SOMEWHERE ELSE? SOME OF US HAVE TO DRIVE TWO HUNDRED MILES IN THE MORNING.
LET'S GO. IT'S A RERUN, ANYWAY.
ROCK STARS.
I KNOW. TSK!
HEY, KID. I'LL GIVE YOU MY LAST CIGARETTE IF YOU MAKE A PHONE CALL FOR ME.
NYEH! I DON'T SMOKE.
PHONE
I'LL GIVE YOU THE REST OF MY BEER, THEN...
NYEH! I DON'T DRINK.
PHONE
C'MON! JUST MAKE THIS CALL FOR ME. THERE'S THIS REALLY HOT CHICK IN CALIFORNIA THAT...
CALIFORNIA?? DOUBLE NYEH!
TAKE THE BEER ANYWAY, YOU FUCKIN' STRAIGHTEDGE FAGGOT!
DID YOU...?
SHUT UP.
APE SEX
4

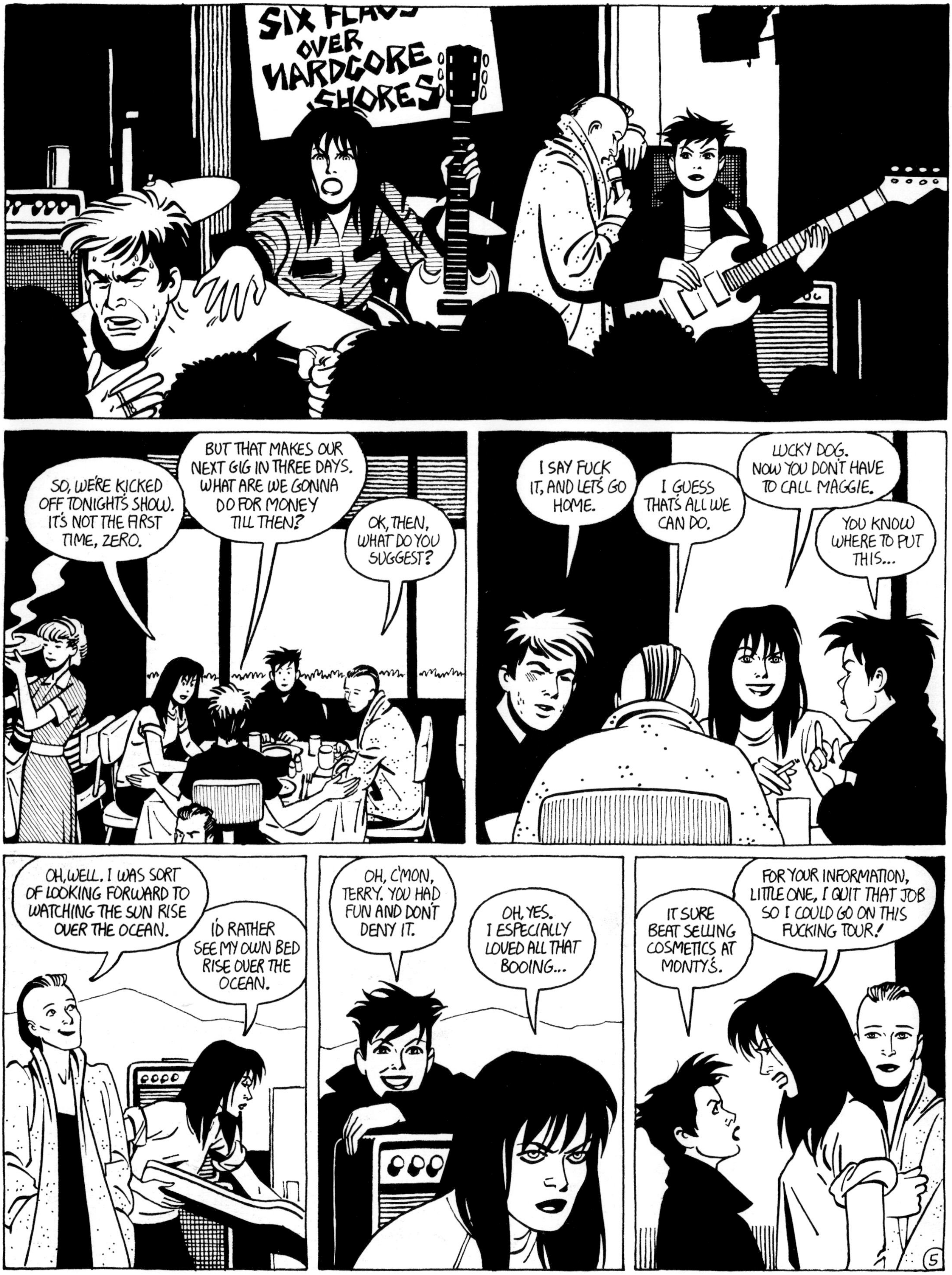
SIX FLAGS OVER HARDCORE SHORES
SO, WE'RE KICKED OFF TONIGHT'S SHOW. IT'S NOT THE FIRST TIME, ZERO.
BUT THAT MAKES OUR NEXT GIG IN THREE DAYS. WHAT ARE WE GONNA DO FOR MONEY TILL THEN?
OK, THEN, WHAT DO YOU SUGGEST?
I SAY FUCK IT, AND LET'S GO HOME.
I GUESS THAT'S ALL WE CAN DO.
LUCKY DOG. NOW YOU DON'T HAVE TO CALL MAGGIE.
YOU KNOW WHERE TO PUT THIS...
OH, WELL. I WAS SORT OF LOOKING FORWARD TO WATCHING THE SUN RISE OVER THE OCEAN.
I'D RATHER SEE MY OWN BED RISE OVER THE OCEAN.
OH, C'MON, TERRY. YOU HAD FUN AND DON'T DENY IT.
OH, YES. I ESPECIALLY LOVED ALL THAT BOOING...
IT SURE BEAT SELLING COSMETICS AT MONTY'S.
FOR YOUR INFORMATION, LITTLE ONE, I QUIT THAT JOB SO I COULD GO ON THIS FUCKING TOUR!
5

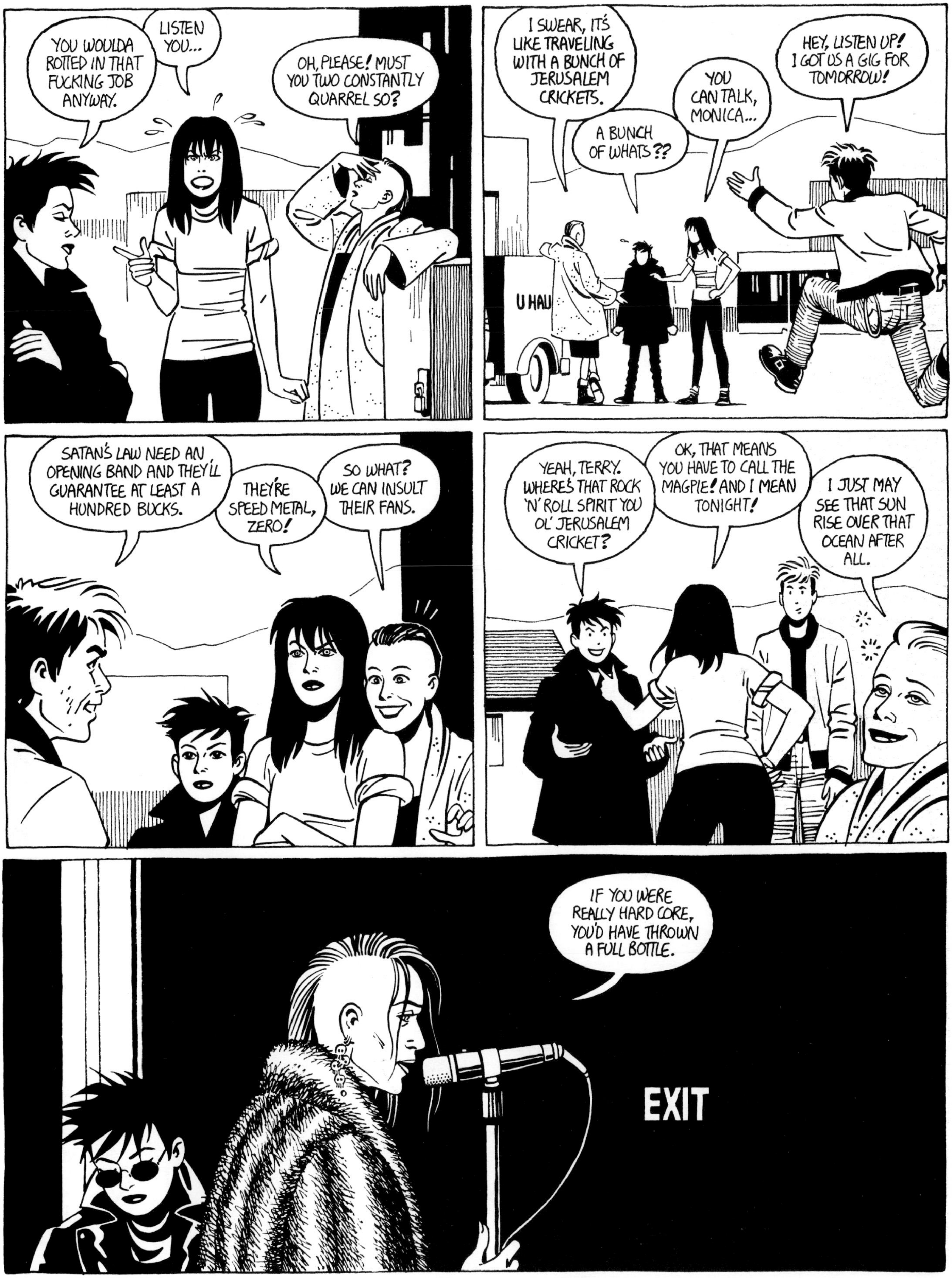
YOU WOULDA ROTTED IN THAT FUCKING JOB ANYWAY.
LISTEN YOU...
OH, PLEASE! MUST YOU TWO CONSTANTLY QUARREL SO?
I SWEAR, IT'S LIKE TRAVELING WITH A BUNCH OF JERUSALEM CRICKETS.
A BUNCH OF WHATS??
YOU CAN TALK, MONICA...
HEY, LISTEN UP! I GOT US A GIG FOR TOMORROW!
U HAU
SATAN'S LAW NEED AN OPENING BAND AND THEY'LL GUARANTEE AT LEAST A HUNDRED BUCKS.
THEY'RE SPEED METAL, ZERO!
SO WHAT? WE CAN INSULT THEIR FANS.
YEAH, TERRY. WHERE'S THAT ROCK 'N' ROLL SPIRIT YOU OL' JERUSALEM CRICKET?
OK, THAT MEANS YOU HAVE TO CALL THE MAGPIE! AND I MEAN TONIGHT!
I JUST MAY SEE THAT SUN RISE OVER THAT OCEAN AFTER ALL.
IF YOU WERE REALLY HARD CORE, YOU'D HAVE THROWN A FULL BOTTLE.
EXIT

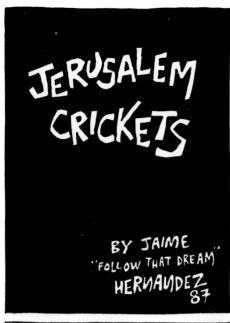

JERUSALEM CRICKETS

BY JAIME
"FOLLOW THAT DREAM"
HERNANDEZ
87

TERRY, I GOTTA HELP LOAD UP OUR SHIT!

IT CAN WAIT. COME ON.

YOU HAVE A CHOICE. TELEPHONE OR LETTER.

LETTER.

WHY ARE YOU SO ANXIOUS FOR ME TO WRITE THE MAGPIE? YOU HATE HER!

YOU HAVE TO CLEAR MY GOOD NAME, LOVE...

YFM

I JUST KNOW SHE THINKS I'M THE ONE RESPONSIBLE FOR LEAVING HER BEHIND ON THIS TOUR.

I KNEW IT WAS MORE THAN JUST THINKING OF MAGGIE...

I AM THINKING OF MAGGIE. SHE STILL MUST BE HEARTBROKEN WITHOUT A WORD FROM YOU YET.

SURE, SURE, OK.

DAMN! HOW DOES ANYONE START ONE OF THESE THINGS?

"DEAREST MAGPIE...

"SORRY I COULDN'T GET IN TOUCH WITH YOU EARLIER, BUT THIS PAST MONTH HAS BEEN VERY HECTIC FOR OUR BAND...

HOW DO YOU SPELL "HECTIC"?

"BY THE WAY, WE'RE ALSO SORRY YOU COULDN'T COME WITH US, BUT WE HAD TO GET AN EARLY START, AND YOU..."

SHE'S NOT GONNA BUY THAT!

66

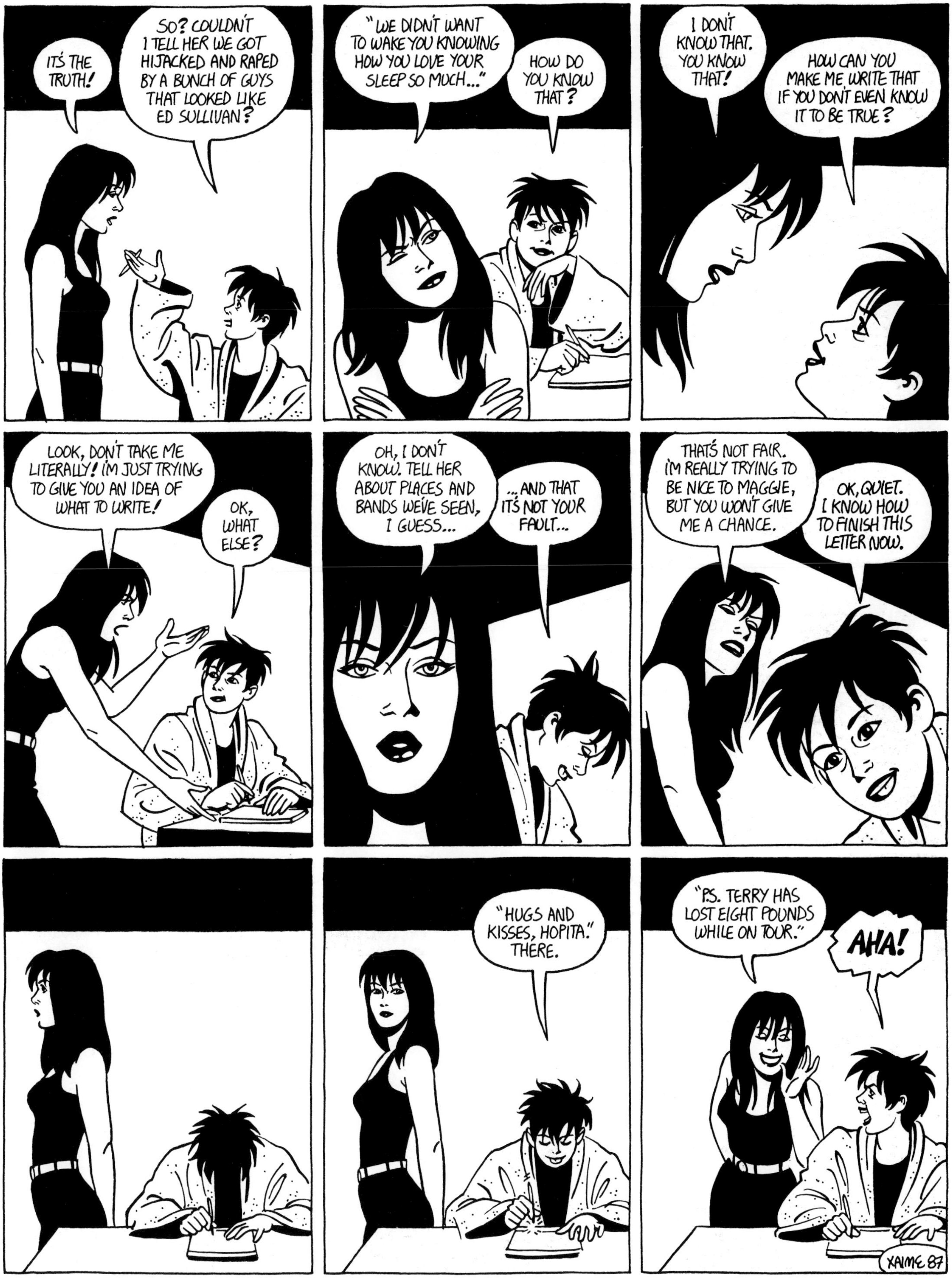
IT'S THE TRUTH!
SO? COULDN'T I TELL HER WE GOT HIJACKED AND RAPED BY A BUNCH OF GUYS THAT LOOKED LIKE ED SULLIVAN?
"WE DIDN'T WANT TO WAKE YOU KNOWING HOW YOU LOVE YOUR SLEEP SO MUCH..."
HOW DO YOU KNOW THAT?
I DON'T KNOW THAT. YOU KNOW THAT!
HOW CAN YOU MAKE ME WRITE THAT IF YOU DON'T EVEN KNOW IT TO BE TRUE?
LOOK, DON'T TAKE ME LITERALLY! I'M JUST TRYING TO GIVE YOU AN IDEA OF WHAT TO WRITE!
OK, WHAT ELSE?
OH, I DON'T KNOW. TELL HER ABOUT PLACES AND BANDS WE'VE SEEN, I GUESS...
...AND THAT IT'S NOT YOUR FAULT...
THAT'S NOT FAIR. I'M REALLY TRYING TO BE NICE TO MAGGIE, BUT YOU WON'T GIVE ME A CHANCE.
OK, QUIET. I KNOW HOW TO FINISH THIS LETTER NOW.
"HUGS AND KISSES, HOPITA." THERE.
"P.S. TERRY HAS LOST EIGHT POUNDS WHILE ON TOUR."
AHA!
XAIME 87

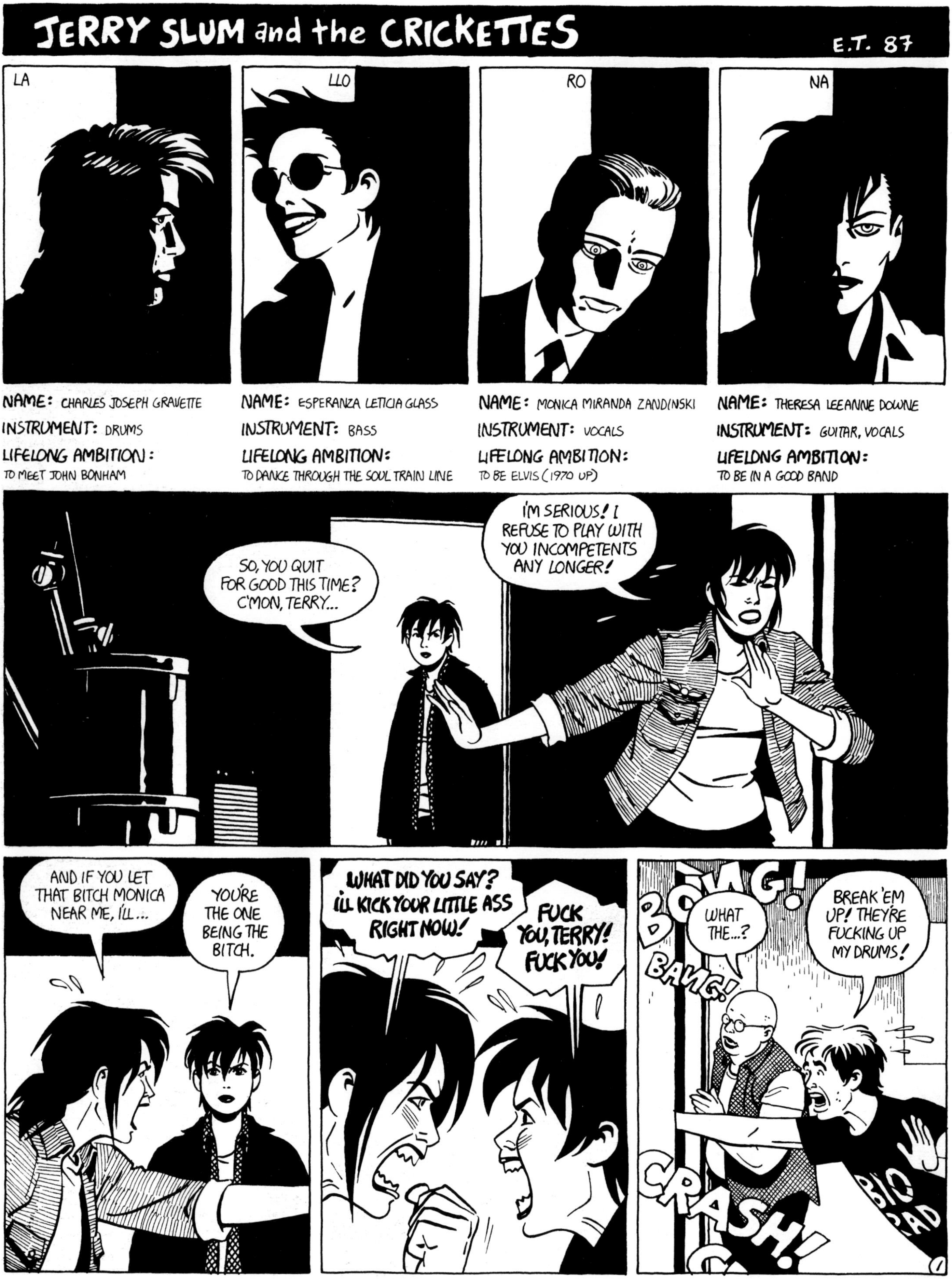
JERRY SLUM and the CRICKETTES
E.T. 87
LA
LLO
RO
NA
NAME: CHARLES JOSEPH GRAVETTE
INSTRUMENT: DRUMS
LIFELONG AMBITION: TO MEET JOHN BONHAM
NAME: ESPERANZA LETICIA GLASS
INSTRUMENT: BASS
LIFELONG AMBITION: TO DANCE THROUGH THE SOUL TRAIN LINE
NAME: MONICA MIRANDA ZANDINSKI
INSTRUMENT: VOCALS
LIFELONG AMBITION: TO BE ELVIS (1970 UP)
NAME: THERESA LEEANNE DOWNE
INSTRUMENT: GUITAR, VOCALS
LIFELONG AMBITION: TO BE IN A GOOD BAND
SO, YOU QUIT FOR GOOD THIS TIME? C'MON, TERRY...
I'M SERIOUS! I REFUSE TO PLAY WITH YOU INCOMPETENTS ANY LONGER!
AND IF YOU LET THAT BITCH MONICA NEAR ME, I'LL...
YOU'RE THE ONE BEING THE BITCH.
WHAT DID YOU SAY? I'LL KICK YOUR LITTLE ASS RIGHT NOW!
FUCK YOU, TERRY! FUCK YOU!
BOING!
WHAT THE...?
BREAK 'EM UP! THEY'RE FUCKING UP MY DRUMS!
BANG!
CRASH!

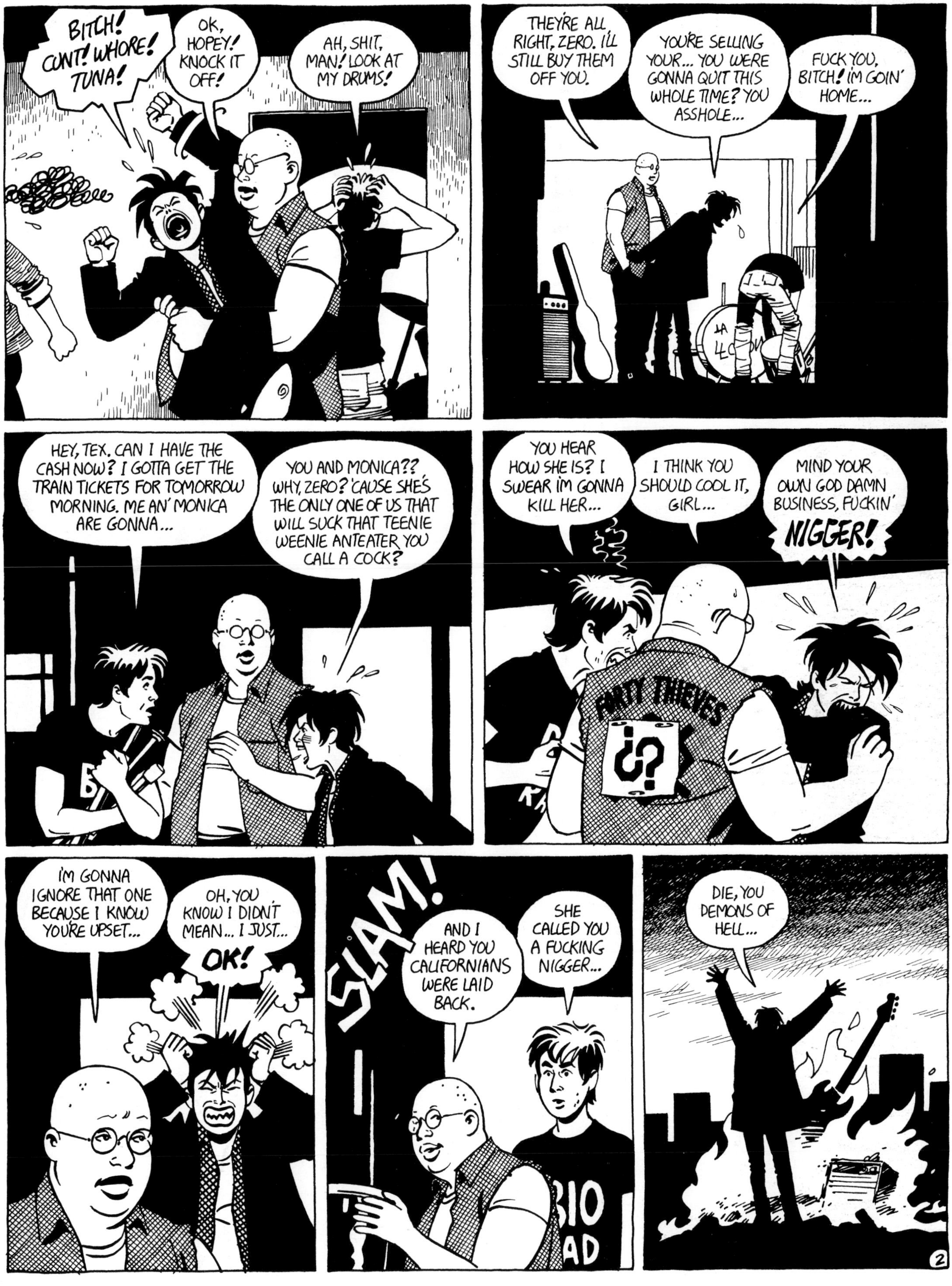
BITCH! CUNT! WHORE! TUNA!
OK, HOPEY! KNOCK IT OFF!
AH, SHIT, MAN! LOOK AT MY DRUMS!
THEY'RE ALL RIGHT, ZERO. I'LL STILL BUY THEM OFF YOU.
YOU'RE SELLING YOUR... YOU WERE GONNA QUIT THIS WHOLE TIME? YOU ASSHOLE...
FUCK YOU, BITCH! I'M GOIN' HOME...
HEY, TEX. CAN I HAVE THE CASH NOW? I GOTTA GET THE TRAIN TICKETS FOR TOMORROW MORNING. ME AN' MONICA ARE GONNA...
YOU AND MONICA?? WHY, ZERO? 'CAUSE SHE'S THE ONLY ONE OF US THAT WILL SUCK THAT TEENIE WEENIE ANTEATER YOU CALL A COCK?
YOU HEAR HOW SHE IS? I SWEAR I'M GONNA KILL HER...
I THINK YOU SHOULD COOL IT, GIRL...
MIND YOUR OWN GOD DAMN BUSINESS, FUCKIN' NIGGER!
FORTY THIEVES
I'M GONNA IGNORE THAT ONE BECAUSE I KNOW YOU'RE UPSET...
OH, YOU KNOW I DIDN'T MEAN... I JUST...
OK!
SLAM!
AND I HEARD YOU CALIFORNIANS WERE LAID BACK.
SHE CALLED YOU A FUCKING NIGGER...
DIE, YOU DEMONS OF HELL...
2

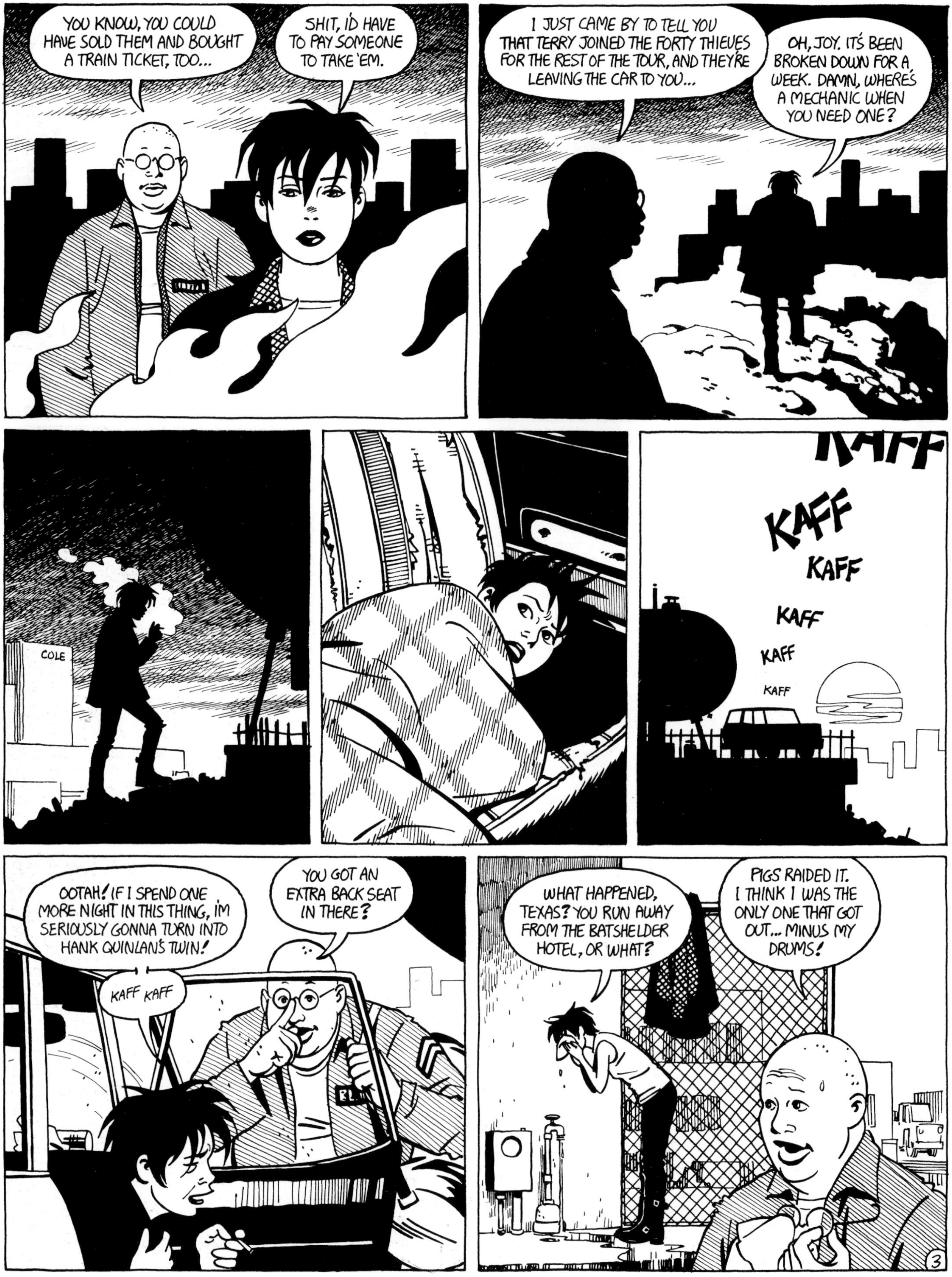

YOU KNOW, YOU COULD HAVE SOLD THEM AND BOUGHT A TRAIN TICKET, TOO...
SHIT, I'D HAVE TO PAY SOMEONE TO TAKE 'EM.
I JUST CAME BY TO TELL YOU THAT TERRY JOINED THE FORTY THIEVES FOR THE REST OF THE TOUR, AND THEY'RE LEAVING THE CAR TO YOU...
OH, JOY. IT'S BEEN BROKEN DOWN FOR A WEEK. DAMN, WHERE'S A MECHANIC WHEN YOU NEED ONE?
COLE
KAFF
KAFF
KAFF
KAFF
KAFF
KAFF
OOTAH! IF I SPEND ONE MORE NIGHT IN THIS THING, I'M SERIOUSLY GONNA TURN INTO HANK QUINLAN'S TWIN!
KAFF KAFF
YOU GOT AN EXTRA BACK SEAT IN THERE?
WHAT HAPPENED, TEXAS? YOU RUN AWAY FROM THE BATSHELDER HOTEL, OR WHAT?
PIGS RAIDED IT. I THINK I WAS THE ONLY ONE THAT GOT OUT... MINUS MY DRUMS!
3

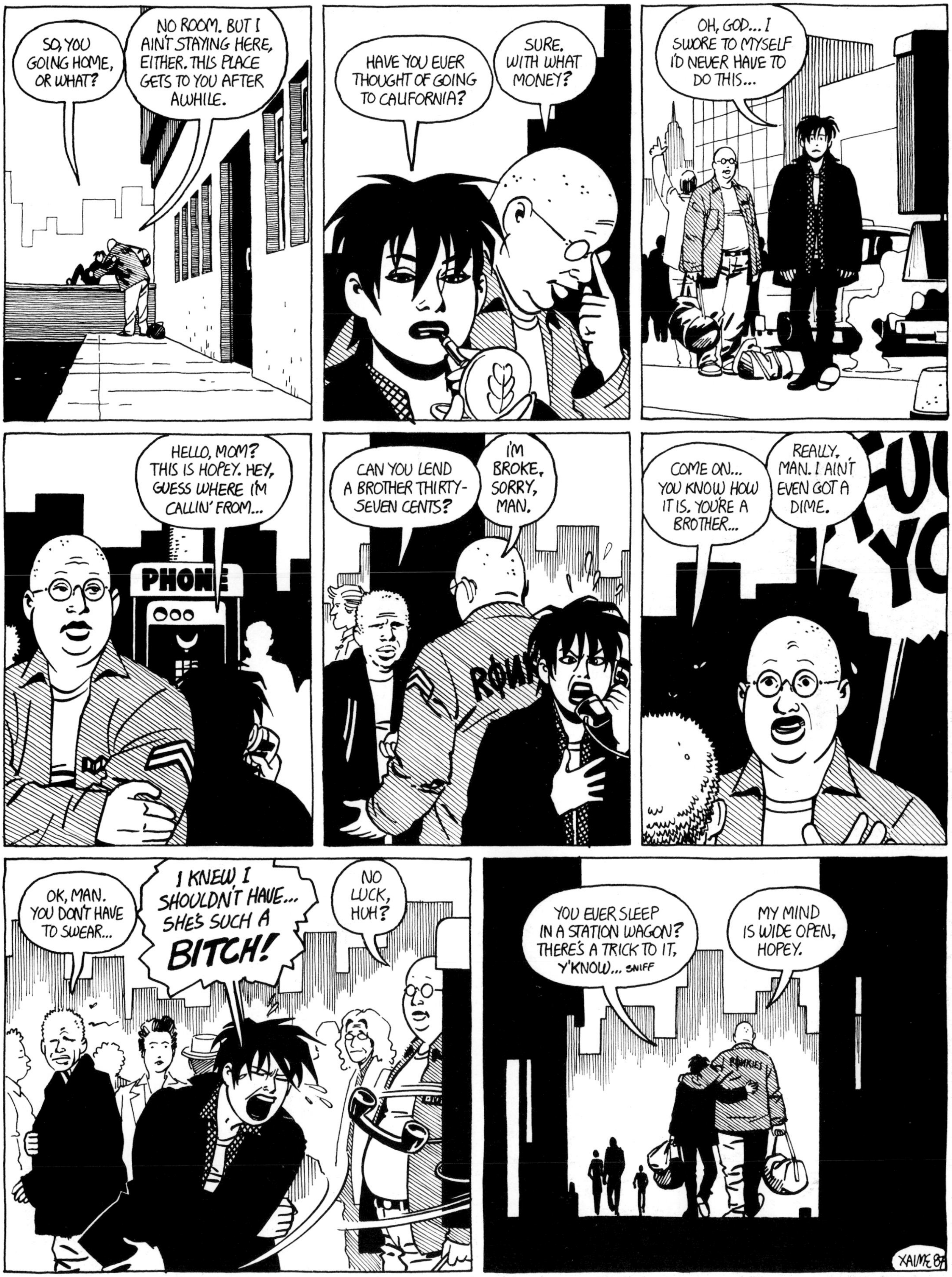

SO, YOU GOING HOME, OR WHAT?
NO ROOM. BUT I AIN'T STAYING HERE, EITHER. THIS PLACE GETS TO YOU AFTER AWHILE.
HAVE YOU EVER THOUGHT OF GOING TO CALIFORNIA?
SURE. WITH WHAT MONEY?
OH, GOD... I SWORE TO MYSELF I'D NEVER HAVE TO DO THIS...
HELLO, MOM? THIS IS HOPEY. HEY, GUESS WHERE I'M CALLIN' FROM...
PHONE
CAN YOU LEND A BROTHER THIRTY-SEVEN CENTS?
I'M BROKE, SORRY, MAN.
COME ON... YOU KNOW HOW IT IS. YOU'RE A BROTHER...
REALLY, MAN. I AIN'T EVEN GOT A DIME.
OK, MAN. YOU DON'T HAVE TO SWEAR...
I KNEW I SHOULDN'T HAVE... SHE'S SUCH A BITCH!
NO LUCK, HUH?
YOU EVER SLEEP IN A STATION WAGON? THERE'S A TRICK TO IT, Y'KNOW... SNIFF
MY MIND IS WIDE OPEN, HOPEY.
XAIME 87

THE NIGHT APE SEX CAME HOME TO PLAY

XAIME 87

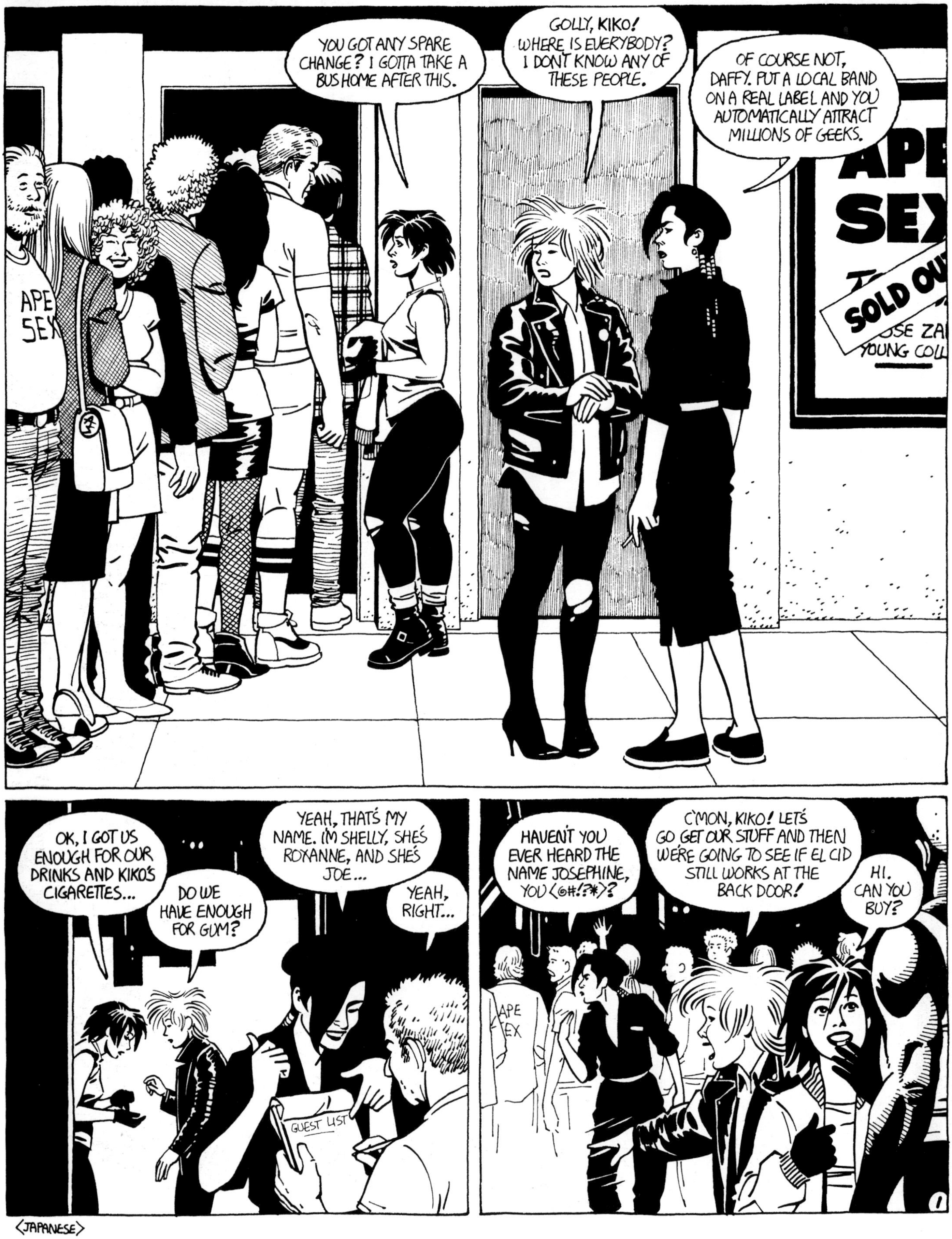

YOU GOT ANY SPARE CHANGE? I GOTTA TAKE A BUS HOME AFTER THIS.
GOLLY, KIKO! WHERE IS EVERYBODY? I DON'T KNOW ANY OF THESE PEOPLE.
OF COURSE NOT, DAFFY. PUT A LOCAL BAND ON A REAL LABEL AND YOU AUTOMATICALLY ATTRACT MILLIONS OF GEEKS.
APE SEX
APE SEX
SOLD OUT
YOUNG COLL
OK, I GOT US ENOUGH FOR OUR DRINKS AND KIKO'S CIGARETTES...
DO WE HAVE ENOUGH FOR GUM?
YEAH, THAT'S MY NAME. I'M SHELLY, SHE'S ROXANNE, AND SHE'S JOE...
YEAH, RIGHT...
GUEST LIST
HAVEN'T YOU EVER HEARD THE NAME JOSEPHINE, YOU <@#!?*>?
C'MON, KIKO! LET'S GO GET OUR STUFF AND THEN WE'RE GOING TO SEE IF EL CID STILL WORKS AT THE BACK DOOR!
HI. CAN YOU BUY?
APE EX
1

<JAPANESE>

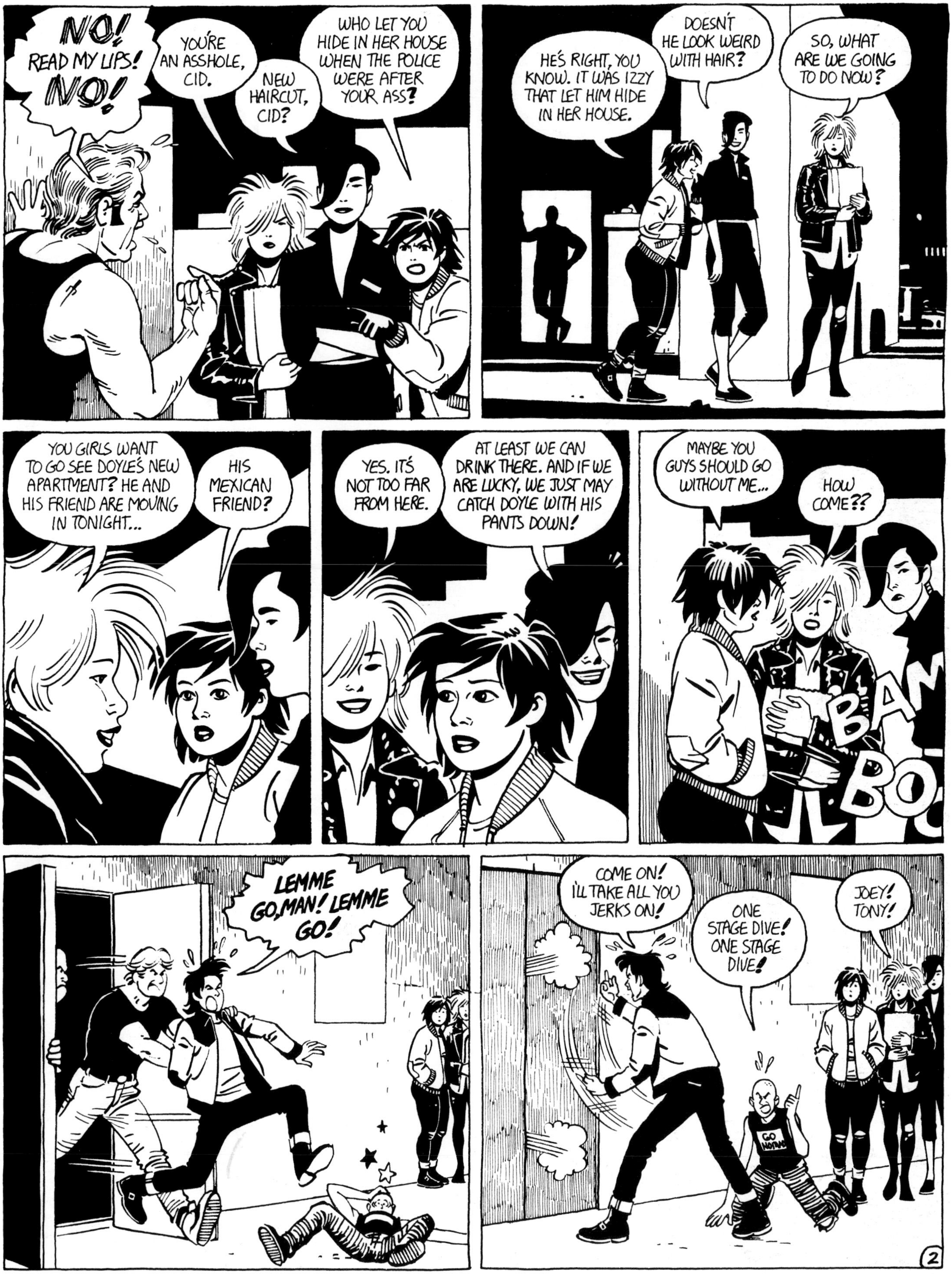
NO! READ MY LIPS! NO!
YOU'RE AN ASSHOLE, CID.
NEW HAIRCUT, CID?
WHO LET YOU HIDE IN HER HOUSE WHEN THE POLICE WERE AFTER YOUR ASS?
HE'S RIGHT, YOU KNOW. IT WAS IZZY THAT LET HIM HIDE IN HER HOUSE.
DOESN'T HE LOOK WEIRD WITH HAIR?
SO, WHAT ARE WE GOING TO DO NOW?
YOU GIRLS WANT TO GO SEE DOYLE'S NEW APARTMENT? HE AND HIS FRIEND ARE MOVING IN TONIGHT...
HIS MEXICAN FRIEND?
YES. IT'S NOT TOO FAR FROM HERE.
AT LEAST WE CAN DRINK THERE. AND IF WE ARE LUCKY, WE JUST MAY CATCH DOYLE WITH HIS PANTS DOWN!
MAYBE YOU GUYS SHOULD GO WITHOUT ME...
HOW COME??
BAM
BO
LEMME GO, MAN! LEMME GO!
COME ON! I'LL TAKE ALL YOU JERKS ON!
ONE STAGE DIVE! ONE STAGE DIVE!
JOEY! TONY!
GO
2

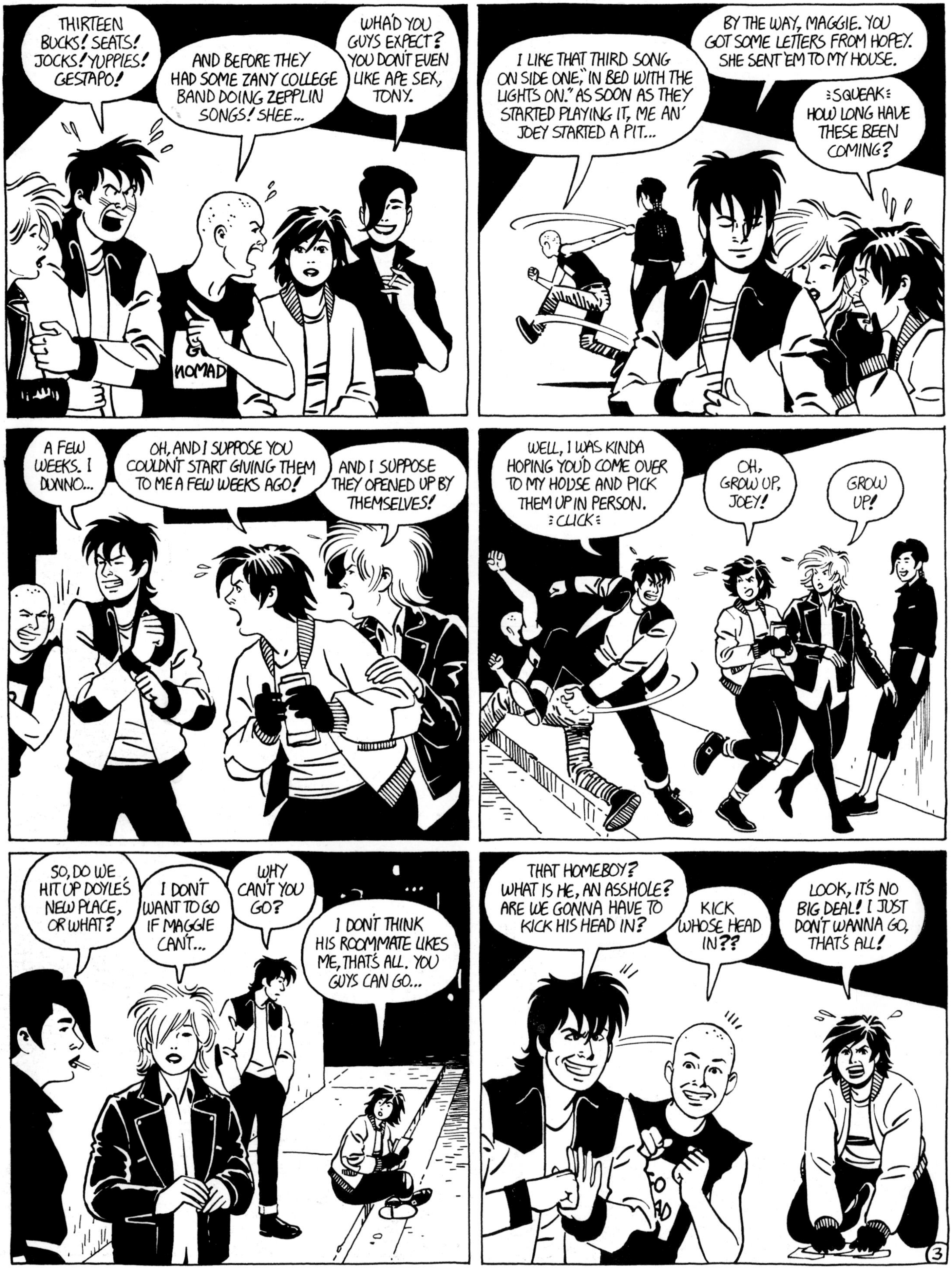
THIRTEEN BUCKS! SEATS! JOCKS! YUPPIES! GESTAPO!
AND BEFORE THEY HAD SOME ZANY COLLEGE BAND DOING ZEPPLIN SONGS! SHEE...
WHA'D YOU GUYS EXPECT? YOU DON'T EVEN LIKE APE SEX, TONY.
NOMAD
I LIKE THAT THIRD SONG ON SIDE ONE, "IN BED WITH THE LIGHTS ON." AS SOON AS THEY STARTED PLAYING IT, ME AN' JOEY STARTED A PIT...
BY THE WAY, MAGGIE. YOU GOT SOME LETTERS FROM HOPEY. SHE SENT 'EM TO MY HOUSE.
SQUEAK
HOW LONG HAVE THESE BEEN COMING?
A FEW WEEKS. I DUNNO...
OH, AND I SUPPOSE YOU COULDN'T START GIVING THEM TO ME A FEW WEEKS AGO!
AND I SUPPOSE THEY OPENED UP BY THEMSELVES!
WELL, I WAS KINDA HOPING YOU'D COME OVER TO MY HOUSE AND PICK THEM UP IN PERSON.
CLICK
OH, GROW UP, JOEY!
GROW UP!
SO, DO WE HIT UP DOYLE'S NEW PLACE, OR WHAT?
I DON'T WANT TO GO IF MAGGIE CAN'T...
WHY CAN'T YOU GO?
I DON'T THINK HIS ROOMMATE LIKES ME, THAT'S ALL. YOU GUYS CAN GO...
THAT HOMEBOY? WHAT IS HE, AN ASSHOLE? ARE WE GONNA HAVE TO KICK HIS HEAD IN?
KICK WHOSE HEAD IN??
LOOK, IT'S NO BIG DEAL! I JUST DON'T WANNA GO, THAT'S ALL!
3

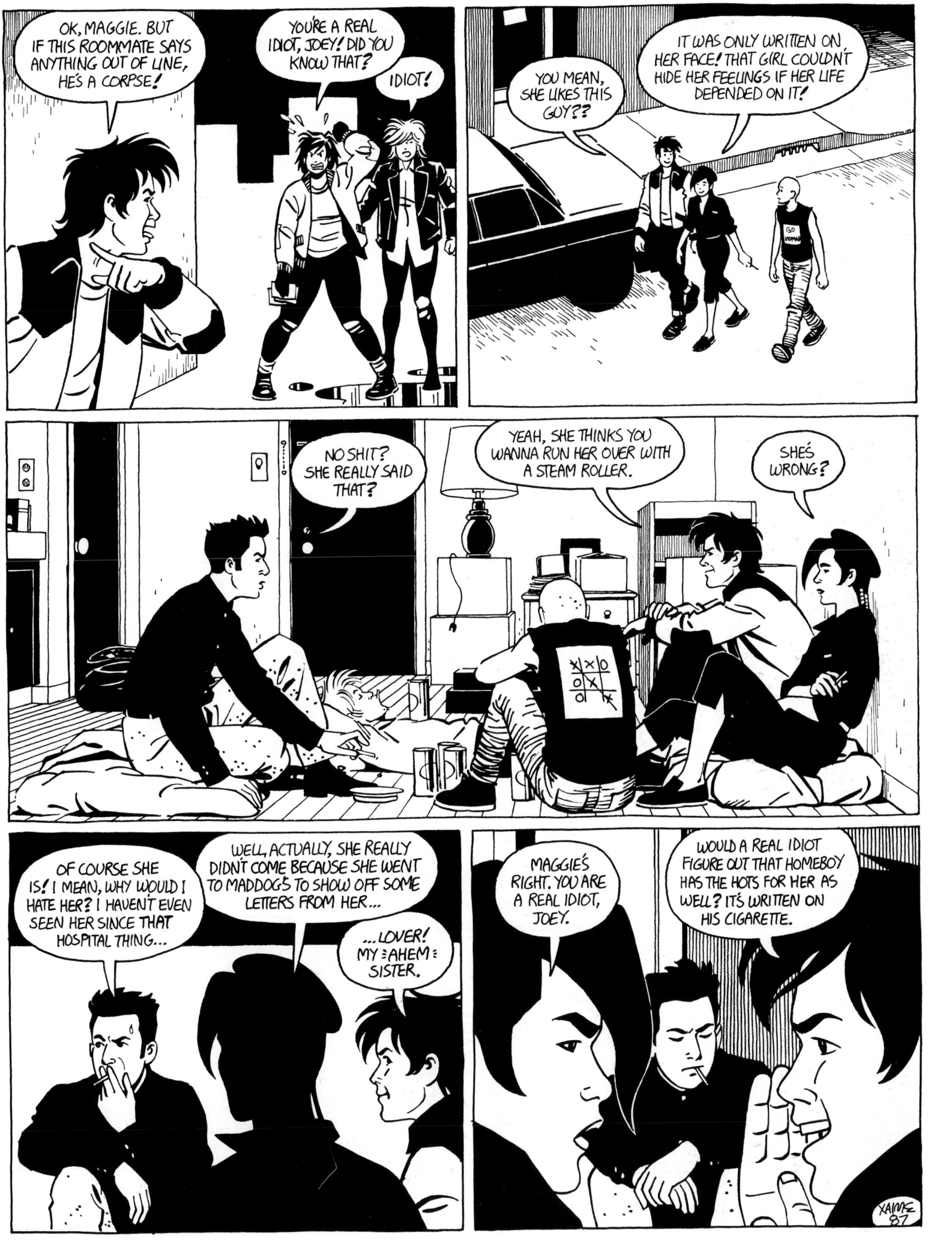

OK, MAGGIE. BUT IF THIS ROOMMATE SAYS ANYTHING OUT OF LINE, HE'S A CORPSE!
YOU'RE A REAL IDIOT, JOEY! DID YOU KNOW THAT?
IDIOT!
YOU MEAN, SHE LIKES THIS GUY??
IT WAS ONLY WRITTEN ON HER FACE! THAT GIRL COULDN'T HIDE HER FEELINGS IF HER LIFE DEPENDED ON IT!
NO SHIT? SHE REALLY SAID THAT?
YEAH, SHE THINKS YOU WANNA RUN HER OVER WITH A STEAM ROLLER.
SHE'S WRONG?
OF COURSE SHE IS! I MEAN, WHY WOULD I HATE HER? I HAVEN'T EVEN SEEN HER SINCE THAT HOSPITAL THING...
WELL, ACTUALLY, SHE REALLY DIDN'T COME BECAUSE SHE WENT TO MADDOG'S TO SHOW OFF SOME LETTERS FROM HER...
...LOVER! MY AHEM SISTER.
MAGGIE'S RIGHT. YOU ARE A REAL IDIOT, JOEY.
WOULD A REAL IDIOT FIGURE OUT THAT HOMEBOY HAS THE HOTS FOR HER AS WELL? IT'S WRITTEN ON HIS CIGARETTE.
XAIME 87

A Mess of Skin...

JAWBONE 87

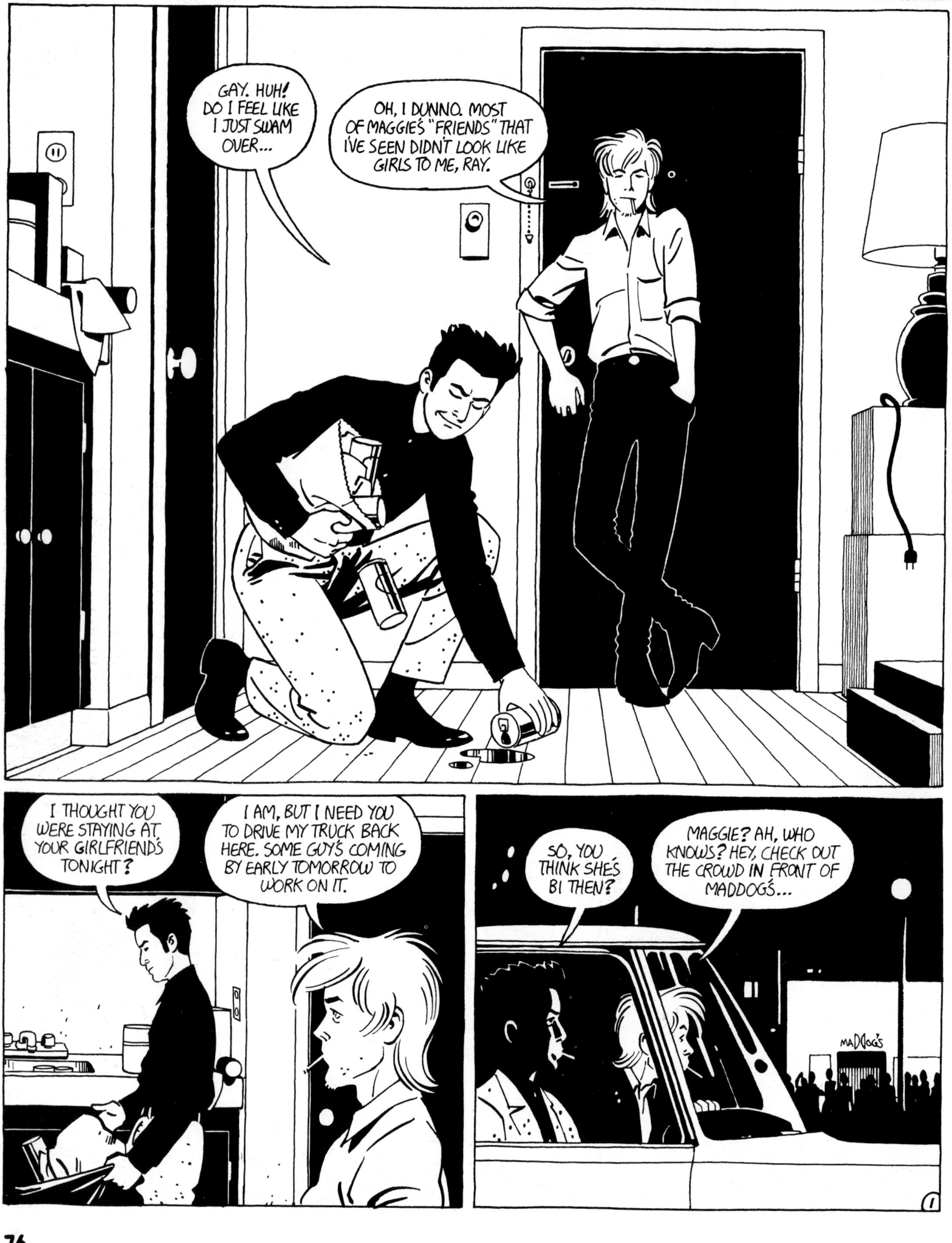
GAY. HUH! DO I FEEL LIKE I JUST SWAM OVER...
OH, I DUNNO. MOST OF MAGGIE'S "FRIENDS" THAT I'VE SEEN DIDN'T LOOK LIKE GIRLS TO ME, RAY.
I THOUGHT YOU WERE STAYING AT YOUR GIRLFRIEND'S TONIGHT?
I AM, BUT I NEED YOU TO DRIVE MY TRUCK BACK HERE. SOME GUY'S COMING BY EARLY TOMORROW TO WORK ON IT.
SO, YOU THINK SHE'S BI THEN?
MAGGIE? AH, WHO KNOWS? HEY, CHECK OUT THE CROWD IN FRONT OF MADDOG'S...
MADDOG'S
1

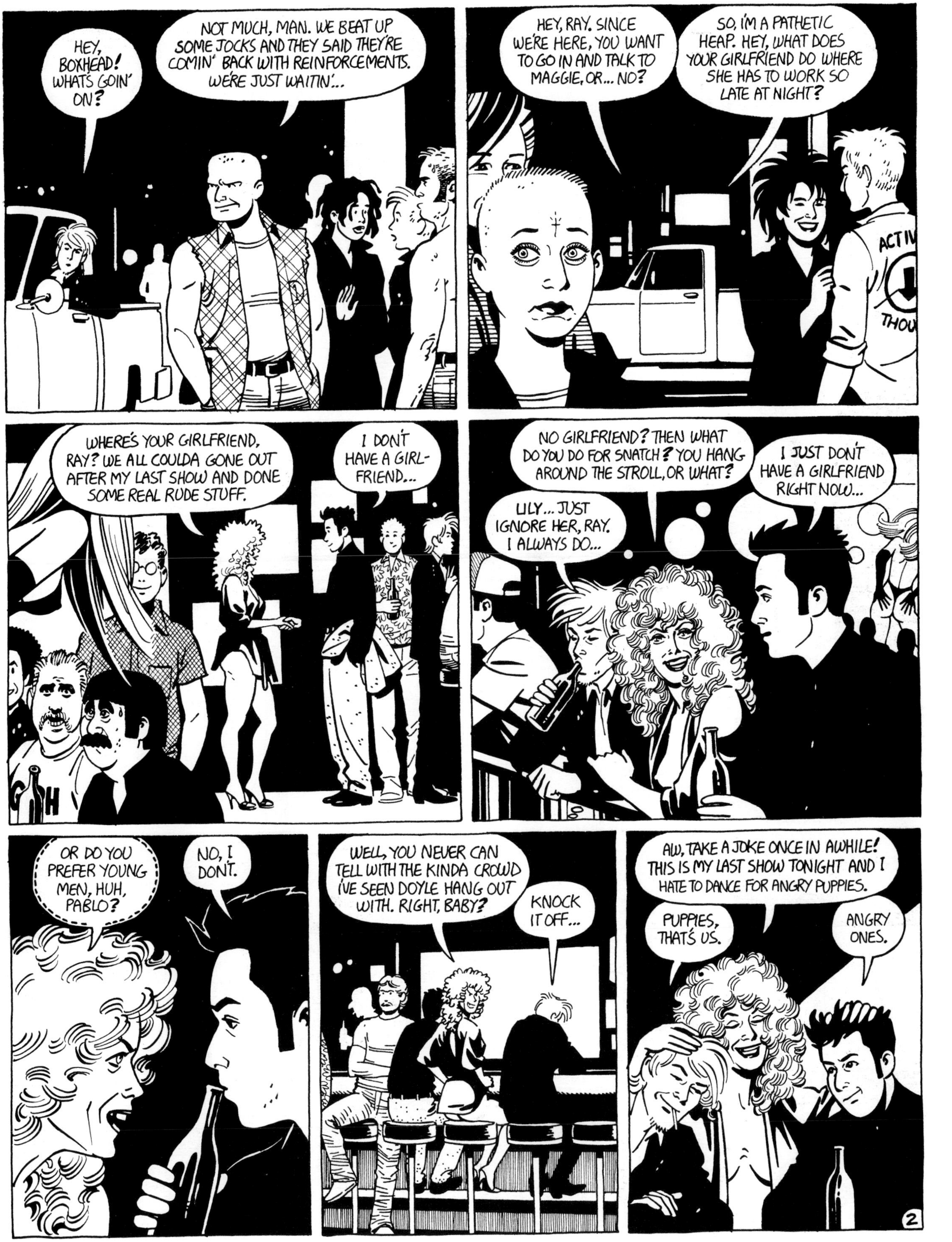
HEY, BOXHEAD! WHAT'S GOIN' ON?
NOT MUCH, MAN. WE BEAT UP SOME JOCKS AND THEY SAID THEY'RE COMIN' BACK WITH REINFORCEMENTS. WE'RE JUST WAITIN'...
HEY, RAY. SINCE WE'RE HERE, YOU WANT TO GO IN AND TALK TO MAGGIE, OR... NO?
SO, I'M A PATHETIC HEAP. HEY, WHAT DOES YOUR GIRLFRIEND DO WHERE SHE HAS TO WORK SO LATE AT NIGHT?
ACTIV
THOU
WHERE'S YOUR GIRLFRIEND, RAY? WE ALL COULDA GONE OUT AFTER MY LAST SHOW AND DONE SOME REAL RUDE STUFF.
I DON'T HAVE A GIRL-FRIEND...
NO GIRLFRIEND? THEN WHAT DO YOU DO FOR SNATCH? YOU HANG AROUND THE STROLL, OR WHAT?
I JUST DON'T HAVE A GIRLFRIEND RIGHT NOW...
LILY... JUST IGNORE HER, RAY. I ALWAYS DO...
OR DO YOU PREFER YOUNG MEN, HUH, PABLO?
NO, I DON'T.
WELL, YOU NEVER CAN TELL WITH THE KINDA CROWD I'VE SEEN DOYLE HANG OUT WITH. RIGHT, BABY?
KNOCK IT OFF...
AW, TAKE A JOKE ONCE IN AWHILE! THIS IS MY LAST SHOW TONIGHT AND I HATE TO DANCE FOR ANGRY PUPPIES.
PUPPIES, THAT'S US.
ANGRY ONES.
2

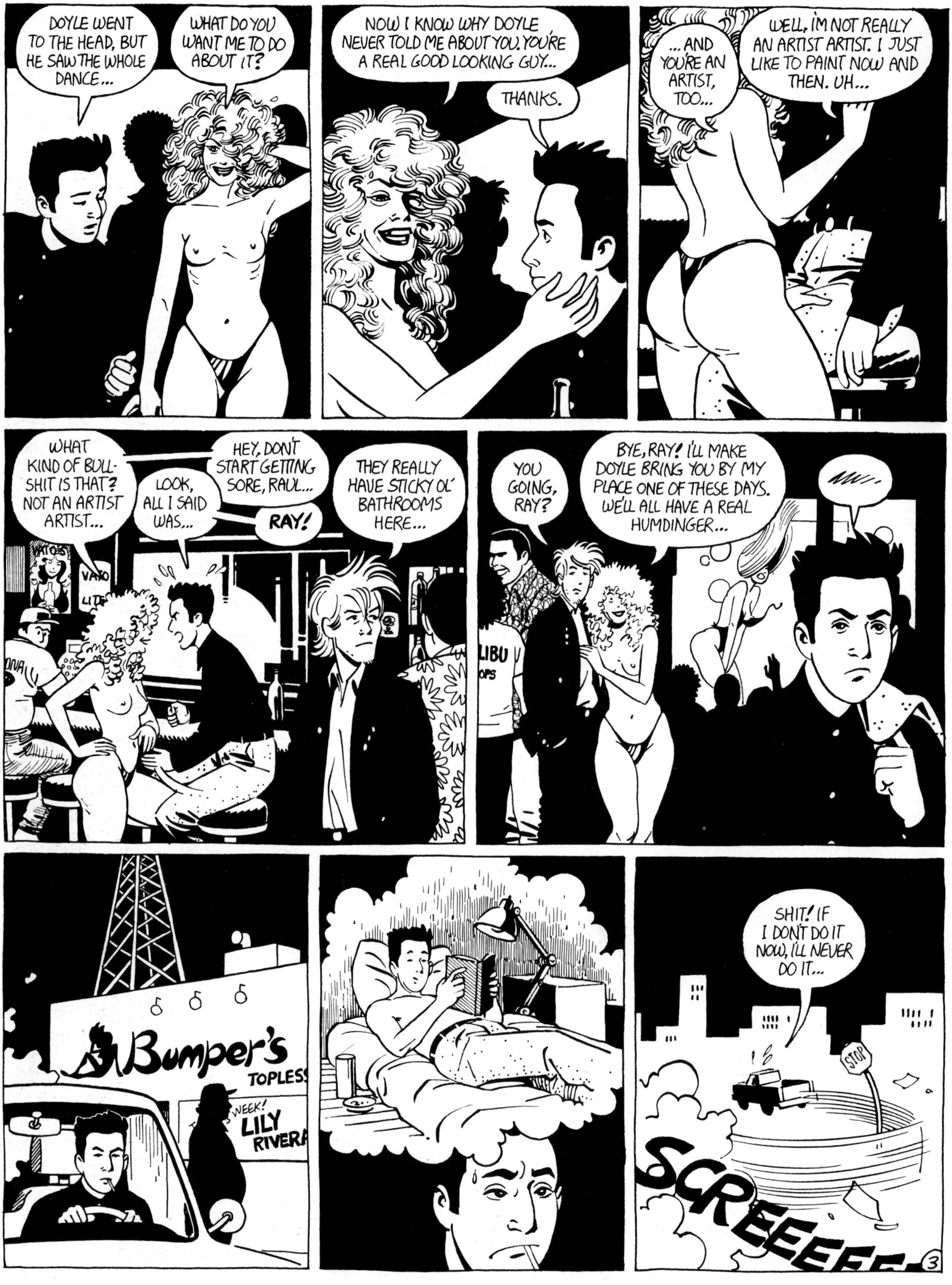
DOYLE WENT TO THE HEAD, BUT HE SAW THE WHOLE DANCE...
WHAT DO YOU WANT ME TO DO ABOUT IT?
NOW I KNOW WHY DOYLE NEVER TOLD ME ABOUT YOU. YOU'RE A REAL GOOD LOOKING GUY...
THANKS.
...AND YOU'RE AN ARTIST, TOO...
WELL, I'M NOT REALLY AN ARTIST ARTIST. I JUST LIKE TO PAINT NOW AND THEN. UH...
WHAT KIND OF BULL-SHIT IS THAT? NOT AN ARTIST ARTIST...
LOOK, ALL I SAID WAS...
HEY, DON'T START GETTING SORE, RAUL...
RAY!
THEY REALLY HAVE STICKY OL' BATHROOMS HERE...
YOU GOING, RAY?
BYE, RAY! I'LL MAKE DOYLE BRING YOU BY MY PLACE ONE OF THESE DAYS. WE'LL ALL HAVE A REAL HUMDINGER...
Bumper's
TOPLESS
WEEK!
LILY RIVERA
SHIT! IF I DON'T DO IT NOW, I'LL NEVER DO IT...
STOP
SCREEEEEE
3

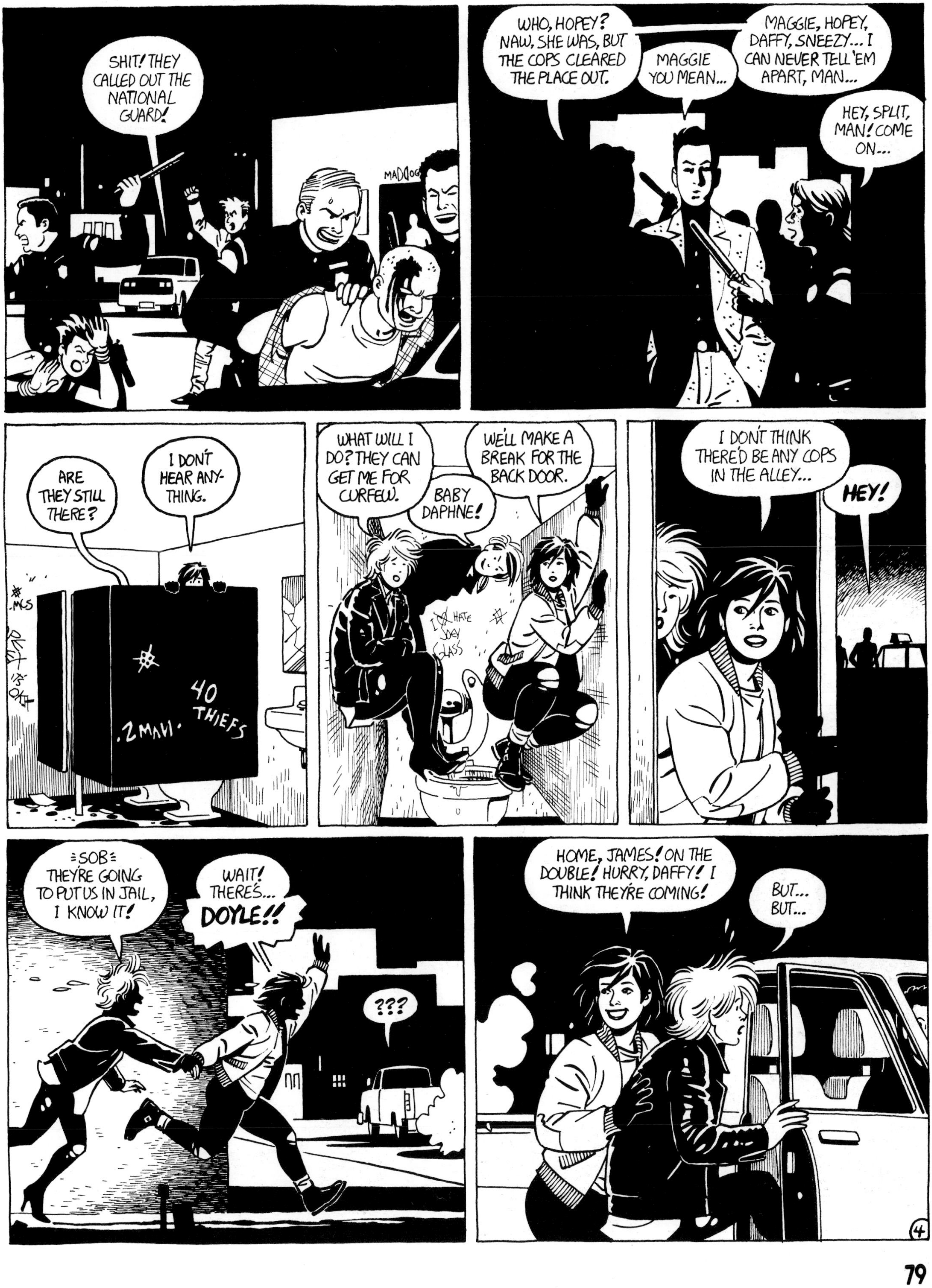
SHIT! THEY CALLED OUT THE NATIONAL GUARD!
MADDOG
WHO, HOPEY? NAW, SHE WAS, BUT THE COPS CLEARED THE PLACE OUT.
MAGGIE YOU MEAN...
MAGGIE, HOPEY, DAFFY, SNEEZY... I CAN NEVER TELL 'EM APART, MAN...
HEY, SPLIT, MAN! COME ON...
ARE THEY STILL THERE?
I DON'T HEAR ANY-THING.
40 THIEFS
WHAT WILL I DO? THEY CAN GET ME FOR CURFEW.
BABY DAPHNE!
WE'LL MAKE A BREAK FOR THE BACK DOOR.
I HATE JOEY GLASS
I DON'T THINK THERE'D BE ANY COPS IN THE ALLEY...
HEY!
SOB
THEY'RE GOING TO PUT US IN JAIL, I KNOW IT!
WAIT! THERE'S... DOYLE!!
???
HOME, JAMES! ON THE DOUBLE! HURRY, DAFFY! I THINK THEY'RE COMING!
BUT... BUT...
4

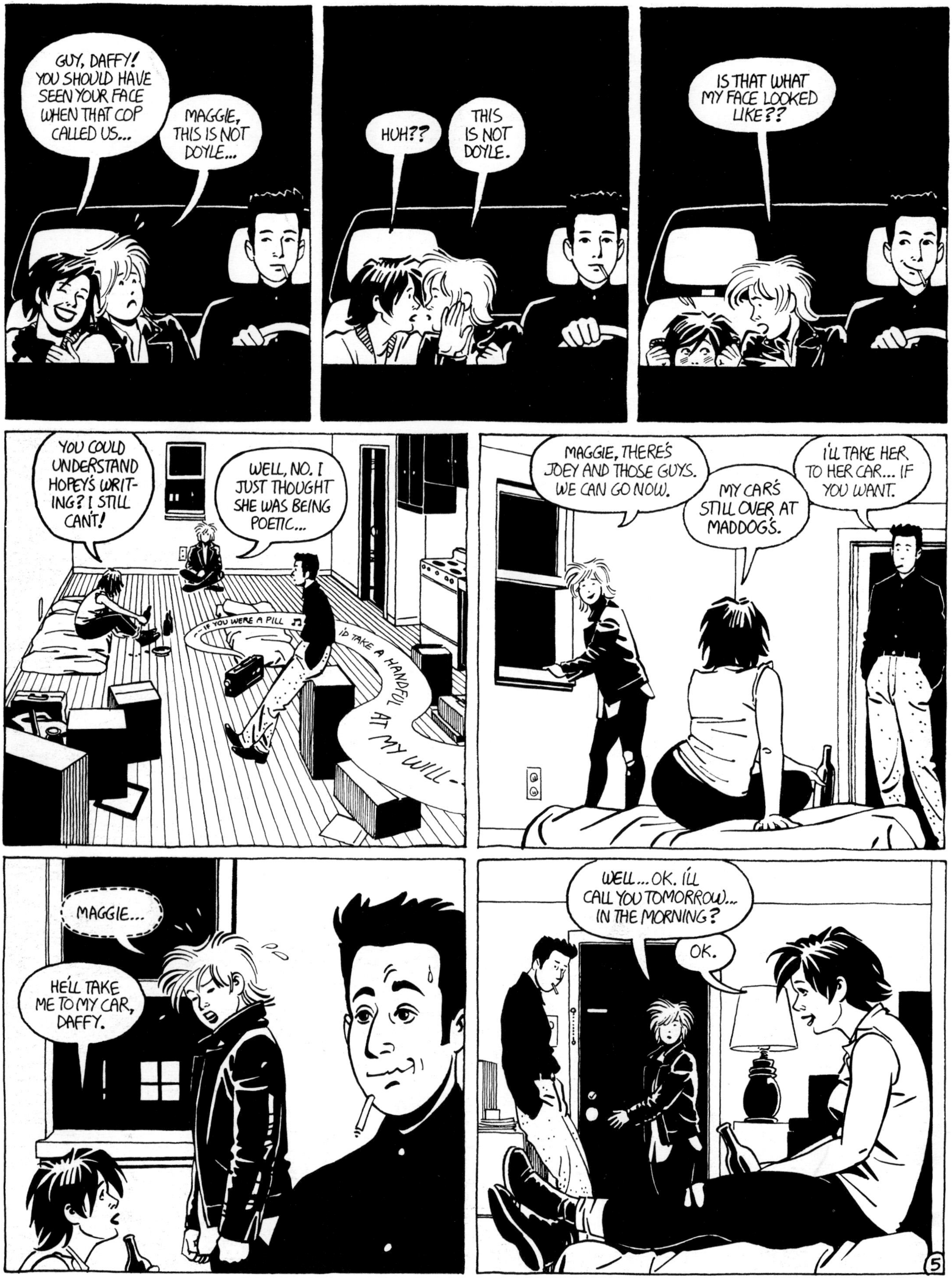
GUY, DAFFY! YOU SHOULD HAVE SEEN YOUR FACE WHEN THAT COP CALLED US...
MAGGIE, THIS IS NOT DOYLE...
HUH??
THIS IS NOT DOYLE.
IS THAT WHAT MY FACE LOOKED LIKE??
YOU COULD UNDERSTAND HOPEY'S WRIT-ING? I STILL CAN'T!
WELL, NO. I JUST THOUGHT SHE WAS BEING POETIC...
...IF YOU WERE A PILL ♫ I'D TAKE A HANDFUL AT MY WILL-
MAGGIE, THERE'S JOEY AND THOSE GUYS. WE CAN GO NOW.
MY CAR'S STILL OVER AT MADDOG'S.
I'LL TAKE HER TO HER CAR... IF YOU WANT.
MAGGIE...
HE'LL TAKE ME TO MY CAR, DAFFY.
WELL... OK. I'LL CALL YOU TOMORROW... IN THE MORNING?
OK.
5

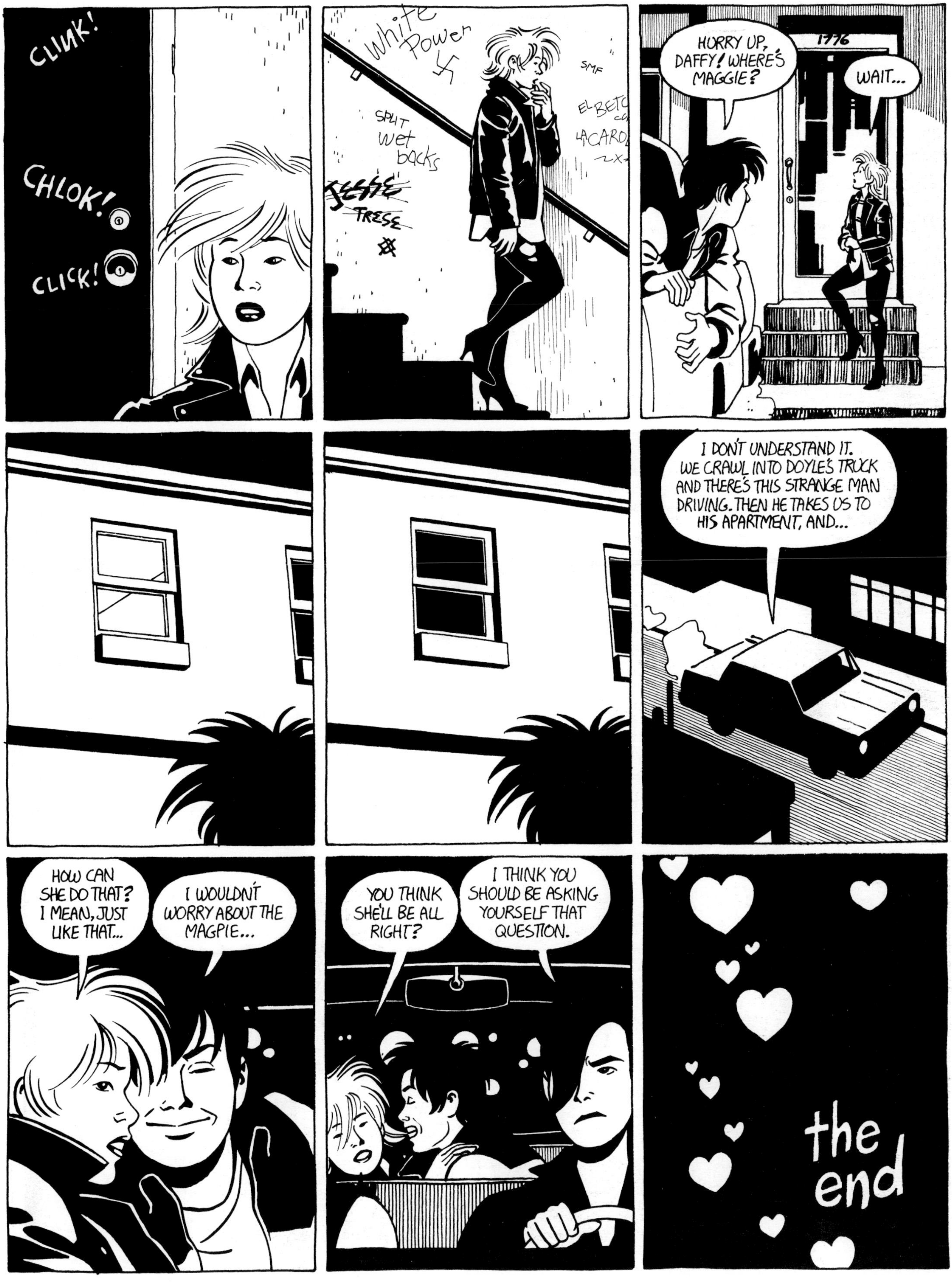
CLINK!
CHLOK!
CLICK!
White Power
SMF
SPLIT wet backs
EL BETO
LA CAROL
TRESE
HURRY UP, DAFFY! WHERE'S MAGGIE?
1776
WAIT...
I DON'T UNDERSTAND IT. WE CRAWL INTO DOYLE'S TRUCK AND THERE'S THIS STRANGE MAN DRIVING. THEN HE TAKES US TO HIS APARTMENT, AND...
HOW CAN SHE DO THAT? I MEAN, JUST LIKE THAT...
I WOULDN'T WORRY ABOUT THE MAGPIE...
YOU THINK SHE'LL BE ALL RIGHT?
I THINK YOU SHOULD BE ASKING YOURSELF THAT QUESTION.
the end

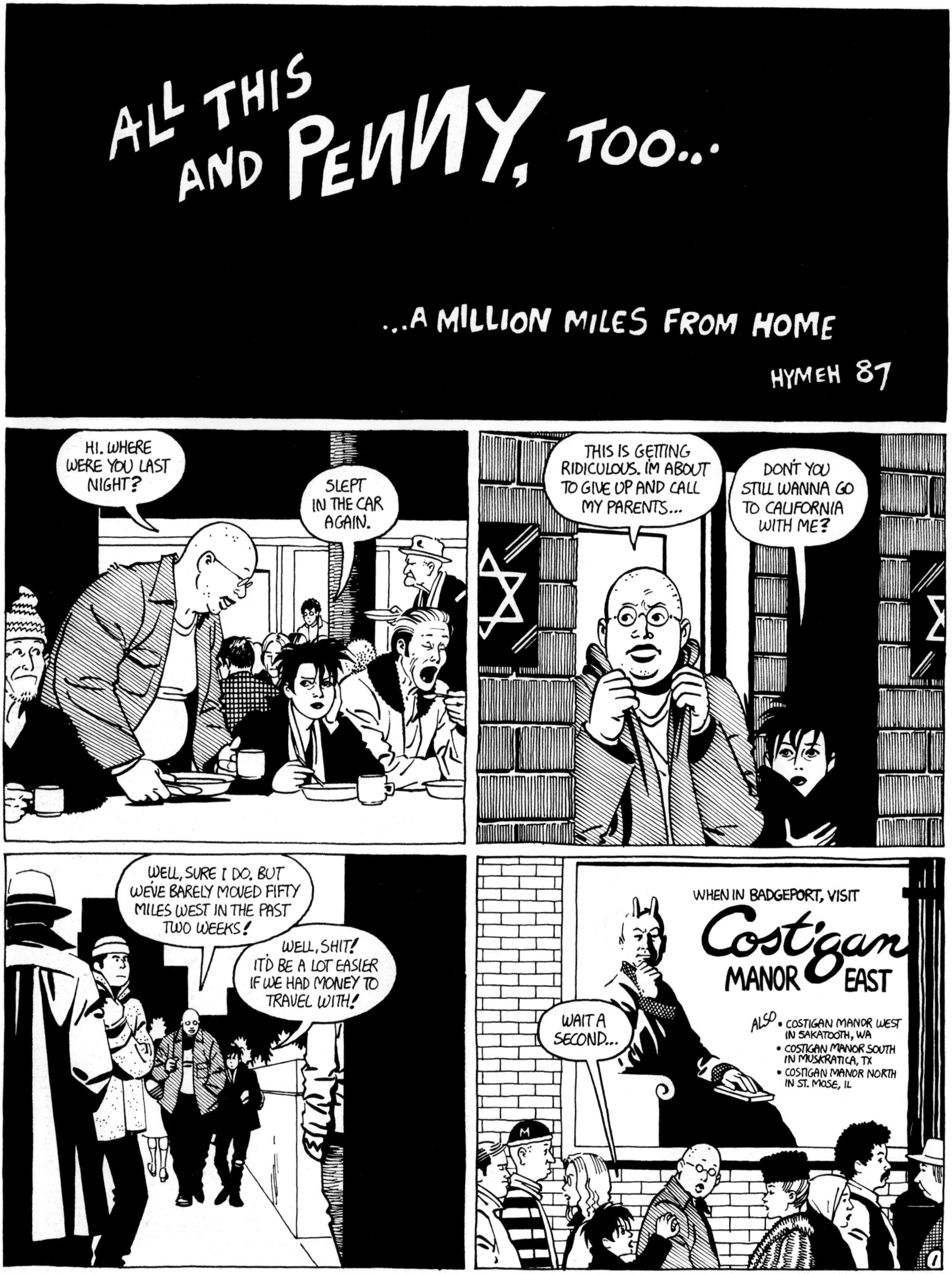
ALL THIS AND PENNY, TOO...
...A MILLION MILES FROM HOME
HYMEH 87
HI. WHERE WERE YOU LAST NIGHT?
SLEPT IN THE CAR AGAIN.
THIS IS GETTING RIDICULOUS. I'M ABOUT TO GIVE UP AND CALL MY PARENTS...
DON'T YOU STILL WANNA GO TO CALIFORNIA WITH ME?
WELL, SURE I DO. BUT WE'VE BARELY MOVED FIFTY MILES WEST IN THE PAST TWO WEEKS!
WELL, SHIT! IT'D BE A LOT EASIER IF WE HAD MONEY TO TRAVEL WITH!
WHEN IN BADGEPORT, VISIT
Costigan MANOR EAST
ALSO • COSTIGAN MANOR WEST IN SAKATOOTH, WA
• COSTIGAN MANOR SOUTH IN MUSKRATICA, TX
• COSTIGAN MANOR NORTH IN ST. MOSE, IL
WAIT A SECOND...
1

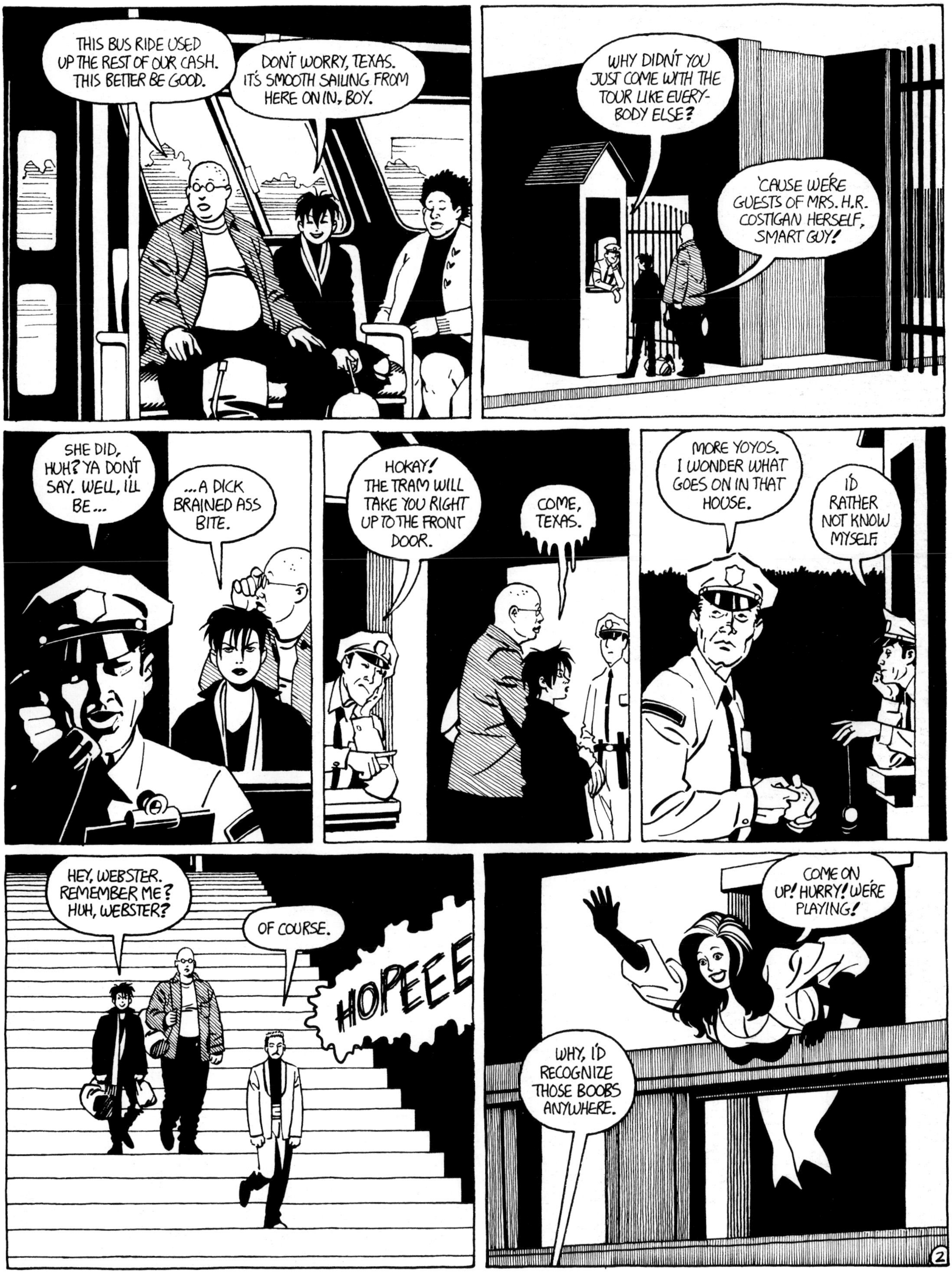
THIS BUS RIDE USED UP THE REST OF OUR CASH. THIS BETTER BE GOOD.
DON'T WORRY, TEXAS. IT'S SMOOTH SAILING FROM HERE ON IN, BOY.
WHY DIDN'T YOU JUST COME WITH THE TOUR LIKE EVERY-BODY ELSE?
'CAUSE WE'RE GUESTS OF MRS. H.R. COSTIGAN HERSELF, SMART GUY!
SHE DID, HUH? YA DON'T SAY. WELL, I'LL BE...
...A DICK BRAINED ASS BITE.
HOKAY! THE TRAM WILL TAKE YOU RIGHT UP TO THE FRONT DOOR.
COME, TEXAS.
MORE YOYOS. I WONDER WHAT GOES ON IN THAT HOUSE.
I'D RATHER NOT KNOW MYSELF.
HEY, WEBSTER. REMEMBER ME? HUH, WEBSTER?
OF COURSE.
HOPEEE
COME ON UP! HURRY! WE'RE PLAYING!
WHY, I'D RECOGNIZE THOSE BOOBS ANYWHERE.
2

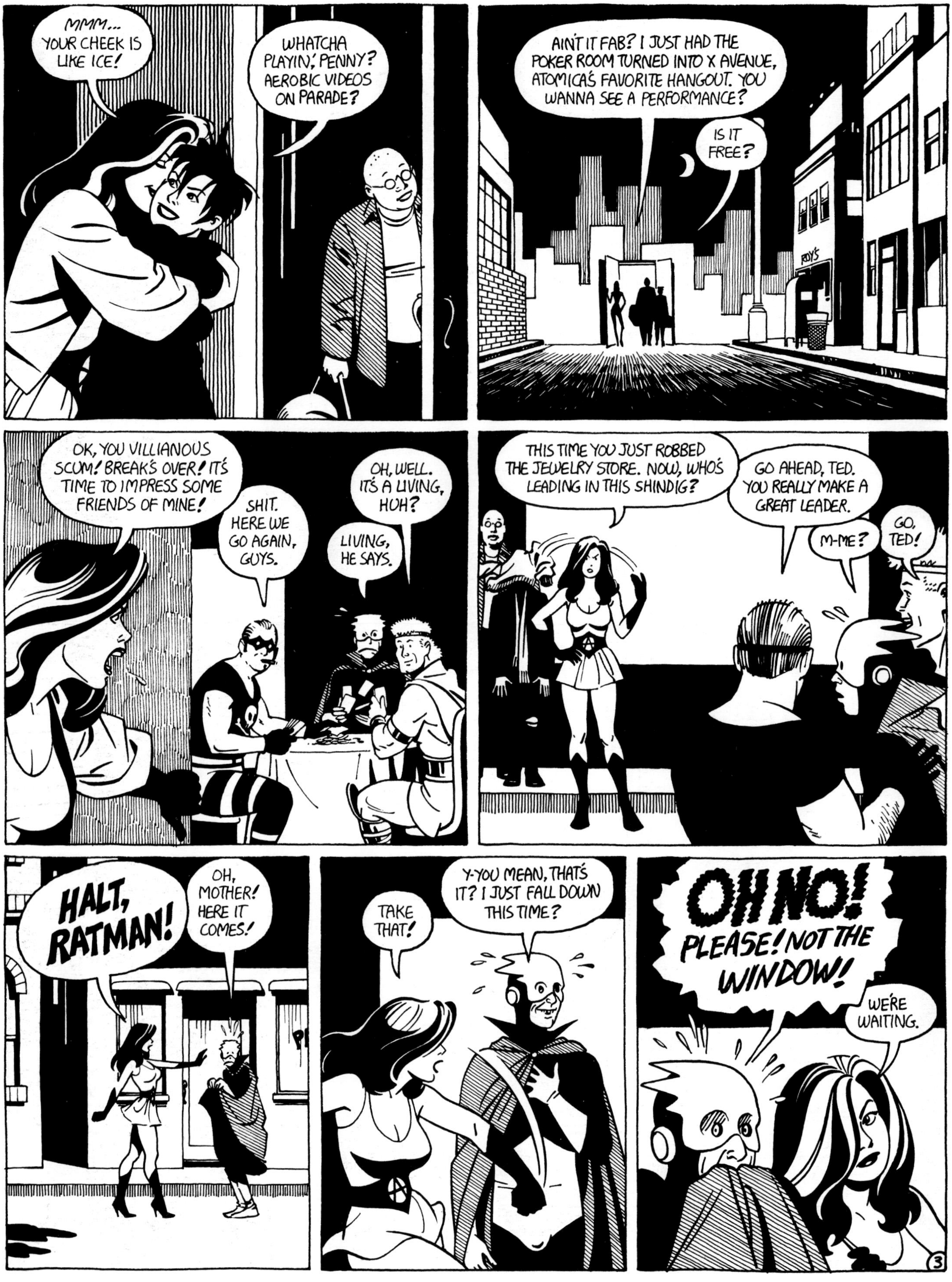
MMM... YOUR CHEEK IS LIKE ICE!
WHATCHA PLAYIN,' PENNY? AEROBIC VIDEOS ON PARADE?
AIN'T IT FAB? I JUST HAD THE POKER ROOM TURNED INTO X AVENUE, ATOMICA'S FAVORITE HANGOUT. YOU WANNA SEE A PERFORMANCE?
IS IT FREE?
OK, YOU VILLIANOUS SCUM! BREAK'S OVER! IT'S TIME TO IMPRESS SOME FRIENDS OF MINE!
SHIT. HERE WE GO AGAIN, GUYS.
OH, WELL. IT'S A LIVING, HUH?
LIVING, HE SAYS.
THIS TIME YOU JUST ROBBED THE JEWELRY STORE. NOW, WHO'S LEADING IN THIS SHINDIG?
GO AHEAD, TED. YOU REALLY MAKE A GREAT LEADER.
M-ME?
GO, TED!
HALT, RATMAN!
OH, MOTHER! HERE IT COMES!
TAKE THAT!
Y-YOU MEAN, THAT'S IT? I JUST FALL DOWN THIS TIME?
OH NO! PLEASE! NOT THE WINDOW!
WE'RE WAITING.
3

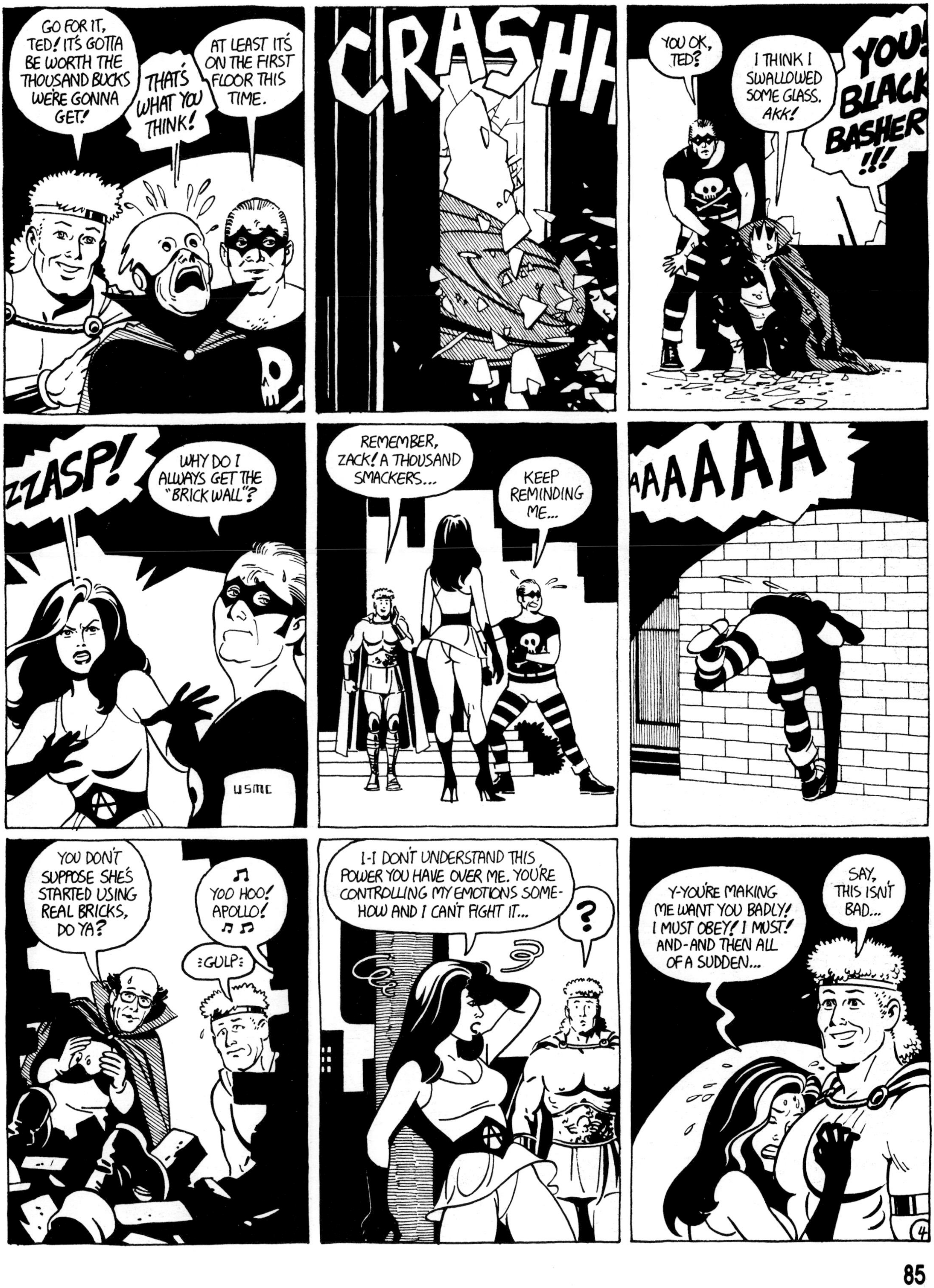
GO FOR IT, TED! IT'S GOTTA BE WORTH THE THOUSAND BUCKS WE'RE GONNA GET!
THAT'S WHAT YOU THINK!
AT LEAST IT'S ON THE FIRST FLOOR THIS TIME.
CRASHH
YOU OK, TED?
I THINK I SWALLOWED SOME GLASS. AKK!
YOU! BLACK BASHER!!!
ZZASP!
WHY DO I ALWAYS GET THE "BRICK WALL"?
USMC
REMEMBER, ZACK! A THOUSAND SMACKERS...
KEEP REMINDING ME...
AAAAAA
YOU DON'T SUPPOSE SHE'S STARTED USING REAL BRICKS, DO YA?
YOO HOO! APOLLO!
GULP
I-I DON'T UNDERSTAND THIS POWER YOU HAVE OVER ME. YOU'RE CONTROLLING MY EMOTIONS SOMEHOW AND I CAN'T FIGHT IT...
?
Y-YOU'RE MAKING ME WANT YOU BADLY! I MUST OBEY! I MUST! AND-AND THEN ALL OF A SUDDEN...
SAY, THIS ISN'T BAD...
4

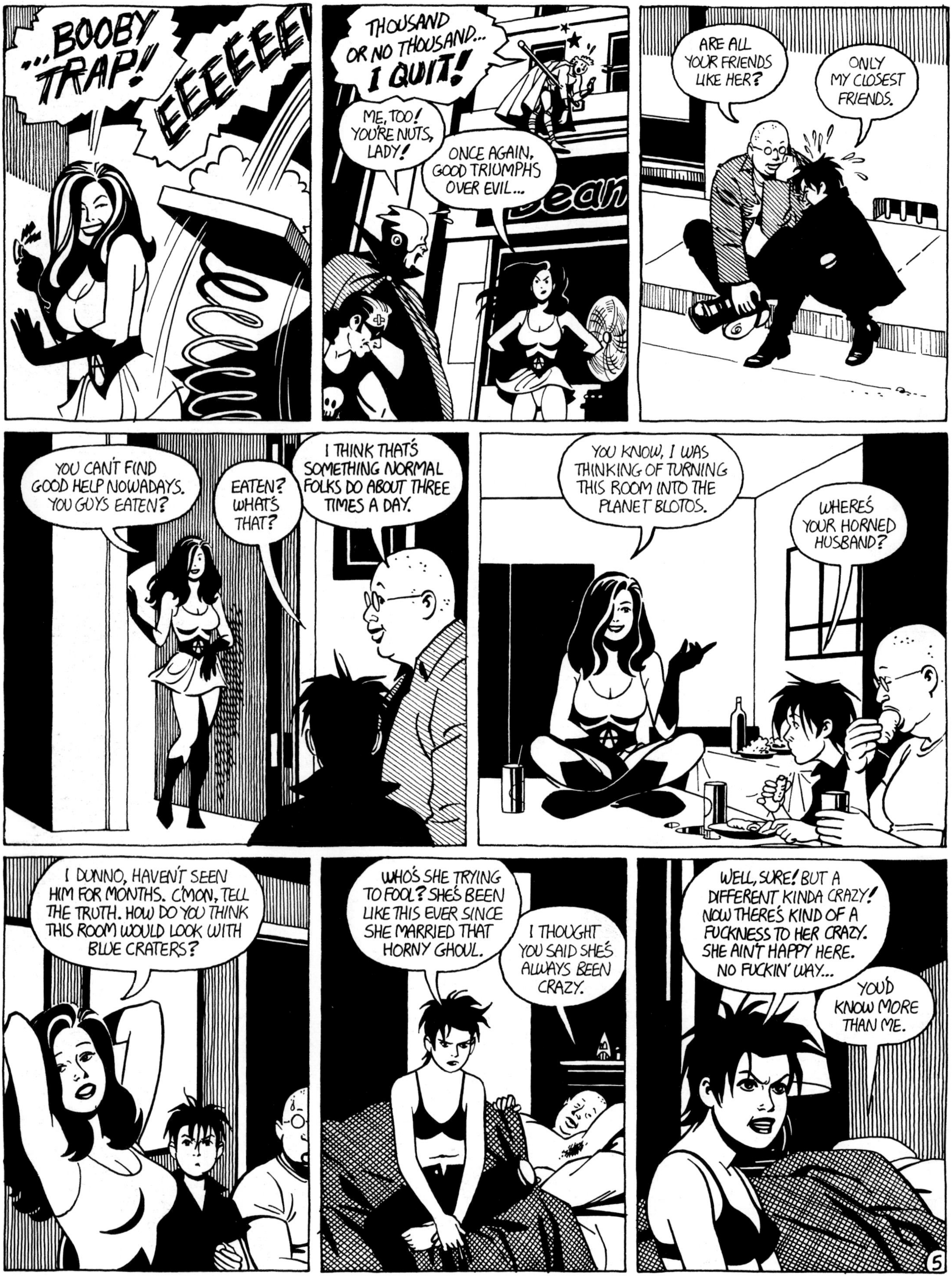
...BOOBY TRAP!
EEEEEEE
THOUSAND OR NO THOUSAND... I QUIT!
ME, TOO! YOU'RE NUTS, LADY!
ONCE AGAIN, GOOD TRIUMPHS OVER EVIL...
Bean
ARE ALL YOUR FRIENDS LIKE HER?
ONLY MY CLOSEST FRIENDS.
YOU CAN'T FIND GOOD HELP NOWADAYS. YOU GUYS EATEN?
EATEN? WHAT'S THAT?
I THINK THAT'S SOMETHING NORMAL FOLKS DO ABOUT THREE TIMES A DAY.
YOU KNOW, I WAS THINKING OF TURNING THIS ROOM INTO THE PLANET BLOTOS.
WHERE'S YOUR HORNED HUSBAND?
I DUNNO, HAVEN'T SEEN HIM FOR MONTHS. C'MON, TELL THE TRUTH. HOW DO YOU THINK THIS ROOM WOULD LOOK WITH BLUE CRATERS?
WHO'S SHE TRYING TO FOOL? SHE'S BEEN LIKE THIS EVER SINCE SHE MARRIED THAT HORNY GHOUL.
I THOUGHT YOU SAID SHE'S ALWAYS BEEN CRAZY.
WELL, SURE! BUT A DIFFERENT KINDA CRAZY! NOW THERE'S KIND OF A FUCKNESS TO HER CRAZY. SHE AIN'T HAPPY HERE. NO FUCKIN' WAY...
YOU'D KNOW MORE THAN ME.
5

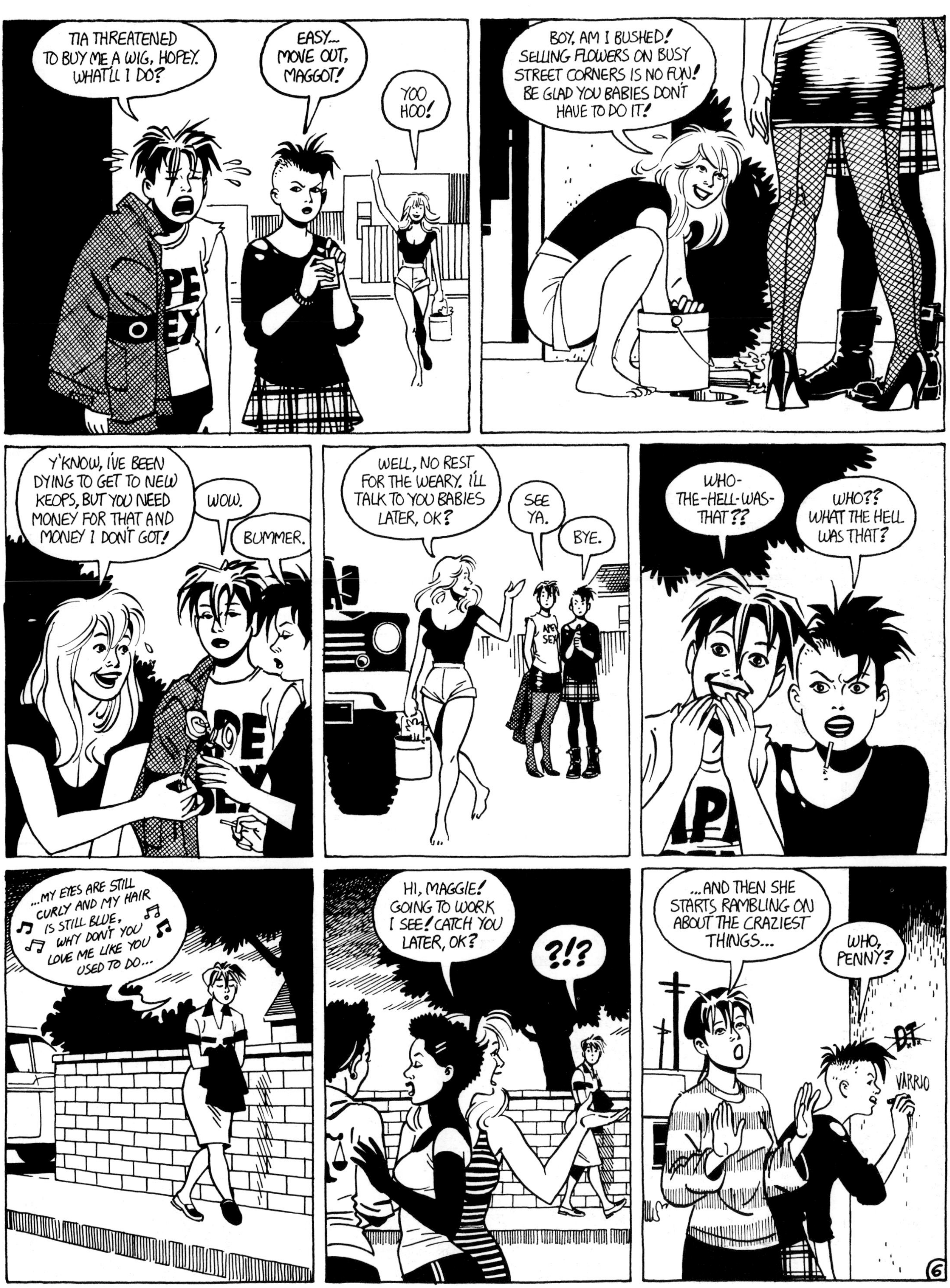
TIA THREATENED TO BUY ME A WIG, HOPEY. WHAT'LL I DO?
EASY... MOVE OUT, MAGGOT!
YOO HOO!
BOY, AM I BUSHED! SELLING FLOWERS ON BUSY STREET CORNERS IS NO FUN! BE GLAD YOU BABIES DON'T HAVE TO DO IT!
Y'KNOW, I'VE BEEN DYING TO GET TO NEW KEOPS, BUT YOU NEED MONEY FOR THAT AND MONEY I DON'T GOT!
WOW.
BUMMER.
WELL, NO REST FOR THE WEARY. I'LL TALK TO YOU BABIES LATER, OK?
SEE YA.
BYE.
WHO-THE-HELL-WAS-THAT??
WHO?? WHAT THE HELL WAS THAT?
...MY EYES ARE STILL CURLY AND MY HAIR IS STILL BLUE, WHY DON'T YOU LOVE ME LIKE YOU USED TO DO...
HI, MAGGIE! GOING TO WORK I SEE! CATCH YOU LATER, OK?
?!?
...AND THEN SHE STARTS RAMBLING ON ABOUT THE CRAZIEST THINGS...
WHO, PENNY?
D.T.
VARRIO
6

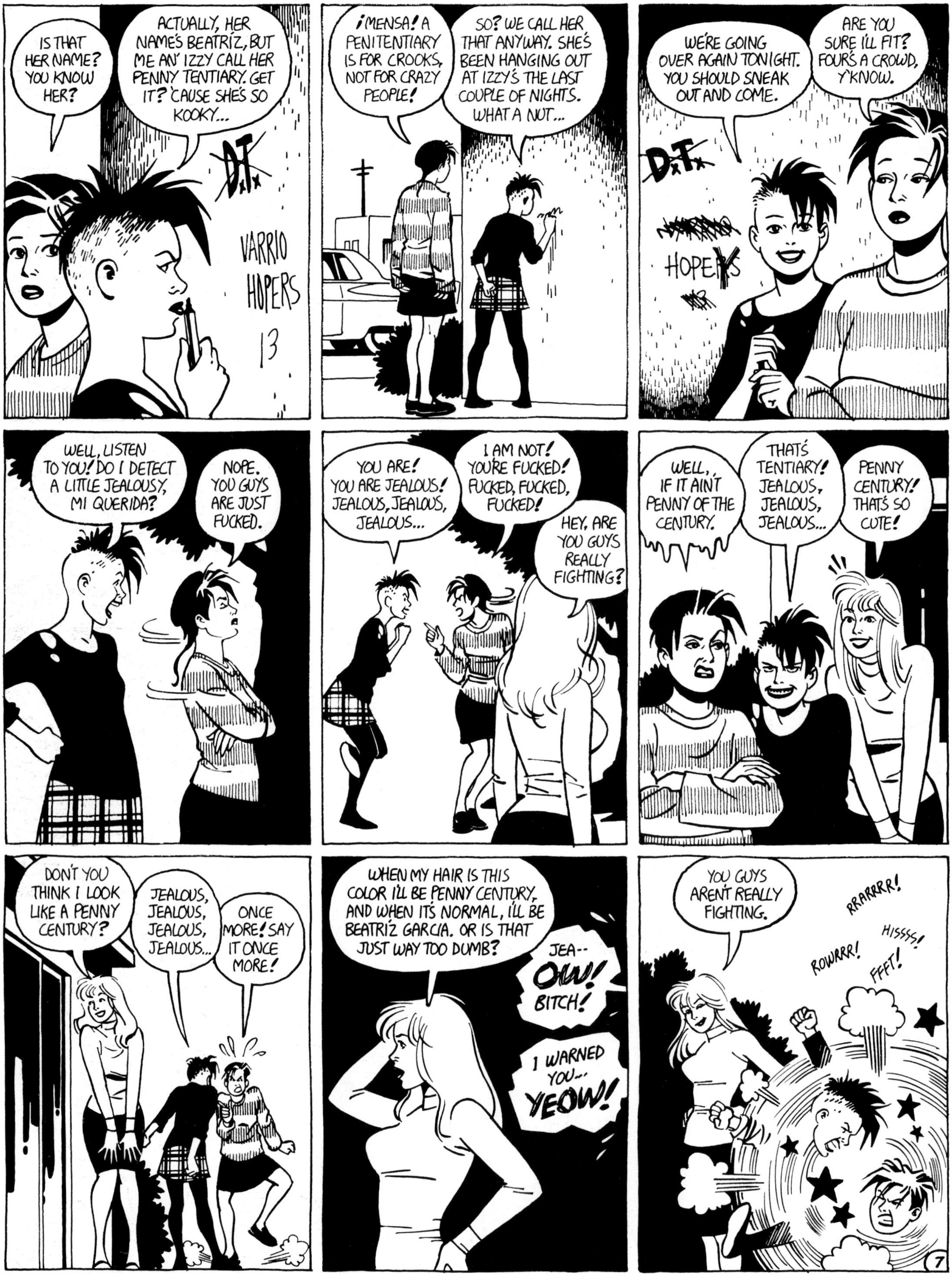
IS THAT HER NAME? YOU KNOW HER?
ACTUALLY, HER NAME'S BEATRÍZ, BUT ME AN' IZZY CALL HER PENNY TENTIARY. GET IT? 'CAUSE SHE'S SO KOOKY...
D.T.
VARRIO HOPERS 13
¡MENSA! A PENITENTIARY IS FOR CROOKS, NOT FOR CRAZY PEOPLE!
SO? WE CALL HER THAT ANYWAY. SHE'S BEEN HANGING OUT AT IZZY'S THE LAST COUPLE OF NIGHTS. WHAT A NUT...
WE'RE GOING OVER AGAIN TONIGHT. YOU SHOULD SNEAK OUT AND COME.
ARE YOU SURE I'LL FIT? FOUR'S A CROWD, Y'KNOW.
WELL, LISTEN TO YOU! DO I DETECT A LITTLE JEALOUSY, MI QUERIDA?
NOPE. YOU GUYS ARE JUST FUCKED.
YOU ARE! YOU ARE JEALOUS! JEALOUS, JEALOUS, JEALOUS...
I AM NOT! YOU'RE FUCKED! FUCKED, FUCKED, FUCKED!
HEY, ARE YOU GUYS REALLY FIGHTING?
WELL, IF IT AIN'T PENNY OF THE CENTURY.
THAT'S TENTIARY! JEALOUS, JEALOUS, JEALOUS...
PENNY CENTURY! THAT'S SO CUTE!
DON'T YOU THINK I LOOK LIKE A PENNY CENTURY?
JEALOUS, JEALOUS, JEALOUS, JEALOUS...
ONCE MORE! SAY IT ONCE MORE!
WHEN MY HAIR IS THIS COLOR I'LL BE PENNY CENTURY, AND WHEN IT'S NORMAL, I'LL BE BEATRÍZ GARCIA. OR IS THAT JUST WAY TOO DUMB?
JEA-- OW! BITCH!
I WARNED YOU... YEOW!
YOU GUYS AREN'T REALLY FIGHTING.
RRARRRR!
HISSSS!
ROWRRR!
FFFT!
7

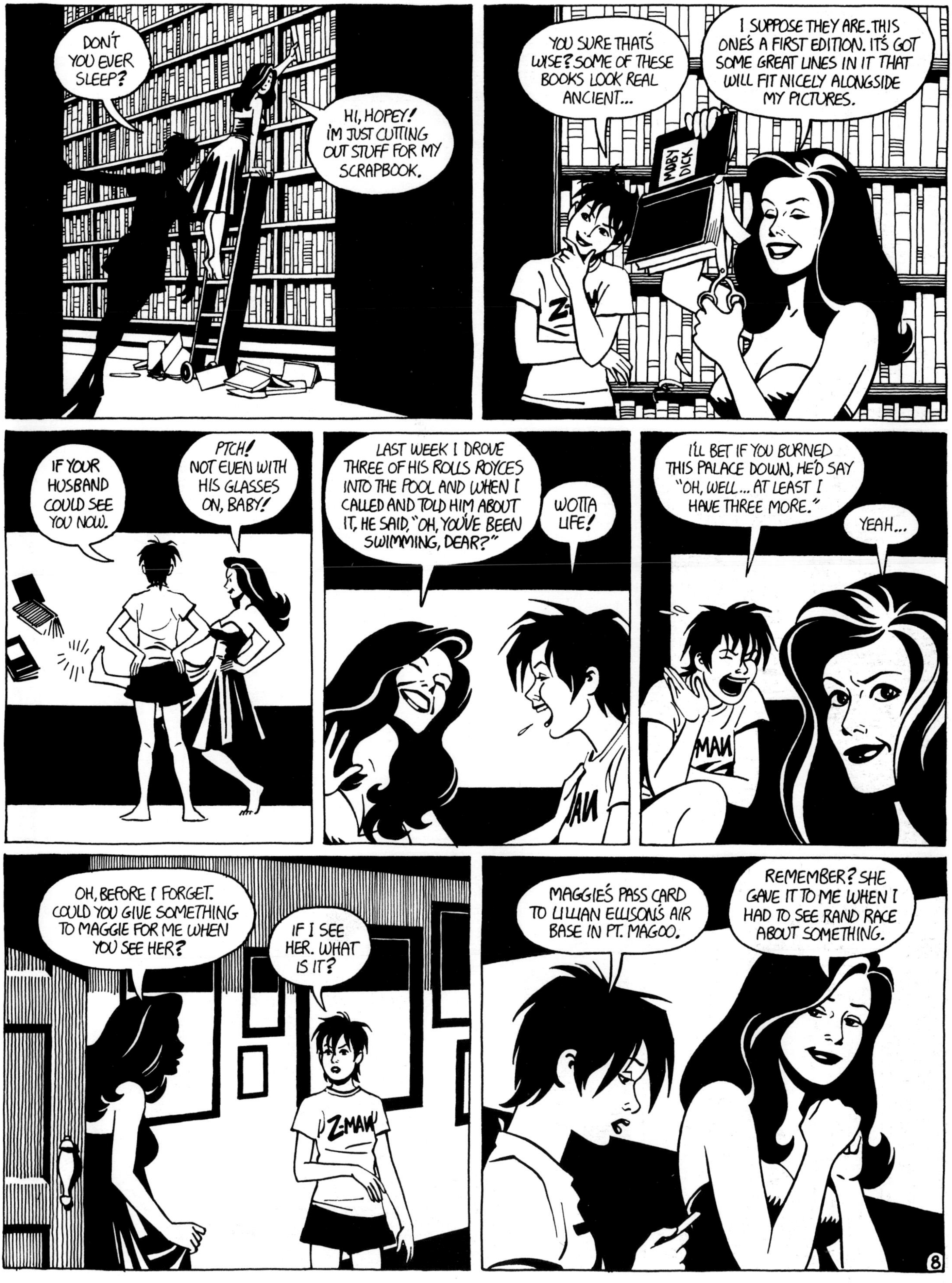
DON'T YOU EVER SLEEP?
HI, HOPEY! I'M JUST CUTTING OUT STUFF FOR MY SCRAPBOOK.
YOU SURE THAT'S WISE? SOME OF THESE BOOKS LOOK REAL ANCIENT...
I SUPPOSE THEY ARE. THIS ONE'S A FIRST EDITION. IT'S GOT SOME GREAT LINES IN IT THAT WILL FIT NICELY ALONGSIDE MY PICTURES.
MOBY DICK
Z-MAN
IF YOUR HUSBAND COULD SEE YOU NOW.
PTCH! NOT EVEN WITH HIS GLASSES ON, BABY!
LAST WEEK I DROVE THREE OF HIS ROLLS ROYCES INTO THE POOL AND WHEN I CALLED AND TOLD HIM ABOUT IT, HE SAID, "OH, YOU'VE BEEN SWIMMING, DEAR?"
WOTTA LIFE!
I'LL BET IF YOU BURNED THIS PALACE DOWN, HE'D SAY "OH, WELL... AT LEAST I HAVE THREE MORE."
YEAH...
OH, BEFORE I FORGET. COULD YOU GIVE SOMETHING TO MAGGIE FOR ME WHEN YOU SEE HER?
IF I SEE HER. WHAT IS IT?
Z-MAN
MAGGIE'S PASS CARD TO LILLIAN ELLISON'S AIR BASE IN PT. MAGOO.
REMEMBER? SHE GAVE IT TO ME WHEN I HAD TO SEE RAND RACE ABOUT SOMETHING.
8

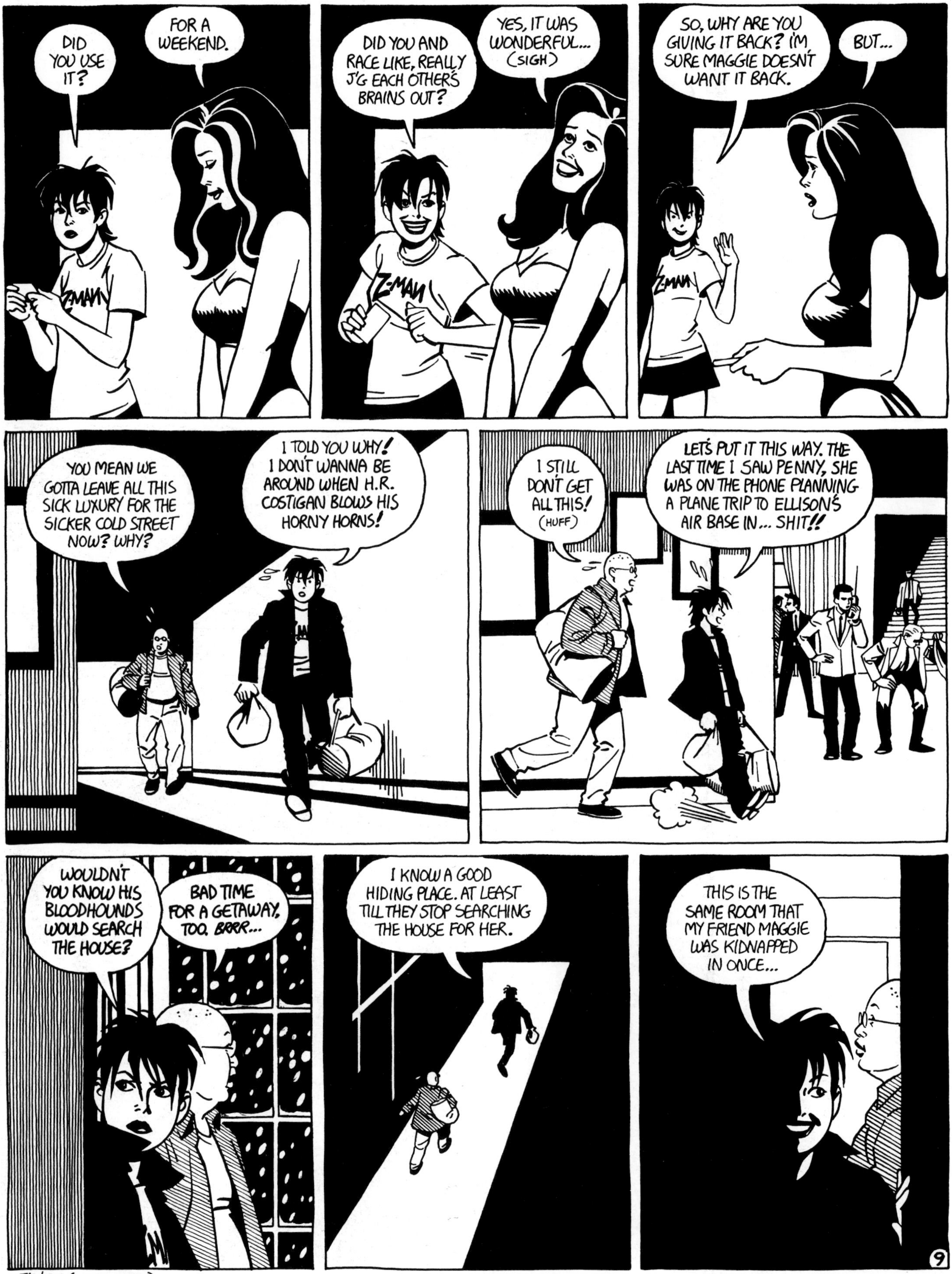
DID YOU USE IT?
FOR A WEEKEND.
DID YOU AND RACE LIKE, REALLY J'G EACH OTHER'S BRAINS OUT?
YES, IT WAS WONDERFUL... (SIGH)
Z-MAN
SO, WHY ARE YOU GIVING IT BACK? I'M SURE MAGGIE DOESN'T WANT IT BACK.
BUT...
YOU MEAN WE GOTTA LEAVE ALL THIS SICK LUXURY FOR THE SICKER COLD STREET NOW? WHY?
I TOLD YOU WHY! I DON'T WANNA BE AROUND WHEN H.R. COSTIGAN BLOWS HIS HORNY HORNS!
I STILL DON'T GET ALL THIS! (HUFF)
LET'S PUT IT THIS WAY. THE LAST TIME I SAW PENNY, SHE WAS ON THE PHONE PLANNING A PLANE TRIP TO ELLISON'S AIR BASE IN... SHIT!!
WOULDN'T YOU KNOW HIS BLOODHOUNDS WOULD SEARCH THE HOUSE?
BAD TIME FOR A GETAWAY, TOO. BRRR...
I KNOW A GOOD HIDING PLACE. AT LEAST TILL THEY STOP SEARCHING THE HOUSE FOR HER.
THIS IS THE SAME ROOM THAT MY FRIEND MAGGIE WAS KIDNAPPED IN ONCE...
9

J'G/JUG (PRONOUNCED JIG)

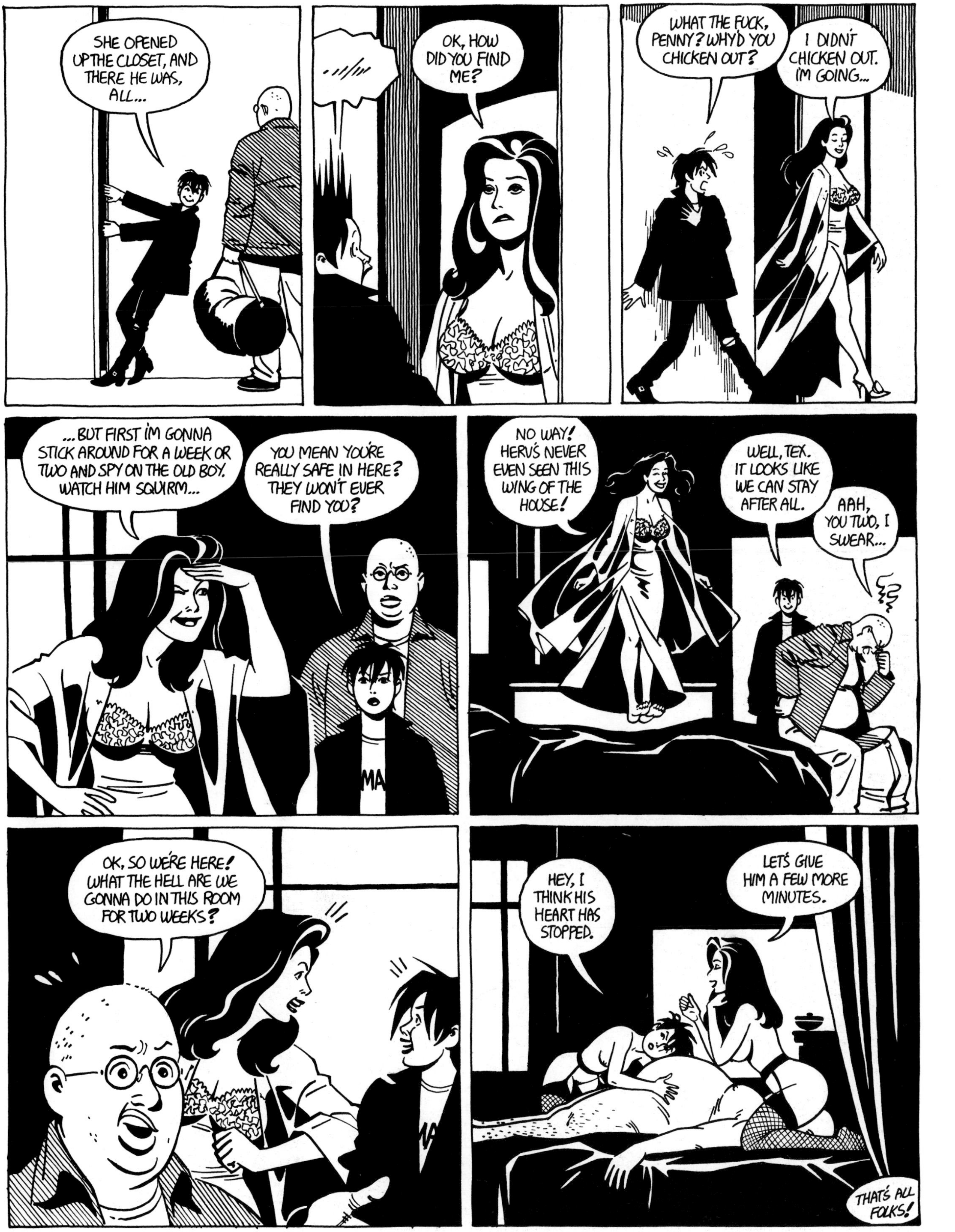

SHE OPENED UP THE CLOSET, AND THERE HE WAS, ALL...
OK, HOW DID YOU FIND ME?
WHAT THE FUCK, PENNY? WHY'D YOU CHICKEN OUT?
I DIDN'T CHICKEN OUT. I'M GOING...
...BUT FIRST I'M GONNA STICK AROUND FOR A WEEK OR TWO AND SPY ON THE OLD BOY. WATCH HIM SQUIRM...
YOU MEAN YOU'RE REALLY SAFE IN HERE? THEY WON'T EVER FIND YOU?
NO WAY! HERV'S NEVER EVEN SEEN THIS WING OF THE HOUSE!
WELL, TEX. IT LOOKS LIKE WE CAN STAY AFTER ALL.
AAH, YOU TWO, I SWEAR...
OK, SO WE'RE HERE! WHAT THE HELL ARE WE GONNA DO IN THIS ROOM FOR TWO WEEKS?
HEY, I THINK HIS HEART HAS STOPPED.
LET'S GIVE HIM A FEW MORE MINUTES.
THAT'S ALL FOLKS!

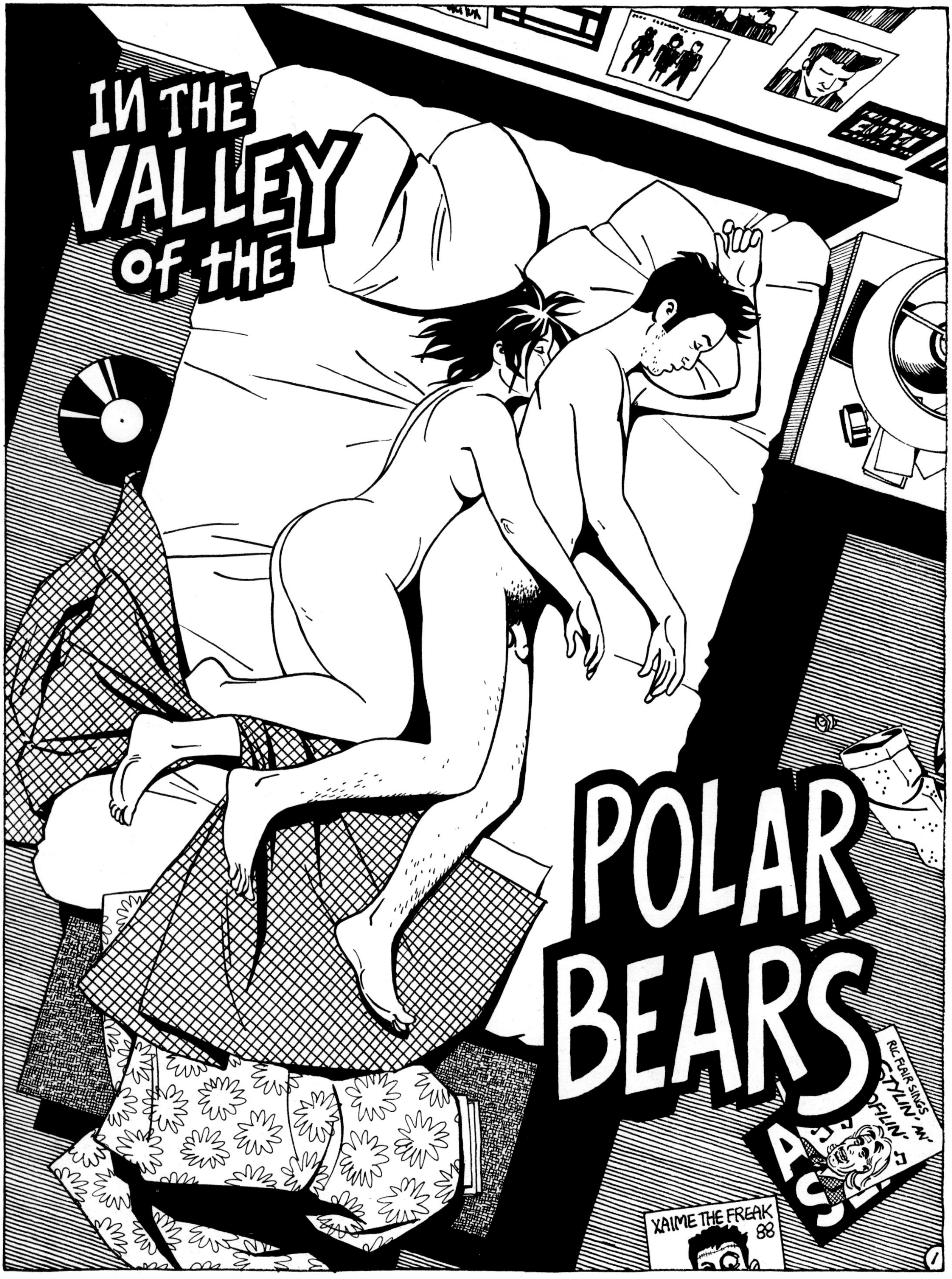
IN THE VALLEY OF THE POLAR BEARS
RIC FLAIR SINGS
STYLIN' AN'
XAIME THE FREAK 88
1

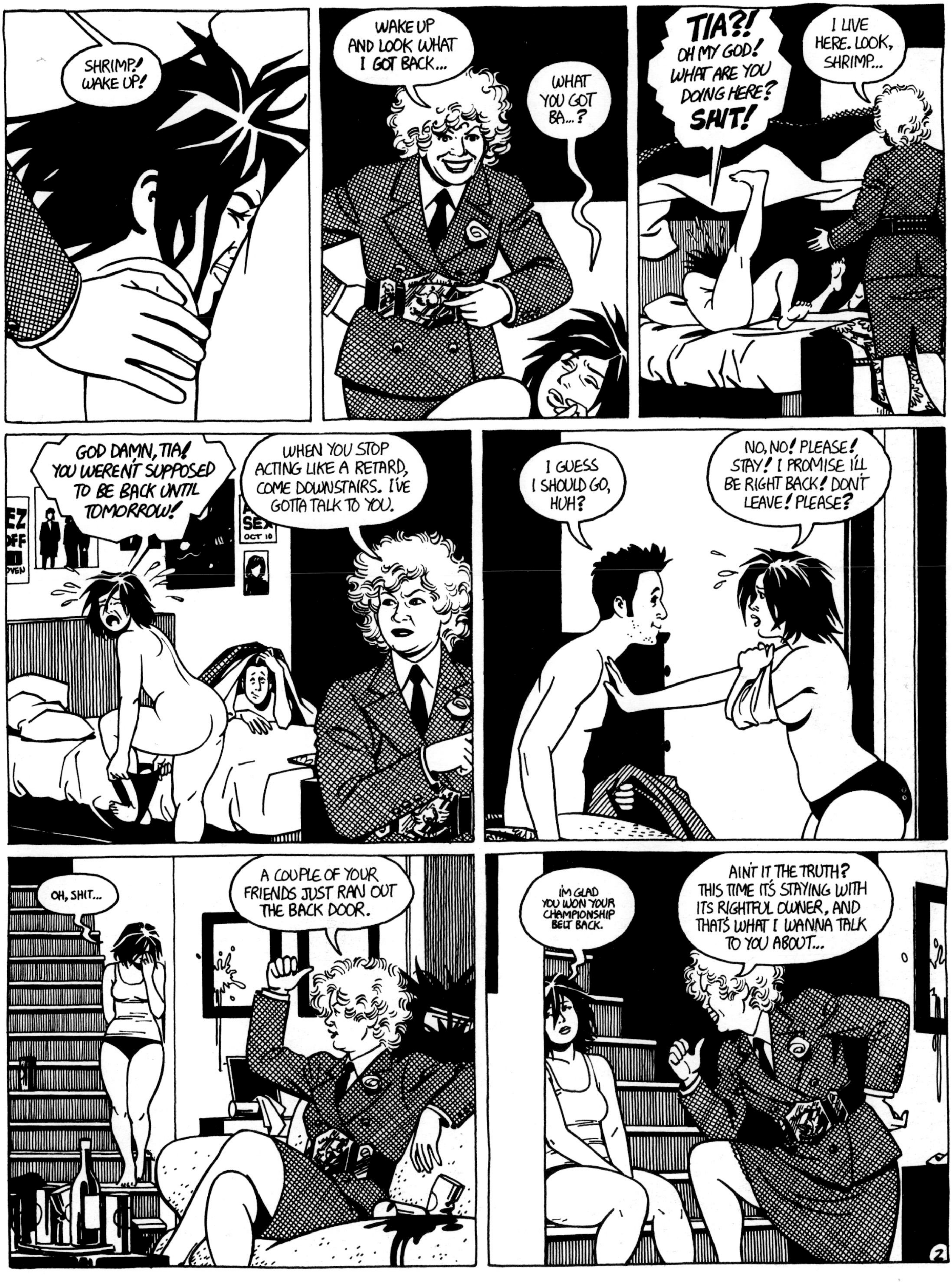
SHRIMP! WAKE UP!
WAKE UP AND LOOK WHAT I GOT BACK...
WHAT YOU GOT BA...?
TIA?! OH MY GOD! WHAT ARE YOU DOING HERE? SHIT!
I LIVE HERE. LOOK, SHRIMP...
GOD DAMN, TIA! YOU WEREN'T SUPPOSED TO BE BACK UNTIL TOMORROW!
WHEN YOU STOP ACTING LIKE A RETARD, COME DOWNSTAIRS. I'VE GOTTA TALK TO YOU.
SEX
OCT 10
I GUESS I SHOULD GO, HUH?
NO, NO! PLEASE! STAY! I PROMISE I'LL BE RIGHT BACK! DON'T LEAVE! PLEASE?
OH, SHIT...
A COUPLE OF YOUR FRIENDS JUST RAN OUT THE BACK DOOR.
I'M GLAD YOU WON YOUR CHAMPIONSHIP BELT BACK.
AIN'T IT THE TRUTH? THIS TIME IT'S STAYING WITH ITS RIGHTFUL OWNER, AND THAT'S WHAT I WANNA TALK TO YOU ABOUT...
2

IS THE COAST CLEAR, DAFFY?

I'M NOT SURE, TOM TOM.

LET'S GO OUT THE BACK WAY IN CASE THEY'RE IN THE FRONT ROOM.

MAGGIE?! WHERE IS YOUR AUNT?

SHE STEPPED OUT AWHILE.

NO SCARS, NO BRUISES. WHAT DID SHE DO? WHAT DID SHE SAY?

BELIEVE IT OR NOT, SHE OFFERED ME A JOB.

HOME SWEET HOME

HUH?!

SERIOUS. SHE'S STARTING A NATIONWIDE WRESTLING TOUR TOMORROW AND SHE WANTS ME TO GO ALONG. I DON'T KNOW WHAT I GOTTA DO, BUT SHE SAYS I'LL MAKE REAL GOOD MONEY.

SHE SAID, "I'M DOING THIS FOR YOU, SHRIMPO, BECAUSE I'M MOVING OUTTA STATE AFTER THIS TOUR AND I WOULDN'T WANNA LEAVE YOU OUT IN THE COLD. Y'ALL UNDERSTAND WHAT I'M SAYING?

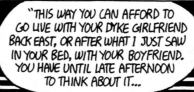

"THIS WAY YOU CAN AFFORD TO GO LIVE WITH YOUR DYKE GIRLFRIEND BACK EAST, OR AFTER WHAT I JUST SAW IN YOUR BED, WITH YOUR BOYFRIEND. YOU HAVE UNTIL LATE AFTERNOON TO THINK ABOUT IT...

"...SO GET OFF YOUR FAT ASS AND CLEAN THIS GOD DAMNED HOUSE BEFORE I RETURN!"

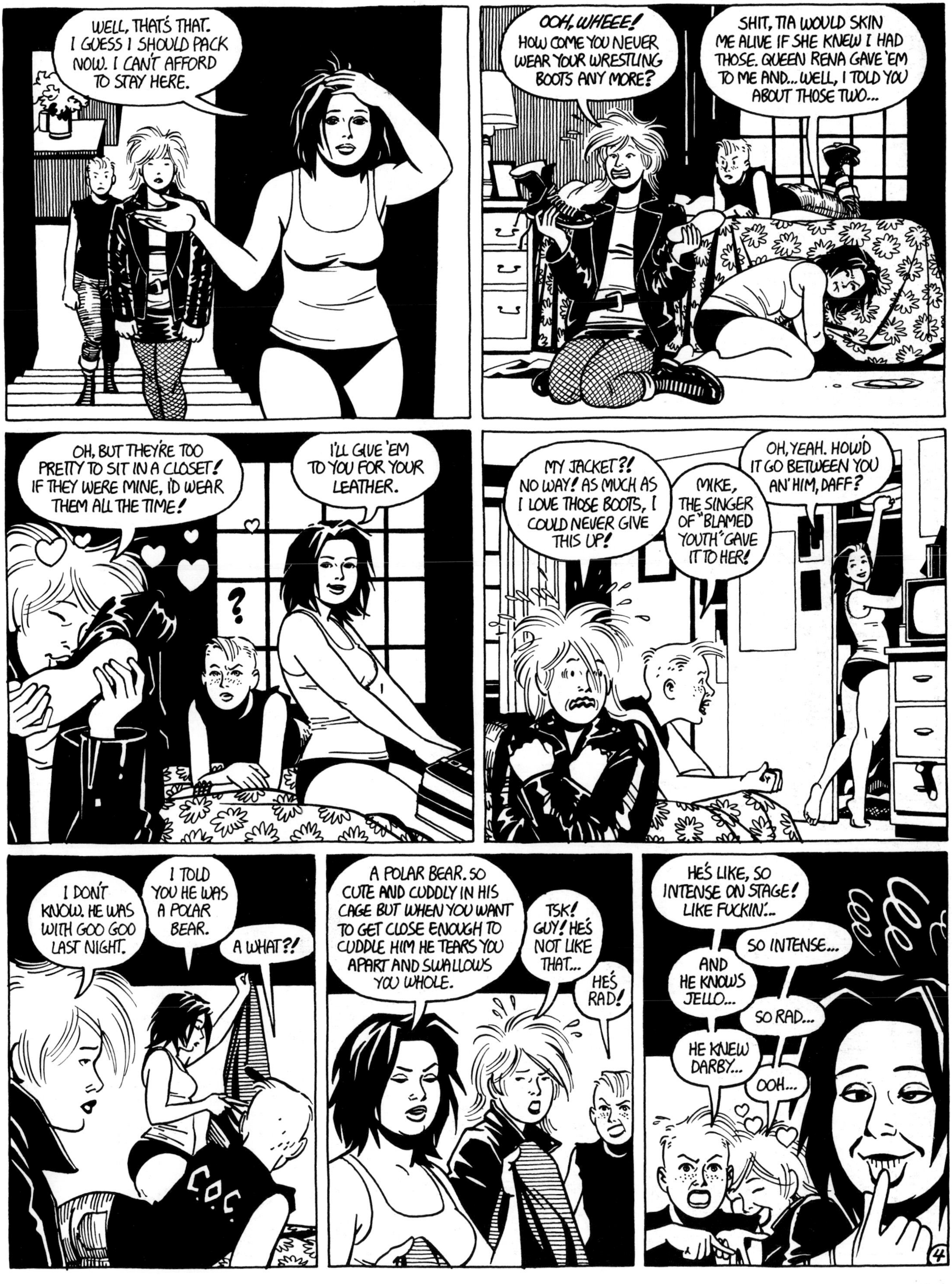
WELL, THAT'S THAT. I GUESS I SHOULD PACK NOW. I CAN'T AFFORD TO STAY HERE.
OOH, WHEEE! HOW COME YOU NEVER WEAR YOUR WRESTLING BOOTS ANY MORE?
SHIT, TIA WOULD SKIN ME ALIVE IF SHE KNEW I HAD THOSE. QUEEN RENA GAVE 'EM TO ME AND... WELL, I TOLD YOU ABOUT THOSE TWO...
OH, BUT THEY'RE TOO PRETTY TO SIT IN A CLOSET! IF THEY WERE MINE, I'D WEAR THEM ALL THE TIME!
I'LL GIVE 'EM TO YOU FOR YOUR LEATHER.
?
MY JACKET?! NO WAY! AS MUCH AS I LOVE THOSE BOOTS, I COULD NEVER GIVE THIS UP!
MIKE, THE SINGER OF "BLAMED YOUTH" GAVE IT TO HER!
OH, YEAH. HOW'D IT GO BETWEEN YOU AN' HIM, DAFF?
I DON'T KNOW. HE WAS WITH GOO GOO LAST NIGHT.
I TOLD YOU HE WAS A POLAR BEAR.
A WHAT?!
C.O.C.
A POLAR BEAR. SO CUTE AND CUDDLY IN HIS CAGE BUT WHEN YOU WANT TO GET CLOSE ENOUGH TO CUDDLE HIM HE TEARS YOU APART AND SWALLOWS YOU WHOLE.
TSK! GUY! HE'S NOT LIKE THAT...
HE'S RAD!
HE'S LIKE, SO INTENSE ON STAGE! LIKE FUCKIN'...
SO INTENSE...
AND HE KNOWS JELLO...
SO RAD...
HE KNEW DARBY...
OOH...
4

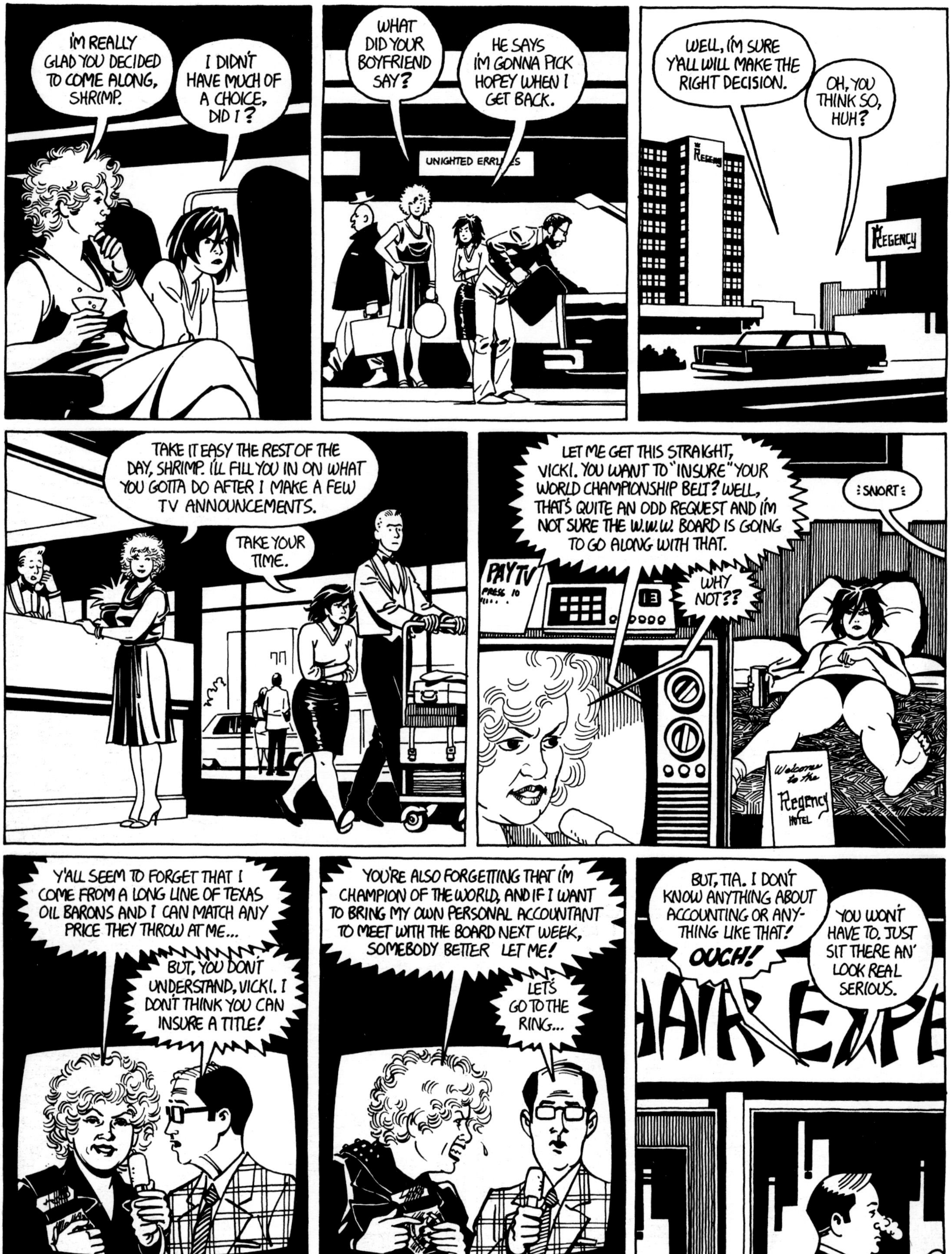
I'M REALLY GLAD YOU DECIDED TO COME ALONG, SHRIMP.
I DIDN'T HAVE MUCH OF A CHOICE, DID I?
WHAT DID YOUR BOYFRIEND SAY?
HE SAYS I'M GONNA PICK HOPEY WHEN I GET BACK.
UNIGHTED ERRL ES
WELL, I'M SURE Y'ALL WILL MAKE THE RIGHT DECISION.
OH, YOU THINK SO, HUH?
REGENCY
TAKE IT EASY THE REST OF THE DAY, SHRIMP. I'LL FILL YOU IN ON WHAT YOU GOTTA DO AFTER I MAKE A FEW TV ANNOUNCEMENTS.
TAKE YOUR TIME.
LET ME GET THIS STRAIGHT, VICKI. YOU WANT TO "INSURE" YOUR WORLD CHAMPIONSHIP BELT? WELL, THAT'S QUITE AN ODD REQUEST AND I'M NOT SURE THE W.W.W. BOARD IS GOING TO GO ALONG WITH THAT.
SNORT
PAY TV
WHY NOT??
Welcome to the Regency HOTEL
Y'ALL SEEM TO FORGET THAT I COME FROM A LONG LINE OF TEXAS OIL BARONS AND I CAN MATCH ANY PRICE THEY THROW AT ME...
BUT, YOU DON'T UNDERSTAND, VICKI. I DON'T THINK YOU CAN INSURE A TITLE!
YOU'RE ALSO FORGETTING THAT I'M CHAMPION OF THE WORLD, AND IF I WANT TO BRING MY OWN PERSONAL ACCOUNTANT TO MEET WITH THE BOARD NEXT WEEK, SOMEBODY BETTER LET ME!
LET'S GO TO THE RING...
BUT, TIA. I DON'T KNOW ANYTHING ABOUT ACCOUNTING OR ANYTHING LIKE THAT! OUCH!
YOU WON'T HAVE TO. JUST SIT THERE AN' LOOK REAL SERIOUS.
HAIR EXPE
5

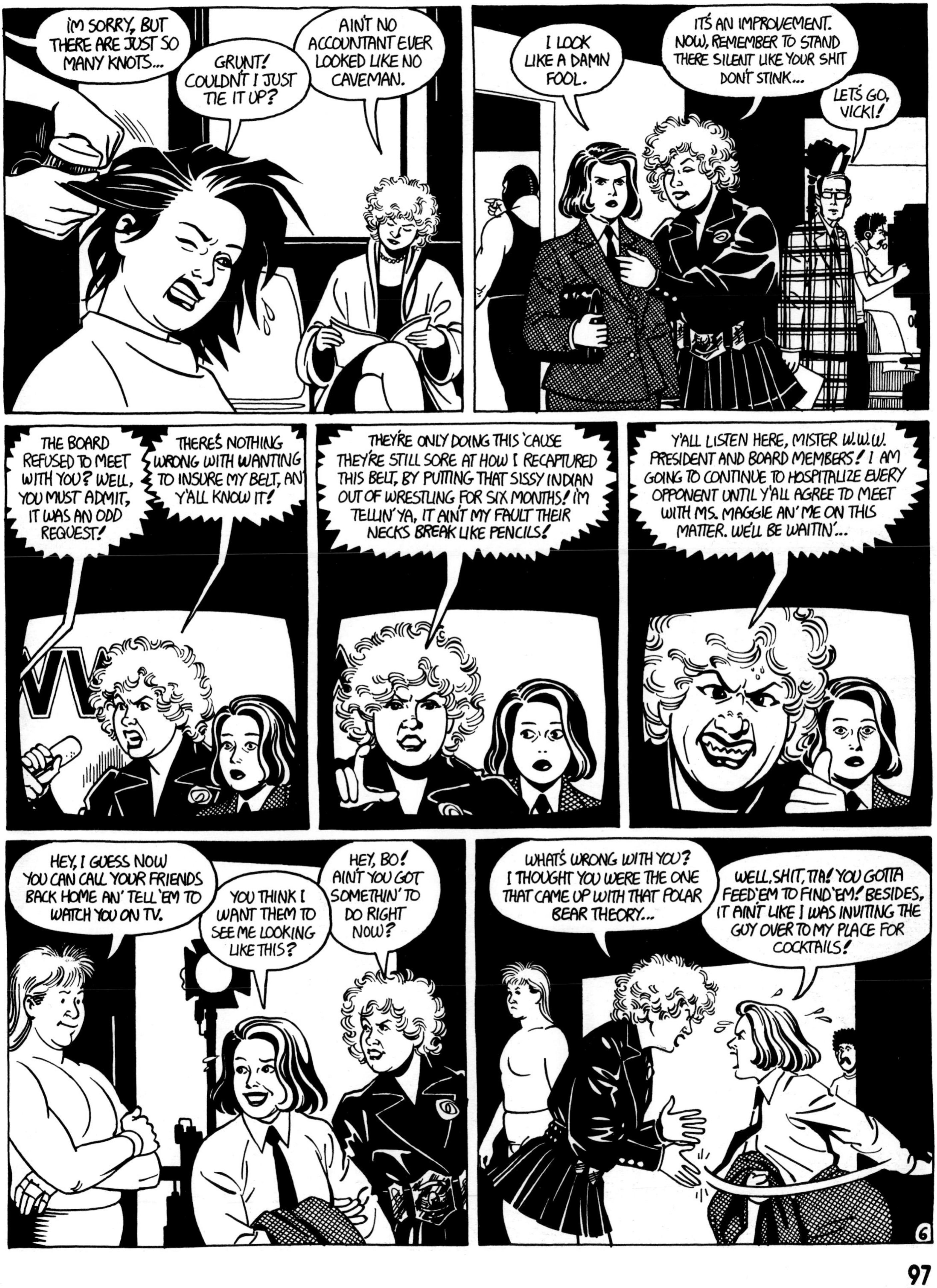
I'M SORRY, BUT THERE ARE JUST SO MANY KNOTS...
GRUNT! COULDN'T I JUST TIE IT UP?
AIN'T NO ACCOUNTANT EVER LOOKED LIKE NO CAVEMAN.
I LOOK LIKE A DAMN FOOL.
IT'S AN IMPROVEMENT. NOW, REMEMBER TO STAND THERE SILENT LIKE YOUR SHIT DON'T STINK...
LET'S GO, VICKI!
THE BOARD REFUSED TO MEET WITH YOU? WELL, YOU MUST ADMIT, IT WAS AN ODD REQUEST!
THERE'S NOTHING WRONG WITH WANTING TO INSURE MY BELT, AN' Y'ALL KNOW IT!
THEY'RE ONLY DOING THIS 'CAUSE THEY'RE STILL SORE AT HOW I RECAPTURED THIS BELT, BY PUTTING THAT SISSY INDIAN OUT OF WRESTLING FOR SIX MONTHS! I'M TELLIN' YA, IT AIN'T MY FAULT THEIR NECKS BREAK LIKE PENCILS!
Y'ALL LISTEN HERE, MISTER W.W.W. PRESIDENT AND BOARD MEMBERS! I AM GOING TO CONTINUE TO HOSPITALIZE EVERY OPPONENT UNTIL Y'ALL AGREE TO MEET WITH MS. MAGGIE AN' ME ON THIS MATTER. WE'LL BE WAITIN'...
HEY, I GUESS NOW YOU CAN CALL YOUR FRIENDS BACK HOME AN' TELL 'EM TO WATCH YOU ON TV.
YOU THINK I WANT THEM TO SEE ME LOOKING LIKE THIS?
HEY, BO! AIN'T YOU GOT SOMETHIN' TO DO RIGHT NOW?
WHAT'S WRONG WITH YOU? I THOUGHT YOU WERE THE ONE THAT CAME UP WITH THAT POLAR BEAR THEORY...
WELL, SHIT, TIA! YOU GOTTA FEED 'EM TO FIND 'EM! BESIDES, IT AIN'T LIKE I WAS INVITING THE GUY OVER TO MY PLACE FOR COCKTAILS!
6

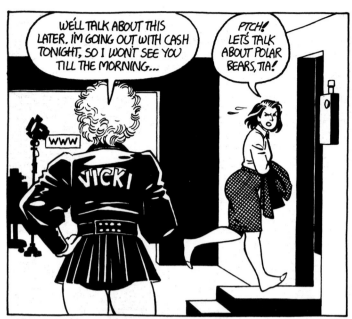

WE'LL TALK ABOUT THIS LATER. I'M GOING OUT WITH CASH TONIGHT, SO I WON'T SEE YOU TILL THE MORNING...

PTCH! LET'S TALK ABOUT POLAR BEARS, TIA!

VICKI

YOU GUYS WILL GET IT ON CHANNEL FIVE AT NINE, YOUR TIME, SO DON'T GET TOO SCARED WHEN YOU SEE A FAT, BLOATED MONSTER INVADE YOUR TV SCREEN.

WHICH REMINDS ME. HOPEY CALLED EARLIER.

SHE DID?! GUY! WHEN? WHAT DID SHE SAY??

SHE RAGGED ABOUT YOUR TIA'S ANSWERING MACHINE THEN THE OPERATOR CUT US OFF.

YEAH... IT'S SO STUPID... SHE GOT ME THIS YUPPIE SUIT AND THIS YUPPIE HAIRCUT AND STOOD ME IN FRONT OF A CAMERA, AND... GOD. IT WAS SO STUPID...

YEAH? HA! CAN'T WAIT TO SEE IT. SO... THEN I'LL SEE YOU WHEN YOU GET BACK, HUH? OK, SEE YA...

I'M GONNA KILL THIS HOPEY PERSON...

HUH? WE KEEPING YOU UP, RAY?

JMMM...

7

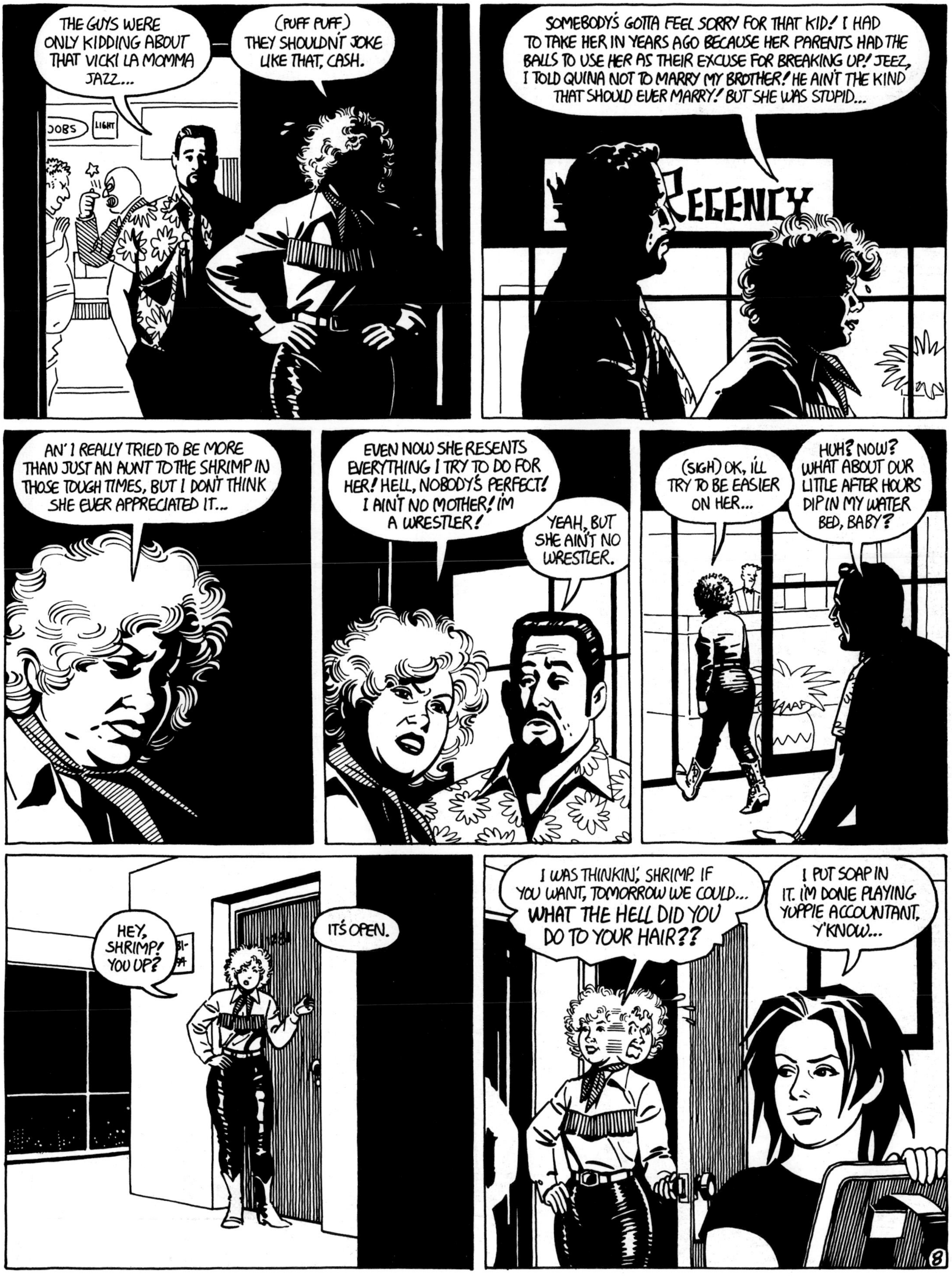
THE GUYS WERE ONLY KIDDING ABOUT THAT VICKI LA MOMMA JAZZ...
(PUFF PUFF) THEY SHOULDN'T JOKE LIKE THAT, CASH.
JOBS
LIGHT
SOMEBODY'S GOTTA FEEL SORRY FOR THAT KID! I HAD TO TAKE HER IN YEARS AGO BECAUSE HER PARENTS HAD THE BALLS TO USE HER AS THEIR EXCUSE FOR BREAKING UP! JEEZ, I TOLD QUINA NOT TO MARRY MY BROTHER! HE AIN'T THE KIND THAT SHOULD EVER MARRY! BUT SHE WAS STUPID...
REGENCY
AN' I REALLY TRIED TO BE MORE THAN JUST AN AUNT TO THE SHRIMP IN THOSE TOUGH TIMES, BUT I DON'T THINK SHE EVER APPRECIATED IT...
EVEN NOW SHE RESENTS EVERYTHING I TRY TO DO FOR HER! HELL, NOBODY'S PERFECT! I AIN'T NO MOTHER! I'M A WRESTLER!
YEAH, BUT SHE AIN'T NO WRESTLER.
(SIGH) OK, I'LL TRY TO BE EASIER ON HER...
HUH? NOW? WHAT ABOUT OUR LITTLE AFTER HOURS DIP IN MY WATER BED, BABY?
HEY, SHRIMP! YOU UP?
IT'S OPEN.
I WAS THINKIN', SHRIMP. IF YOU WANT, TOMORROW WE COULD... WHAT THE HELL DID YOU DO TO YOUR HAIR??
I PUT SOAP IN IT. I'M DONE PLAYING YUPPIE ACCOUNTANT, Y'KNOW...
8

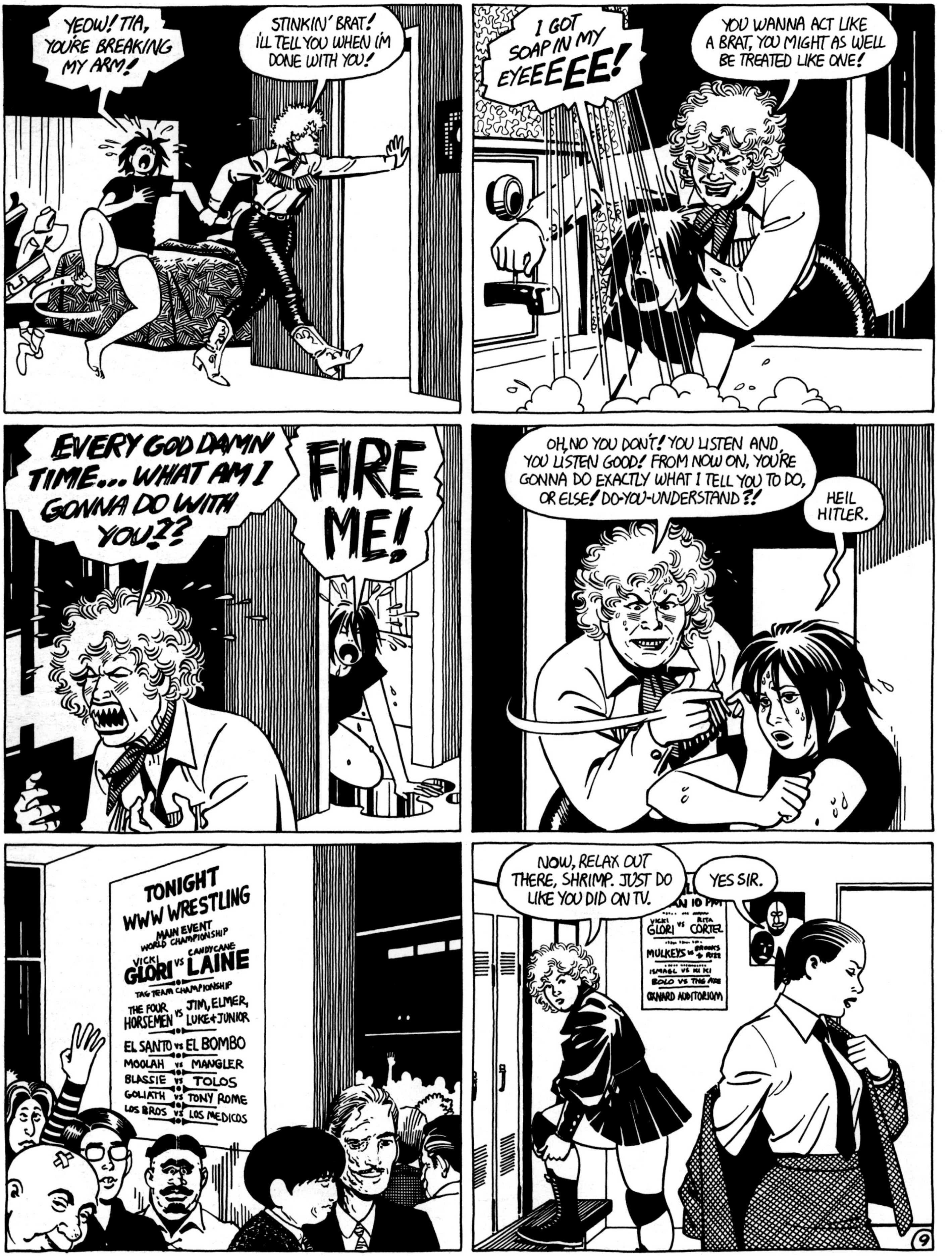
YEOW! TIA, YOU'RE BREAKING MY ARM!
STINKIN' BRAT! I'LL TELL YOU WHEN I'M DONE WITH YOU!
I GOT SOAP IN MY EYEEEEEE!
YOU WANNA ACT LIKE A BRAT, YOU MIGHT AS WELL BE TREATED LIKE ONE!
EVERY GOD DAMN TIME... WHAT AM I GONNA DO WITH YOU??
FIRE ME!
OH, NO YOU DON'T! YOU LISTEN AND, YOU LISTEN GOOD! FROM NOW ON, YOU'RE GONNA DO EXACTLY WHAT I TELL YOU TO DO, OR ELSE! DO-YOU-UNDERSTAND?!
HEIL HITLER.
TONIGHT
WWW WRESTLING
MAIN EVENT
WORLD CHAMPIONSHIP
VICKI GLORI vs CANDYCANE LAINE
TAG TEAM CHAMPIONSHIP
THE FOUR HORSEMEN vs JIM, ELMER, LUKE & JUNIOR
EL SANTO vs EL BOMBO
MOOLAH vs MANGLER
BLASSIE vs TOLOS
GOLIATH vs TONY ROME
LOS BROS vs LOS MEDICOS
NOW, RELAX OUT THERE, SHRIMP. JUST DO LIKE YOU DID ON TV.
YES SIR.
VICKI GLORI vs RITA CORTEZ
OXNARD AUDITORIUM
9

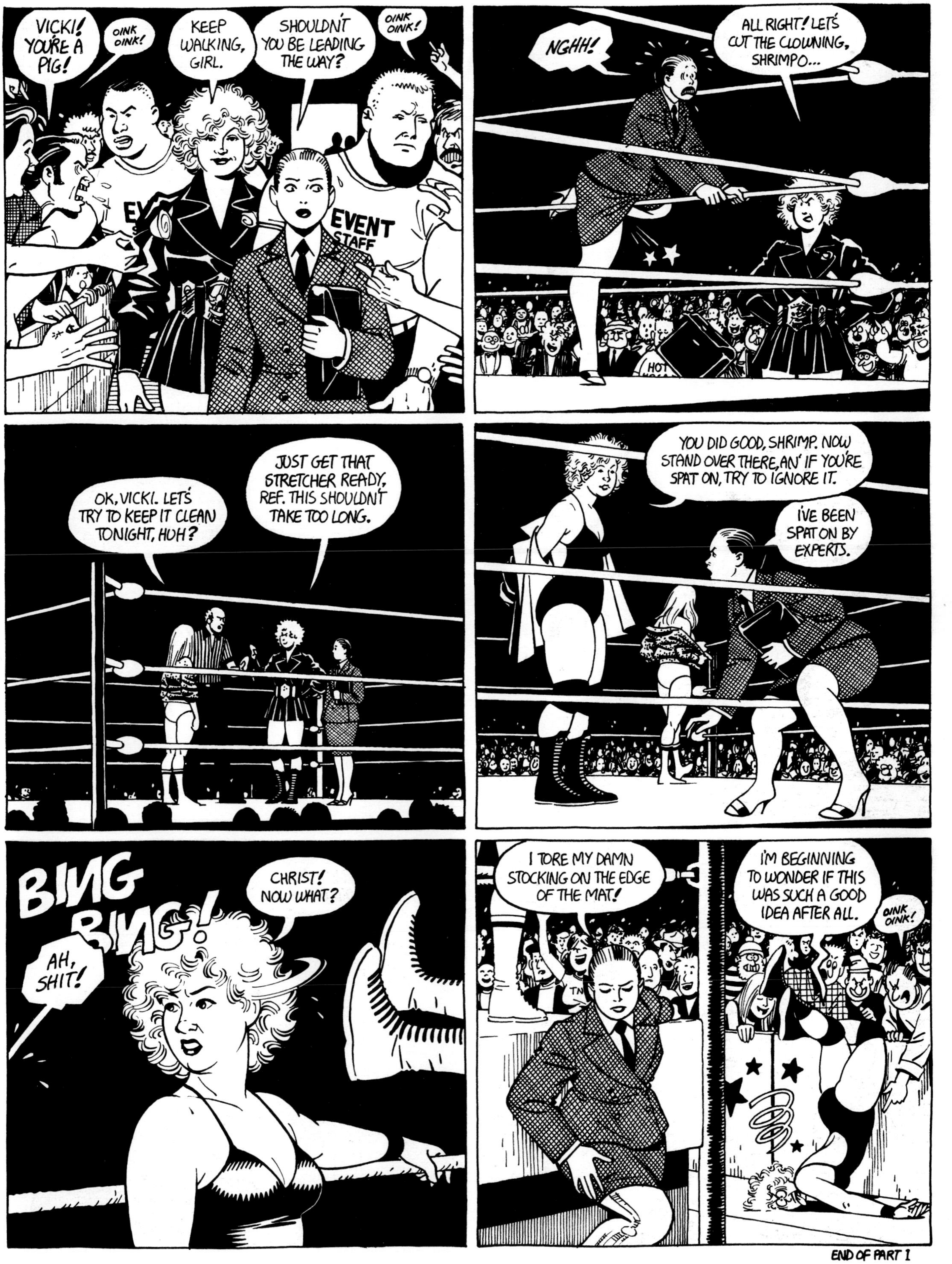
VICKI! YOU'RE A PIG!
OINK OINK!
KEEP WALKING, GIRL.
SHOULDN'T YOU BE LEADING THE WAY?
OINK OINK!
EVENT STAFF
NGHH!
ALL RIGHT! LET'S CUT THE CLOWNING, SHRIMPO...
OK, VICKI. LET'S TRY TO KEEP IT CLEAN TONIGHT, HUH?
JUST GET THAT STRETCHER READY, REF. THIS SHOULDN'T TAKE TOO LONG.
YOU DID GOOD, SHRIMP. NOW STAND OVER THERE, AN' IF YOU'RE SPAT ON, TRY TO IGNORE IT.
I'VE BEEN SPAT ON BY EXPERTS.
BING BING!
AH, SHIT!
CHRIST! NOW WHAT?
I TORE MY DAMN STOCKING ON THE EDGE OF THE MAT!
I'M BEGINNING TO WONDER IF THIS WAS SUCH A GOOD IDEA AFTER ALL.
OINK OINK!

END OF PART I

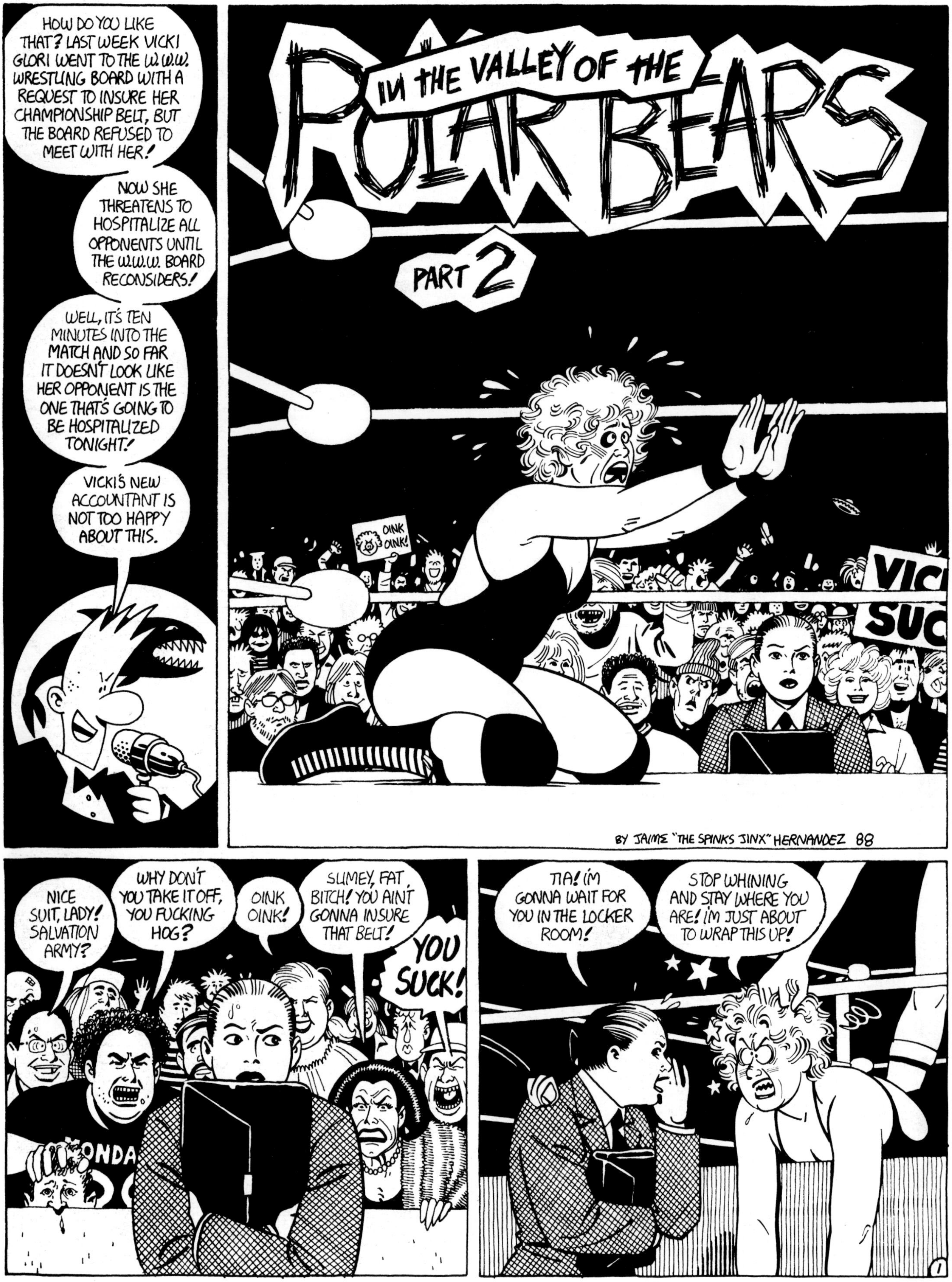
IN THE VALLEY OF THE POLAR BEARS
PART 2
HOW DO YOU LIKE THAT? LAST WEEK VICKI GLORI WENT TO THE W.W.W. WRESTLING BOARD WITH A REQUEST TO INSURE HER CHAMPIONSHIP BELT, BUT THE BOARD REFUSED TO MEET WITH HER!
NOW SHE THREATENS TO HOSPITALIZE ALL OPPONENTS UNTIL THE W.W.W. BOARD RECONSIDERS!
WELL, IT'S TEN MINUTES INTO THE MATCH AND SO FAR IT DOESN'T LOOK LIKE HER OPPONENT IS THE ONE THAT'S GOING TO BE HOSPITALIZED TONIGHT!
VICKI'S NEW ACCOUNTANT IS NOT TOO HAPPY ABOUT THIS.
OINK OINK!
VICKI SUC
BY JAIME "THE SPINKS JINX" HERNANDEZ 88
NICE SUIT, LADY! SALVATION ARMY?
WHY DON'T YOU TAKE IT OFF, YOU FUCKING HOG?
OINK OINK!
SLIMEY, FAT BITCH! YOU AIN'T GONNA INSURE THAT BELT!
YOU SUCK!
HONDA
TIA! I'M GONNA WAIT FOR YOU IN THE LOCKER ROOM!
STOP WHINING AND STAY WHERE YOU ARE! I'M JUST ABOUT TO WRAP THIS UP!
1

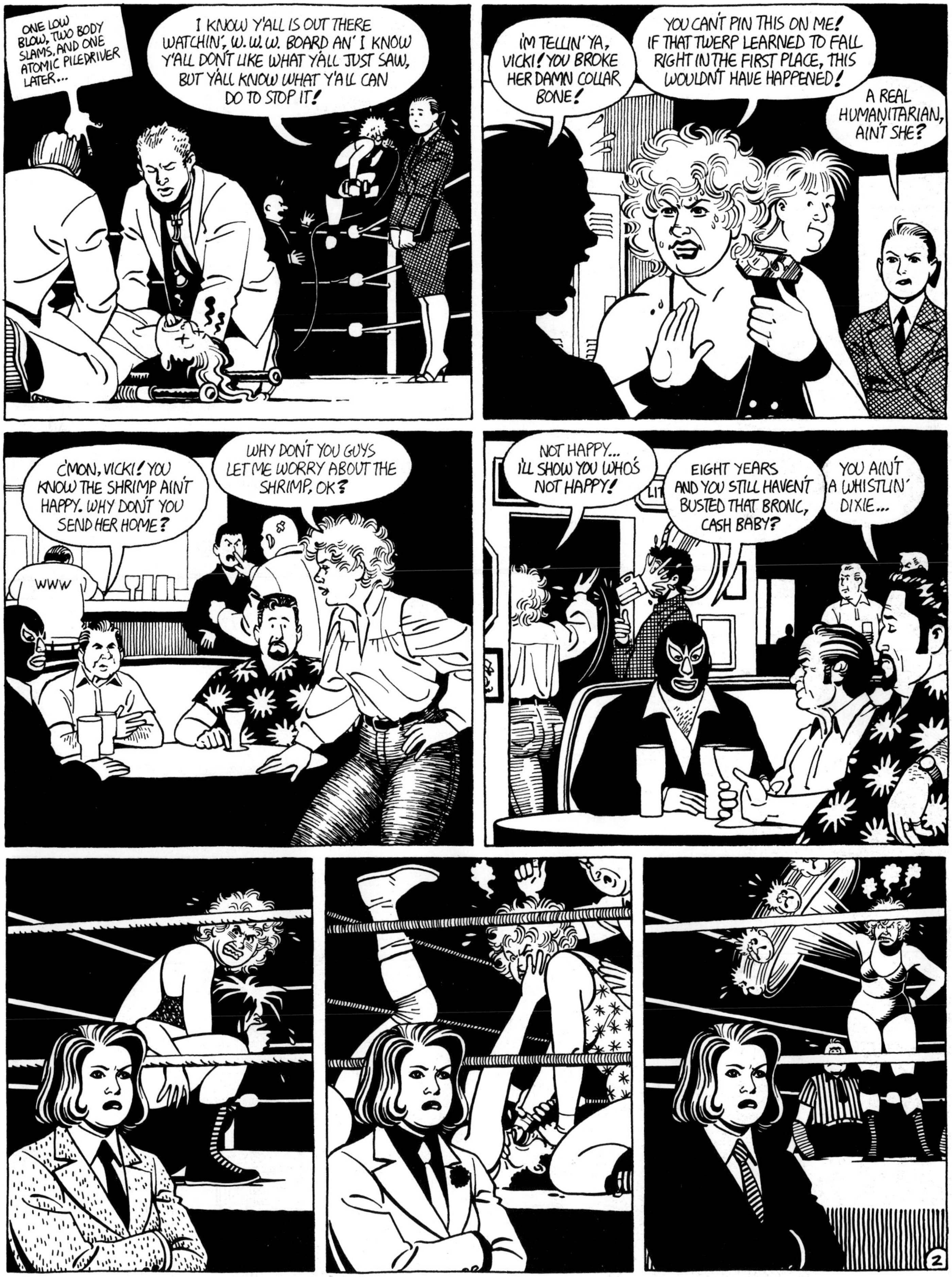
ONE LOW BLOW, TWO BODY SLAMS, AND ONE ATOMIC PILEDRIVER LATER...
I KNOW Y'ALL IS OUT THERE WATCHIN', W.W.W. BOARD AN' I KNOW Y'ALL DON'T LIKE WHAT Y'ALL JUST SAW, BUT Y'ALL KNOW WHAT Y'ALL CAN DO TO STOP IT!
I'M TELLIN' YA, VICKI! YOU BROKE HER DAMN COLLAR BONE!
YOU CAN'T PIN THIS ON ME! IF THAT TWERP LEARNED TO FALL RIGHT IN THE FIRST PLACE, THIS WOULDN'T HAVE HAPPENED!
A REAL HUMANITARIAN, AIN'T SHE?
C'MON, VICKI! YOU KNOW THE SHRIMP AIN'T HAPPY. WHY DON'T YOU SEND HER HOME?
WHY DON'T YOU GUYS LET ME WORRY ABOUT THE SHRIMP, OK?
WWW
NOT HAPPY... I'LL SHOW YOU WHO'S NOT HAPPY!
EIGHT YEARS AND YOU STILL HAVEN'T BUSTED THAT BRONC, CASH BABY?
YOU AIN'T A WHISTLIN' DIXIE...
2

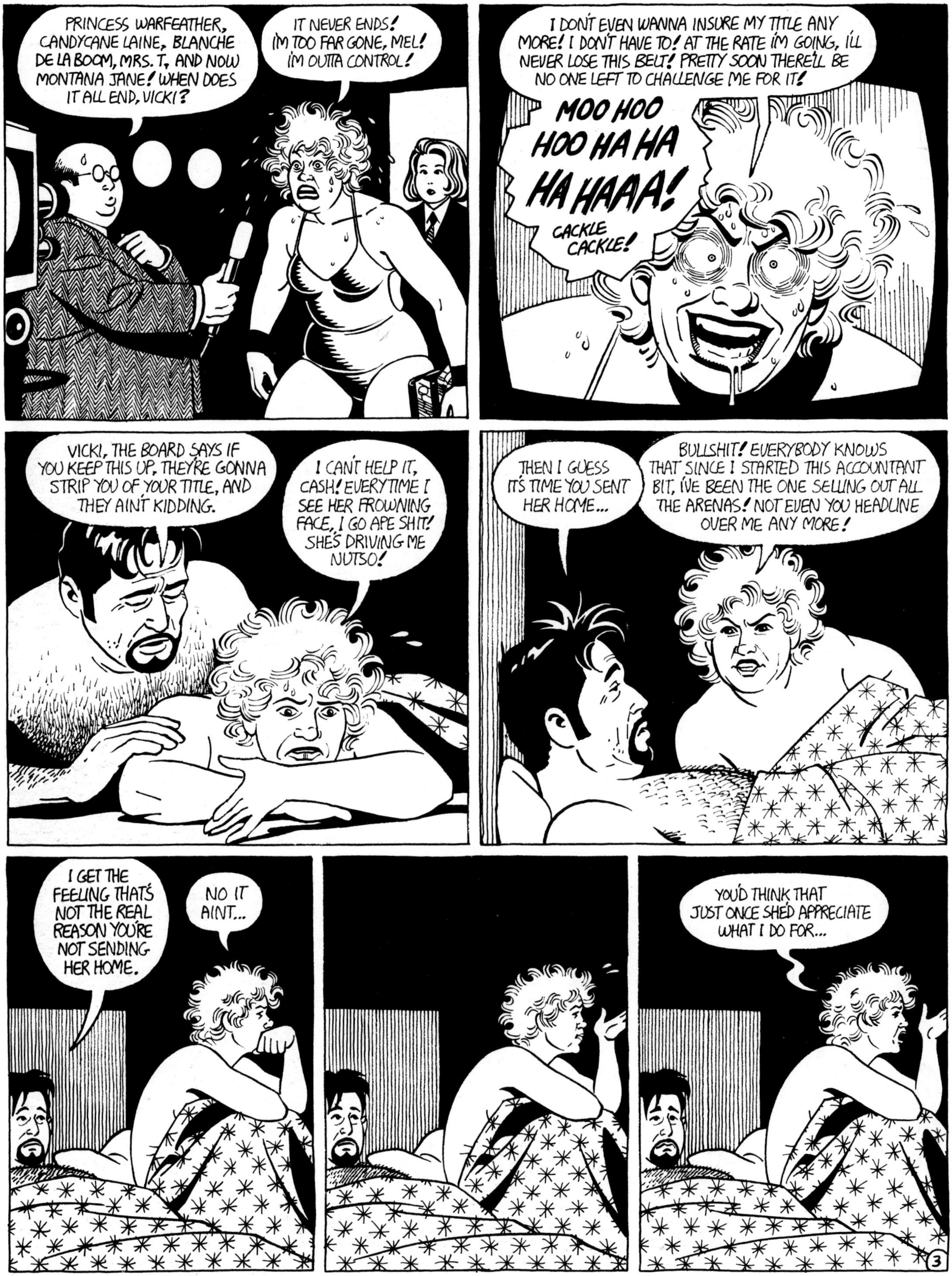

PRINCESS WARFEATHER, CANDYCANE LAINE, BLANCHE DE LA BOOM, MRS. T, AND NOW MONTANA JANE! WHEN DOES IT ALL END, VICKI?
IT NEVER ENDS! I'M TOO FAR GONE, MEL! I'M OUTTA CONTROL!
I DON'T EVEN WANNA INSURE MY TITLE ANY MORE! I DON'T HAVE TO! AT THE RATE I'M GOING, I'LL NEVER LOSE THIS BELT! PRETTY SOON THERE'LL BE NO ONE LEFT TO CHALLENGE ME FOR IT!
MOO HOO HOO HA HA HA HAAA!
CACKLE CACKLE!
VICKI, THE BOARD SAYS IF YOU KEEP THIS UP, THEY'RE GONNA STRIP YOU OF YOUR TITLE, AND THEY AIN'T KIDDING.
I CAN'T HELP IT, CASH! EVERYTIME I SEE HER FROWNING FACE, I GO APE SHIT! SHE'S DRIVING ME NUTSO!
THEN I GUESS IT'S TIME YOU SENT HER HOME...
BULLSHIT! EVERYBODY KNOWS THAT SINCE I STARTED THIS ACCOUNTANT BIT, I'VE BEEN THE ONE SELLING OUT ALL THE ARENAS! NOT EVEN YOU HEADLINE OVER ME ANY MORE!
I GET THE FEELING THAT'S NOT THE REAL REASON YOU'RE NOT SENDING HER HOME.
NO IT AIN'T...
YOU'D THINK THAT JUST ONCE SHE'D APPRECIATE WHAT I DO FOR...
3

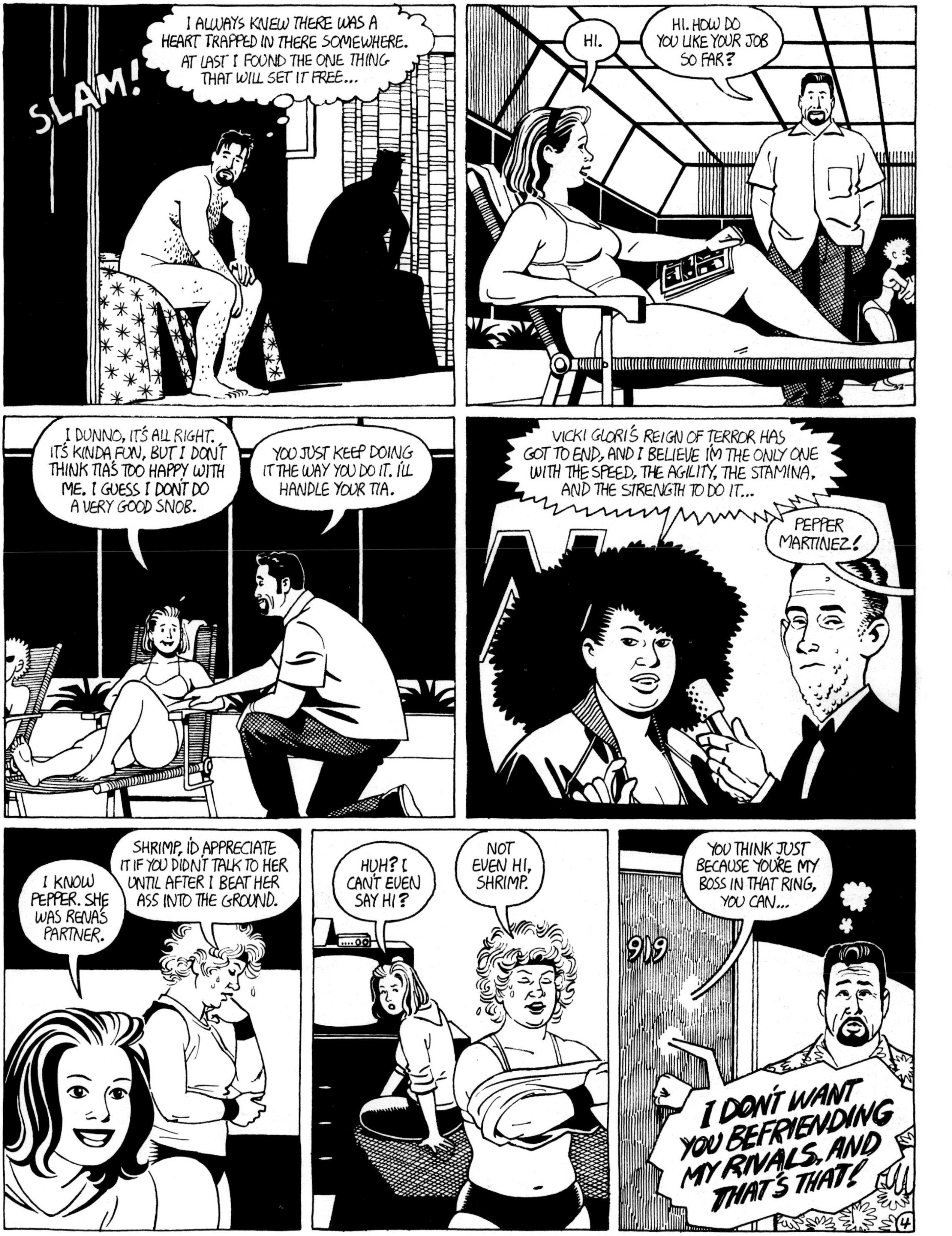
SLAM!
I ALWAYS KNEW THERE WAS A HEART TRAPPED IN THERE SOMEWHERE. AT LAST I FOUND THE ONE THING THAT WILL SET IT FREE...
HI.
HI. HOW DO YOU LIKE YOUR JOB SO FAR?
I DUNNO, IT'S ALL RIGHT. IT'S KINDA FUN, BUT I DON'T THINK TIA'S TOO HAPPY WITH ME. I GUESS I DON'T DO A VERY GOOD SNOB.
YOU JUST KEEP DOING IT THE WAY YOU DO IT. I'LL HANDLE YOUR TIA.
VICKI GLORI'S REIGN OF TERROR HAS GOT TO END, AND I BELIEVE I'M THE ONLY ONE WITH THE SPEED, THE AGILITY, THE STAMINA, AND THE STRENGTH TO DO IT...
PEPPER MARTINEZ!
I KNOW PEPPER. SHE WAS RENA'S PARTNER.
SHRIMP, I'D APPRECIATE IT IF YOU DIDN'T TALK TO HER UNTIL AFTER I BEAT HER ASS INTO THE GROUND.
HUH? I CAN'T EVEN SAY HI?
NOT EVEN HI, SHRIMP.
YOU THINK JUST BECAUSE YOU'RE MY BOSS IN THAT RING, YOU CAN...
919
I DON'T WANT YOU BEFRIENDING MY RIVALS, AND THAT'S THAT!
4

THAT'S IT. THAT'S REALLY IT. I CAN'T TAKE THIS SHIT NO MORE.

WAIT, KID. LISTEN TO ME FOR A SECOND...

916 - 999 →

SHE SAID THAT, HUH? SO WHAT AM I SUPPOSED TO DO, FEEL SORRY FOR HER WHEN SHE BREAKS MY ARM? SHEEE...

AW, DON'T GIVE UP! SHE NEEDS YOU!

HELL, I NEED YOU...

"...SO DON'T JUDGE HER TOO HARSHLY. SHE REALLY DOES CARE ABOUT YOU, Y'KNOW."

MY GOD, I KNOW I'M GONNA REGRET THIS...

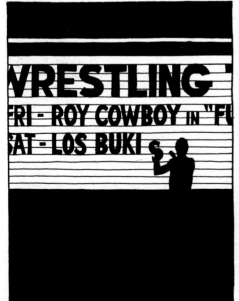

WRESTLING

FRI - ROY COWBOY IN "FU

SAT - LOS BUKIS

I WAS EASY ON THOSE OTHER SAPS COMPARED TO WHAT I'M GONNA DO TO THAT FAT MONSTER! SHE'S GONNA WISH SHE NEVER LEFT PUERTO RICO!

SOMEONE MUSTA DROPPED HER ON HER HEAD WHEN SHE WAS LITTLE 'CAUSE SHE AIN'T PLAYIN' WITH A FULL DECK! WHAT I'M GONNA DO TO HER, NONE OF HER TEXAS MILLIONS WILL BE ABLE TO REPAIR!

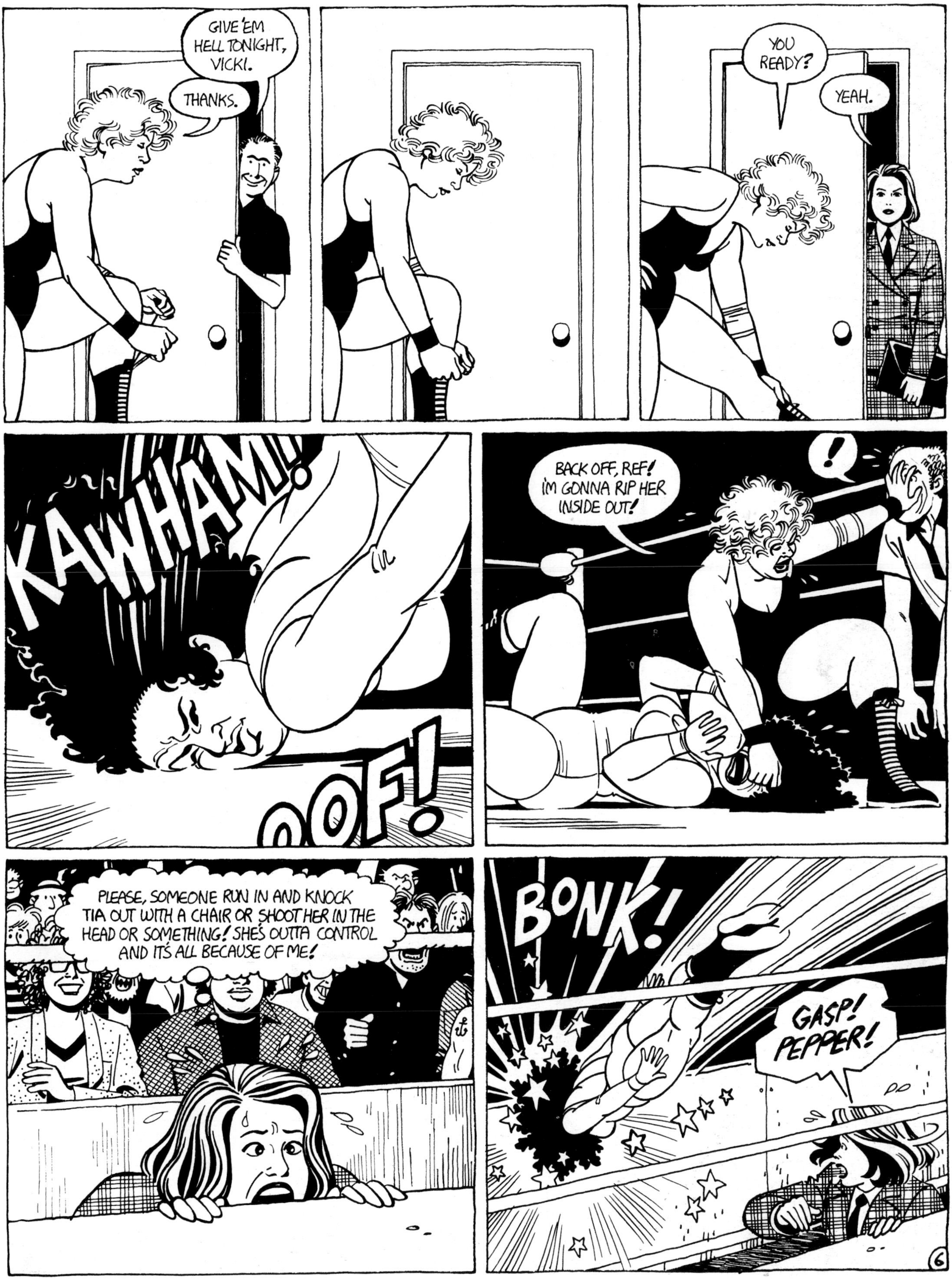
GIVE 'EM HELL TONIGHT, VICKI.
THANKS.
YOU READY?
YEAH.
KAWHAM!!
OOF!
BACK OFF, REF! I'M GONNA RIP HER INSIDE OUT!
!
PLEASE, SOMEONE RUN IN AND KNOCK TIA OUT WITH A CHAIR OR SHOOT HER IN THE HEAD OR SOMETHING! SHE'S OUTTA CONTROL AND IT'S ALL BECAUSE OF ME!
BONK!
GASP! PEPPER!
6

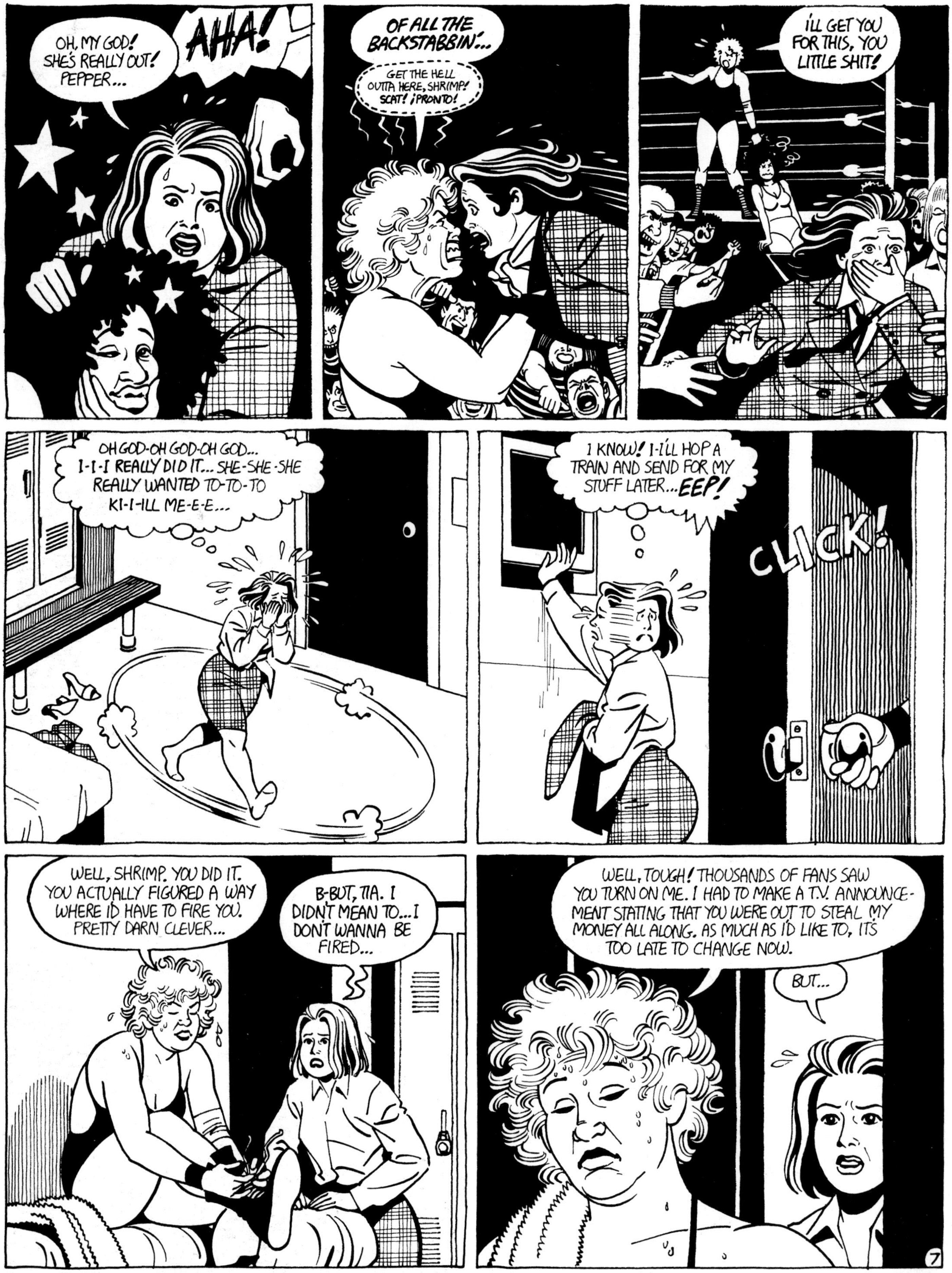
OH, MY GOD! SHE'S REALLY OUT! PEPPER...
AHA!
OF ALL THE BACKSTABBIN'...
GET THE HELL OUTTA HERE, SHRIMP! SCAT! ¡PRONTO!
I'LL GET YOU FOR THIS, YOU LITTLE SHIT!
OH GOD-OH GOD-OH GOD... I-I-I REALLY DID IT... SHE-SHE-SHE REALLY WANTED TO-TO-TO KI-I-ILL ME-E-E...
I KNOW! I-I'LL HOP A TRAIN AND SEND FOR MY STUFF LATER... EEP!
CLICK!
WELL, SHRIMP. YOU DID IT. YOU ACTUALLY FIGURED A WAY WHERE I'D HAVE TO FIRE YOU. PRETTY DARN CLEVER...
B-BUT, TIA. I DIDN'T MEAN TO... I DON'T WANNA BE FIRED...
WELL, TOUGH! THOUSANDS OF FANS SAW YOU TURN ON ME. I HAD TO MAKE A T.V. ANNOUNCEMENT STATING THAT YOU WERE OUT TO STEAL MY MONEY ALL ALONG. AS MUCH AS I'D LIKE TO, IT'S TOO LATE TO CHANGE NOW.
BUT...
7

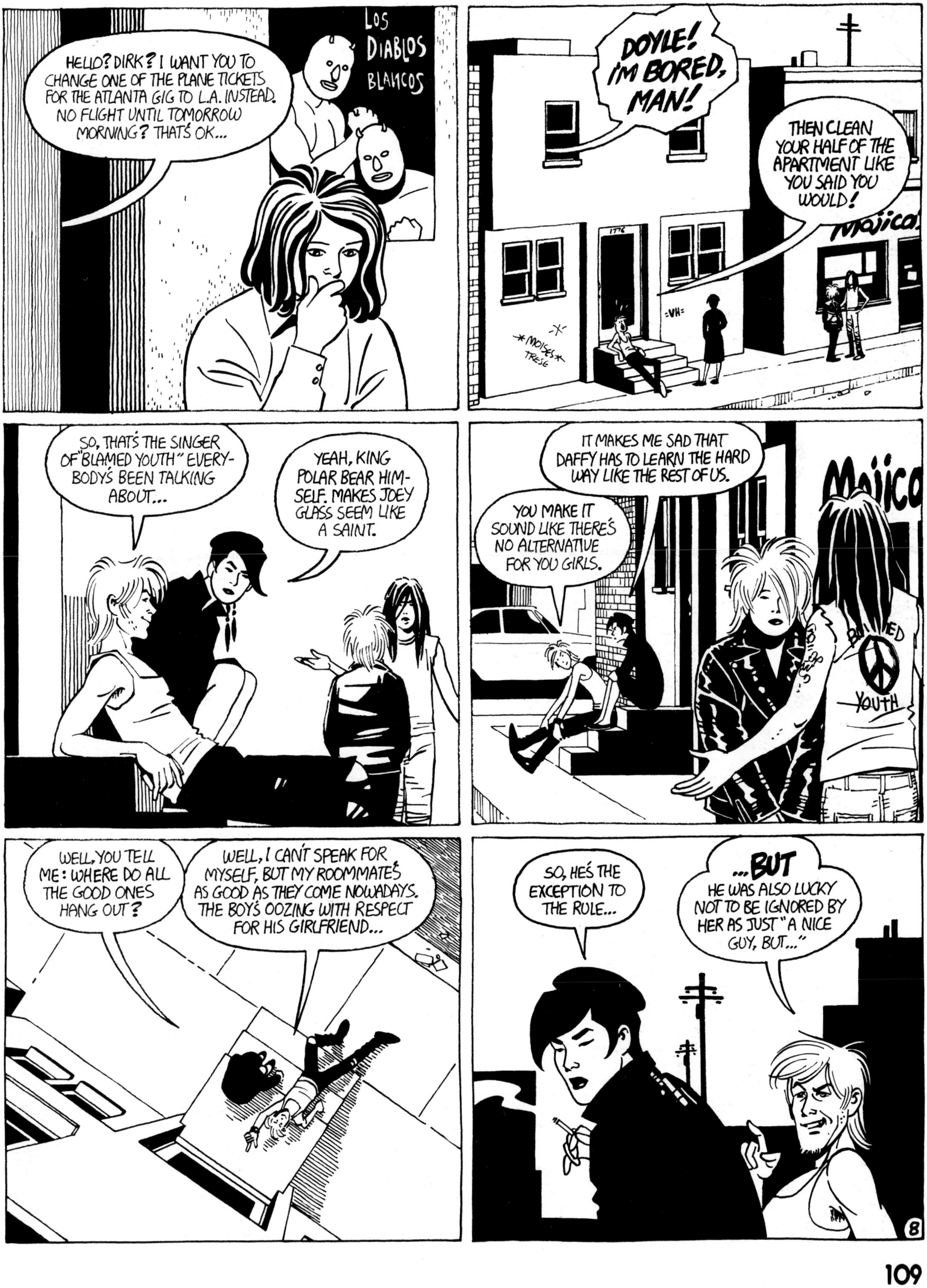
LOS DIABLOS BLANCOS
HELLO? DIRK? I WANT YOU TO CHANGE ONE OF THE PLANE TICKETS FOR THE ATLANTA GIG TO L.A. INSTEAD. NO FLIGHT UNTIL TOMORROW MORNING? THAT'S OK...
DOYLE! I'M BORED, MAN!
THEN CLEAN YOUR HALF OF THE APARTMENT LIKE YOU SAID YOU WOULD!
SO, THAT'S THE SINGER OF "BLAMED YOUTH" EVERYBODY'S BEEN TALKING ABOUT...
YEAH, KING POLAR BEAR HIMSELF. MAKES JOEY GLASS SEEM LIKE A SAINT.
IT MAKES ME SAD THAT DAFFY HAS TO LEARN THE HARD WAY LIKE THE REST OF US.
YOU MAKE IT SOUND LIKE THERE'S NO ALTERNATIVE FOR YOU GIRLS.
WELL, YOU TELL ME: WHERE DO ALL THE GOOD ONES HANG OUT?
WELL, I CAN'T SPEAK FOR MYSELF, BUT MY ROOMMATE'S AS GOOD AS THEY COME NOWADAYS. THE BOY'S OOZING WITH RESPECT FOR HIS GIRLFRIEND...
SO, HE'S THE EXCEPTION TO THE RULE...
...BUT HE WAS ALSO LUCKY NOT TO BE IGNORED BY HER AS JUST "A NICE GUY, BUT..."
8

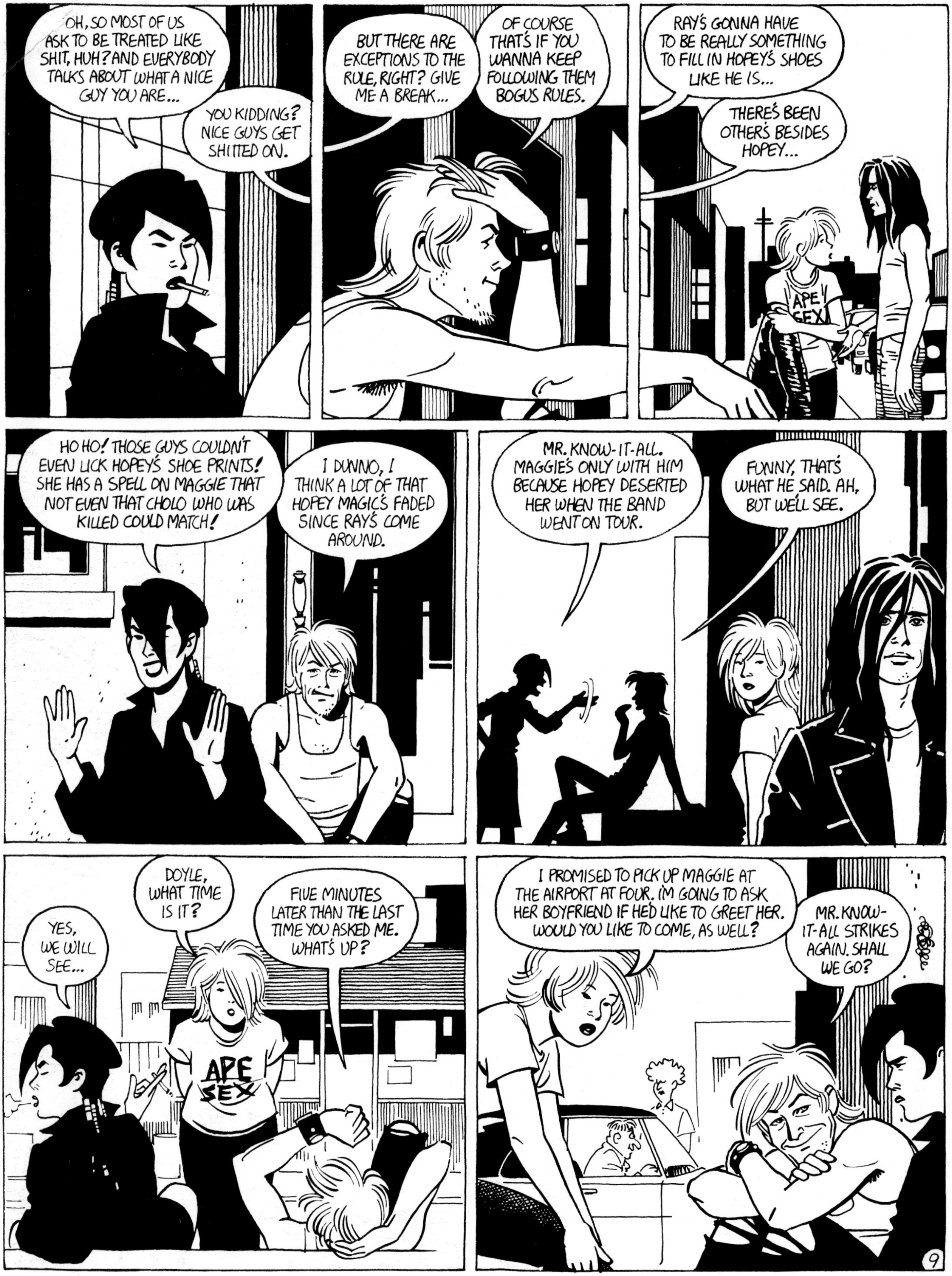
OH, SO MOST OF US ASK TO BE TREATED LIKE SHIT, HUH? AND EVERYBODY TALKS ABOUT WHAT A NICE GUY YOU ARE...
YOU KIDDING? NICE GUYS GET SHITTED ON.
BUT THERE ARE EXCEPTIONS TO THE RULE, RIGHT? GIVE ME A BREAK...
OF COURSE THAT'S IF YOU WANNA KEEP FOLLOWING THEM BOGUS RULES.
RAY'S GONNA HAVE TO BE REALLY SOMETHING TO FILL IN HOPEY'S SHOES LIKE HE IS...
THERE'S BEEN OTHER'S BESIDES HOPEY...
APE SEX
HO HO! THOSE GUYS COULDN'T EVEN LICK HOPEY'S SHOE PRINTS! SHE HAS A SPELL ON MAGGIE THAT NOT EVEN THAT CHOLO WHO WAS KILLED COULD MATCH!
I DUNNO, I THINK A LOT OF THAT HOPEY MAGIC'S FADED SINCE RAY'S COME AROUND.
MR. KNOW-IT-ALL. MAGGIE'S ONLY WITH HIM BECAUSE HOPEY DESERTED HER WHEN THE BAND WENT ON TOUR.
FUNNY, THAT'S WHAT HE SAID. AH, BUT WE'LL SEE.
YES, WE WILL SEE...
DOYLE, WHAT TIME IS IT?
FIVE MINUTES LATER THAN THE LAST TIME YOU ASKED ME. WHAT'S UP?
APE SEX
I PROMISED TO PICK UP MAGGIE AT THE AIRPORT AT FOUR. I'M GOING TO ASK HER BOYFRIEND IF HE'D LIKE TO GREET HER. WOULD YOU LIKE TO COME, AS WELL?
MR. KNOW-IT-ALL STRIKES AGAIN. SHALL WE GO?
9

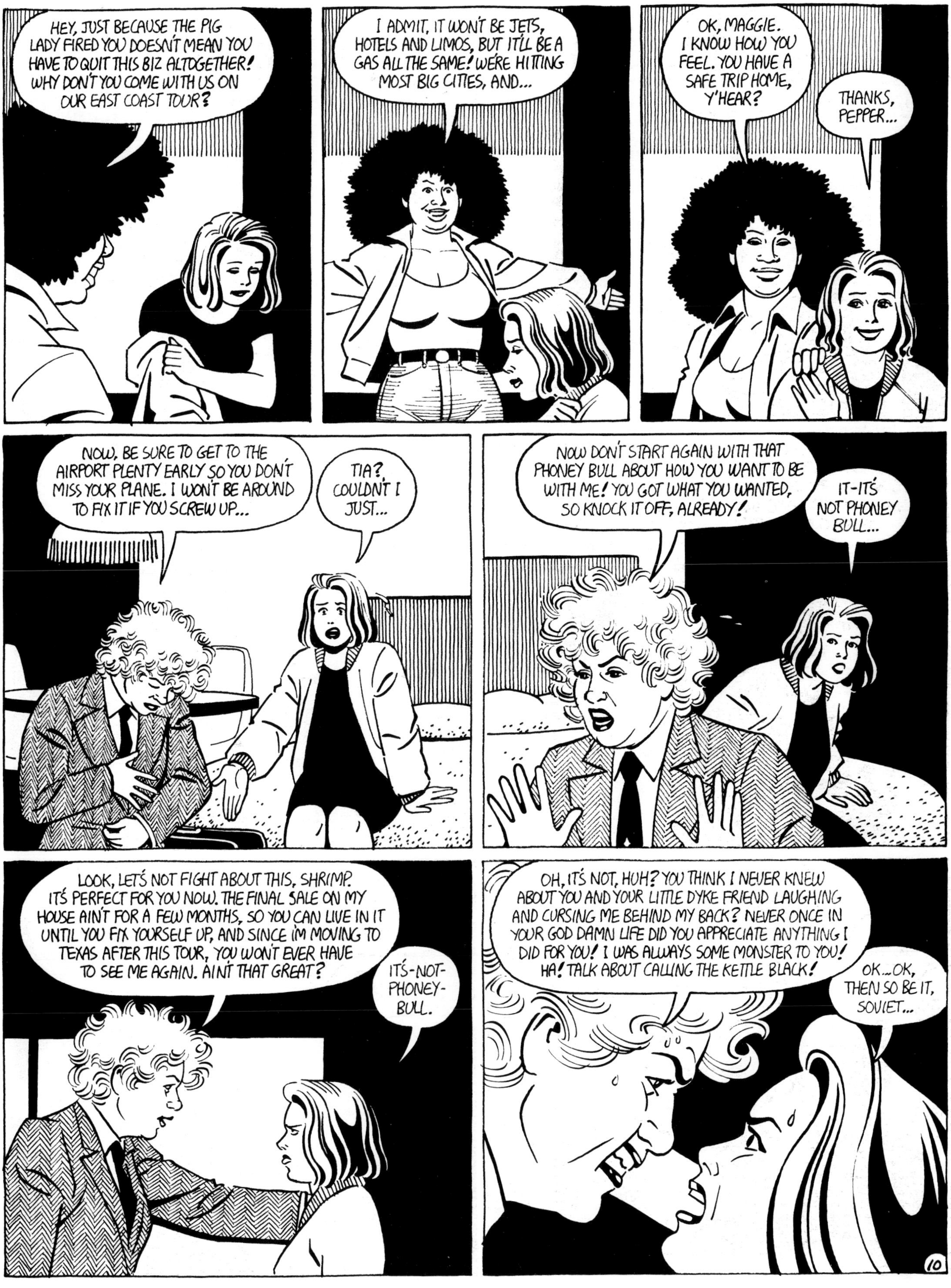
HEY, JUST BECAUSE THE PIG LADY FIRED YOU DOESN'T MEAN YOU HAVE TO QUIT THIS BIZ ALTOGETHER! WHY DON'T YOU COME WITH US ON OUR EAST COAST TOUR?
I ADMIT, IT WON'T BE JETS, HOTELS AND LIMOS, BUT IT'LL BE A GAS ALL THE SAME! WE'RE HITTING MOST BIG CITIES, AND...
OK, MAGGIE. I KNOW HOW YOU FEEL. YOU HAVE A SAFE TRIP HOME, Y'HEAR?
THANKS, PEPPER...
NOW, BE SURE TO GET TO THE AIRPORT PLENTY EARLY SO YOU DON'T MISS YOUR PLANE. I WON'T BE AROUND TO FIX IT IF YOU SCREW UP...
TIA? COULDN'T I JUST...
NOW DON'T START AGAIN WITH THAT PHONEY BULL ABOUT HOW YOU WANT TO BE WITH ME! YOU GOT WHAT YOU WANTED, SO KNOCK IT OFF, ALREADY!
IT-IT'S NOT PHONEY BULL...
LOOK, LET'S NOT FIGHT ABOUT THIS, SHRIMP. IT'S PERFECT FOR YOU NOW. THE FINAL SALE ON MY HOUSE AIN'T FOR A FEW MONTHS, SO YOU CAN LIVE IN IT UNTIL YOU FIX YOURSELF UP, AND SINCE I'M MOVING TO TEXAS AFTER THIS TOUR, YOU WON'T EVER HAVE TO SEE ME AGAIN. AIN'T THAT GREAT?
IT'S-NOT-PHONEY-BULL.
OH, IT'S NOT, HUH? YOU THINK I NEVER KNEW ABOUT YOU AND YOUR LITTLE DYKE FRIEND LAUGHING AND CURSING ME BEHIND MY BACK? NEVER ONCE IN YOUR GOD DAMN LIFE DID YOU APPRECIATE ANYTHING I DID FOR YOU! I WAS ALWAYS SOME MONSTER TO YOU! HA! TALK ABOUT CALLING THE KETTLE BLACK!
OK...OK, THEN SO BE IT, SOVIET...
10

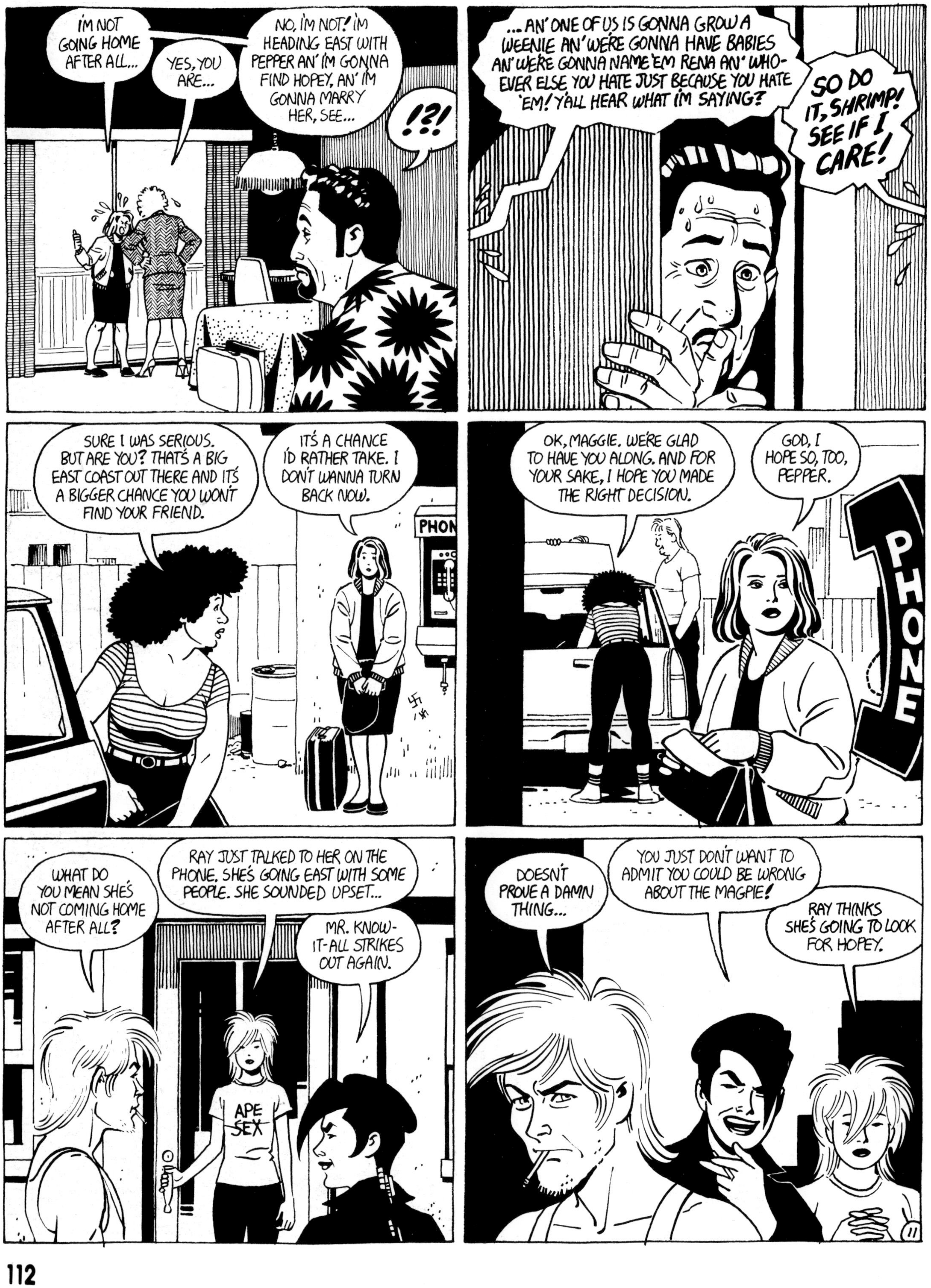

I'M NOT GOING HOME AFTER ALL...
YES, YOU ARE...
NO, I'M NOT! I'M HEADING EAST WITH PEPPER AN' I'M GONNA FIND HOPEY, AN' I'M GONNA MARRY HER, SEE...
!?!
...AN' ONE OF US IS GONNA GROW A WEENIE AN' WE'RE GONNA HAVE BABIES AN' WE'RE GONNA NAME 'EM RENA AN' WHO-EVER ELSE YOU HATE JUST BECAUSE YOU HATE 'EM! Y'ALL HEAR WHAT I'M SAYING?
SO DO IT, SHRIMP! SEE IF I CARE!
SURE I WAS SERIOUS. BUT ARE YOU? THAT'S A BIG EAST COAST OUT THERE AND IT'S A BIGGER CHANCE YOU WON'T FIND YOUR FRIEND.
IT'S A CHANCE I'D RATHER TAKE. I DON'T WANNA TURN BACK NOW.
PHON
OK, MAGGIE. WE'RE GLAD TO HAVE YOU ALONG. AND FOR YOUR SAKE, I HOPE YOU MADE THE RIGHT DECISION.
GOD, I HOPE SO, TOO, PEPPER.
PHONE
WHAT DO YOU MEAN SHE'S NOT COMING HOME AFTER ALL?
RAY JUST TALKED TO HER ON THE PHONE. SHE'S GOING EAST WITH SOME PEOPLE. SHE SOUNDED UPSET...
MR. KNOW-IT-ALL STRIKES OUT AGAIN.
APE SEX
DOESN'T PROVE A DAMN THING...
YOU JUST DON'T WANT TO ADMIT YOU COULD BE WRONG ABOUT THE MAGPIE!
RAY THINKS SHE'S GOING TO LOOK FOR HOPEY.
11

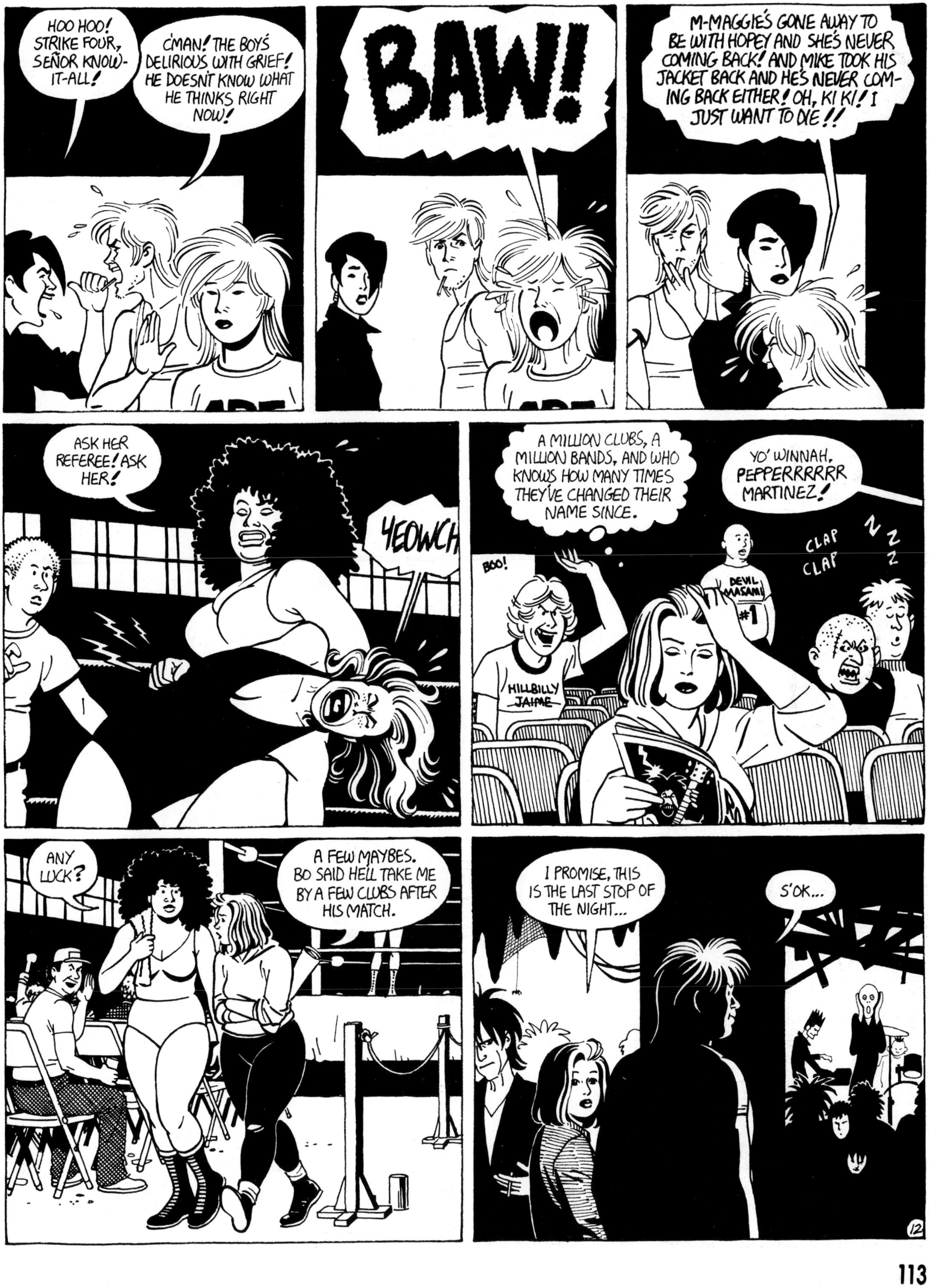
HOO HOO! STRIKE FOUR, SEÑOR KNOW-IT-ALL!
C'MAN! THE BOY'S DELIRIOUS WITH GRIEF! HE DOESN'T KNOW WHAT HE THINKS RIGHT NOW!
BAW!
M-MAGGIE'S GONE AWAY TO BE WITH HOPEY AND SHE'S NEVER COMING BACK! AND MIKE TOOK HIS JACKET BACK AND HE'S NEVER COMING BACK EITHER! OH, KI KI! I JUST WANT TO DIE!!
ASK HER REFEREE! ASK HER!
YEOWCH
A MILLION CLUBS, A MILLION BANDS, AND WHO KNOWS HOW MANY TIMES THEY'VE CHANGED THEIR NAME SINCE.
YO' WINNAH, PEPPERRRRRR MARTINEZ!
BOO!
CLAP CLAP
Z Z Z
DEVIL MASAMI #1
HILLBILLY JAIME
ANY LUCK?
A FEW MAYBES. BO SAID HE'LL TAKE ME BY A FEW CLUBS AFTER HIS MATCH.
I PROMISE, THIS IS THE LAST STOP OF THE NIGHT...
S'OK...
12

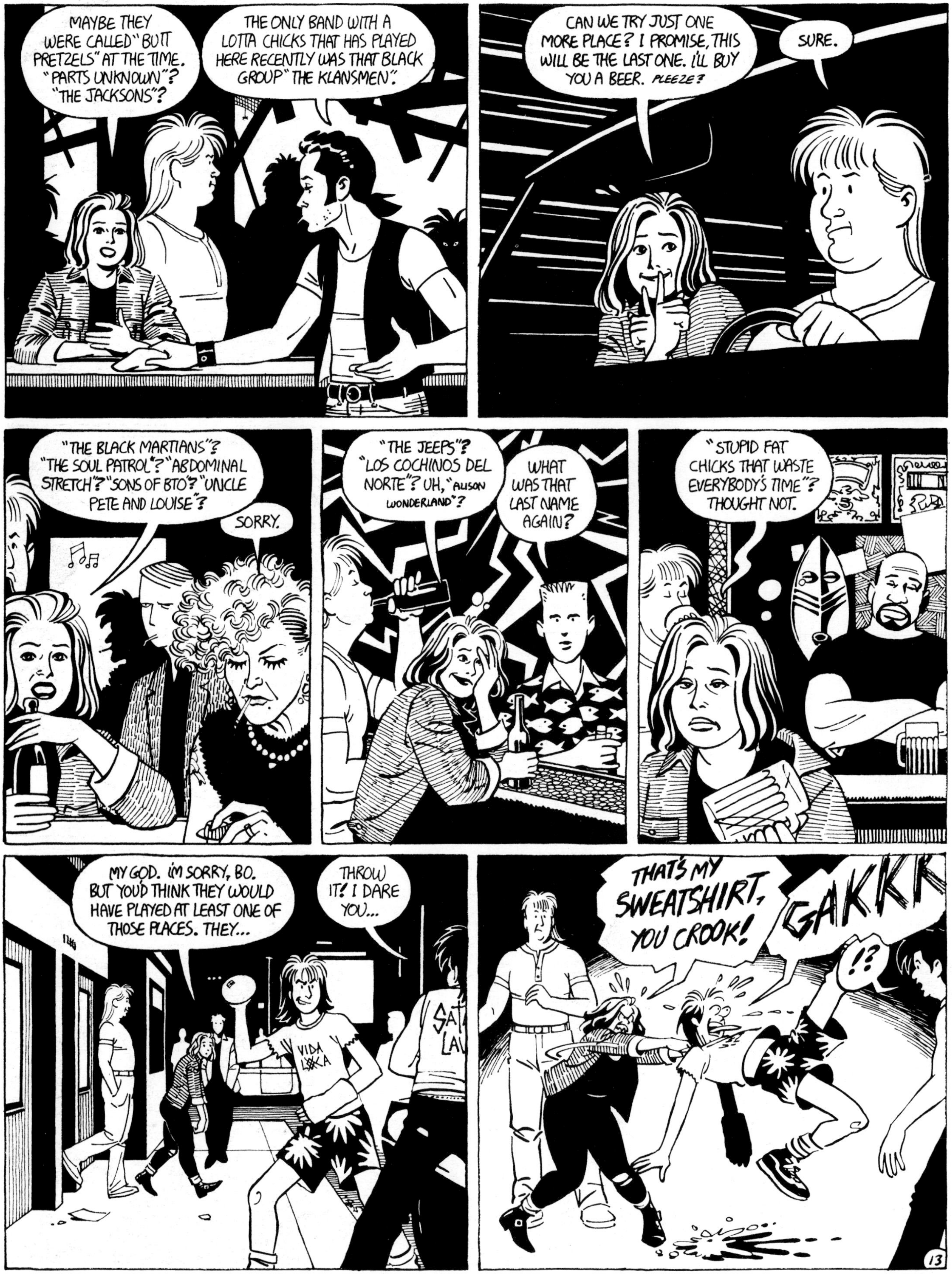
MAYBE THEY WERE CALLED "BUTT PRETZELS" AT THE TIME. "PARTS UNKNOWN"? "THE JACKSONS"?
THE ONLY BAND WITH A LOTTA CHICKS THAT HAS PLAYED HERE RECENTLY WAS THAT BLACK GROUP "THE KLANSMEN".
CAN WE TRY JUST ONE MORE PLACE? I PROMISE, THIS WILL BE THE LAST ONE. I'LL BUY YOU A BEER. PLEEZE?
SURE.
"THE BLACK MARTIANS"? "THE SOUL PATROL"? "ABDOMINAL STRETCH"? "SONS OF BTO"? "UNCLE PETE AND LOUISE"?
SORRY.
"THE JEEPS"? "LOS COCHINOS DEL NORTE"? UH, "ALISON WONDERLAND"?
WHAT WAS THAT LAST NAME AGAIN?
"STUPID FAT CHICKS THAT WASTE EVERYBODY'S TIME"? THOUGHT NOT.
MY GOD. I'M SORRY, BO. BUT YOU'D THINK THEY WOULD HAVE PLAYED AT LEAST ONE OF THOSE PLACES. THEY...
THROW IT! I DARE YOU...
VIDA LOCA
THAT'S MY SWEATSHIRT, YOU CROOK!
GAKKK
!?
13

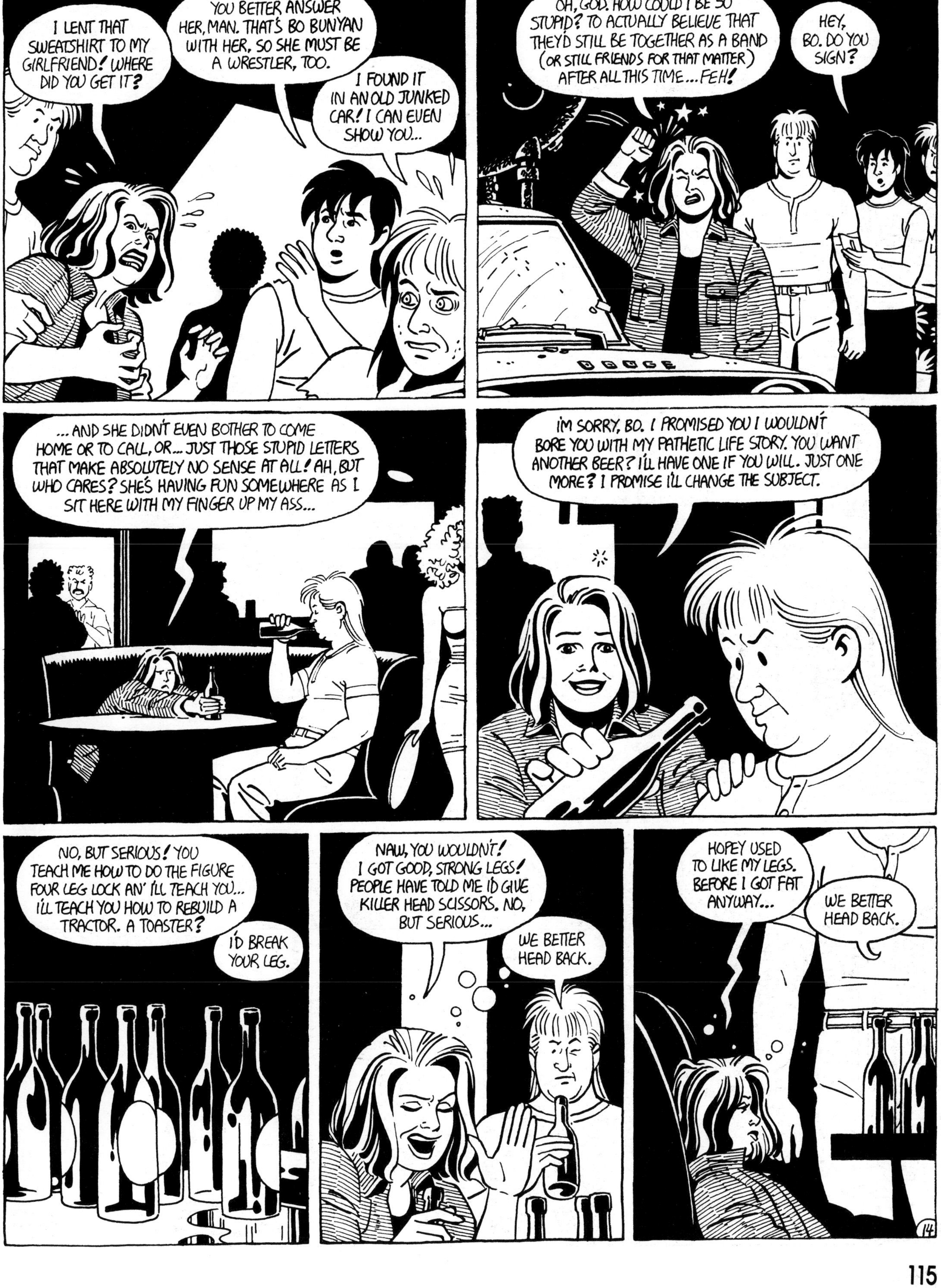

I LENT THAT SWEATSHIRT TO MY GIRLFRIEND! WHERE DID YOU GET IT?
YOU BETTER ANSWER HER, MAN. THAT'S BO BUNYAN WITH HER, SO SHE MUST BE A WRESTLER, TOO.
I FOUND IT IN AN OLD JUNKED CAR! I CAN EVEN SHOW YOU...
OH, GOD. HOW COULD I BE SO STUPID? TO ACTUALLY BELIEVE THAT THEY'D STILL BE TOGETHER AS A BAND (OR STILL FRIENDS FOR THAT MATTER) AFTER ALL THIS TIME... FEH!
HEY, BO. DO YOU SIGN?
DODGE
... AND SHE DIDN'T EVEN BOTHER TO COME HOME OR TO CALL, OR... JUST THOSE STUPID LETTERS THAT MAKE ABSOLUTELY NO SENSE AT ALL! AH, BUT WHO CARES? SHE'S HAVING FUN SOMEWHERE AS I SIT HERE WITH MY FINGER UP MY ASS...
I'M SORRY, BO. I PROMISED YOU I WOULDN'T BORE YOU WITH MY PATHETIC LIFE STORY. YOU WANT ANOTHER BEER? I'LL HAVE ONE IF YOU WILL. JUST ONE MORE? I PROMISE I'LL CHANGE THE SUBJECT.
NO, BUT SERIOUS! YOU TEACH ME HOW TO DO THE FIGURE FOUR LEG LOCK AN' I'LL TEACH YOU... I'LL TEACH YOU HOW TO REBUILD A TRACTOR. A TOASTER?
I'D BREAK YOUR LEG.
NAW, YOU WOULDN'T! I GOT GOOD, STRONG LEGS! PEOPLE HAVE TOLD ME I'D GIVE KILLER HEAD SCISSORS. NO, BUT SERIOUS...
WE BETTER HEAD BACK.
HOPEY USED TO LIKE MY LEGS. BEFORE I GOT FAT ANYWAY...
WE BETTER HEAD BACK.
14

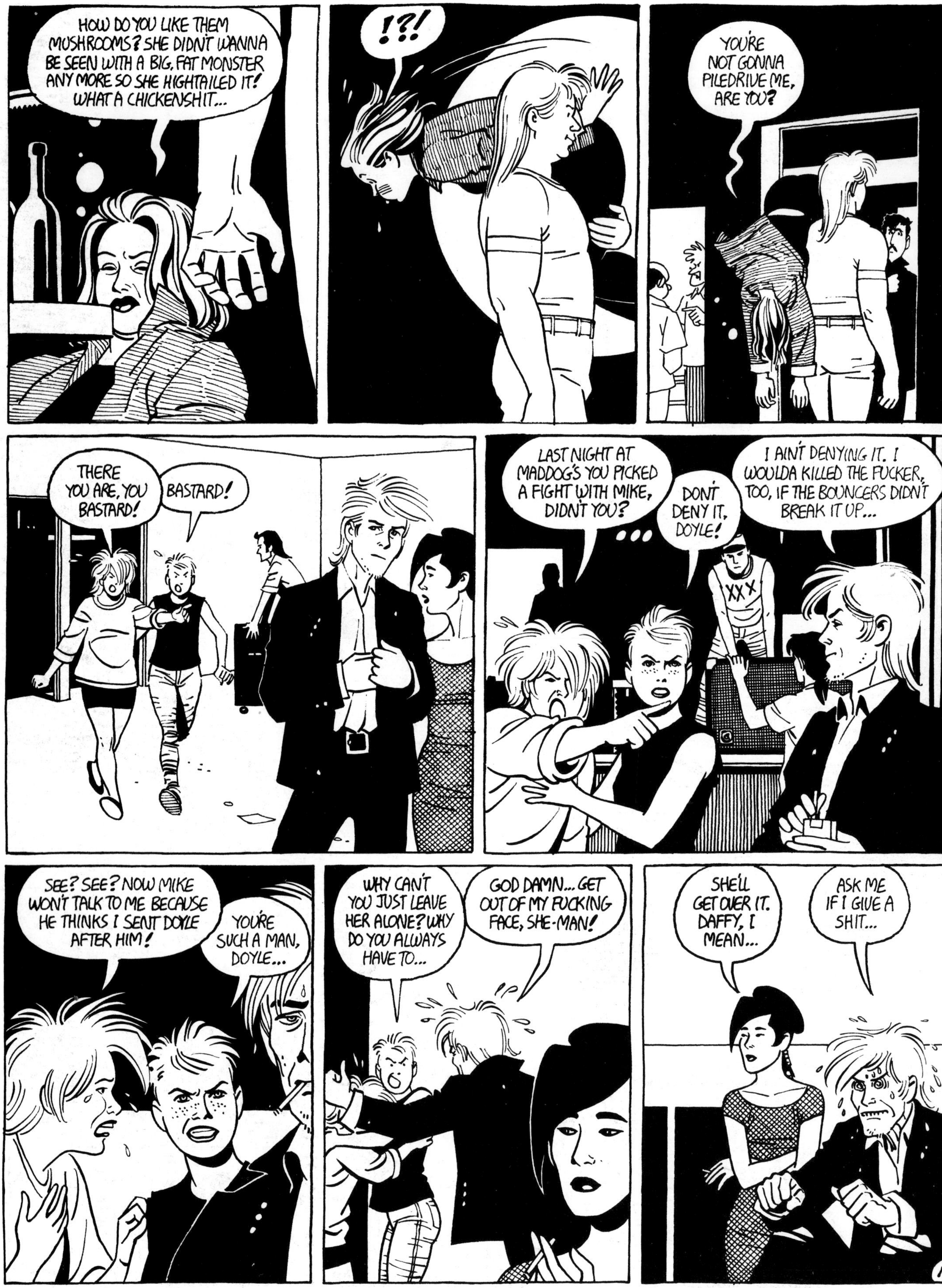
HOW DO YOU LIKE THEM MUSHROOMS? SHE DIDN'T WANNA BE SEEN WITH A BIG, FAT MONSTER ANY MORE SO SHE HIGHTAILED IT! WHAT A CHICKENSHIT...
!?!
YOU'RE NOT GONNA PILEDRIVE ME, ARE YOU?
THERE YOU ARE, YOU BASTARD!
BASTARD!
LAST NIGHT AT MADDOG'S YOU PICKED A FIGHT WITH MIKE, DIDN'T YOU?
...
DON'T DENY IT, DOYLE!
I AIN'T DENYING IT. I WOULDA KILLED THE FUCKER, TOO, IF THE BOUNCERS DIDN'T BREAK IT UP...
SEE? SEE? NOW MIKE WON'T TALK TO ME BECAUSE HE THINKS I SENT DOYLE AFTER HIM!
YOU'RE SUCH A MAN, DOYLE...
WHY CAN'T YOU JUST LEAVE HER ALONE? WHY DO YOU ALWAYS HAVE TO...
GOD DAMN... GET OUT OF MY FUCKING FACE, SHE-MAN!
SHE'LL GET OVER IT. DAFFY, I MEAN...
ASK ME IF I GIVE A SHIT...
15

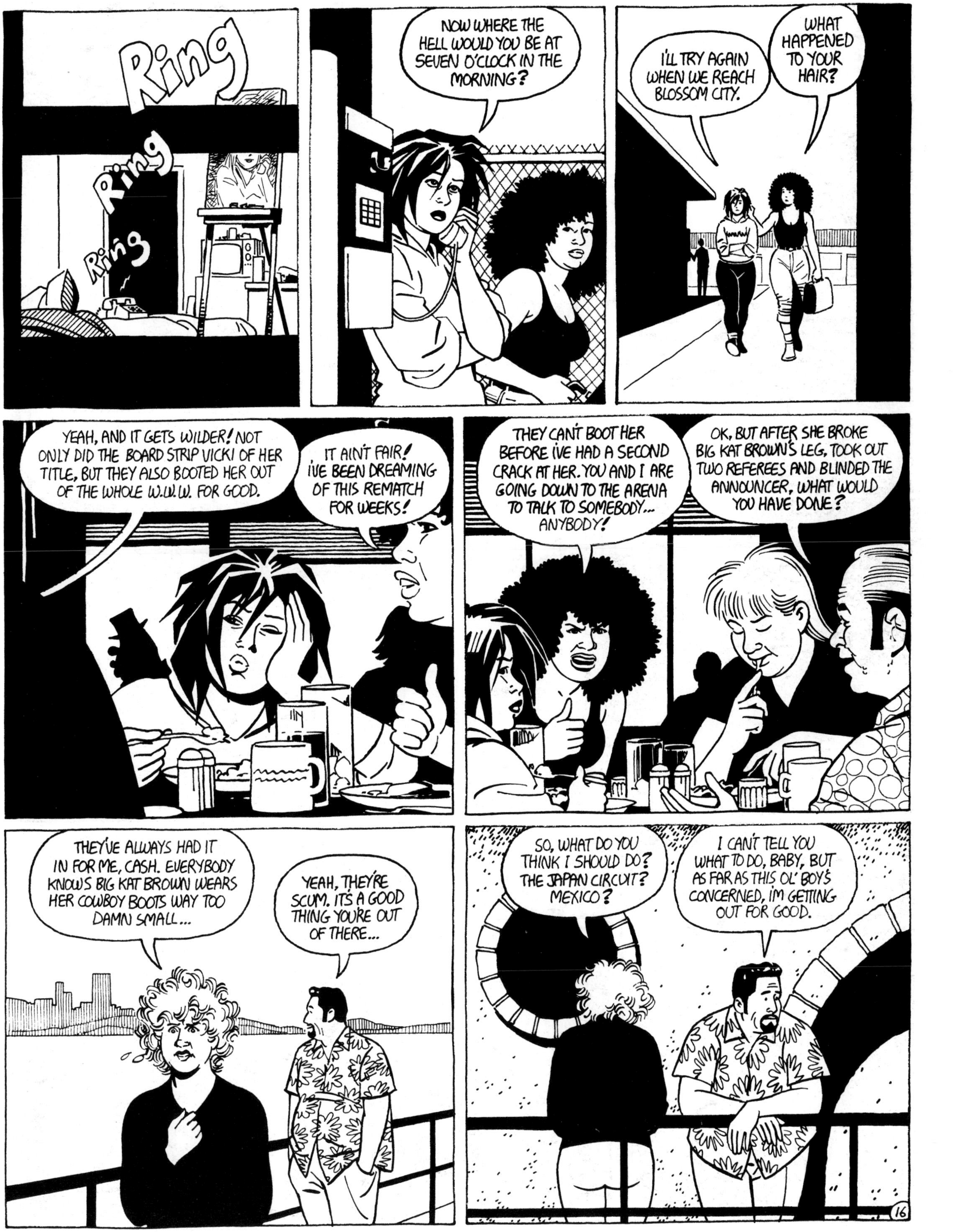
Ring
Ring
Ring
NOW WHERE THE HELL WOULD YOU BE AT SEVEN O'CLOCK IN THE MORNING?
I'LL TRY AGAIN WHEN WE REACH BLOSSOM CITY.
WHAT HAPPENED TO YOUR HAIR?
YEAH, AND IT GETS WILDER! NOT ONLY DID THE BOARD STRIP VICKI OF HER TITLE, BUT THEY ALSO BOOTED HER OUT OF THE WHOLE W.W.W. FOR GOOD.
IT AIN'T FAIR! I'VE BEEN DREAMING OF THIS REMATCH FOR WEEKS!
THEY CAN'T BOOT HER BEFORE I'VE HAD A SECOND CRACK AT HER. YOU AND I ARE GOING DOWN TO THE ARENA TO TALK TO SOMEBODY... ANYBODY!
OK, BUT AFTER SHE BROKE BIG KAT BROWN'S LEG, TOOK OUT TWO REFEREES AND BLINDED THE ANNOUNCER, WHAT WOULD YOU HAVE DONE?
THEY'VE ALWAYS HAD IT IN FOR ME, CASH. EVERYBODY KNOWS BIG KAT BROWN WEARS HER COWBOY BOOTS WAY TOO DAMN SMALL...
YEAH, THEY'RE SCUM. IT'S A GOOD THING YOU'RE OUT OF THERE...
SO, WHAT DO YOU THINK I SHOULD DO? THE JAPAN CIRCUIT? MEXICO?
I CAN'T TELL YOU WHAT TO DO, BABY, BUT AS FAR AS THIS OL' BOY'S CONCERNED, I'M GETTING OUT FOR GOOD.
16

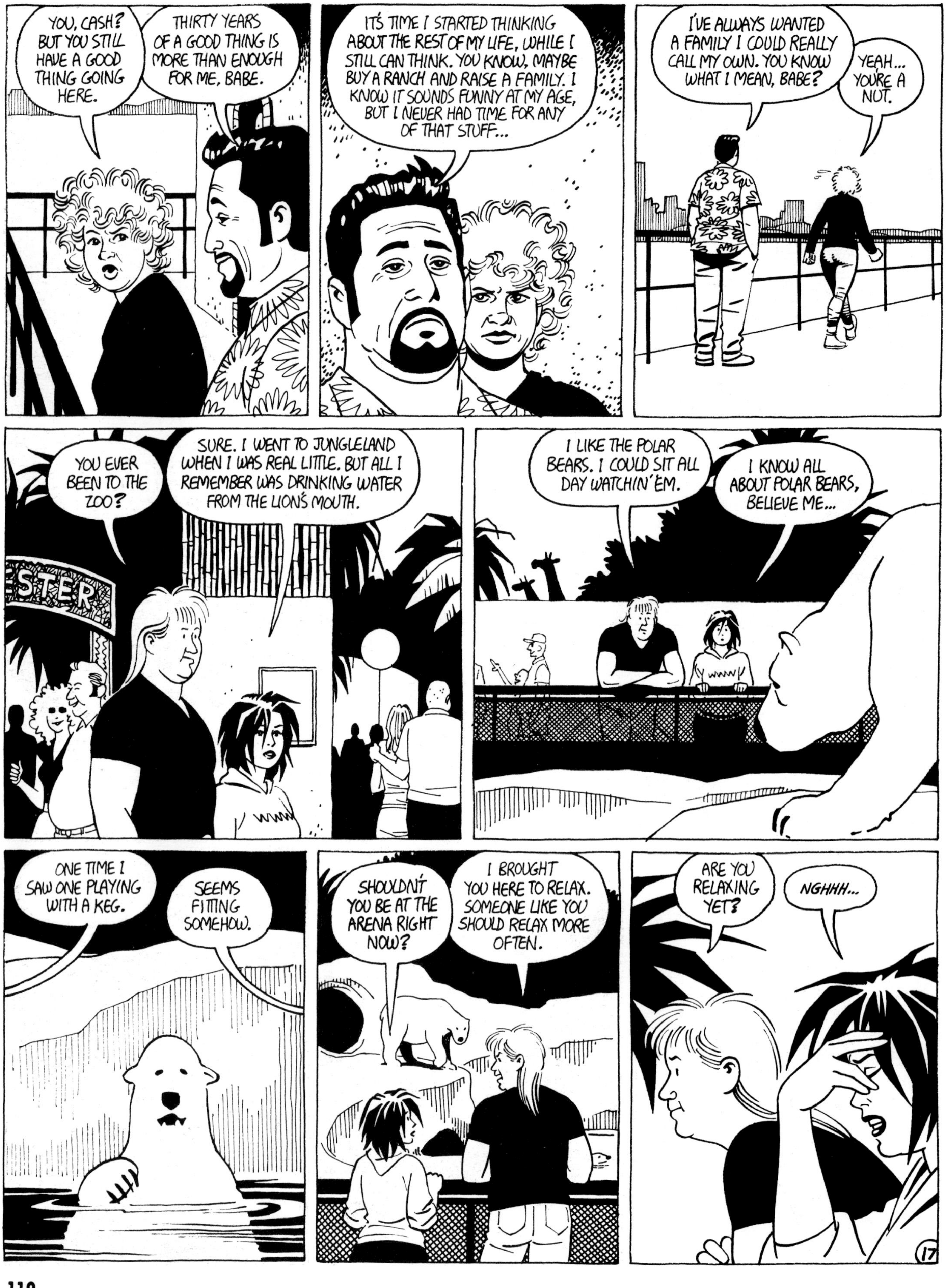
YOU, CASH? BUT YOU STILL HAVE A GOOD THING GOING HERE.
THIRTY YEARS OF A GOOD THING IS MORE THAN ENOUGH FOR ME, BABE.
IT'S TIME I STARTED THINKING ABOUT THE REST OF MY LIFE, WHILE I STILL CAN THINK. YOU KNOW, MAYBE BUY A RANCH AND RAISE A FAMILY. I KNOW IT SOUNDS FUNNY AT MY AGE, BUT I NEVER HAD TIME FOR ANY OF THAT STUFF...
I'VE ALWAYS WANTED A FAMILY I COULD REALLY CALL MY OWN. YOU KNOW WHAT I MEAN, BABE?
YEAH... YOU'RE A NUT.
YOU EVER BEEN TO THE ZOO?
SURE. I WENT TO JUNGLELAND WHEN I WAS REAL LITTLE. BUT ALL I REMEMBER WAS DRINKING WATER FROM THE LION'S MOUTH.
ESTER
I LIKE THE POLAR BEARS. I COULD SIT ALL DAY WATCHIN' 'EM.
I KNOW ALL ABOUT POLAR BEARS, BELIEVE ME...
ONE TIME I SAW ONE PLAYING WITH A KEG.
SEEMS FITTING SOMEHOW.
SHOULDN'T YOU BE AT THE ARENA RIGHT NOW?
I BROUGHT YOU HERE TO RELAX. SOMEONE LIKE YOU SHOULD RELAX MORE OFTEN.
ARE YOU RELAXING YET?
NGHHH...
17

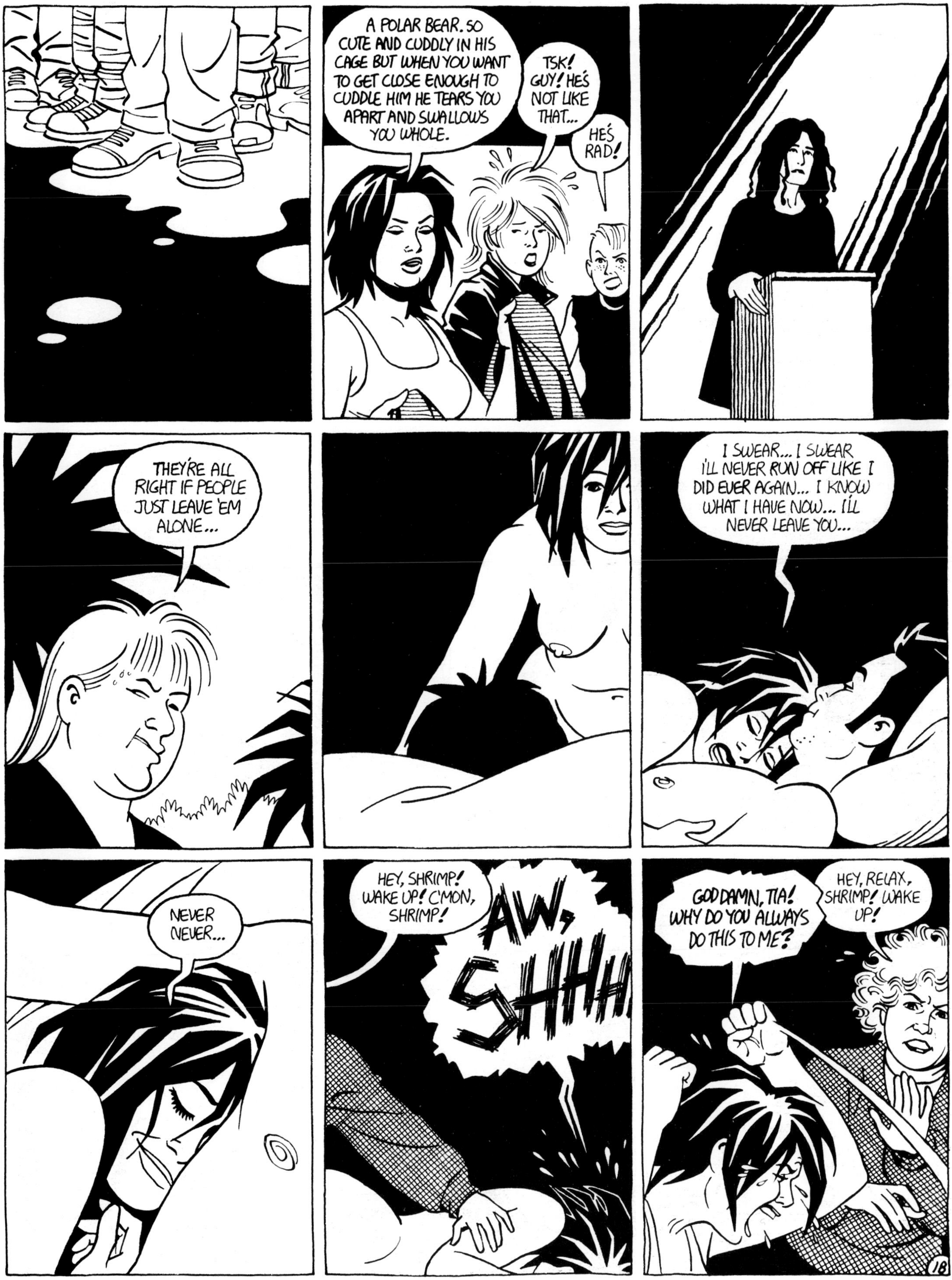
A POLAR BEAR. SO CUTE AND CUDDLY IN HIS CAGE BUT WHEN YOU WANT TO GET CLOSE ENOUGH TO CUDDLE HIM HE TEARS YOU APART AND SWALLOWS YOU WHOLE.
TSK! GUY! HE'S NOT LIKE THAT...
HE'S RAD!
THEY'RE ALL RIGHT IF PEOPLE JUST LEAVE 'EM ALONE...
I SWEAR... I SWEAR I'LL NEVER RUN OFF LIKE I DID EVER AGAIN... I KNOW WHAT I HAVE NOW... I'LL NEVER LEAVE YOU...
NEVER NEVER...
HEY, SHRIMP! WAKE UP! C'MON, SHRIMP!
AW, SHHH
GOD DAMN, TIA! WHY DO YOU ALWAYS DO THIS TO ME?
HEY, RELAX, SHRIMP! WAKE UP!
18

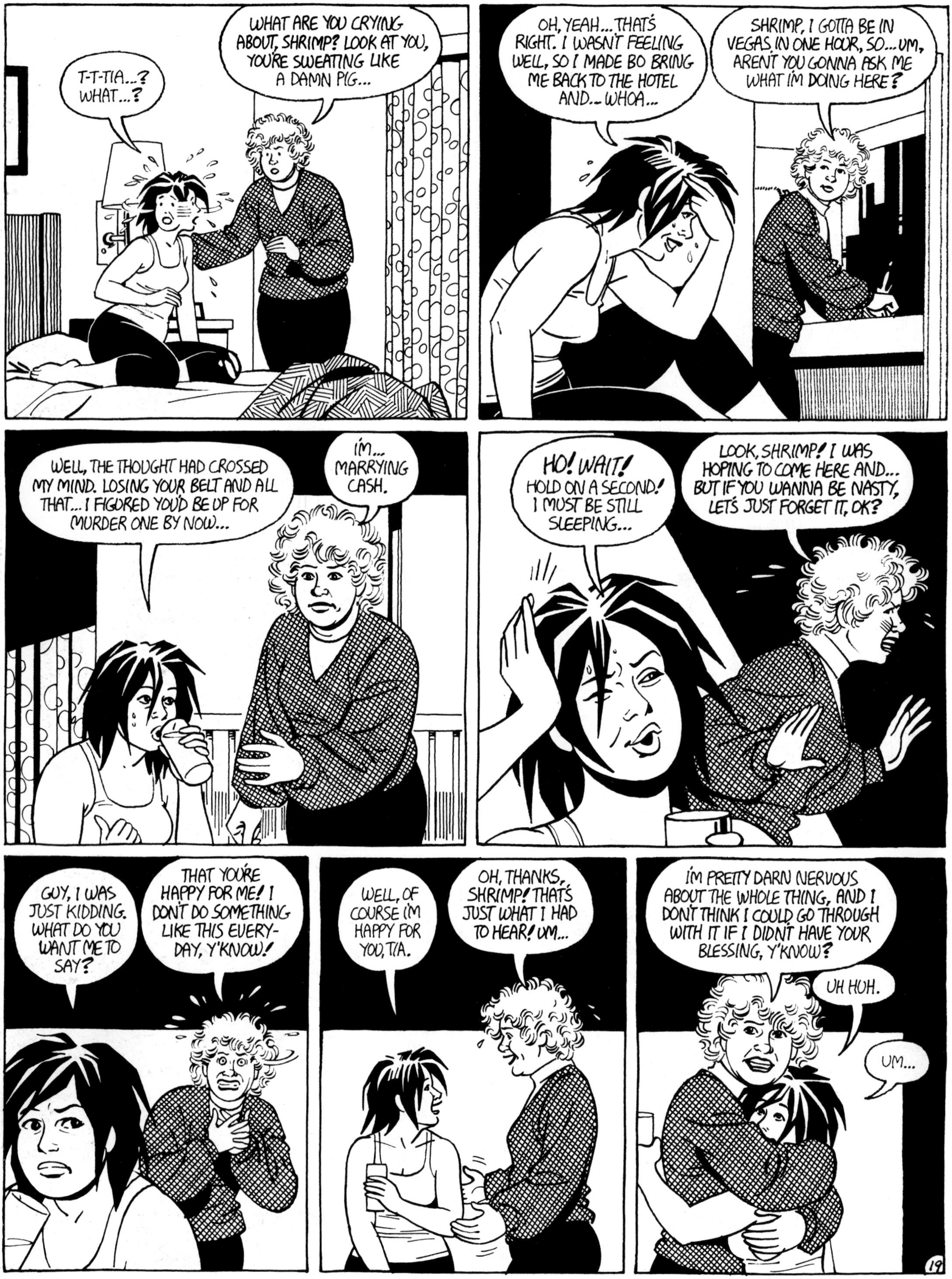
T-T-TIA...? WHAT...?
WHAT ARE YOU CRYING ABOUT, SHRIMP? LOOK AT YOU, YOU'RE SWEATING LIKE A DAMN PIG...
OH, YEAH... THAT'S RIGHT. I WASN'T FEELING WELL, SO I MADE BO BRING ME BACK TO THE HOTEL AND... WHOA...
SHRIMP, I GOTTA BE IN VEGAS IN ONE HOUR, SO... UM, AREN'T YOU GONNA ASK ME WHAT I'M DOING HERE?
WELL, THE THOUGHT HAD CROSSED MY MIND. LOSING YOUR BELT AND ALL THAT... I FIGURED YOU'D BE UP FOR MURDER ONE BY NOW...
I'M... MARRYING CASH.
HO! WAIT! HOLD ON A SECOND! I MUST BE STILL SLEEPING...
LOOK, SHRIMP! I WAS HOPING TO COME HERE AND... BUT IF YOU WANNA BE NASTY, LET'S JUST FORGET IT, OK?
GUY, I WAS JUST KIDDING. WHAT DO YOU WANT ME TO SAY?
THAT YOU'RE HAPPY FOR ME! I DON'T DO SOMETHING LIKE THIS EVERY-DAY, Y'KNOW!
WELL, OF COURSE I'M HAPPY FOR YOU, TIA.
OH, THANKS, SHRIMP! THAT'S JUST WHAT I HAD TO HEAR! UM...
I'M PRETTY DARN NERVOUS ABOUT THE WHOLE THING, AND I DON'T THINK I COULD GO THROUGH WITH IT IF I DIDN'T HAVE YOUR BLESSING, Y'KNOW?
UH HUH.
UM...
19

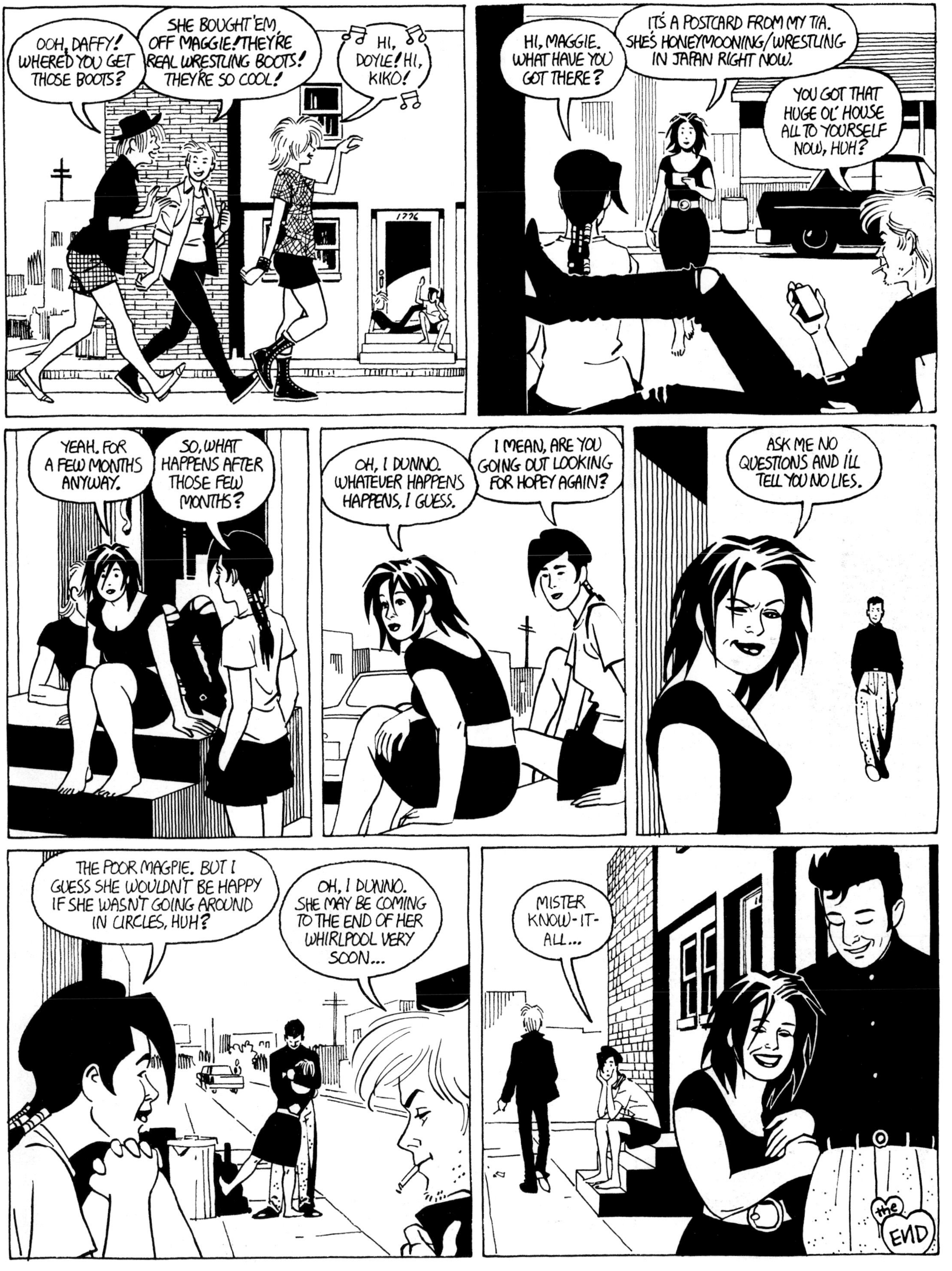
OOH, DAFFY! WHERE'D YOU GET THOSE BOOTS?
SHE BOUGHT 'EM OFF MAGGIE! THEY'RE REAL WRESTLING BOOTS! THEY'RE SO COOL!
HI, DOYLE! HI, KIKO!
1776
HI, MAGGIE. WHAT HAVE YOU GOT THERE?
IT'S A POSTCARD FROM MY TIA. SHE'S HONEYMOONING/WRESTLING IN JAPAN RIGHT NOW.
YOU GOT THAT HUGE OL' HOUSE ALL TO YOURSELF NOW, HUH?
YEAH. FOR A FEW MONTHS ANYWAY.
SO, WHAT HAPPENS AFTER THOSE FEW MONTHS?
OH, I DUNNO. WHATEVER HAPPENS HAPPENS, I GUESS.
I MEAN, ARE YOU GOING OUT LOOKING FOR HOPEY AGAIN?
ASK ME NO QUESTIONS AND I'LL TELL YOU NO LIES.
THE POOR MAGPIE. BUT I GUESS SHE WOULDN'T BE HAPPY IF SHE WASN'T GOING AROUND IN CIRCLES, HUH?
OH, I DUNNO. SHE MAY BE COMING TO THE END OF HER WHIRLPOOL VERY SOON...
MISTER KNOW-IT-ALL...
the END

COVER GALLERY

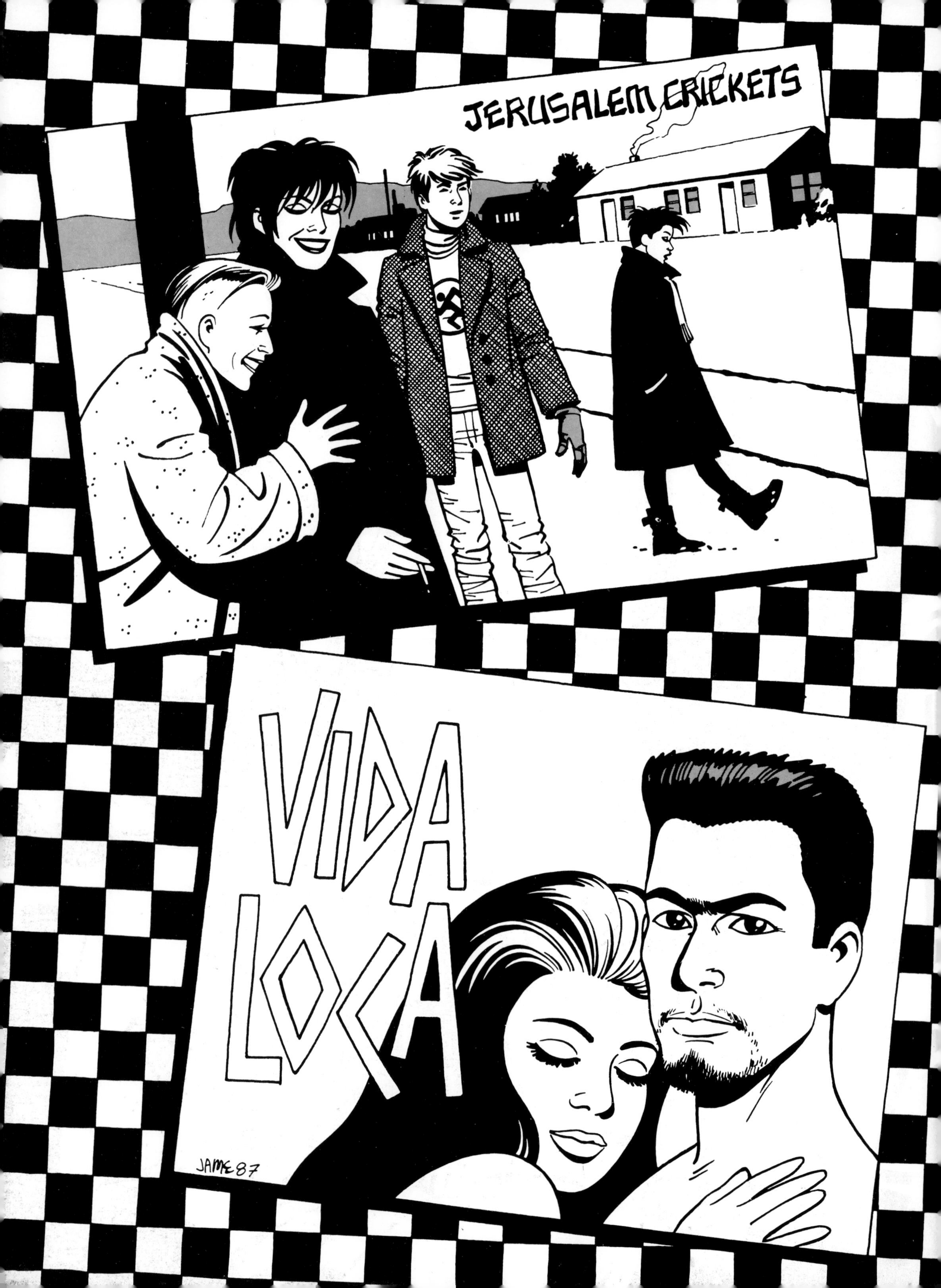
JERUSALEM CRICKETS
VIDA LOCA
JAIME 87

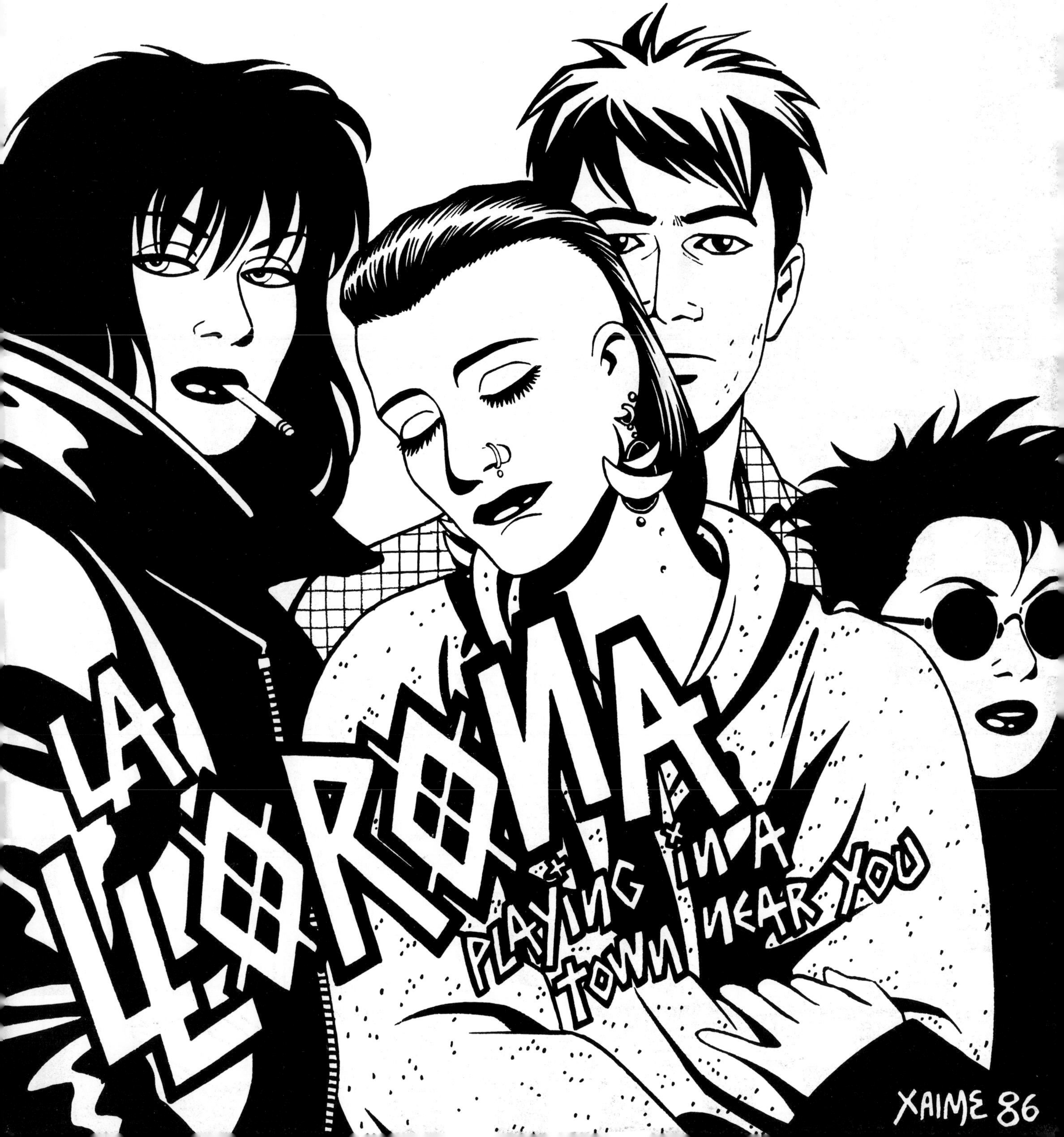

LA LLORONA
PLAYING IN A TOWN NEAR YOU
XAIME 86

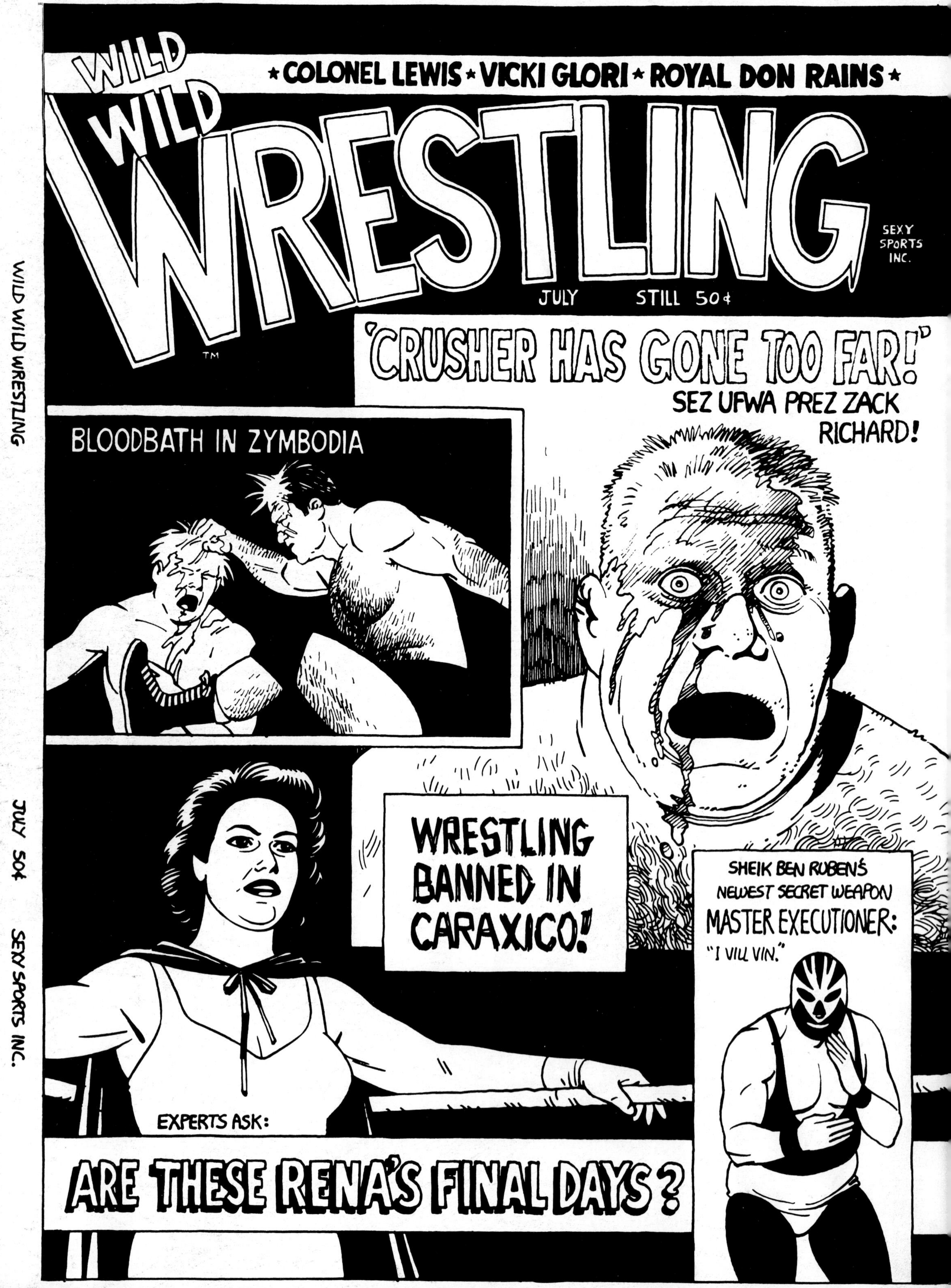
WILD WILD WRESTLING
★ COLONEL LEWIS ★ VICKI GLORI ★ ROYAL DON RAINS ★
TM
SEXY SPORTS INC.
JULY STILL 50¢
"CRUSHER HAS GONE TOO FAR!"
SEZ UFWA PREZ ZACK RICHARD!
BLOODBATH IN ZYMBODIA
WRESTLING BANNED IN CARAXICO!
SHEIK BEN RUBEN'S NEWEST SECRET WEAPON
MASTER EXECUTIONER:
"I VILL VIN."
EXPERTS ASK:
ARE THESE RENA'S FINAL DAYS?
WILD WILD WRESTLING
JULY 50¢
SEXY SPORTS INC.

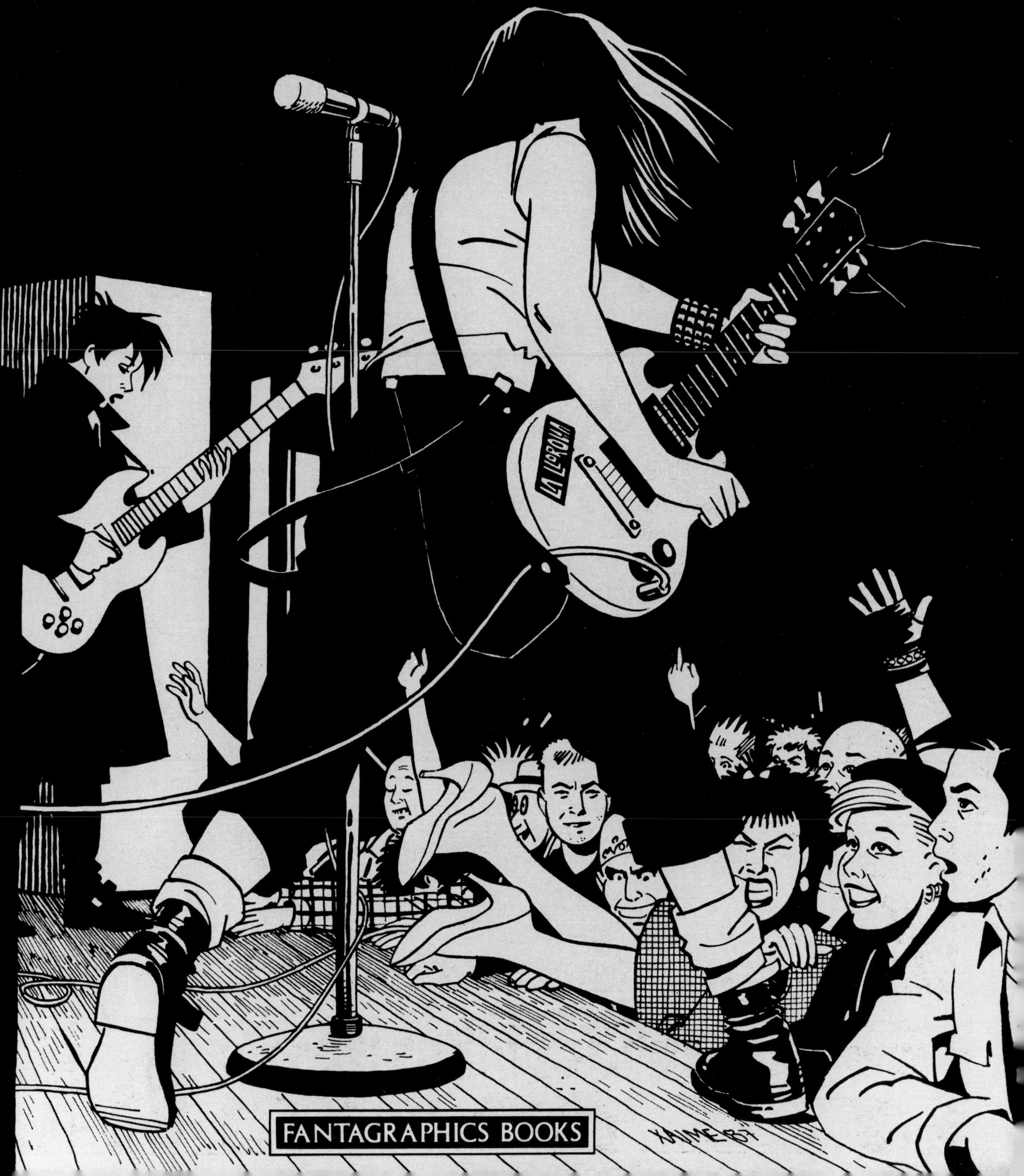
LA LLORONA
FANTAGRAPHICS BOOKS

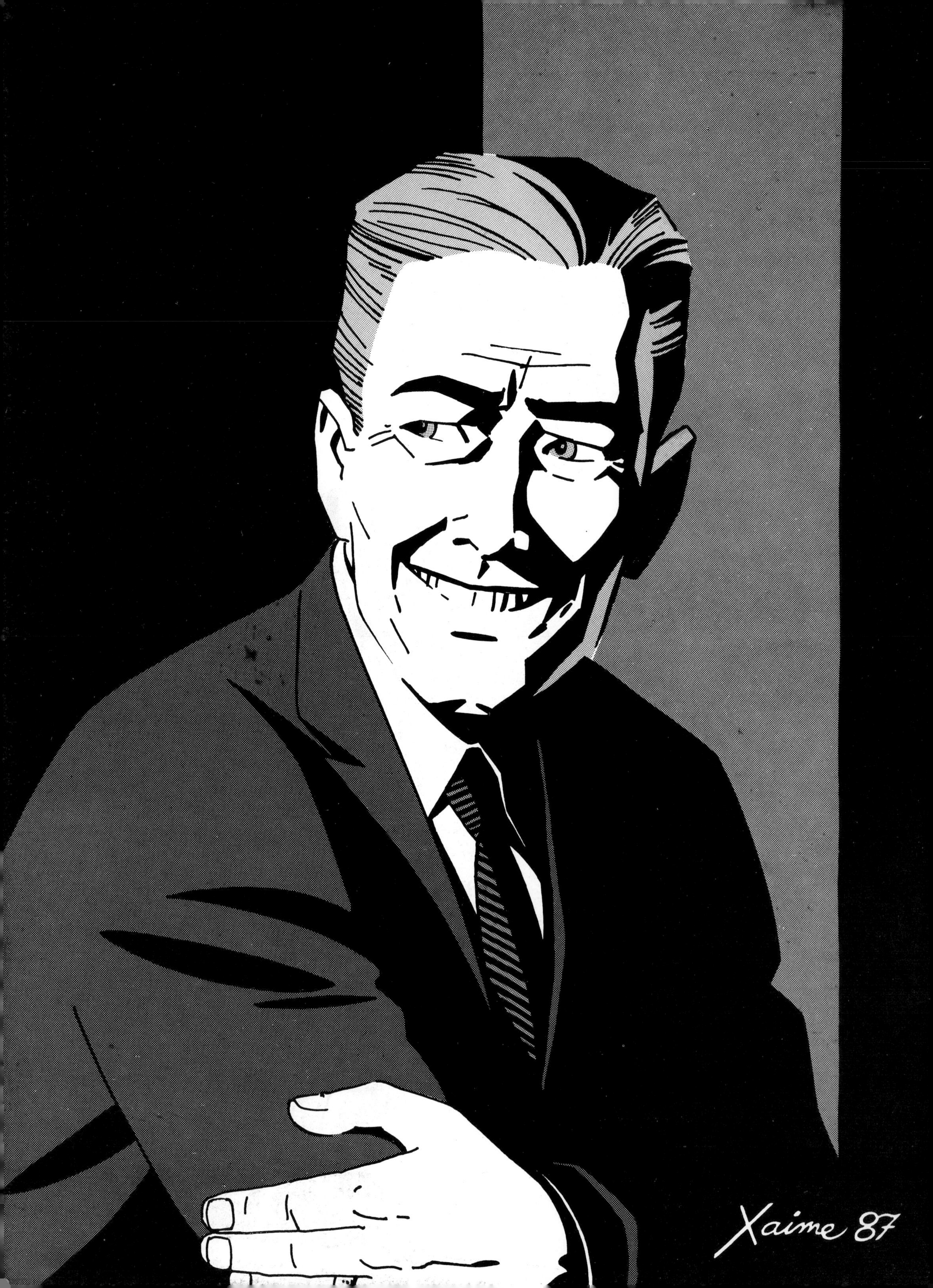
Xaime 87

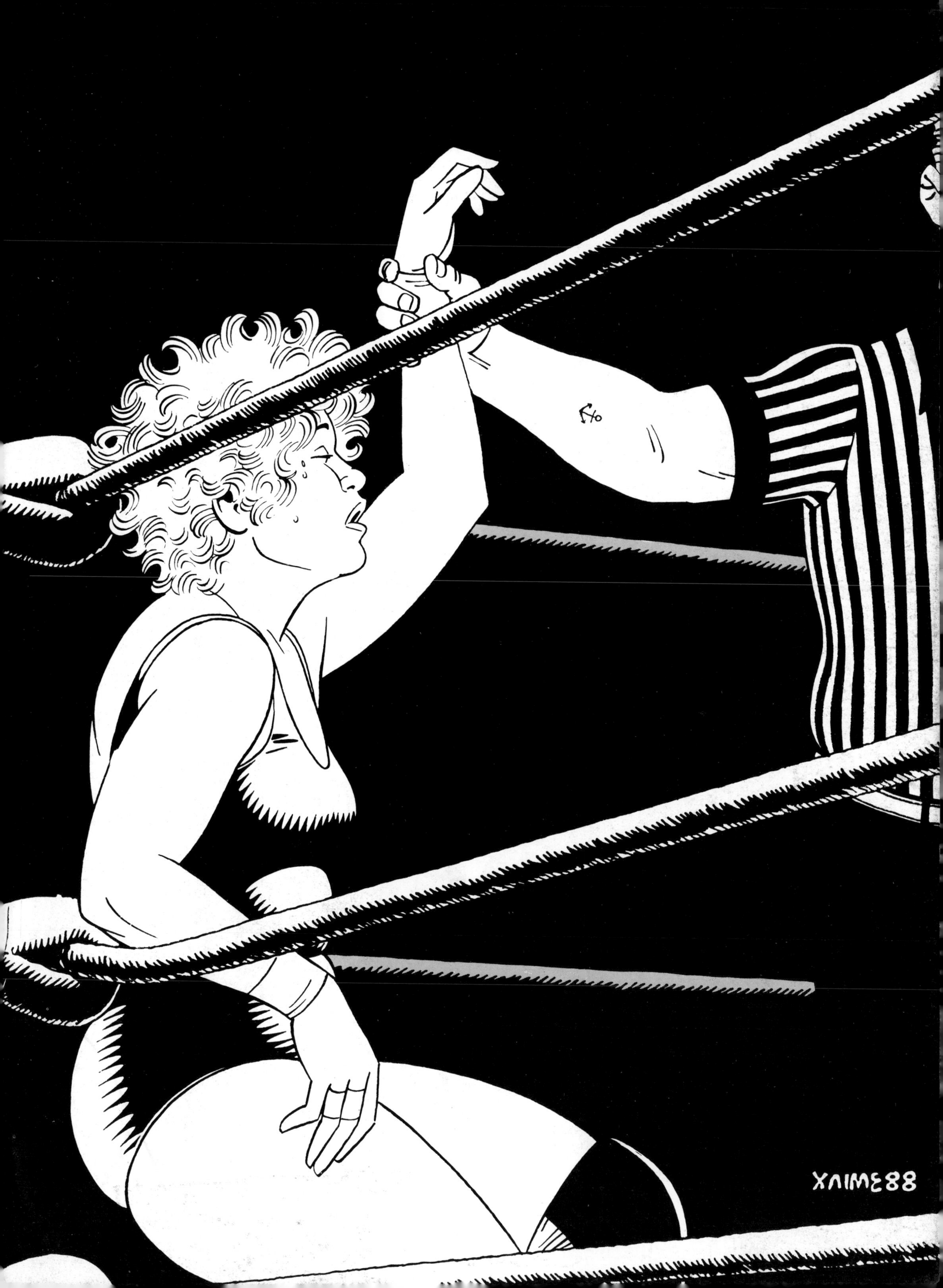

IF YOU ENJOYED THIS BOOK...

Fantagraphics Books has also published the following books by Los Bros. Hernandez.

Love and Rockets Books 1-6, 8 ($12.95 each). In the same format as the tome currently clutched in your hands, these volumes combined reprint the entirety of the first 26 issues of the **Love and Rockets** comic –plus a selection of new stories as well.

Love and Rockets: Short Stories and **The Lost Women** ($10.95 each) Two compact volumes (6" x 9"), each reprinting over 130 pages of Jaime Hernandez's strips–including the "Locas/Mechanics" series and "Rocky." Introductions by Carter Scholz and Brad Holland.

Heartbreak Soup and Other Stories and **The Reticent Heart** ($10.95 each) In the same format as the Jaime Hernandez solo books, the first two installments of Gilbert Hernandez's Palomar saga–plus "Errata Stigmata," and more. Introductions by Alan Moore and Harvey Pekar.

The Love and Rockets Sketchbook ($19.95) Not just a sketchbook (although there's hundreds of roughs and finished drawings from the Bros. in here too), but a collection of pre-**L&R** comics and illustrations, including SF strips by Gilbert and Mario Hernandez, and a very early "Mechanics" yarn by Jaime Hernandez. 180 pages, oversize format.

Love and Rockets Calendars 1989 and **1990** ($9.95) Many brand new full-page illustrations by Gilbert and Jaime Hernandez (plus a few dozen small ones), as well as an eclectic collection of dates to remember.

*Each of these can be had by mail for $1.00 postage and handling from Fantagraphics Books, 7563 Lake City Way, Seattle, WA 98115. You can also subscribe to **Love and Rockets** for six issues ($15.00)–or just send us a postcard to get our catalogue of new & classic comics work by R. Crumb, Jules Feiffer, Berni Wrightson, Vaughn Bode, Stan Sakai, Frank Frazetta, Hal Foster, E.C. Segar, Kaz, Peter Bagge, Winsor McCay, and many others.*